The Fountain at the Centre of the World

The Fountain at the Centre of the World

ROBERT NEWMAN

VERSO

London • New York

First published by Verso 2003
© Robert Newman 2003
This paperback edition first published by Verso 2004
© Robert Newman 2004

The moral rights of the author have been asserted

1 3 5 7 9 10 8 6 4 2

Verso
UK: 6 Meard Street, London W1F 0EG
USA: 180 Varick Street, New York, NY 10014-4606
www.versobooks.com

Verso is an imprint of New Left Books

ISBN 1-84467-523-8

British Library Cataloguing in Publication Data
A catalogue record for this book is available from the British Library

Library of Congress Cataloging-in-Publication Data
A catalog record for this book is available from the Library of Congress

Printed and bound in the UK by Bookmarque, Croydon, Surrey

To Mum and Ann

CHAGAS DISEASE, or *American trypanosamias,* is a disease widespread in Central and South America, and caused by the *Trypanosoma cruzi* . . . There is no effective drug treatment. It has been suggested that Charles Darwin acquired the disease during his historic voyage on *The Beagle* and that it was the chronic form that . . . was ultimately responsible for his death in 1882.

Black's Medical Dictionary, 39th edition

The Fountain at the Centre of the World

Part One
Spring 1999

1

Evan Hatch is listening to the radio in his kitchen. He is standing in an azure cotton shirt and blue silk tie. He likes to be dressed before he has breakfast. The white coffee cup hangs in midair. He is listening to a *Today* story about Colombian president Pastrana's visit. He is listening the way a piano teacher listens to her pupil play a nocturne.

Evan knows this story because he's read it in the original. It's the one where all your preconceived ideas about a Colombian ruling elite turn out to be very wrong. It's the one where the president's in strategy meetings with the British government (joint ventures, shared concerns, acting together), where he's asking the drug tsar for help *against* the narco-traffickers and the death squads.

He has his coat on and stands holding keys and case, still waiting for the story to end. He jingles the keys in his hand. The acoustics in his flat are like they are when you first move into a new place before you've unpacked the boxes.

It's the story that ends when Reporter asks Defence Minister why for God's sake Britain doesn't increase military aid to Colombia.

Walking to Angel tube he wondered if he'd get a gloating e-mail from Lenny at Sawyer Miller. Sawyer Miller had the Colombia contract. (Nine point seven million dollars initial signing-on fee, and then three million for every year that the threat of sanctions diminishes.)

Morden via Bank. The train bent and swayed and ignored the nursery-coloured map.

Dispatch riders have to hunt for a moment before finding a small logo-plaque by the recessed buzzer bearing the lower-case legend: poley bray communications. The buzzer when pressed makes no noise. The motorcycle courier, even with helmet off and damp hair steaming the tinted glass, hears nothing until the door clicks open.

Nor does the lobby of Poley Bray say: This is what we do, this is how massive we are. A punch-number door seals a corridor and the decor is modest, like a mid-rent video production company. There are no plasma screens, no in-house video, no low-table presentation pack. Just a few glossies and newspapers—a bit like a dentist's waiting room. But there is one giveaway . . .

Anyone left sitting in the lobby for more than a few minutes—waiting for an appointment perhaps—might find their eyes wandering to the wall behind reception. Here they will see a map of the world: black countries on a black background with spidery white borders. On this chart Poley Bray's business offices are mapped out in electric red dots. If you're kept waiting long enough you might get 'round to counting them. There are sixty red dots in thirty blacked-out countries. And behind the sixty red dots in thirty dark countries, behind the multi-billion annual turnover, behind Poley Bray lies a single, precise calculation. *It is easier and less costly to change the way people think about reality than to change reality.*

On the fourth and final floor Evan has almost reached his office-cube when he hears a voice behind him: You're not very tanned!

Evan turns round to see Stella, half in the corridor, half in her glass-walled office. She's peering at him, kind of curiously and mock-curiously at the same time. You've been working, haven't you? she says. You didn't go on holiday at all.

How are *you?* replies Evan, disappearing into his own glass hutch.

He hasn't been on holiday. But he hasn't been working either. Now he can, though. Now he can. Except that even now, even today, his first day back, he's going to have to leave at noon to see the doctor.

Clicking on his in-tray icon here's something new. An invitation to speak in Seattle: an issues management conference hosted by the Washington Board of Trade and Development. But no. Sorry, no. His strategy right now is to cut out everything nonessential.

To work. Translations clipped off a whole world's news bulletins relevant to each of his client accounts wait for him a double click away. Come home all my pretty pigeons.

He lifts his jacket away from his shirt a moment. Not too much sweat. Good.

You're not very tanned. He hates getting tanned anyway.

What you're doing wrong here, said Evan, is you're trying to win the argument.

At the end of his first morning back for a fortnight, Evan was over-seeing Richard Sizer and Heidi Spenney on some "regulatory capture." You don't have to win the argument, said Evan. It's more like you just want to put a weight of impressions on the public mind so that people will have doubts and lack motivation to take action. You just want them to go: *Oh things are really complicated—it's not so simple as I thought.* So to do this we just keep getting our *balancing information* into the stream from trustworthy sources. There's no need for a clear-cut victory. That's the point I'm making. Don't over-reach. You just keep gently increasing the public's doubts about this being any kind of clear-cut situation. And that's all you need to do. There's the fairy-tale forest, elves and pixies on the one hand, and here's MFP on the other, with the Sustainable Forest Foundation behind them, saying, well, in the real world it's more important to the logging companies to *preserve* the rich diversity of forest. We nurture because we have a real concern, not a sentimental one, a *real* concern in all the diversity of the forest and its—

Evan felt a cold draught as the door opened, smelt perfume and heard Jenna's voice: Excuse me, sorry, Evan, only the Seattle people need an answer by—

What am I doing? asked Evan, looking halfway between her and the table. He then repeated the question, but casually as if it were a query: What am I doing?

I'm sorry, she said, withdrawing and shutting the door, slower and quieter than its weighted hinges would have managed alone.

There was a persistent economy to Evan's movements: only one thing moved at a time. He might move his forearm at the elbow or turn his close-cropped head to listen—but not at the same time. Evan always moved like someone recovering from slight whiplash, a recovery which looked sensuous; the glow of nerves heating up again as the circuit was renewed, a subtle return of feeling.

Evan Hatch was not the only workaholic who, were it not for designer glasses and a handsome suit, would have looked like he'd been sleeping rough until a few power-shower weeks ago. But to Spenney and Sizer there was a weird corporate glamour about Evan's wizened look, the alert, brown eyes in a pale, dry face. Even the slightly receding temples looked to the juniors like a badge of having got beyond self into pure incorporation.

The best issues management work, Evan now told them, you should never notice: you just notice your opinions slowly changing.

Integrated Communications. That was where it was at, and that was Evan's job. Hands-on control of the intellectual thermostat, active agenda setting, journals and briefing documents for ministers, special little conferences for journalists, intelligence gathering on activist/civic/ political groups. Once there was a time when Evan used to wish he was in lobbying or government relations. But not now. Trade liberalization had pulled flaks into the front line. Poley Bray was on the WTO Industrial Sector Advisory Committee and Evan had a seat on the Business Council for Sustainable Development where the talk was war-like and macho. They spoke of battlelines, firefights, and a return to the trenches; of corporate activism, guerrilla campaigns, and rear-guard actions, of blood on the carpet and body count. This was way closer to power than government relations. Evan was treetops now.

Fists in the pockets of fawn crombie with black velvet collar, Evan skipped down the three steps on to the pavement. It was a short walk from Poley Bray to the doctor's. Evan Hatch liked the fact that his new specialist was actually on Harley Street. With money and power, it seemed, London shrunk down to its con-stituent nineteenth-century villages and the city made sense, its geography took shape. Power was the perspective from which a confusing urban layout became legible. To Evan it was just like those Aztec earthworks whose geometrical patterns could only be made out from a helicopter; a nod and a wink from one long-gone elite to another. The shadow of a Lear jet on a revealed decahedron, a coherence emerging, the true pattern of London. He pressed the buzzer of the listed building. He was impatient to get back to work. He hoped it wouldn't take too long.

Bone marrow! Bone fucking marrow! What has that got to do with me? Tissue match! Stem cell! Why even go to the specialist when I was feeling better? Why spoil the up-time? Why didn't I just go when I had to go?

He looked up. Poley Bray. Already. How could it be such a short walk back to the office? He went round the block, and then the next one and the next. Crossing over from the sunny side of a street he passed through damp and chilly shadows. Alone here in his own gloomy biosphere, he remembered.

The prognosis had been simply and straightforwardly put, but the words describing what would happen to him were impossibly large. He felt like someone watching a landslide coming toward him who just stares at the thundering rocks because the scale's so impossibly wrong (this long-distance stuff in the near distance). Because it's not in the agreed nature of things that he should not have time to run. Because the sound has yet to catch up. And yet this is the prognosis, thought Evan. This is what will happen to me unless I can get some bone marrow. No, unless I can get some blood *and* bone marrow. Jesus!

He tried to let the sound catch up with the words he had heard: one in four. There's a one in four chance of a tissue match if I can find my brother.

Evan walked past buildings he knew nothing about. He came to a park and stood by a bench looking down at the empty wooden slats.

If I can find my brother. How? A tracing agent? I could die waiting for the dog-eared folders of a Mexican records department. An ad in *La Prensa*? Can he even read? (The Spanish word now came to Evan before the English: *analfabeto*. Illiterate.) Or use a free-media plant: a story about an Englishman looking for his long-lost brother. Yeah, and get loads of impostors. No they'll see me coming! And when the bone marrow doesn't match, well, perhaps I'd still like to come to dinner, see some old photos, buy a farm. Yes. Plus word would get out to the biz. Long-term plans disappear if they find out I'm ill.

Evan lived in the shadow of the fear that they'd find out about his illness at Poley Bray. Just over a fortnight earlier, his last lapse had begun with a trembling fit in his glass-walled office. Evan had gone to sit in the toilets for a few minutes until it had passed. Fourteen hours later he'd been discovered by the Kenyan office cleaners. On coming round he'd washed himself as best he could before walking to Tottenham Court Road in damp and soiled kecks. In a curtained cubicle he put on the trousers and boxers he'd just bought and wore them out, leaving his old clothes next to a litter bin still heaped with the junk of last night. Back in the office he'd given the cleaners fifty pounds hush-money.

My brother might still be around the same area I was born . . . Evan reflected, as he reached the three steps of Poley Bray.

He stood in his office as if it was someone else's. And in a way it was, because the decision he now made was the complete reverse of what he'd decided in this same office a couple of hours ago. Previously he'd been cutting out non-essential assignments, but this trip to Seattle would act as a cover for going to Mexico. He'd just not be going *straight* to Seattle. (In fact, if he said he was going to *America* he wouldn't even be lying.) By the time I get back, thought Evan, I'll still have done all the meetings, only taken slightly longer about it. The only thing is I'll have to write the Seattle speech now, in case I wobble in the week before the conference.

This stockpiling was his strategy: each time he rounded the sunny side of the moon he set about stacking up enough work to cover him before he went out of view again.

His coat still on, Evan slowly paced the loud floor of his cold flat like an estate agent waiting for a view-by-appointment.

The one good thing about a definite diagnosis, he thought, is that now at least I can tell someone. It'll be a relief to tell someone I can trust. Patrick, not Sophie. (Thinking about Sophie, it now seemed to Evan that chucking her had been an act of selfless renunciation so that she wouldn't be left grieving. He hadn't known he was ill at the time, but still he felt he was only now able to see his actions in their true light. It would almost be worth getting in touch to show her how selfless he'd been.)

Evan imagined what he'd say to Patrick when they met up. How he'd say it: *So, er, yeah, I've got to go and seek out my brother . . . Mexico, as it happens . . . Yes, as a matter of fact, that's, ah, that's actually where I was born . . . Myelogenous leukaemia it would appear . . . Well, no, not if you catch it early, really . . .*

2

But what can a protest march achieve? asked Chano Salgado.

We have to do something, right? replied Oscar, his forearm flat on the table like the shadow on a sundial pointing at Chano. The others at El Café Fuente were all looking at Chano too. Yes, they'd known him a long time—but a long time ago. Did they still?

Of course you have to act, Chano replied, but we need to find, well, some other way, a new way.

Yes, said Ayo intently and Oscar nodded easily. But only Yolanda—Yolanda who worked in the *caseta telefónica*—had heard Chano correctly. She alone had heard his secret hope that he wouldn't have to be involved in finding this new way because he was sure that it wouldn't work any better than the old. No one, she thought, is more concerned with the practicalities of action than those who never do anything. Ayo meanwhile had heard something different again. Something altogether different.

Only a few miles away the Ethylclad toxic-waste plant was pumping out sixty thousand gallons of groundwater a day. Protests last year had held up construction for ten months. But now not only was the plant up and pumping but the people of Tamaulipas state had to pay Ethylclad ninety million dollars compensation for the ten months' lost profits. Ninety million was more than the combined annual income of everyone in Tamaulipas, but private power's writ was absolute. (And alphabet soup: NAFTA through WTO's International Centre For The Settlement of Investment Disputes.)

Chano Salgado climbed the steep, wooded cemetery on the edge of Tonalacapan, pulling himself up by branches and roots. He came out at the top of the copse. The half-moon and night pollution from distant Calderon flared over a wide flat expanse, glazing the clear canola fields below with a dim glow. He went down the hill sideways, carefully. How long has it been? one of the old crowd at El Café Fuente had asked him. How long since you were here with us all? It had been years. But perhaps he'd thrown El Café Fuente over too quickly.

He entered the field and walked a long, thin runway between strips of canola.

Dona, who'd brought him up, would always tell him off for throwing things over too quickly. (Chano was four when his mother died and his baby brother was adopted by an English couple. He'd gone to Dona and Guido, his mother's aunt and uncle, who were both quite old.) The evening English lessons Dona gave him were more a lesson in sticking at things, an example underscored by the fact that she herself had already been out teaching English all day. But since she would have energy for another hour, then he, with all his youth, should too.

Unrelentingly, she'd teach him to adapt what he already knew with the single purpose of showing him that he could always do more than he thought. *You already know this, Mariano.* (She never called him Chano, the short form of Mariano.)

How do you say "*Aprendimos a nadar en el río*"?

No sé.

Yes, you do, she'd counter in the insistent English of unavoidable things. How do you say "*incendiar*"?

Burn.

And what did the prince of hearts do with the tarts? she asked.

Burned.

Burn. To burn. It's an "rn" verb. She touched the battered and taped text book open on the table before them. And what's this called? she asked, turning the front cover just enough to show him the title before flattening it out again on the page they were on.

"We Are Learning English."

Of course. Now what does that mean?

Aprendieron inglés.

Yes. To learn is an 'rn' verb like 'burn'—learn, burn—so in that case how do you—

Learned.

Bueno. Río . . . ?

River.

Aprendimos a nadar en el río? she resumed with that frowning look the elderly sometimes assume with children, a look which disguises their need to be involved in beginnings, newness, and growth, their need to love. *Aprendimos a nadar en el río*, she repeated.

We learned to swim in river.

In . . . ?

The river.

Good.

No más, said Chano.

No . . . ?

More. No *more.*

Bueno.

From the other room Guido, who'd had a former life at the Detroit Bridgewater tire plant, called out in gnarly old English: Don' swim in no river! You die of poison, boy!

That was when there still *were* rivers, thought Chano, passing the buckled white metal sign for Calderon and Ejido El Reparo El Refugio.

Tamaulipas, the northeasternmost state of Mexico, is a land of dead rivers. The dead rivers are more diverse than live ones. In the Sierra de Cruillas foothills they're a fiery shale of bauxite cinders and rusty iron filings. Higher up are rockeries of suspended gravel (like an art teacher doing a waterfall by pouring grit down a gully of glue). In the clay flats dry gorges have carved out a Model-World Grand Canyon; and on the limestone plains around Tonalacapan the riverbeds are gob-stoppered with bleached stone. These pebble ditches may, from time to time, puddle with mud and water but will never be a river again. They remain geological relics, curios of the Water Age, just as a flat-bottomed valley can be covered in ice and snow but will never be a glacier again.

Chano clanged an empty propane cylinder on to the shed's stone floor. Today he had fifty brown bottles—*canela jora*—and ten crates of clear bottles—*fresa upi*—to do.

Chano's tall shed at the Taxco Santos Chicha Co-op stood fifty paces from the main still where *chicha*—the local corn beer—was pitch-fermented. The tall shed had a flat, felt roof and a stainless steel chimney. Only Chano had the key. He was as self-employed as it was possible to be in a co-op. The past ten years Chano had spent working in this little sterilizing shack. Though he'd never dropped in on El Café Fuente, he'd never been that far away either. His time with the sulphite purifying solution meanwhile had made his skin like wax-paper, his hair salt-thick and clumpy, and his fingernails ridged and brittle.

There came a banging on the door. Lunchtime! We're going downtown, shouted a voice from a scampered distance. Coming?

Chano suppressed his irritation enough to call out in a pleasant voice: Not possible right now. *Orale-bye.* He held himself still until they moved off. He wrapped a withered, sterilized sheet round a few crates of empties and stacked them a few feet outside the door, where the mummified bottles made a muffled clink.

On a clear day like this Chano could see the tip of the Sierra de Cruillas, a mountain range the Mayans had believed the centre of the world, because when the snow disappears from its peak the world will end. His mind went back to the wayward fountain at El Café Fuente, which last night had slumped and plumed as if registering sine waves of distant forces. He wondered whether the fountain was a seismograph, its erratic flow some kind of readout. It was possible, he considered, since it was a hydraulic fountain, powered solely by water pressure and gravity. Maybe it was the fountain at the centre of the world, responding minutely to everything that's going on everywhere on earth. Then again, he thought, perhaps the Ethylclad plant has killed the groundwater already.

By five the main still was empty again. Everyone else had gone home. The siphon-tubing, pitch-bins, and plastic kegs from the main still were stacked outside. He took them in, glancing nervously at the road. A strange orange sun hung low and round and further away than usual, and the sky was a bit misted up, like cloudy lemon juice.

A little later Chano went out to empty some rinse water and again looked at the road. And this time—with a sharp, sinking feeling—he finally saw what he'd been waiting for. Here came Ayo, walking his bow-legged, head-rolling walk with a kind of loping inevitability. Ayo's thin, patchy beard jutted forward on the horizontal, parallel to his peaky bangs, as though a grizzly bear's jaws were closing on the back of his head. Chano went back into the shack's thick fog and fumes and turned off the gas stove which was cooking up the sulphur.

Ayo knocked and stepped into the smoke-cloud hut. He'd just begun speaking when a coughing fit sent him staggering straight back out. Chano joined him outside. Wheezing and eyes streaming, Ayo said: *Puta madre!* Only you and the Devil can live in there, my friend!

Sodium metabisulphite, said Chano, smiling and handing him a bottle of tap water, which Ayo poured over his face before sitting on a crate of bottles. Don't sit on that one, Chano said sharply. Sit there.

OK.

Ayo wiped his eyes with the tips of his fingers, blinked once, twice, until he could see again. He drank a little water and put it down on the ground very carefully as if the dirt outside Chano's shack was a brand-new carpet. You were right, what you said last night, Ayo began in his tight, strangulated voice, a croaky squawk. What can a protest march achieve? Nothing. Chano looked back toward his shack and its warm smoky interior. Here you have the chemicals, said Ayo, the knowledge—

No, no, no, replied Chano, feeling poisoned, but Ayo continued in the same slow pace of speech with which he'd begun:

—with which to blow the pipes—

No, Ayo, see—

—the organo-phosphates to make a fertilizer bomb, he said, pouring some water on his neck and spreading it around under his jagged Eskimo hair. All you need is ammonia, he added, kicking the bag at his feet.

No, Ayo. You heard me wrong. I meant . . . what I meant was who will hear us? That's all. Unless it's a really big march. We have to speak truth to power. That's what we have to do.

No, no, no, Ayo replied with easy dismissiveness. He'd thought about the conversation they would have. He knew Chano would behave like people at one of those tedious meetings where they were always finding a committee-type, procedural way out of doing anything there and then (and always managed to sound more revolutionary than everybody else in the process), where they'd broaden everything out to big consultations. He'd expected Chano to have lots of ready-made phrases and positions set up like road blocks this way and that. And so he was patient.

Yes, countered Chano. We take our demands downtown and we say, "This is what we demand—what are you going to do about it?"

It's time, said Ayo, to stop asking what they are going to do about it, and start deciding what we are going to do.

Yes, I agree with that, said Chano. Community action, from the ground up. But I just meant we have to find a way to make sure it gets picked up by the media, to make it national, form links between trade unions, the land unions, the peasants, Maya, church groups. That sort of thing.

Speak truth to power, *pinto*? You think power don't *know*?

Chano flinched minutely. *Pinto*. In calling Chano *pinto*—or ex-con—Ayalo had broken a small, local taboo. No one ever alluded to Chano's past. Ayo knew about the wall of brittle dignity called the Past, behind which Chano claimed immunity from all collective, political action in the present. And this, Ayo thought, in a land where . . .

well, *que viva la raza!* It's not like he's the only one with a story. And it's not even as if his story is entirely his own.

Who but you, he asked, knows how to do this thing, *pinto?* To do it safely?

I'm not a terrorist, Chano replied.

It's only the fact that it's a bomb makes it seem like terrorism!

Oh Jesus!

It's sabotage. Sabotage.

But that's not how the military or police will see it—

What sort of argument is that? asked Ayo. When did we ever—

—if a bomb's involved.

It's not terrorism, said Ayo softly. Terrorism is putting a bomb on a subway train and killing ordinary, working-class people.

Or any people . . .

Or any people . . . but this is . . . they're the terrorists, Ethylclad. They're the ones indiscriminately killing people whose names they don't even know. This—what we're doing—this is anti-terrorism, this is self-defence. Self-defence. Soon the land will be so salty nothing else will grow here if we just let them keep pumping it out. It's self-defence.

All right. But not this. This is never the way. And not me, no.

The pipes are miles from any human, squawked Ayo. No one will even hear it. Pop! A little pop in the distance. "What was that?" If we could drill through the steel and iron pipes with a pneumatic drill we'd do that, but we can't.

Not me, Ayo.

Then who?

Then no one.

Then no one, repeated Ayo.

Right.

And the crops and the farmers and the children and the sickness and the villages and the savings and the money? While we wait for power?

No, this isn't the way. Violence is always the first thing infiltrators do, first thing they try to get everyone else to do. And why's that?

Violence, scoffed Ayo, it's not violence—

Because then we lose the sympathy of the people, said Chano. That's why we have to speak truth to power.

Sixty thousand gallons a day are being pumped out, squawked Ayo. And then the dry land will get so thirsty it will suck all the toxins in the sludge straight back out again, right back down into the groundwater. And when that happens? Crops, people, livestock— everything will be poisoned. Poisoned. For hundreds of miles around. It's a dirty bomb. And you want to speak truth to power?

You're dismissing the whole, great history of demonstrations. Many rights have been won by speaking truth to power. We show them the big picture, the real human cost of what they're doing.

They can never change, said Ayo, emphasizing every syllable.

We can change them, replied Chano, his mouth dry.

Ayo sensed that Chano's jabber now was merely the canary chatter you make as the air of your belief gets thinner and thinner and so he let Chano talk himself out. Then he said: I'll leave this here, anyway.

Take it away.

You don't have to plant the bomb.

No, said Chano in sudden bitter fury. If I make it, I'll take it.

Ayalo shot him a look, but Chano had turned and slammed the door of the shed behind him. End of meeting.

Alone, Ayo took a big yellow bag of fertilizer out of his backpack, put it next to the ammonia and walked quickly away.

Chano still has some siphon-tubes to purify. He lowers the hinged and perforated stainless-steel crate with the big lever on the side like a one-armed bandit into the vat of sodium metabisulphite solution. He stops. He sits down on his chair, a draining tray in his hand. The shack's dense mist has begun thinning. He gazes at the curlicues of smoky sulphur cloud twisting and shaping in the light.

Pinto. Hundreds and hundreds of miles down south is Cerro Hueco prison where the cells have no numbers. No one knows how many *olvidados* are in there at any one time, *incomunicados* from all over Mexico (they call it the Trade Union Conference). In Cerro Hueco he has imaginary conversations with Daniel. No sooner does Chano learn something new (what to do if you end up in prison, for example) than he imagines sharing it with the boy, except in the telling it comes out salty with age as if from a mysterious cache of old wisdom.

In the polythene-lined shack Chano wonders whether he jinxed their future by imagining conversations he'd one day have with Daniel as he grew up, whether by putting the future in the present he used it all up.

Four A.M. and the baby howling. Chano gets out of bed, lifts Daniel into his arms and carries him into the other room while Marisa sleeps. Daniel is bawling, his face raw, wet, and sore.

Putting some water on to boil, Chano frees first one hand and then the other to warm it at the gas ring's flame, before laying the hand on Daniel's face and head.

The kitchen is the short bit of the L-shaped room; in the long bit he walks up and down holding the baby.

Can you hear that, Danilito? Yes, it's your mother snoring. Yes. Isn't it loud?... Yes, it is, isn't it? You're such a lucky boy, because your mother knows everything. Yes she does. And she's never wrong. No, she never is. And you look like her, so you'll be smart, too.

Dog-tired and wholly oblivious of the steam slowly filling the room as the saucepan boils down on the propane ring, Chano sits on a chair, hooks his feet up off the cold floor and perches Daniel on the table, holding him by the chubby wrists. He has run out of baby noises and soothing words and begins to wonder whether an adult, conversational tone might have some magic sedative properties. And so begins the first long conversation he ever has with his son. And the last.

But there is one thing I see in you that is like me, he says and clicks his thumbs either side of Daniel's head. The baby slowly registers the sound and works his spindly-gyro neck upright. After some hunting around, his gaze finds his father's face again. Yes, says Chano, that's it. You are not present, you're off somewhere else, el soñador! *Isn't the world all surprising and new! And you will need us here.*

Daniel stops crying. Instead his big eyes seem vaguely alarmed by the continuous rolling address.

But how much to tell you? Without you becoming like all the others? For if the others are playing chess but you're playing checkers you'll never fall for the traps they set for you. There it is, hijo. *There it is.*

The baby's face is red and hot. The saucepan boiling down on the hob begins to rattle and Chano discovers that the room is thick with steam. He lays Daniel on the floor. In dense fog he nips round the corner of the room and bumps into the invisible trash can. He turns off the gas and pours cold water over the saucepan. As the black hissing expends itself, its fury doused to mere reproach, Chano hears the baby crying. Daniel has remembered that he's hungry and won't, by the sound of it, get fooled again.

Back in the tiny steam-filled front room, Daniel has tipped on to his side. Tiny hands up by his red and streaming face, he is crying uncontrollably again. Chano stops. He looks down at his curled-up son. Something moves geologically within his heart, a powerful emotion he can't name. It has something to do with seeing Daniel lying there on his own; lying on the floor like on a microscope slide, like he's abandoned. Chano crouches down a foot away from him and strokes his damp hair.

Don't cry, my baby, don't cry, he says. It's all right, it's all right.

He can hear Marisa getting up now.

Ay! What's going on? asks Marisa. There's so much steam in here I almost stepped on the baby!

I wonder at what age they feel love? he asks.

Eh? Too soon, too soon.

Want a coffee? he asks.

She nods and picks up breast-cloth and baby, wondering what bare minimum of consciousness she can do this in.

Chano looks around the shed, watching steamy clouds of sulphite solution unravel and flee. A last trail of head-height sulphur smoke is curling into thin air. He says the word out loud in the sterilizing shack. *Pinto.*

The night after Marisa's assassination, Chano drives out in a pick-up with two other student activists, three rifles and a pistol. They go to do they know not what. Army roadblock. Soldiers. Bright lights. Shouting. Two run. Both are shot dead. Chano stays at the wheel. His corpse is never found. Desaparecido, *the people say. Disappeared like in El Salvador, Chile, Argentina or somewhere like that. Rumour says that after the first two bodies were found, the military or White Guards, or* el pulpo *or whoever the assassins were, went and buried Chano Salgado's body some place else. A place it would never be found. But what now to do with the orphan Daniel?*

It takes two weeks from Chano's release from Cerro Hueco jail, at the end of his two-year stretch, until he steps off an Oriente bus on the highway by the

straight, white road which leads into Tonalacapan; little knowing that the
worst news left in the world is only half a mile's walk ahead of him.

And now, putting the draining tray on the floor, Chano once again
entertains that other fantasy. The one where he just gets on a bus to
Costa Rica. The one where he calculates how long it would take him
to sift through all of fourteen million people to find only one. His
son. Daniel. He gets up stiffly, opens the door and carries the ammonia and fertilizer back into his shed at the Taxco Santos Co-op, locks
up and heads for home.

Stepping off the bus in Calderon, Chano walked through the chain-
store shopping mall where there was a man selling bunches of helium
balloons and an ancient Toltec woman begging. He cut across the
plaza, crossing the grass outside Calderon's university. He passed a student demonstration, and paused to read the banners. The student
strike, he learned, was against the introduction of tuition fees.

Like many others, Chano had moved away from political involvement since his student days. He supposed he still believed what he
always had—which is, of course, the same as not believing anything
any more. Occasionally at, say, a table in the steamy One Dollar Diner
in Calderon, he'd get worked up about an issue he heard being discussed. But when he did so it was with a slightly hectic sense that
everyone else was missing something massively simple. That was his
interest: the oversight more than the issue. And so in the One Dollar
Diner his voice would get this urgent, oddly sing-song tone. He would
repeat himself and grow heated that the owner or the guys at the next
table weren't slapping their foreheads, getting on the phone, passing
it on like wildfire and weren't, in general, acting like the scales had
fallen from their eyes. And then, a few minutes later, Chano wasn't
bothered by the oversight or by the whole issue at all. It had gone
from him. And the other men in the diner who'd carried on arguing
would glance over at him, thinking they'd offended him, until they
noticed his complete absorption in his paper, or his meal, or in the
view from the window. For Chano Salgado had optimism of the intellect and pessimism of the will.

Standing by the student picket line, Chano noticed a short police-man with crumbling, chalky skin who kept twitching his small moustache, incessantly waggling his top lip side to side. Chano tried twitching his own moustache to see what it felt like. He looks like someone about to sneeze except he never does, thought Chano. No, he looks more like his small moustache is too tight for his face. The policeman began staring directly at Chano. For a few seconds Chano stared back in an absent-minded daze, still twitching, then looked sharply away. When he looked back the policeman was still looking at him. Chano walked away, heading for home in the peripheral *barrios* on the northern outskirts of Calderon.

Chano's home was a small triangular patch of land at the junction of Calles Morales and Benito Juarez, two small, dusty streets in the res-idential grid in El Refugio. His one-storey, two-room *choza* was in the narrow corner of the triangle, and had a car seat propped next to the front door. What looked like a scrapyard or private dump were all the bits of salvage and pipes which he hadn't been able to fit into the puzzle of his house-building and so had left out of the equation. The rusted hood of Oscar's old 68 Chevy formed part of his fence, Christmas lights coiled around a drainpipe and estafiata sprouted from a Commex paint can nailed to the wall.

This was the same home he'd once shared with his wife and son. Back then El Refugio El Reparo had been a separate pueblo, but over the years Calderon had extended a long, clanking arm of hub-caps nailed on to clapboard mechanics, stalking signposts, and the black steel columns of low-slung PeMex garages.

Chano sat down at his kitchen table with a glass of water. His gaze rested, at first blindly, on cans and bags on the shelves. Thinking about what he'd have to do tomorrow the cans and bags quickened before his eyes. Looking at the vinegar he now saw acetic acid; the talc became magnesium silicate; the iron rust on his saucepan, ferric oxide; the chalk was calcium carbonate; and the battery sulphuric acid and zinc. It was as if the real nature of things that had been ossi-fied was only now coming to life. Now here they were. As reckless and unstable as ever. This was how they'd always been, they'd never been away, only sleeping. He began, dejectedly, to think of combinations toward chloride of azole, picric acid and mercury fulminate, to work out his stabilizing agent, texturizer, and blasting cap, his own small thoughts and memories prisoners within the orbit of ammonium nitrate.

Chano stood out in his backyard. He looked at yesterday's half-empty cup of coffee, at the sweatshirt he'd used as a pillow last night, at the *Uno Mas Uno* he'd never got round to reading. They looked like a roped-off museum exhibit called "How We Lived Yesterday." Artifacts from another life. The same hammock, the same paper, the same sweatshirt—except that now they were all gone from him. And Chano knew exactly why this had happened, knew just why he now stood among the ordered wreckage of a lost life. It was because he had opened his heart to it. Found peace here. Because he had loved it.

3

A heavy squall burst over the potato pickers in the black field. Fat drops shuttled through them like a loom, before pattering away into the far trees to leave the air in misty stupefaction. The boy threw a potato at the bag from a few yards away and missed.

The yellow sacks kept keeling over. The boy tried to set one straight but the vinyl was slippery with rain, and the old fertilizer sack heavy with potatoes. He angrily grabbed the sack with both hands and lapelled it upright.

If a sack had just seven pounds in, or was even a few ounces under, or if the potatoes had too much mud on them, then the whole sack didn't count. And that was forty minutes wasted. *Putada.*

You could get a system going with bell peppers. With the bell peppers you could get into a rhythm, swoop and scoop and catch the stalks snug in the join at the base of your fingers. But in this field you were crouching and on your knees. He looked over at Paciencia: short and stocky and five bags ahead. Eleven neat bags all in a row. For once he wished he wasn't tall.

At first, he'd thought it was good: seventy-five cents a bag. Better than the day rate in the packing room he'd reckoned. But today, filling bags in the rain, the boy was tired in wet clothes, with the dark, clogged earth heavy on his calf muscles, his socks chafing and his cold hands clumsy.

Last week was better. But not much. Cleaning out a barn over on the Cargill mega-ranch. Scraping up the encrusted cow shit, feathers and fertilizer. Two spades, one barn and a hundred square yards of buried floor. Sometimes it would come easy, as satisfying and salivary as picking a scab, his spade zzzhinging the stone floor and a whole chunk lifting clean away. But other times he'd scrape and stab and dig and chisel and get nowhere, nothing, no joy. There seemed to be a fossilized dirt layer more compact than stone. And of course, he remembered, dragging a yellow sack to the next furrow, the one time he'd stopped to rest what had happened? The foreman had come in, his walk all smart and crisp like the tail-wagging labrador beside him.

I don't see you doing much work, Daniel, he'd said.

It's just there's a few patches that won't lift so easy, and it's . . . I was just . . . eh, Daniel had begun, holding his spade-handle in midair, neither using it nor feeling he could rest it on the ground. (He had unconsciously adopted that compromised position—stooping with a slight knee-bend—of half-pretending to be half-working.) Having stared him into silence, the foreman snatched up a rusted-thin, bucket-scoop shovel that Daniel had earlier found useless and discarded. The foreman set about working full-tilt for thirty seconds. Thirty seconds of wild, up-and-at-'em activity lifted away a tough, encrusted patch. He then straightened up, all nifty and full of beans.

There you go! See how simple it is if you go at it with a bucket scoop and the right attitude, he announced, drumming head with middle finger and staring at Daniel. Then he very precisely held the scoop shovel out to Daniel by the handle. Daniel, who was already holding one shovel by the handle in midair, took it in his free hand. Holding two spades off the ground is, for a boy, a bit like being strung up on powerful, opposing magnets. He buckled and the clanging metal shovel heads crash-landed on to the loud patch of concrete just cleared by the foreman. Daniel looked up to find the foreman's smug eyes on him. It was as if this subtly humiliating touch had been the cost of the lesson, the penalty for making the foreman do thirty seconds of exhibition work. And with that, the foreman left as suddenly as he'd come, the labrador trotting vaingloriously beside him. I expect it done by four, the *cargillero* had called out without turning. He'd stepped through the door, cocked a leg, farted, and was gone. Daniel had then hoisted a shovel-load up into a tall, wooden crate and half the spadeful had fallen back on him.

He cleared mud from a divot in a crooked potato, packing his fingernails with dirt. His hands were wet and cold. He loaded his forearms with seven potatoes and walked carefully back to the sack. He concentrated on balancing them along his arms and also on resisting the urge to look at Paciencia who was bending over in her black, woollen tracksuit trousers. He dumped the potatoes in the yellow fertilizer bag.

It was easy for the *cargillero* foreman, he thought. Easy. I could nip into a barn and make scraping the floor look easy. *For thirty seconds.* Anyone can do that for thirty seconds, but not for a whole day. And yet that *cargillero* goes on as if it's all in the right attitude, all in the mind. (Daniel saw again the foreman rapping middle finger on head.) No effort at all. But that energy comes from his whole day being full of lots of short, fast buttings-in and goings-out again. In. Out. For him it *is* all in the mind. And yet he makes out as if the whole reason he's a supervisor now is because once upon a time he *did* use to work like that all day long, as if that's how come they made him foreman. But then, if that were true, they'd have never let him stop. *Pinche cabron!*

The faded, saggy sun is drying out as Daniel walks the six miles home. His black sweatshirt exhales steam in the late dusk, weed spores speckle his wet and sorry trainers. Herons follow a tractor in the two ploughed lanes of a green field as if they've just been ploughed up as they are: perfectly formed, perfectly white, perfect herons. He likes the walk home. He isn't tired now like when he's at work. Or at least it's a different kind of tired from when he's at the *finca*. There he aches and every hour is grindingly slow and all he can think about is lying down in dry clothes. But he always finds that as soon as he's free, like now, he's alright. Maybe, he vaguely considers, *el cargillero*'s right and I am a shirker.

He looks down. It's happened again. His hands are full of leaves. Once again he's walking along with stalks or leaves in his hand which he can't remember having torn off bush, hedge, or tree. He's never caught himself in the act of plucking them. It's only ever some time after that he becomes aware of spindling stripped stalks between his fingers, of wearing reed brass knuckles. He drops the green pirule stalk and wipes his palms clean of the shredded leaves. Right, he thinks, next time I'll catch myself doing it. OK. Hands empty now. He fixes in his mind the hacienda he's just passing so as to locate the starting point of this control experiment. At this point both hands are empty, Daniel says out loud.

The rottweiler at the gate barks. Daniel sees the dog is on a long chain spiked to the yard. As low as his fourteen-year-old pipes will go he growls at the rottweiler in the back of his throat. Wide-eyed with first disbelief then outrage the dog goes livid, throwing himself at the gate in a killing frenzy. Daniel runs down the lane laughing. He slows to a walk, arms swinging free, and then, as if scooted along by a new and sudden breeze, goes running and laughing again. Still the dog barks. Daniel hears the long chain snapping taut again and again like a failed trap.

Daniel slows a little. Then he slows some more. He begins to wonder how slow he'd go if he was just a body without a mind. He staggers and reels around the narrow lane: a guerrilla completing an arduous jungle trek, the last drops from his bullet-holed canteen having scorched cracked lips fifty jungle-miles ago; blind head slumped and nodding on chest and shoulder. Every dozen steps he forces his heavy eyes open. Must. Stay. Awake. Can't go on much longer . . . Until the guerrilla makes a discovery: exhaustion is all in the mind. So, using only the power of positive thinking, *el guerrillero* tricks himself into thinking he's just left base camp shaved and showered after a lemon tea. And, miraculously, he begins to walk as upright and smartly as if he was only just now *starting* his journey; as free and easy as a fourteen-year-old boy strolling home on a cool evening. That's what I'll do, thinks Daniel, if I'm ever a guerrilla in the jungle after the first hundred miles. Or, he judiciously amends, any similar situation (and drums a middle finger against his temple).

He leaves the road before La Guarari at the FCV mural (Frente Costarricence de la Vivienda), and follows his favourite dirt track toward Oscar Felipe pueblo.

Daniel Salgado knows some of the story of how he came from Mexico as a two-year-old to live in Costa Rica with Beto and Arlinda. His parents—Marisa and Chano—were both dead. There was a girl called Yessica, who looked after him and was some kind of relation of his mother or just from the same village in Mexico. A village called Tonalacapan. Yessica had married Arlinda and Beto's son, a trawler-man from Costa Rica. She'd died. Her husband had gone to Los Angeles. Daniel stayed with Arlinda and Beto.

The dirt track cuts across the fields to where the old man will be cursing a new machine, hitting it on its side with a wrench too big for its tiny, tiny parts. Beto is often still out there even at this hour since they've all changed to just corn.

Everyone has had to change the way they farm. From growing a variety of pulses and vegetables they've all had to shift to corn. It's not working. Now they need expensive pesticides, gas, insecticides and machine-rentals.

Fifty paces away Daniel sees Beto standing in his field. The old man has his head down, one arm across his solar plexus, as if he's halfway through crossing his arms but has forgotten the knot. At twenty paces Daniel notices that Beto's glasses are in one hand. At ten a tight adrenalin clip tells the boy it's all wrong. Dropping the torn estafiata leaves from his fingers, Daniel walks up to him.

The next noise he hears shocks him. A hawking, cawing sound. The old man is crying, but aridly. Chha! Chha! Little staccato barks, like someone who sneezes with just their mouth. Without looking up, Beto puts his hand out to lay it on Daniel's shoulder and misses. Daniel moves closer in case he tries again, but somehow he can't put his own hand on the old man. Abruptly, with thumb and forefinger, Beto wipes eyes and face in a single downward stroke, leaving a wet film on his raised and raddled face. Looking about him, his gaze falls on Daniel as if on a random object. It's not my field where I'm stand-ing, he says. Shouldn't even be here now. Ah, you see, we've all done it. Same here as in every field far as the eye can see. It seems to Daniel as if Beto's trying to enter an unreal world where it's not he but Daniel who's so bewildered by this, not he but Daniel who needs reas-suring words. No, when you got a responsibility, says Beto, you have to get out, got to cut your losses.

Beto puts on his glasses, makes a squaring-his-shoulders kind of harrumph, sniffs conclusively and turns to face the house. They start walking back. The old man stops. He puts both his hands in his pock-ets. Turning fresh eyes on Daniel he asks, in a disarmed and absolutely matter-of-fact undertone that scares the boy: What will happen to my land?

Daniel is doing his schoolwork by the light of the TV. The sound is turned down. His note pad lies flat on a sky-blue formica table—most of which is taken up by the portable TV—but he's no longer putting numbers in neat rows. Arlinda and Beto are arguing. He's never heard them fight like this before. He goes cold. Silently he puts his pencil down. His eyes rest on the screen. A silent marmoset leaves a silent tunnel on a silent plain and, stranded in its deafness, falls prey to a slow-motion eagle.

One afternoon a few days later, squeezing in among a standing-room-only crowd, Daniel weaved his way through a rammed café, where all heads were watching the breaking news on the top-corner TV like it was the Copa America. The entire Mexican trawler fleet, the news was saying, has been grounded!

It had happened like this. In the United States, the Sierra Club had forced a Congressional ban on tuna fishing with purse-sein nets, the Endangered Species Act (known as the Dolphin Death Act). The new, dolphin-friendly tuna laws immediately grounded the seventy-strong, privatized Mexican tuna fleet, gutted its canneries and scraped clean the slabs of its market stalls.

Good news for *los Ticos*. Their own fishing industry killed by de-regulation, their own waters off-limits, here was an opening for Costa Rican fishermen. Most boats could never make it to Europe, but they could now go to shallow-trawl dormant seas ripe with bigeye, albacore, blue-fin, skipjack and yellow-fin. But those with access to fishing boats had to hurry because they didn't know how long the grounding of the Mexican trawler fleet would last. It might only be as long as it took for a refit and a quick inspection. And as it happened *los Ticos* were dead right. For the Dolphin Death Act coincided with strange events . . .

At first no one saw the connection. But on the Frankfurt Eurex and in London Bridge City, on the Dow Jones and Tokyo Nikkei, the numbers were going up and down and all around and no one knew why. Green screens howled like amps wailing feedback from an undiscovered electrical source. All was confusion until, with an apologetic cough, the US Drug Enforcement Agency stepped forward and explained.

The Mexican trawler fleet, said the DEA, is the Cali cartel's fishing fleet of choice, the preferred delivery service to export cocaine to the docks of Bologna, Rotterdam, and Liverpool, which was why finance houses that had long handled these high-yield, see-no-evil blind trusts suddenly had burst condoms in the belly. Thus the Mexican fishing fleet was to get a rapid dolphin-friendly refit and its grounding was, in the event, to last only ten days.

Three nights after the news first broke in Costa Rica, however, Daniel was once again pretending to do some schoolwork by the flickery light of the TV. Again he couldn't concentrate. But Arlinda and Beto weren't fighting this time. There was another reason. He would have to tell them. Tell them now.

He stood up and went into the back room. His foster parents looked up at him while he began his announcement. He hadn't got more than a few words in when Arlinda interrupted him: You're going to leave home. You're going on a fishing boat to Mexico. You're going to find the village where you were born. Tonalacapan!

Daniel was astonished. Arlinda appeared to him in his amazement like the wise old woman in a fairy tale. How had she been able to read his mind? Always too old to pass for his mother, now was the one time her appearance fitted her role. (He was not, of course, the only fourteen-year-old boy to have believed himself more inscrutable than he really was.)

Yes, he replied, with Stefano. But he said to ask you.

Arlinda got up, humming a single note over and over and waving a hand over her frown as if to say, Well, whatever you've decided to do you'll do, and there's no talking you out of it. She then stood facing Daniel. She was much shorter and stronger than him.

I have no doubt you will go, she said. Her tone sounded as if she was washing her hands of him. For a moment Daniel feared she would deny him her two cents' worth which, he knew, was the same as her blessing. He stood facing her attentively. I have no doubt you'll get to Tonalacapan, she said. If you want. But you probably won't even find a wooden cross with his name on it.

Then I'll ask if anyone knew someone called Chano.

Well, if that was his name . . . It may have been his nickname.

It was all a long time ago, said Beto, knowing, as Arlinda knew, that Daniel's nature would respond more to sand in the gears than a red light. Daniel knew they spoke out of love. They were trying to prevent him putting himself in danger.

It was his name, said Daniel.

Daniel, I'm going to ask you to do something now, said Arlinda.

Yes, OK.

Don't tell anyone in Tonalacapan who your father was.

Why not?

Just don't.

Is it because he was—

Yes.

What if they were his friends? The people from the same organization?

How will you know? she asked. Daniel didn't know how he would know. Well, she continued, there it is. But I have no doubt you *will* tell someone. I have no doubt you *will* ask around.

No, I'll wait before I—

You *can't* wait, she said. But you should *try* to wait. And you should think about going where the jobs are instead. If you *could* wait then you would stay with Stefano on the boat, making money and then when you go away you would—well. There. You can do nothing other than you've always done.

Daniel's arms hung by his side and he now felt her cold, damp hands clamp his wrists while she gave him a long and searching look. Then she dropped his arms without a word and set about preparing dinner.

Daniel went for a walk around the dark block, along high, cement pavements with jumbo DIY drains set in them like ice-hockey goals, past broken glass and a pack of stray dogs.

He began to wonder what people mean when they talk about someone's "nature". He seemed to be hearing phrases like "human nature" mentioned more and more often. He knew that couldn't be right, that he must have heard the phrase plenty before. All the time. But it was only now that it had snagged his attention, that parts of his being had been set vibrating by the concept, that the saying had set him off.

That's just like you, she says, he reflected, or *That's not like you, Daniel,* she says; but what is like me? And is being like me a good thing? What if my true nature is bad? Is my nature a good thing? Is everyone's?

Sometimes when his teacher scolded him or when Arlinda lost patience with him it was like his nature was something he wasn't living up to—a clear outline of himself hanging just above him in the same way that his clean shirts hung from the kitchen-light flex when Arlinda was ironing. Other times, from what she said, it was like there was altogether too much of his own nature going on.

I can do this or I can do that, he thought, but what is being true to my nature? How do I know what to be true to? How do I know what's me and what's how other people want me to be? . . . What if someone's brave but then something terrifying happens to him so that he loses all his courage and he acts like a coward for the rest of his life? And suppose there's a friend of his who's born with exactly the same amount of bravery, but nothing really terrifying ever happens to him, and so he goes through his whole life being just as brave as he always was . . . Is one of the two men braver than the other? Daniel didn't know the answer.

He wondered why he was thinking about this word nature just now. He suspected the answer might be to do with his coming of age. He had fine down on his upper lip, his voice had dropped, and his arms and legs were beveling a little.

He stopped by a bush. There was that stench again, perhaps a maggoty dead dog. He'd noticed the smell the last few times he walked past this patch of scrub. He parted the bush with a trainer but couldn't see any dog. He'd have a look for it in daylight. Except no, he thought, because I won't be here tomorrow. I'll be gone! I am only one meal, one night's sleep, and two hugs away from leaving. Leaving for ever. And yet here I am walking past the same pack of stray dogs and broken glass, the same shops, the same smells of yam, cassava, and burnt rice.

On board the *Jennifer Lopez* all the fishermen were jabbering with the flush of being fishermen again, if only for a week. And all the banter and chat Daniel heard was sea stuff, was boat stuff, was paint, tuna, and packing-ice stuff. The crew were belting out all the talk and running jokes they used to share, but it was such a rapid, pell-mell banter that they were like a tribute band covering all their old standards in a medley. No one spoke of the jobs they'd never found since they were last at sea. Instead it was factory ships, subsidies and did you hear about Mario? Oxyacetalened his boat for scrap the day before the news broke!

Throughout all the spraff and spray the diesel engine was thudding good under the *Jennifer Lopez* (whose name meant they could say they were going into her, spent the night and most of the morning on her, etc). Someone unfurled the filthy sail of faded green tarpaulin just to air it. This got another cheer. For the hell of it. Why not? Dust and dead cockroaches, bits of grey polythene, cochineals and wood-chippings slid out, caught in the wind and got in everyone's eyes and mouths and down their necks. This got a cheer, too. Grins cracked the worn and waxed faces of these dust-blown ex-fishermen whose filthy clothes were only work clothes now.

4

Still with his coat on, keys in hand, Evan burrows in the cupboard under the stairs. He searches through old A4 folders, through shopping bags full of photos, under zipped-up tennis racquets, demoted phones, clattering cassettes, old curtains, student camp-beds, and buckled lampshades. The more he searches the more there gathers in a band across his forehead a sickly memory: his bouts of compulsive searching . . .

In the drinking days he'd come home reeking and decide that there was really *only one* video he had to watch in his last ten minutes of consciousness, *only one* cassette he had to hear, *only one* old sweater that he definitely needed to check he hadn't lost, *only one* old photograph of one ex-girlfriend he had to find. And so he would search. And next morning, his upstairs neighbours would have left a note in the hall, complaining about being woken by the up-ending of moving boxes or the hurling of a tool box or the slinging of fold-up patio chairs. But tonight he's searching for real.

Evan excavates sedimentary layers of his past. School photos and rough books. Gateway Comprehensive, Leicester. Evan, you should know this word, it's the same as in Spanish, his French teachers would say. A laaast request griiinngo, the boys would go. We've always believed it's very important you should learn Spanish, his mum would announce to him, in a self-conscious, speechifying tone. A chunk of chocolate on the striped tablecloth while he learned the regular verbs: ar, er, ir. *Amar. Temer. Partir.* Yeah, thought Evan, that's what my mother taught me. To love, to fear, to leave. (And somewhere in Nuneaton a confused and wandering Unitarian sat and wondered why his constant accusations had been exchanged for total absence.)

Graduation certificate. A starred first in History at Gonville & Caius College, Cambridge. History, as taught to Evan, was a puerile maturity of knowing that every faith shall be destroyed and every hope turn out like the last one. The real function of such an education was to prepare the money by teaching it the folly of social change; how a belief in humanity is only available to those who have no knowledge of it.

Block-mounted copies of Evan's *PR Week* front cover and his profile in *O'Dwyers*, both acclaiming the VNR triumph which first won him industry-wide recognition.

VNRs or video news releases are short segments packaged to look like news items. Evan had joined Poley Bray just after the Greenpeace Piper Alpha campaign had been won on the back of VNRs, action shots the news media could never have got themselves, and Poley Bray had big British oil on the books.

The first couple of moves in Evan's counter-offensive were routine "two-step communications." He mobilized the independent think tanks to write op-ed articles which argued that editorial decisions on TV news were being led by sexy footage from NGOs (non-governmental organizations such as pressure groups and charities). He then coordinated the different departments of Poley Bray to use their different contacts toward a single end until he was in consultation with the BBC and the Independent Broadcasting Authority. What Evan Hatch then pulled off became industry legend. BBC News categorically banned VNRs from NGOs but *only* from NGOs. They didn't ban corporate VNRs: those deep-in-the-jungle shots of Colombian narco-traffickers in handcuffs courtesy of Sawyer Miller; that talking-head scientist explaining the cleaner, greener BP fuel. VNRs had always been popular with cash-strapped TV news budgets, but there was now a twist which made Evan's master stroke a double-bubble: *the absence of NGO VNRs meant that corporate VNRs got even more air-time.*

He was transferred to the Competitive Enterprise Institute in New York for a year. Here his job was mainly laying astroturf, an industry in-joke meaning fake grassroots. Evan had helped set up the Clean Air Working Group (coal companies against the US Clean Air Act), the Coalition For Sensible Regulation (developers) and the Sea Lion Defense Fund, a trawler consortium fighting limits on factory fishing. Consumer Alert, meanwhile, campaigned against safety regulations for consumer goods.

He treads on his school photo and leaves a wet, muddy footprint. The stamp of death on a now-never-to-be-recovered past. He swears at the top of his voice, only just controlling himself from screaming and roaring. Which he doesn't want to do this time, because, of course, he's actually looking for something. He kicks over a box of files to do with blocking BSE legislation.

And then . . . he simply masters himself. Suddenly, and almost as if he's known where to find it all along, he steps out of the cupboard under the stairs, steps on to a chair, reaches up to a shelf and pulls out a large book.

He finds the letter he's looking for hidden between two pages of the *AA Book of the British Countryside.* A single sheet of ruled paper slipped into the double-page spread on Limestone Regions—Relics of Ancient Seas.

The top right-hand corner of the cheap, lined paper is rubber-stamped: Midlands New Families International (Leicester Diocesan InterCountry Adoption Services). The blue ballpoint script is in Spanish. The letter is a little explanatory note written by a nurse or social worker: *Tienes un hermano que se llama Mariano (4 años).*

A town, a village, a surname: *Calderon. Tonalacapan. Salgado.*

And a little goodwill message which he translates: *Enjoy life and live every day!*

The curtains thin and the first housemartin chirrups outside, as early as the office cleaners it has traced and followed all the way from Kenya.

5

The stench of boiling fertilizer had made Chano vomit three times. His red eyes were streaming into the bandana tied over his nose and mouth. He gagged, retching on empty, the bandana lifting like a beak with each empty hawking caw. He emptied three-quarters of the nitrate fertilizer into the vat and dodged his face out of the up-gust of sulphur-steam. Then he had to go outside again. It was ten minutes outside the shed for every five he prepped.

The evil noxious fumes had spread outside the shed. Even at twenty paces the air was rotten. He was walking further and further away from the shack just to breathe deep lungfuls of good clean air. He was worried the toxic stench would carry into Taxco Santos. Maybe it would even stop the villagers waking up.

Chano himself had given up on sleep just after midnight. Watching TV he'd caught a few minutes of late-night Channel Telemun—*Donna Express* and *Secretos Decorativos*—and had felt removed from the innocent world of cross-dressing, infidelity and home-and-garden tips. He'd locked the door of his house in pelting rain. The rain had suddenly stopped when it saw him and he'd walked in eerie black silence, except for his feet disturbing puddles, and plastic bunting flapping like the echo of rain.

Over the years in the sterilizing shack, lack of supplies meant Chano often had to improvise a home-made Campden powder formula from whatever ingredients were to hand. The golden rule in all sulphite detours is that you never want to find out that you've made ammonium nitrate. Like I'm doing now, he thought, and, shivering in the cold, went back to the shed.

Chano began working on the mercury fulminate which would detonate the ammonium nitrate high explosive. Since he was going to use straight paraffin as his texturizer, this would be the last task he had to do. He shook a teaspoon of pure mercury over seven times as much nitric acid solution. He turned down the gas ring to low heat. The solution bubbled and turned green as the silver mercury dissolved. He poured the solution slowly into his free-standing tin thermos. He knocked it slightly. It wobbled but didn't fall, ballasted as it was with two-parts ethyl alcohol. Chano poured in the rest, then quickly stood back. Red fumes poured out of the top. He clutched hand over scarf over nose and mouth, and staggered out again.

Twenty-five paces this time. On the horizon, first light was simmering. He dropped the bandana to his chin. He wouldn't have to go in again for half an hour now, not until the red fumes had turned white. Green, red, white. Yes, that was it.

Green, red, white: the task had purified too. The sabotage had become as purely technical as decisions made in Fidelity Investment boardrooms.

Back in his shed, Chano filtered the entire solution through a fine-mesh flour sieve. And there they were: tiny and multitudinous, mercury fulminate crystals. Chano stared at the pure, white crystals. How curious that they had been there all along, stashed inside a colour-coded combination lock, all the time waiting to do their trick, to reveal their true nature.

Chano washed the crystals in distilled water, drying them with a kitchen towel between his palms. He washed and dried them a few more times, before testing the crystals with litmus paper to make sure no acid traces remained. The litmus paper wasn't convinced. He lightly dusted the crystals with baking soda until they were definitely, positively, absolutely alkali.

Next he sawed the top off a sterilized can of Fanta and poured the mercury fulminate crystals inside the can, tamping them with his forefinger (still safely basted with baking soda), and careful not to pack it too tightly. He then taped a magnifying glass over the top of the Fanta can. This was his non-electrical blasting cap, the low-explosive mercury fulminate which would ignite the high explosive. The explosion from the first would ignite the other fertilizer bombs. He loaded the detonator into one of the bombs.

Outside—at thirty paces—he sat on a Coca-Cola crate and began to calculate the minimum safety distance for the twenty-seven pounds of explosives. He'd just worked out that it would be three hundred yards when he looked up and saw Ayo at half that distance, his short, bow-legged figure walking rapidly. Chano plucked a cluster of broad leaves from a gigante bush to scrub his hands and forearms. He checked over the detonator pack inside the long, blue, nylon sports bag between his legs, examining the wired-up can of Fanta to make sure that its black lid—half an old hardback book cover—hadn't slipped and exposed the magnifying glass. He let his eyes rest on the incongruous orange can with its faded logo. Bound and gagged, the can looked like some innocent shopper snatched from among the tinned produce and taken hostage during an armed robbery.

Did you sleep? asked Ayo.

No. I went to the dock.

Calderon?

No. Villegas. The cargo terminal. To get charcoal.

Right. Yes. Good. Ayo had a martial briskness about him this morning which irritated Chano deeply. His peaky bangs were too peaky, his jutty, scrappy beard too jutty and scrappy, his broad and beaky nose too beaky and broad. Chano was too on edge to be much interested in the words he heard himself say, but spoke anyway to calm his nerves. There's, uh, a yard with loose coal . . . lying about all stacked up in rotting bags. I needed some charcoal . . . Chano fell silent again, feeling like a wasp bundled out of his patterns by a gale. He stared at the ground where the scrunched leaves he'd cleaned his hands with lay. What a mess he'd made of them with the woodmeal, vaseline and charcoal.

What are you using? asked Ayo.

It's a kind of slow-acting detonator.

How long?

I don't know, it could be five minutes or forty. If everything goes right it should be at least forty to an hour.

They set off across the fields, Ayo carrying two blue nylon sports bags and a coil of rope around his shoulders, and Chano the third blue sausage bag and a can of diesel oil.

Dawn was cracking a combustible compound: gaseous greens, cobalt blues, sulphurous yellows and ferrous reds leaked into each other with massive instability. The sound of truck brakes half a mile away on the highway made both men nervous. The air was very still and noise would carry a long way today.

Chano and Ayo reached the last field before Ethylclad's perimeter fence. Three black steel pipes ran horizontally in rows about five feet above the earth. The pipes came fat and curving out of the ground and flew low in formation through the fence of the toxic-waste plant, giant straws sucking all the marrow out of the land.

Chano knelt on one knee by the fertilizer bag. He ran the rope through the handles of one blue bag and round the pipe, then repeated this action with the next pipe and the next bag.

Chano and Ayo now stood three pipes apart. In one tug of war they hoisted two bags up flush with the pipes. The two men each bound their end of rope to the pipe. Chano balanced the last blue sports bag crosswise on top of the middle pipe, allowing each of its sausage ends to sag down slightly. This was the bag containing the Fanta-can detonator. He unzipped the bag and flipped back the hardback lid on its gaffer-tape hinge, exposing the magnifying glass and mercury fulminate to the day. Chano looked up and the sky was gently dissolving the dawn gases into white light.

They ran stooping across the fields to the trees, both heads darting this way and that to make sure no one was around to see them. No *campesinos*, security guards, poachers, *transuentes*. Chano followed Ayo winding through the trees, struggling to keep up as Ayo bobbed and weaved at a clip, taking the long way round.

Está chingón, Ayo, said Chano half an hour later and between breaths when he saw where they'd come out. It was well done. They were no longer in a straight line from the Ethylclad pipes. They had emerged into corn fields. Over the brow of the next undulating field would be Taxco Santos.

Ayalo wiped a fine film of sweat off his face, took a swig of water as he walked, and offered the plastic bottle to Chano. Chano took a swig of water—except it wasn't water, it was strong rum. This made Chano speechless with rage. He had relied on Ayo's self-possession to convince himself that blowing up the pipeline was no wild stunt, that it was an act within the bounds of acceptable risk, where possible outcomes could be calculated and balanced.

Ayo was oblivious to Chano's silent fury. Still walking, drying his face with the bottom of his T-shirt, droplets of rum in his ragged, wispy beard, he said: This gives us time . . . when you get down to the village make yourself public, knock them up in the shop, get a coffee at the PeMex, buy a paper, be seen around town. Then when the bang goes off you're with everyone else when you hear it, and no one will point a finger at you and—

A massive explosion cracked the air. A NASA blast-off. They froze. The sky was being rocked *ahead* of them not behind. A few hundred yards away. Near enough now to hear timber and concrete bang at each other as they fell back to earth.

Chano knew first, knew instantly. His shack had blown up. In his polythene-lined shack the damp morning's condensation had refluxed the fulminating ammonium nitrate vapours. Softly, delicately, lightly they had settled on sulphur.

A small hope formed far in the back of his mind. An explosion in his shed was just an accident that could happen anytime. He would still be OK as long as the other bomb didn't go off. Just then—from exactly where the small hope had been—he heard a small thud far behind them. An attenuated explosion two miles back. A bump so muted that perhaps only two men standing absolutely still and straining every nerve would ever have heard it. Pop.

No! No! *Me chingaron!*

Puta madre!

Ay! Chingadazo! Now they'll know it's me! They'll know it's me.

It will be all right.

The military and—*madrazo!*

Que madrazo!

My whole life!

OK, let's see, now—uh—

Yes, yes. Let's reason it out, announced Chano stopping and turning. He went blank.

Yes, said Ayo, also blank with terror.

I've not been around much, said Chano, so most people don't know my old ties with—with everyone.

You will have to go into hiding, Chano.

If I don't tell anyone where I'm going I don't put anyone else in danger.

I'll bring you food and money, said Ayo. And maybe there's still time for me to break into your house. I can bring you documents and things.

But where? Where to?

Just a bit into the *reserva*, yes. Where the cement pipes are. I'll leave things there. For now. And then we can think of a longer plan.

No, I've got to get out, Ayo. I've got to leave. I've got to get away.

Yes, but the *reserva* now. For now.

The vast *reserva ecológica* began five miles away. It was an environmental set-aside forest, wide as a city. To get there, however, Chano would have to skirt villages and cross open fields and use the road when he lost his way.

OK, said Chano. OK. Let's go.

No, said Ayo. I'll lead off. You stay back about two hundred yards. Keep it like that. Chano nodded. Ayo emptied a few crumpled notes and shrapnel from his oily jeans into Chano's palms, then led off.

Forty minutes later Ayo stopped, turned round and pointed the way. Chano waved a hand, then Ayo headed off in the opposite direction.

The last road of the last village before the *reserva ecológica*. Chano walked down a steep and flinty narrow gully between the white adobe walls of tiny two-room peasant *cantones* either side. Pecking roosters stopped in their pecking to eye him suspiciously. Now and then an old couple were sitting in an open doorway and Chano would nod *buenos dias* as casually as he could. Just out for a saunter. But there was, he felt, too much clarity, precision and full-colour definition around here for him to get away with it. Last night's rain still shone on the brilliant white walls and clean, sharp flint protruded from the narrow dirt road. In tidy tin trays stood accurate rows of exact pink knapweed and precise yellow pansies, each with a distinct bull's-eye. Explicit hanging baskets drip-dried the bright green leaves of steamed white gentians.

An old *campesino,* sitting in his own open doorway on his own wooden chair in his own clean white shirt, watched the passing stranger in his own sweet time, the bare gloom of his one-room behind him. The old *campesino*'s brown face was deep with creases and folds. His wet or greased-back hair shone black. His face wore that peasant look which at one and the same time says "Don't mind me, I don't know anything," as well as saying: "I see what you don't see and I see through you." Chano saw him late. Too late to nod. Chano performed instead a kind of nervous-horse-head half-greeting. Their eyes met. He's heard the blast, thought Chano, he knows everything. Chano was sure of it. So sure that when, for some reason, the *campesino* gave Chano the merest twitch of a smile, an almost imperceptible flicker of his lower-face wrinkles and a passing flash of his deep-set brown eyes, Chano felt sure he'd survive the next few days without capture.

And he felt the same way still, when a mile into the bio-zone forest he set about building a bivouac near the half-buried giant cement pipes of a ring-main project begun but never completed after the peso crash.

I'll live for now at least. But oh Jesus, what am I going to do? Find a *coyote* and cross to the other side? Cross the border and start a new life? Or move to another town in another state? *Madre de la chingada*, he cried, what am I going to do now? He felt a sudden gust of hate. He hated Ayo. And Yola. And Ruiz. And Oscar. And he hated himself for that night when he should never have gone back to El Café Fuente but did.

I'll never see my home again, he thought, my last connection with Marisa and Daniel. Never hear the pipes knock-knock-knocking. Never solve the riddle of the pipes.

For the last fifteen years, every time the plumbing knock-knock-knocked—which was every time Chano turned a tap—he'd felt her looking at him, amused that he couldn't see something—he never knew what—which was staring him in the face. For when Marisa was alive and Chano pontificating away, she'd knock-knock-knock on his head, on a door frame, or, if she was sitting at the table, knock on the table legs. His stupidity alluded to, he had seldom liked to confirm it by asking what her cryptic signal meant. He knew it was a reference to the pipes which knocked whenever the tap was turned and then for a few hours after, the pipes which were part of an immense plumbing grid he'd salvaged then ruined, but more than that he didn't know. He'd never got the connection. And why the knocking? he used to ask her. Why did she do that? To which she had, of course, just knocked some more and so he had been left to ponder both his own obtuseness and its connection to the puzzle of the plumbing grid and the riddle of the pipes.

The keen mental torture of eviction, fire, flood, hurricane, or exile is slowly to lose the thousand secrets of a home. Chano felt as remote as his *choza*, which now stood abandoned miles away with all its intimacies invisible, meaningless and doomed.

. . . And not just that, there's lots of other things as well that I've been wanting to say and which—

Do you want a coffee? she asks.

What?

I'm having one, she says, her voice coming from around the corner of the L-shaped room.

Yes, yes, thank you. I do. Yes.

He hears her put the pot on the ring, and strike a match. But he has more to say: It's very important that we have this talk because, and this is the main thing, how can you say I don't do my share with the baby, with Daniel? And you say you can't go to meetings if I'm going too, but when did I ever specifically say "You can't go to your meeting"? When did I say that? Can you tell me? Because I know, I definitely know, as much as I know anything, that I didn't say that, because that's simply not something I'd ever say. You must know it's not. And as for talking over you in the café, that's just plain crazy. It was only that I hadn't seen Oscar for a long time, we were catching up. You didn't have to sit there if you didn't want to listen. But this is the whole point: if you never tell me when you're annoyed then how am I ever to know? Why only tell me much later rather than at the time? If we could talk like we are now, then we could discuss things before they get blown up out of all proportion. That's why it's good that we're having this talk now because it's clearing the air, it's establishing ground rules. And I'm sure that you've got things, many things probably, that you want to say, too. But if the spirit's right, then . . . then we can have this kind of open exchange. So. Now. What are the things you want to say? Marisa? Marisa?

Is she silent because she's contrite? he wonders. Has his tone of voice been harsher than he meant? Marisa? He gets off his stool. Listens. Is she crying? He goes into the kitchen. She's not there. He touches the coffee pot. Cold. Lifts the lid. Empty.

And then he gets it: she left the house moments after he began. Just walked out the kitchen door, holding a lit match. He frowns a little, and then, as reluctantly as if she were still in the room to watch him, laughs.

Later, the people of two villages, Nahualhuas and Tonalacapan, pieced together her last hours. A neighbor said she'd seen Marisa walking down the street laughing her head off, swinging her arms, and then, as the laughter took her again, running in a spurt down the street. (Chano had imagined small sea birds that scoot on flat sand when the wind gets behind them.) She'd gone to Yolanda's house, and had that coffee after all. Together they'd gone on to the Unión de Ejidos Uniones hall, to the strike meeting of the Ford maquillas. And that night, at about eleven, after the meeting ended, shots were fired from the trees across the street at people in the doorway of the Uniones hall. Only one was hit. Nobody special, no reason for it to be her. Nothing personal. It was important to send a message. Just someone, anyone, who was leaving the meeting. ·

Oscar and Yola identified the body for him. Shot in the head and neck.

He'd left and come back to his *choza* twice before. Once after Cerro Hueco jail—during which time it had been locked up, empty and decaying—and again when he went north to work for eighteen months in a Crown Heights pharmaceutical warehouse—during which time Bad Medicine had lived there. But now he could never go back to his *choza* again. Fifteen years in the L-shaped kitchen, he thought, walking into the forest, and I never solved it.

And what would happen to the Taxco Santos Chicha Co-op now? What have I done to them? he asked himself. Will the police shut it down? What have I done? Has all the women's work come to nothing? That would be a tragedy.

Ten years ago a few women in Taxco Santos had decided to see if *chicha* could be made by pitch-fermentation. *Chicha* had always been made by spontaneous fermenting, where the corn mash is left out in the open air in big wooden tubs and all sorts of airborne yeasts and bacteria fly in to mix with the sugar. But people were getting ill from it. Since each and every ingredient was also used in other foods, the women deduced that the devil must be in the air. The crop-spraying, the *maquilladora* incinerator chimneys, the fat flies in the flammable river and the chemical froth in the irrigation trenches.

With spontaneous fermenting you can't sterilize because it kills the flavor, but you can with pitch-fermenting because the flavor's added later. If they were to pitch, however, then everything would have to be sterile: the bin, the tubing used for siphoning, the bottles and the plastic keg, everything. The Taxco Santos women offered the job to

Chano Salgado, who was known to have two-thirds of a chemistry degree.

Fumes of sodium metabisulphite solution were so strong that a separate shed had been built for him about fifty paces from the still. This way Chano had had, as it were, his own private place of work. He locked up the shack at night and let himself in in the morning. No one else ever went in there or, if they could help it, near there. *Chicha* may be spiced with anything, and the women added cinnamon, orange peel, bell peppers, chilies, lime rinds, and *jalapinos* to the ferment. Chano sterilized the equipment for pitch-fermenting as well as the recycled bottles the *chicha* was sold in. It sold quite well, not brilliantly, but enough to keep the co-op going. Chano couldn't touch the money while he was still at work because of contamination from thumbed and fingered, licked and hidden notes, and so, on Fridays, the women left his wages under a stone outside his door like a prayer offering. But now, thought Chano, the sterilizing shack is detonated in a thousand little pieces not much taller than that stone.

Further into the *reserva* forest he found a branch exactly the size he'd been looking for. He broke it off and, binding the branch with creepers to the mainframe, recalled the way the old *campesino* with the lined brown face had looked at him. It was as if the man had been appraising him; a look which had seemed—in Chano's fantasy—to be weighing up parts foolish and parts unavoidable in the action he'd taken, the deed he'd done. Chano saw the look again as if still fixed on him even now, and just as suddenly as hate had come it left, and he set about finding another branch the same size as the last one.

6

A trillion dollars a day were flying around the global financial markets. It all had to be offset by collateral and sent everything and everyone scattering all over the planet. Crocuses marching up the Alps to the cold air; ships passing with no lights in the night; Hotpoint fridge-freezers heading north; ice-packs splitting up and floating south; beluga whales with molten black bubbles on their backs twisting rickety spines south from Moray Firth; seawater algae clogging the

Akosombo River downstream from the World Bank Dam. Geiger-counter dolphins clickety-clicking past Dungeness; night foxes padding through Hackney Wick train station; Afghans waking up in cold-storage trucks on the German border; and the *Jennifer Lopez*, an unregistered, unlicensed Costa Rican fishing smack, chugging for three nights and four dawns in the Gulf of Mexico.

The men are silent as the boat docks. They look at the quay. It is modernized beyond recognition and almost deserted. The container yard facility is new, so too the drop-lock steel shutters, each with a big number painted on them.

A few Mexican small boats have unloaded here as well. But there's way too many fishmongers and wholesalers for the supply and so the Costa Ricans get a nod from these Mexican crews, almost a welcome.

Once off the boat the crew are noisy again. Trestles are knocked up on concrete, four-ply boards slammed on trestles, crates banged down on the boards. Cash flies about. Stefano's ice-wet hands reach over heads, through arms, around bodies, taking money like some DF street trader with a clap-up box of stolen watches, while his brother Jordi calls the weight from the scales. Every now and then, when paid in greenbacks, Stefano cheers *Dólares!* This gets a response cheer from the crew—*Dólares!*—while they pack and stack and weigh and scale and cut.

Passing between the boat and the boards, carrying a full crate of blue-fin, Jordi leans his head toward Stefano and asks: Are we smarter taking the rest of the catch home? There's about a quarter left. What's the exchange?

Stefano makes some runny ink jottings on his wet hand, then says: No, we're here now and if we go back with it there's tax and . . . Thank you. *Dólares!* . . . Keep a crate back for family, he tells Jordi, but no more.

They were cleaned out. The buyers had all gone and *Jennifer Lopez* was the only boat left on the quay.

Jordi was dispatched to find a snack shop and a gallon of bottled water. Daniel wished they'd asked him to go instead. Here he was on the poured-cement border of a whole other country, but he couldn't start his new life in Mexico yet. In the stained crates, ice munched itself in the heat, collapsing in tinkly scurries.

He carried his knapsack off the boat. A lone traveler with sole responsibility for his own welfare, he checked all its fastenings once again. The brown leather strap wasn't long enough to take in the rolled blanket so he'd tied a bit of string between the strap's last hole and its buckle. This he undid and retied again.

Daniel sat on a post a little way from the others and looked inland at the dock buildings, his brain still bobbing with the motion of the waves. He heard the crew go quiet in their talk. He looked up. All seven came shuffling toward him. Stefano spoke for the delegation with somber concentration: Me and the boys have talked it over and this is what we've come up with.

Daniel smiled sunnily.

Stefano continued with frowning rectitude: Since you're not coming back the only way to do this right is if you get a rough estimate of the share here. Properly this should be done later when we know how much diesel we've used. So it's just a rough estimate. OK? And it's a half-share, seeing as you've only come one way. Agreed? Does this sound fair to you?

Yes, yes, Stefano, answered Daniel grinning and not really listening.

OK, Stefano said gravely and divvied up flaky pesos from a friable clutch of notes worn smooth at the folds.

The lucky mascot! said Jordi, setting down the plastic gallon of water. The crew were pleased they had got Daniel. He worked hard and he'd brought good luck. But most of all they liked him because he was only taking a half-share.

Thursday or Friday we'll be back, said Stefano. No later but it could be sooner.

I'll come down to the dock every day to check.

No. *Thursday or Friday.* And if you want a ride home then, we'll take you.

Ah no, said Jordi, by then it will be too late. Daniel will have gone back to the wild by then, he'll be a total Mexican.

The crew began putting on dodgy Mexican accents, adenoidal and sing-song:

Orale-bye, mano, manito,
Que onda gueii-iee-yyy, man!

If you need a peeemp, Daniliiito, I only take half from my bitches and you won't have to work Sundays. Not the Virgin Mary's special day, man. No way, mano!

Orale-bye, manito!

Daniel felt he knew these people better than any he'd ever known. His hands still cold and red from packing the fish in ice, he watched them climb back into the boat and crowd round to get the engine going, and as he did so he made a secret wish: that all their combined strength, manliness, guile, mob-handed confidence, and fearless laughing could somehow come with him and be part of him. He stood watching the flaky white boat move away, toward the orangey violet light behind them.

Daniel walked between towering stacks of ribbed container crates, like a street in some steel Chicago. Seaco, Geest, Tiphook, Linea Mexicana, ShangYin, SeaLand, Capital, DSG Senator. One day he'd speak English and know what all these words meant. Maersk, K-Line, MOL, Pandoro, Hinjun, CalArk, Astro. He walked on through the cold shadows of this windy valley and out into light and heat.

A line of trucks off the freight ferry were waiting to get through immigration. Intercontinental pantechnicons with bounce buckets and air-con, silver stove-pipe Kenworth Kenmex artics, freight-liner semis, chunky little flatbeds with drop-flaps and wooden fences, Quaker State oil tankers and combination cargo wagons with faded, orange, ragged banners on the back saying *Precaución: Doble Semi-Remolque.*

Daniel began to work his way up the line. The first driver on to whose silver footplate he climbed waved him away without a word, not even moving chin off hand to do so. Daniel dropped down from the steps. He thinks I'm selling oranges, he thought, or that I'm begging. I'll walk round the front of the next truck I come to.

Daniel raised his index finger when he caught the next driver's eye. By the time Daniel got round the cab, the driver had leaned out of his window and was looking down from the turret: What?

Daniel looked at the rungs but now thought it might seem aggressive if he climbed them. Shielding his eyes from the sun he called up to the man: Are you going to Tonalacapan?

Where?

Tonalacapan?

No. Highway, highway all the way. Where's that you say?

It's called Tonalacapan.

Never heard of it.

Daniel thanked him. And walked away. The horn bellowed. Daniel jumped. *Oye!* called the driver. Daniel went back. You want to try the smaller trucks if it's a small town, said the trucker.

Thanks. Yes. OK.

From his sprung perch the driver watched the boy go and as he did so reflected that he might not talk to another soul until Mexico City. In DF he'd hand a docket to some *vato*, ask where the toilets were and then come back again. *Que viva la raza* . . .

Daniel walked further down the line passing silver hulks and flatbeds. All empty.

Where do you want to go?

Daniel looked round. Sitting on the verge was a man in overalls with a green cap on. Tonalacapan?

I'm going to Calderon.

Oh, said Daniel, not knowing whether this was good or bad, a yes or a no.

Calderon, the man repeated as if Daniel hadn't heard. And you want to go to Tonalacapan? Daniel nodded attentively, dumbly. It's on the way, said the man.

Excellent!

Well, at least, I can drop you on the high road and then it's . . . two miles? A straight road into town. That's if we get through here some time today, of course.

The boy looked up at the line, gauging how long it was. The man laughed. We will. That's my truck there, he said gesturing toward an old, yellow Ford. Here, he told Daniel, pulling out some coins and a crumpled blue peso. Get me a coffee from the stand and a Dime bar. And get yourself one too.

No, it's OK, I've got some money. I'll get my own.

By the time Daniel came back from the kiosk the truck had gone. He looked up and saw the old yellow truck about to go through the gate.

Heh-heh, cackled the driver when Daniel caught up with him. You almost missed it, *chavo*!

Daniel handed up the coffee, which had burnt his hands, and went round to the passenger side.

You didn't get yourself one, said the trucker when Daniel was aboard.

Dropped it, said Daniel.

They went through the gate with just a lazy wave at the uniform guy. The driver must know him, thought Daniel.

After the wide expanse of asphalt free-for-all had settled into lanes, and the crashing gears had found fourth at fifty, the driver asked: Where've you come from?

Costa Rica.

Ah, *un Tico*! And what's in Tonalacapan?

Not wanting to appear friendless or helpless, Daniel made up a story about looking up relatives in Tonalacapan, telling his tale in that authoritative and self-important tone with which fourteen-year-olds lie. The driver kept his eyes on the road and, with a complacent grin, said: So, you've left home to start a new life elsewhere! Daniel was startled to find yet another mind-reader. First Arlinda, now him! Very good, very good, said the driver with such simple, matter-of-fact approval that for a moment Daniel wondered whether he hadn't, after all, said, I've left home to start a new life elsewhere.

There's no such thing as a free ride. Hitch-hiking is a transaction. A confessor parrot has flown in through the window. That's the deal. Length of road traveled, times receptiveness of listener, times simplicity of route determine both how much of the trucker's personal tachometer the passenger will get and what type of preoccupations the driver will share.

No, he wasn't a man for regret but he had married too soon . . .

Tonalacapan arrived before the trucker had calculated and he wore a faintly offended smile as if Daniel hadn't heard him out. The trucker made an elaborate show of locking the handbrake and kept tapping the revs with his foot as he waved Daniel goodbye. From the truck he pointed with his whole hand down the turn-off like a cleaver slicing a course straight down thataway.

Daniel stood in Mexico. He bought a lemonade from the stall at the side of the road. He was inland now and his future was all around him. He could smell it in the dust stirred by the truck driving off. He could feel the future in the warm, diesel gust on his face and in the chilly coins and cold, wet bottle in his hand. He could see it in the lemonade woman's preoccupied frown, big teeth and long Mayan hair.

Tonalacapan? he asked, already pointing in the right way down the white-dust road which ran perpendicular off the highway.

Yes, said the woman curtly, as if she had a line of other customers at the desk. But when Daniel smiled broadly and thanked her she smiled back, exposing her long teeth, and nodded at him. And it seemed to Daniel in that instant they'd shared a secret, him and the Mayan lemonade woman, and that she somehow knew that he'd come back to the place of his birth, and was herself sure that he'd have living relatives who remembered his parents, knew all about him and would help him find work here. (Mexico, said the TV news back home, was booming and was now, technically, almost a First World country.) His journey blessed, Daniel set off along the white dust and potholes, walking down the long, straight road, and before long he was pulling a dusty estafiata leaf to pieces between his fingers.

The graves rose on a steep incline between twisted, ragged trees; the little crossed sticks looked like fixed points in a landslide. Daniel picked his way up, seeing if he could go right to the top without touching the ground, without pulling himself up by root or branch.

He looked for a Marisa or a Chano Salgado. He found a Marisa but there was no surname. He stood there solemnly for a while until out of the corner of his eye he spotted another Marisa. Then three. And then some letter Ms. He started looking for a Chano. Found none. Daniel climbed back down the cemetery hill, a plan forming. Since Marisa seemed to be such a common name hereabouts, he'd ask if anyone had known a Chano. That, he concluded, would be the best way of finding someone who had known his parents. Then, if they had also known a Marisa she would be Chano's Marisa. Excellent.

Tonalacapan was all shut up. He saw a *caseta telefónica,* the one silent business in a silent street. The phone shack was a three-sided, concrete box open to the road. There was a desk inside and a beige phone on the wall.

A woman sat inside adding up some numbers in a battered and grubby spiral-bound note pad. She had very large, plastic glasses and wore a green and white headscarf wrapped up high like an African woman. Daniel thought he'd just start chatting and let his enquiry slip into conversation. But then he looked again at the woman. No, he thought, she didn't look in the mood to chat with a boy. He decided therefore just to ask her straight out. As soon as she looked up. Seeing how small the village was he felt lucky. He reckoned she was the same age as his father. In fact, the more he thought about it, the more certain he became that his father and this woman had been teenage lovers, and that when he asked her if she'd ever known a man of that name she'd be sure to smile and blush.

Buenos dias, said Yolanda with a brief smile.

Hola. I wonder if you . . . Daniel began in a by-the-way tone of voice (even though there was no "way" for it to be "by") . . . if you ever knew a man called Chano? Chano Salgado?

No, she replied with a bored voice. Her face now back at her figures, she asked: You want to use the phone?

No, it's OK, said Daniel. No thanks. And with that the strange boy shouldered his backpack and Yolanda watched him walk off down the road.

She wondered what she should do. Was he a spy? Or could he have been sent by Chano from wherever he was holed up. He looked very lost. Maybe she should call him back. But if he is a spy, she considered, then that would be a disaster. Why did they send a boy? Because he's just a boy. And not so young either, she thought, for he was only a year or so younger than the spotty soldier boys you saw in their stiff green uniforms, skinny and self-conscious behind sandbags in the town squares.

After two hours tramping around Tonalacapan, Daniel felt as if every sideways look from every doorway, every shutter, every passing bus, shopkeeper, and pedestrian was against him. He turned one corner and then another. He tried to count the cash in his pocket without getting it out. Did he have enough to last until Tuesday or Wednesday when the boat came in? He saw a fitful fountain on a patchy square of dust across the way from an isolated café. Drawing nearer he could hear the fountain's odd gargle and spatter. He'd buy a drink, fill his army-green plastic water bottle at the limping fountain, then go.

He bought a lemon tea at the café and sat on a moulded, job-lot Pepsi chair at a red plastic table in the shade. Daniel couldn't hear what they were saying but knew they were talking about him. No, he wouldn't ask anyone here. He'd just drink his drink then leave.

That's him there, said Yolanda. Why is he asking now?

This is bad, said Oscar. Very bad. So soon.

Alma-Delia came and wiped the boy's table. It didn't need wiping and Daniel took this as a sign that she wanted him to go.

Angered by this, he no longer cared what they thought about him or how they reacted. Years ago, he asked bombastically, did you know a man called Chano?

Her circular wiping action slowed down. (Maybe she's thinking back, thought Daniel, trying to remember.) Slowly, slowly the J-cloth went round and round, like the run-in band of old vinyl before the stylus recalls the song.

Here? she asked.

Yes. He lived here. Or near here.

No, she said, resuming normal wipe-speed, before heading abruptly back toward the café.

Daniel didn't like these people. And he wasn't going to ask again. Mexicans were mean and unfriendly. Fuck them. Fuck. Them.

Meanwhile old Ruiz Gatica, whose nickname was Bad Medicine because his face, winched into a permanent grimace, looked like he'd just swallowed some, had sat at the next table and, stirring his own lemon tea, a notion was forming in his mind.

Hello, young man.

Tardes, Daniel replied in what he hoped was a jaded, world-weary grunt of bare-minimum politeness from a reclusive, mysterious traveler.

Where've you come from? asked the old man, squinting behind the thick scratched lenses of his brown plastic glasses.

The docks.

The docks, here?

I'm . . . we're working on a fishing boat, said Daniel.

You're a fisherman? Good. Good. That's a fine trade, fisherman. But hard, no?

Daniel nodded, but was disturbed by the old man's weird smile of secret relish. He must be a pimp, thought Daniel. A pimp who thinks

I'm his next *puto*. Why else was the old man enjoying their conversation so much? Unless he was getting his jollies or preparing a little business offer?

Ah! But there's no boats going out at the moment, said the pimp, enjoying the little trap he'd set.

This one came in.

Where from?

Costa Rica.

Costa Rica, the old man repeated, in the same slow and abstracted way as the waitress who had wiped the table.

What a bunch of *chinches raros*—fucking weirdos—thought Daniel. Yes, and I've got to go now, he said, left too few pesos on the table and walked quickly away. He changed direction with an awkward swerve and made for the fountain. Standing on its rim, he held his bottle out to where the water tumbled. In one spiteful lunge, the fountain soaked his trainers.

Standing between the red plastic tables, Yolanda, Oscar, Ruiz, Erik and Alma-Delia gathered in a huddle and watched Daniel as he walked back up the street away from fountain and café.

Ruiz broke the news of the boy's identity to them with these words: He's come from Costa Rica.

But we can't be sure it's him, said Alma-Delia.

He's come from Costa Rica, repeated Ruiz flatly.

He looks like Marisa, said Yolanda.

What shall we do? asked Oscar.

We mustn't tell Chano, said Yolanda. He'll come straight out of hiding and get caught.

No, said Ruiz, his face squinting behind his scratched bottle-lenses, we've *got* to tell him. Straightaway. We've got to find him and tell him. Today. This hour.

We don't know where he is, she replied. So we can't anyway.

But Ayo could tell him—

While the El Café Fuente crowd debated what to do, a young man on the corner of the street was fixing the low-pressure jet in the engine of his Kawasaki 750. He switched to do some unnecessary work on the front axle, all the better to observe this muttering huddle. He couldn't hear what they said but saw each cast quick looks over at the boy. The same *chavo* who was now walking toward him, coming his way.

Oye! Hold this will you? he called without looking up. Daniel found himself holding the top half of an air filter and a torque wrench, while Blas Mastrangelo burrowed back into the valve casing. How's business? he asked from down among the gun-metal cylinders and sprockets.

OK, said Daniel, looking back toward the café. Yes, he added.

The man said nothing, but continued tinkering with his front suspension.

Feeling at length that he was expected to say something himself, Daniel asked, falteringly: And for you?

The man straightened up now. Looking at Daniel he responded with a breezy grin and said: Same as everyone—the English are doing very well!

This was a phrase Daniel had heard many times before. Except this time he felt that he wasn't being addressed as a boy, but as a man who was himself involved in all this; someone who knew all about making ends meet.

The *coyote* caught Daniel looking back at El Café Fuente again and then took a chance. Look at them, yallayallayalla . . . What's stirred those old hens now I wonder? he said, but in a tone which meant that he didn't wonder at all because it was sure to be nothing.

Me.

You?

Yes.

How?

Oh, I was just asking if they knew someone who lived round here . . . Once.

Did they?

No.

Sure it was here?

Yes, Daniel replied, downcast. Yes, it was here

Maybe he didn't hang out with *them*. It was a he?

Yes.

Go on.

Well, you're a bit . . . he was older . . . more their age . . .

No problem, said Blas in a tone which suggested he was more than happy to let it slide. His bright emerald eyes, meanwhile, fixed on the boy who was staring off into the distance, head turning first one way then the other.

While Daniel debated with himself whether to trust this stranger, the hens were yallayalla-ing to a conclusion over at El Café Fuente . . .

We will take care of the boy ourselves, said Yolanda, but not act like—

How? asked Ruiz.

—but not act like we have any special reason to. There are spies and snitches everywhere so we must not make the boy look like family. And then, when Chano comes out of hiding, which will be when he is ready, when he's safe, then the boy will be with us.

No, said Ruiz, and walked off. The nickname was used less now that he was old, but it had never been more apt than at this moment when, standing alone in the trees and scrub behind the fountain, Bad Medicine feared history repeating itself.

Yessica is about seventeen when she takes in the "orphaned" baby Daniel. Not long after she meets a Costa Rican trawlerman at a dance in Calderon—a good man who'd take the boy on too. They marry and the three of them go to live in his home town of Limon.

One year on, another trawlerman leaves a letter for Bad Medicine at the harbour terminal. The letter from the husband says Yessica has died of chagas.

Transmitted by a blood-sucking beetle known as the assassin bug, chagas is a Latin American disease of the blood. A nocturnal triatomine beetle, the assassin bug, bites people when they are sleeping. Most often it attacks babies, swapping its trypanosomes for the blood of the soft-skinned newborn. (The succulent botanist is a rarity enjoyed by only the very fittest of the triatomine species.)

There are three stages of chagas: infection, intermediate, and final. But the length of these three stages is wildly unequal. The infection stage lasts six to eight weeks before a slight rash and a little swelling vanish entirely of their own accord even without treatment. Chagas has now entered its intermediate stage during which there are *no* symptoms. None. This stage typically lasts between fifteen and twenty-five years. It takes this long for the trypanosomes circulating in the bloodstream finally to hit critical mass. Now comes the onset of chagas proper. The final stage begins with blackouts and attacks on the heart, intestines, and nervous system. You've then got from between three and nine years tops. If you're lucky. Yessica was not.

Her husband writes that he's moved to the USA and left Daniel in Costa Rica. Yessica's in-laws will now take care of the boy. Beto and Arlinda, the widower's parents, have a good farm where the boy is much loved and goes to school every day, says the letter. But there's no address. Not for the husband, nor the farm.

It's one of the last boats from Limon ever to dock in Calderon. The small boats are replaced by factory ships full of strangers and then—as night follows day—by the collapse of Costa Rica's fishing industry. Contact with Daniel is lost for ever. But Bad Medicine and everyone in Tonalacapan can at least take comfort in the fact that they did right by the memory of Chano and Marisa. The boy now has a life, a family, a future. They did the right thing, they think. Until Chano returns from the dead. Until that ghost steps off an Oriente bus on the highway after two years in Cerro Hueco prison, and begins the long walk down the straight, white road to Tonalacapan toward his reason for living, the son who has been alive only a few months longer than Chano has been in prison.

Bad Medicine rejoined the group outside El Café Fuente and said: We all know it's him. Why not just tell the boy?

Ruiz, said Erik, the boy could be a snitch—just look! Together they all watched Daniel talking to Blas Mastrangelo the *coyote*, who, Yolanda thought, smiled the strange, lop-sided smile of those who belong nowhere.

Those who fear the law, said Yolanda, are near the law, and there was never a grass yet who didn't have a record—and that certainly applies to Blas Mastrangelo. And with that she set off back to work at the *caseta*.

The *coyote* watched the hens disperse. *Orale, gracias manito*, he said, holding out his hand for the tools. Blas then kicked the bike off its stand and delivered the job of balancing its free weight on to Daniel, while he followed the flow of the brake cable. Where you from? he asked.

Costa Rica.

You just got here.

Daniel was about to say yes, but then realized it was a statement not a question. But then thought he should say yes anyway. Yes.

I'm called Blas, said the man, walking round to the other side of the bike.

Daniel.

Daniel. Good.

Daniel was thinking that if he didn't ask and keep asking people if they'd known his father, then he'd be lost in a strange land with four hundred and twenty-seven pesos. He felt a kinship with Blas, who'd also never been invited to join in the group of strange and unfriendly people by the fountain.

Chano, he said.

Eh?

Did you used to know a man called Chano Salgado?

Yeah, oh yeah, said Blas, and, picking up on the past tense, added: He was a good man, too. Or at least I thought so. Blas held the front wheel with his knees, put a small screwdriver between his teeth and worked the brake lever.

You knew him? asked Daniel.

The care Blas took with the action of the brake lever was the care he took with his reply: adjusting its holding-screw by minute turns. Did it sound like the boy thought Chano Salgado was long gone? [turn] Or did he know he was just on the run? [turn]

Yes, I can tell you a lot about his movements, but what's your—why are you interested in Chano? I've got to know where you're coming from. Maybe you're an assassin and I'm giving up one of my people here.

Daniel laughed.

And so it was that Blas became the first to hear it from the boy's own lips. Looking frankly into the *coyote*'s face, Daniel said: He was my father.

Yes, Blas replied somnolently—a long, drawn-out, speculative *sssi-iiiiiiiii*. Yes, he was.

Blas Mastrangelo put his hand on Daniel's shoulder. Hold this screwdriver, he said. Blas lifted the cap of the low-pressure valve while he worked things out: The news had said the terrorist Salgado was from Calderon. But if he was from Tonalacapan originally, then like all good criminals this was where he'd come back to. Back to your roots. The explosion was in Taxco Santos. From Taxco Santos to Tonalacapan wasn't so very far either. Chano . . . Salgado? asked Blas.

Yes, said Daniel excitedly.

Well, let's put it this way, said Blas, popping the filter back down on its catch and pressing it secure. I know many old *compadres* and relatives of Chano, who, if I can track them down, would love to meet you, and possibly, perhaps, may be able to fix the son of Chano Salgado up with a place in Matamoros—just for a little while, and maybe not, and maybe work and maybe not. But I promise nothing and I know you understand.

Oh, yes, *claro, claro.*

Is this where you're staying? asked Blas. Daniel looked around and for want of a better place said yes. Blas Mastrangelo straddled his Kawasaki and put his thumb over the ignition switch. Settling into the saddle, he dropped his haunches a little, stretched his legs out, keeping the soles of his boots flat on the ground in front of him, and said: Give me three days, *caballero.*

Good. Yes.

Blas pressed the ignition, cocked an ear to the engine, and glided away.

7

They can hear the Rio Bravo as they follow the winding dirt path through the night. Blas Mastrangelo is at the rear of the line thinking hard about a problem. The problem is the new Zone Commander or police chief. Calderon's last police chief had been happy with his *mordida*—his kickback—from the *cholos de la frontera,* but took a security job in DF. A new Zone Commander has replaced him.

They say he's young, thinks Blas. And clean. *El incorruptible.* But when I give this new Zone Commander the terrorist, then I'll get my immunity back or whatever words this fine young captain's easy with. Right now, in this exact moment, it's only me who knows that Chano Salgado is the boy's father. I know the Zone Commander will see what I can see. He'll use the son to make the father give himself up. But let's lay hold of this carefully now, because . . .

Compañero?

What? says Blas, irritated to be disturbed in the deep thought needed for this crucial moment in his life. Yes, yes, Blas replies. Straight, straight, just keep going straight . . . *A la verga*, man! he hisses to himself.

Problem is this: the new captain will arrest Daniel as soon as I tell him. Same day. That's no good to me. Then everyone knows I'm the informer—and that would be one more area I can't work, which is more money on gas. And round there's a good spot by the docks and the truck ferry and all and all and yallayalla. But how to work it?

Blas follows his herd through a dirt track, winding through thick, tall pampas south of Rio Bravo, east of Reynosa, Nuevo Leon. Straight on, he tells them, just keep going straight.

To get here the convoy drove west for three hours, switching strategically between highway and *libremente* to avoid checkpoints. The van the *mojados* traveled in was windowless and hot, its airless interior covered in old carpet, two wooden benches bolted to the floor.

A few days ago none of them had ever met Blas Mastrangelo, and now all their lives were in his hands. All from one meeting next to Matamoros bus station, across from the weed-strewn parking lot of the *supermercado*.

Eleven o'clock we go out and hide, he'd told them that day. We cross later. Then we follow the power lines to San Antonio—but don't just spread out and scatter—there's power lines and power lines, and the ones with the worn trail under them are not the ones you wanna follow. You might think, oh this is easy, here's a path, we just go the way of all the other pilgrims—but that's the last path you ever want to take because that's the one *La Migra* know about; that's the one hooked up to the radar machines, that path will have a spy-cam in a helium balloon filming it from the sky day and night. They got night-cam, UV, infrared—all kinds of expensive shit.

For these *mojados* hoping for a new life *al otro lado*—on the other side—there had seemed to be glimpses of the United States in the very body of this Mexican *coyote*. In his emerald eyes, in his wispy mullet with blond highlights, in the T-shirt hanging off his spare frame which said RACE MANAGEMENT TEXACO HAVOLINE on the back, and TEAM on the front.

I know which paths *La Migra* know about, he'd said. Other *pateros* will say, There you go, there's the path, and just leave you. But not me. Why? Because I know all migrants have other family members who will one day also be migrants and want to join you and want *pasado*. And then they'll come to me because you told them about me and where to find me.

After three hours the convoy had swung off the road on to a long fire-track and the *mojados* had bumped their heads on the uncarpeted van ceiling. They emerged from the double doors clutching their bags. By time traveled they guessed they were west of the Gomez Dam. Up ahead Blas Mastrangelo got out of a Dodge Ram and the wetbacks watched as a walkie-talkie was handed to him from a plastic Wal-Mart bag. They watched Blas Mastrangelo go over to the other *pateros* and consult about something. Each migrant sensed the full measure of their powerlessness.

Blas now marches past them to head of the line. The *mojados* follow their *coyote* along a dirt track toward the river.

If I don't tell the captain until I'm about to go out of town . . . how would that be? Yes, that's good. But for this to work, all the hens in Tonalacapan will need to know that Daniel is Chano's son, because they will be the ones who get word to Chano that his long-lost son is in the jail. And if the captain sees how clever I am in having tied up that end for him, then he will know I'm a man that it will be good for him to have around.

Here the river is flowing faster. The soon-to-be Chicanos glimpse little mounds of white water like walnut whips. Under the sound of the stone-knocking river they start murmuring to each other. Blas Mastrangelo turns and hushes them with a furious, urgent stabbing finger. He stops in his tracks until everyone stands still and silent. At which point he starts walking again. Message received and understood.

They don't really need to keep quiet, there's no one around to hear. But how can I think with all this chatter going on? *Entonces* . . . Tomorrow I'll go over to Tonalacapan and tell the boy who it is safe to tell. Now here we are.

Down at the river's edge Blas beckons the wetbacks closer. He waits until they are all huddled round him in a semi-circle before he speaks. *Orale*, if *La Migra* stop us, you don't know me—I'm the only one who stands to get arrested. You just get sent back. OK? OK, clothes in the bag.

While they strip, Blas takes off his boots and socks and wades into the river ahead of them. *Puta madre*! This water is flowing ice! The fuck am I doing standing in the Rio Grande Chingada again? *Puto, puto, puto*. OK. Ropes.

Blas signals to the banks of the Rio Grande. His *compadre* tugs on the US end of a single guide-rope which tears clean from the river a moment, making a little waterfall. Blas signals that he has understood which of the two ropes to use.

Blas receives the big clear polythene bag of clothes from the *mojados*. He ties a section of elasticized rope around its scrunched neck, and then ties Exhibit A to one of the guide-ropes which cross to *el norte*. The *mojados* watch their clothes float away until the cord catches taut and the polythene sack is snatched clear of the water.

Blas selects the biggest among them, the one who looks most likely to be trouble. Here, he tells him, you take the bag of shoes. The man holds up his own little plastic bag with his watch and wallet in as if to say, But then I'll have no arm to swim with. OK, says Blas. Tie the shoe bag to your waist and follow me in.

The good *coyote* wades out a little further with his back to them. He ties an elaborate, specialist knot with the two pieces of climbing rope which each have different markings of tape at intervals on them. Got to get it right, now. OK . . . The rabbit goes round the tree, into the hole, comes back out of the hole and sits cross-legged outside the tree, then waggles its ears. There you go! I'm like a computer! I remember the details. I've got a special processing zone in my head that is all the time sorting out the shit and gravel, just leaving the shiny ore, the quick steel, the gold. To other people a gold tooth in their head is just a gold tooth. Too much money earned too easy. But with me it means something. It means panning out the gold from all the shit.

Blas waves the wetbacks in. Standing in the river he watches them pass. A smooth back, a spotty back, a fat back, a knobbly back. Like the Indians who once waded out with offerings to greet Columbus, the *mojados'* bare brown arms hold gold trinkets and keepsakes above the water; except their San Cristobals, photos, and watches are in sealed plastic bags (like the Indians selling gifts at the traffic lights). Blas counts them out until the last one has gone past, waiting until the water has covered the tattooed shoulder of the man with the shoes.

Blas climbs quickly on to the bank, yanks the rope head height and runs backward like he's launching a kite. This releases the slipknot. The river hooks them away like dry grass in the wind. Blas hears the wetbacks crying out in terror and, worse, some kind of open-throated grief, like the sound of something broken which should never break. Yallayallayalla, he jabbers aloud to himself to drown their nagging heckles. *Vete a la chingada!* he shouts, *vete a la chingada!*, until their noise is all river gargle, until it's hard to tell what's pebble groan and what's not. Not his fault anyway. Half this batch was cash upfront and it was them who ruined things for the others.

Blas starts putting his socks and boots back on, free from gas costs and the tedious gyp of conveying the losers all the way to San Antonio.

Those people at El Café Fuente knew whose son the boy is all right! There it is. And by their secrecy they must know where the terrorist is hiding! I just need in some way to make the boy easily identifiable to the snatch squad so it can be done when I'm not there. But how . . . ?

8

Tall and erect, Yolanda Gutierrez had a peculiar walk. Precise and slow, as if a naturally fast walker were slowed by a sudden thought or consideration crossing her mind. She was wearing her large, plastic glasses, a yellow sweatshirt, and a bottle green skirt, her green and grey headscarf wrapped up high as usual. Her bare shins and plastic-weave sandals were dusty. The sun was going down, igniting the broken-glass verge. The red flatbed was outside. He was home.

So the problem is, said Yolanda walking in from light to dark, from heat to cool, how can we take care of the boy without anyone else knowing that we are taking care of him, and without him knowing either?

She stopped and stared. Her husband was on his knees looking guilty. Eyes trained on the balance distribution of the table legs, Oscar placed both palms on to the red formica top and wobbled the table speculatively. Yolanda saw at once what had happened. She had caught her fellow member of the anarcho-syndicalist Frente Auténtico Trabajista praying. She pretended, however, that she hadn't.

If Daniel asks again, she continued evenly, we all have to keep acting like we never knew Chano.

Oscar leaned round the back door frame, reaching for a saw. That will be hard to do, he said, and lifted the table on to its side.

Well, just until someone's spoken to Chano, she said, now pitching her voice over the sound of sawing. The wood and steel furor alternated with sudden silence while off-cut fell to stone floor in tip-tapping bathos. Which means, I suppose, she resumed more quietly, Ayo's got to see if Chano's still in the same hiding place.

I'm worried about the *coyote*, said Oscar, holding Table Leg One's off-cut against Table Leg Two while he cut a guide nick with the saw. Blas?

Blas Mastrangelo. Mastra-cholo. Why?

He gave Daniel a gold basketball top, said Oscar.

Why?

I don't know, called Oscar over the din of sawing.

That's strange, Yolanda shouted thoughtfully. Tip-tap. Silence.

Well, I say he gave him the top, but he didn't give it to Daniel himself, said Oscar. Some woman with orange hair and lots of make-up driving a Silverado gave it to Daniel, but she said it was from . . . him . . . this Blas.

That I don't like.

We can't tell the boy about Chano? asked Oscar.

No, replied Yolanda, putting half a plucked chicken on the chopping board and opening the knife drawer.

But can't we tell him just about Marisa?

No.

Why not?

If you tell him about his mother he'll ask about his father. And then what do we say? replied Yolanda. Oscar righted the new low table and sat on it.

But what to do? he asked glumly, looking at her.

What to do? she repeated in kind.

Their eyes met. And in that moment both knew the other's mind. For Daniel's arrival had brought Oscar Jr. back to both of them more intimately than usual. As they discussed how to look after a strange boy and somehow convince him that the extraordinary pains they took were quite normal, Oscar Jr.'s presence had entered the room at waist height. They looked at each other with a kind of open-ended look as the past wandered into the present and found all the furniture smaller (which, in the case of the kitchen table, it now was).

In his industrial past Oscar Sr. had worked in Magnetec de Matamoros. Had made light rods. Had used trichloroethylene to wash the grease for soldering. Had used a resin and tar paste so the welding would stick. No face mask, just goggles to protect the eyes. At about the same time Yolanda was working at Componentes Mecánicos Matamoros. She didn't even have the goggles.

When Yolanda had first started at Componentes Mecánicos they'd asked if she was pregnant. That was pretty much the job interview for every woman who wanted to work there. A week later Yolanda had had to show the nurse a bloody Kotex in the toilets; door open in case of cheating and the nurse watching the whole production. It wasn't until you showed a red Kotex that you got your first pay packet.

Componentes Mecánicos was a subsidiary of a famous US make of car. For the next three years, Yolanda had built and repaired steering wheels. She had worked each day with trichloroethylene, alcohol paste, and solvent MIVK, while spray paint was misting the far end of the shed. Yolanda had cleaned the steering wheels with a pink foam which Chano had later identified for her—meaninglessly, uselessly, typically—as pollyole tiossionate. No gloves or mask, no ventilation; three years in an open-necked shirt with just her name on the pocket for protection. Squinting through the funky vapors gave her the standard-issue bifocals of the *maquilla*. Then she got pregnant.

Their son Oscar Jr. was born with *sindrome de Sturge-Weber*, his head swollen by toxic fluid pushing up against his skull. Oscar Sr. had a mental picture of Mr. Sturge and Mr. Weber, the two mysterious North Americans who always traveled together. They wore brown derbies and brown, nineteenth-century, three-piece suits with high, rounded collars and ties. They sent up their calling card to sick rooms, where parents read it out in hushed, confused tones over the encephalitic heads of children: Sturge-Weber syndrome.

The boy would clamp his hands to his head as if it would burst without the tight vice of his eyes screwed shut. From age one to four the pain seemed to get worse every year. Oscar Jr. had learned language as a game of catch-up: first to be able to describe each new pain, then to ask, When will it stop? At five years old he was walking round in a blue plastic, styrofoam-padded bike helmet. His hair was smooth and shiny like a black horse. Too beautiful, thought Yola, to cover with the bike helmet, and sometimes she didn't insist.

Fifty-five thousand pesos. The cost of one-off surgery to put in a valve to draw the fluid from his brain. Even then, the doctor told them, the operation should have been done when he was three, and now he was six.

Yolanda glanced at the stone floor. Oscar caught this look and knew she was remembering their son's convulsions . . . The pee on the floor was only ever spotted after, or if it had stained Oscar's shirt (if he'd picked him up against Yola's shouts—seven convulsions a day was seven arguments a day).

There was another woman, called Elena, whose daughter had also been born with Sturge-Weber syndrome. She visited Yolanda and Oscar in their old flat in Matamoros and told them she'd got Sister Susan from the Coalition for Justice in the Maquilladoras on the case. A one-shot local television interview had brought in cash for magnetic resonance images, she said. Plus she was getting support from Pastoral Juvenil Obrero. She wanted Yolanda in on the campaign.

Why, asked Yolanda, because two heads are better than one?

Yes, replied Elena (ignoring or missing Yolanda's sardonic comment). We want to file a complaint against the company, and get a lawyer.

There's no point, said Yolanda. We can't even raise money for the surgery. If you've got any money for a lawyer you should give it to one of the other mothers or us for surgery bills. All the compensation went on the doctor's bill and the medicine.

There's too many other *maquillas* affected, and not just by this but other birth defects as well.

Elena, let me tell you something: there is no point in getting a lawyer. For me and Oscar there's certainly no point—he was exposed to trichloroethylene as well. So which company could it be? It could be either. And it's not one cause, it's many causes. What about the MIVK? The paint fumes? No ventilation? The long hours?

Well, we file suit on the other company too, said Elena. The point of it all is so that other families don't suffer so the companies have to clean up their act.

That's what happens on the MGM channel. But it's not *one* bad company that has done something wrong, said Yolanda, *one* company that has behaved in a way that other companies don't. It's all companies, it's a whole system. That's why they come here, because they can do this. Suppose you win—

We fight where we can, where we are.

Suppose you win. You win this, suppose you do, which you won't, Elena—but suppose you do, and it's just like the films and the company pays out the money . . . Then they go to Thailand. And maybe *las maquilladoras* win in Thailand. So then they go to China.

Ah, but if the company lose in *China.* Ah! You see, what then? Now they have nowhere left to go until they find little green women in space. What then?

El-e-na! Look around! Then there's another hundred companies here meanwhile all doing the same thing or something else like it, and another and another, streets and streets of them in Matamoros, Reynosa, Juarez, Nogales.

So we do nothing?

We organize. You come to *autogestión* meetings because you believe in that, yes? So. We don't go begging to their courts because, even if you win, it'll just keep happening in other ways in other places.

You say this, my friend, because you have lost hope, because you think, well it's too late for me so to the devil with everyone else, and because—

We hope for different things—

—because you are already preparing for Oscarito's death.

Yolanda looked at her hands in her lap for a moment, then said: Why do you say that? No. He has fewer convulsions now. Some *Sturge-Weberos* become young men.

So you won't help us?

Let's do something else. An occupation, *protesta, manifestación,* a general *maquilladora* strike, yes—but not the courts. *Their* courts.

This is the campaign that's happening, said Elena. This is the one that exists, the one which has support.

Then no.

Though Yolanda did indeed have deep ideological convictions against indulging the law courts, that didn't stop her having other reasons, too. Elena was right. It was too late for Oscar Jr.. And going to court—apart from being in her mind a lost cause—would take too much of the brief time she had left with her son.

Elena left empty-handed but the pressure continued. Notes under the door, name-checked in meetings, a petition begging their involvement in the litigation campaign, and reminders of the date of the next preliminary hearing.

They decided to move. Yolanda didn't have much of a future on *la frontera* anyway. Work three years in the windowless *maquilladoras* until your eyesight goes and they replace you with younger women who can see. (You met your wife, she was fond of reminding Oscar, in the Town of Short-Sighted Women.) And so they had moved back to Tonalacapan, near where they'd both grown up. (Oscar in Tonalacapan itself and Yolanda in Calderon where her friend Marisa still lived.)

A village is better for a boy with Sturge-Weber syndrome anyway. The older kids—like Tavo, Alma-Delia's eldest—were punctilious in their care not to accidentally knock him over. They were stridently self-important when telling other kids, kids new to the park, the special Oscar Jr. rules of soccer. No contact. No headers. No tackling. And every now and then they'd roll Oscar Jr. a long, grasscutter pass, which he'd whack back wildly.

But their son was daily more frustrated. Oscar Sr. remembered how Oscar Jr. used to sit on his own on the wooden mini-slide by the flats, tilting his heavy head as he listened to the distant, squealing, break-time laughter coming from the school. And he remembered how, after first telling his father to read more quickly, his son would end up reading to him about the giraffe whose neck was too tall for his house and who had to have a hole cut in the roof of his car when driving to see his friends the rhino and the anteater whose kite was one day stuck up a tree the rhino and the anteater could not reach up high enough and so they would never get their kite back but the giraffe got it down from the tree with his long neck and so from that day on the rhino and the anteater began to help out the giraffe by tying his shoelaces for which task his long legs were too long and his tall neck too tall and his heavy head too heavy.

Yolanda had smiled when she'd walked out on to the pitch to tell her son's friends that he'd died. Tavo, hot and sweaty and holding the ball, had asked the first question. How did it happen? Yola had thought this was the right question to ask. For it gave her yet another chance to try to contain the death of her son in words, to try again to conceive that edge of things beyond which there was no more Oscar Jr., the point at which he'd stopped existing. It was, in short, the question she'd been asking herself. She began matter-of-factly: He was on a Nintendo high-score and getting off the bus at the same time. (She laughed. They didn't.) He fell over and then he hit his head on one of those cement flower tubs.

Tavo had nodded, frowned, and then, perhaps wishing her answer might explain the incomprehensible, or just to abolish the enormity of the fact, had asked what the high-score was. She hadn't known the answer to that question either.

No more children, they had decided. Oscar was demoted from Oscar Sr. to just Oscar. In perpetuity.

And now this boy had come along—Daniel—with that same sense of being both apart from the life of the *pueblo* yet part of it, too. The boy with the question they couldn't answer. And once more Oscar and Yolanda found themselves discussing how to look after a strange boy, and somehow convince him that the extraordinary pains they took were quite normal and no different from how any other boy might be treated.

Shunting the knife drawer with her hip, Yolanda saw the chicken start to roll off the chopping board. She saved it from flopping to the floor but caught two fingers in the slamming drawer.

Putada! she hissed. Oscar stood up. She grabbed his shoulder and tried to pull his arm from its socket until the pain went away. At which point they both calmly left off. She to prepare the chicken, he to take the saw out back.

That night Oscar and Yolanda went to a dance in Nahualhuas, a Frente Auténtico Trabaja benefit for the coming demonstration against the Ethylclad plant. The dance was in a massive, concrete siding which had once been a slaughterhouse and was now roofless. It was packed.

Oscar danced, watching Yolanda's hands and feet like she was going to ask him to Find the Lady. His burly frame bobbed and bounced with ease, yet he looked around the crowded dance floor wide-eyed and slightly apprehensive, as if fearing that any moment the dance might suddenly change tempo or become a stampede toward the exits, and he didn't, in either eventuality, want to be caught out or left behind.

Once he'd had a few drinks in him—and had become convinced that there were going to be no surprises—he was lit up and wanting to get as much of this as he could before it was banned, bouncing his hands double-time when the beat wasn't speeding up quick enough. He had more energy, Yolanda noticed, when they left at two A.M. than he'd had at five P.M. (having driven all the way from San Luis Potosi in time to scrub up and change). Loud in the park, he pushed out coins with his thumb for roast sunflower seeds.

After a lift back to Tonalacapan, they dawdled on their way home past the dusty, shuttered El Café Fuente. In the close, humid night, they rested aching, tired limbs on the fountain's ledge. The fountain bubbled and boiled and dissolved post-dance tinnitus and the cicadas' livid tumult.

The fountain had enjoyed a short burst of flourishing life after Chano and Ayo blew up Ethylclad's groundwater pipelines. So much so, in fact, that its full-bodied celebration had made everyone nervous. Just a few hours after the explosion the fountain had leapt up with a strange skittering noise, scattering its crystals toward El Café Fuente and leaving the earth smelling damp. Over here! the fountain's blabber-mouthed cry had seemed to say. Here's who you're looking for! Erik and Alma-Delia who ran El Café Fuente, and who, though the fountain belonged to the *ejido* (or communal land tenure), were its primary carers, had frowned from just inside the café door as the fountain sang revolutionary songs day and night.

Ethylclad's sabotaged water pipeline was all over the national news. In *La Prensa* a black-and-white, fourteen-year-old photo showed a thin-faced Mariano a.k.a. Chano Salgado (from his Cerro Hueco arrest sheet), while a colour photo showed his triangular plot in Calderon.

There had already been one near thing. Ayalo had been carrying two bags of Chano's possessions from his *choza* when he'd been vox-popped by the first satellite news van on the scene. What did those in the neighborhood think of the terrorist attack? Who knew the quiet loner? Me no speak only Toltec sorry, Ayo had mumbled in broken Spanish and kept walking. Ethylclad's pipeline had been repaired two days later, the fountain had diminished again and everyone breathed easier.

Behind Oscar and Yolanda's backs the fountain now made a sound like a load of geese taking off, then fell to a faint, weak frizzing. Frrrrzzz-ffffrzzzz, fffrrrrrzzzz-fffffrrzzzzz, fffffrrrrrzzz, ffffrrrrrzzzz . . .

The reason people delight in the sound of fountains, said Yolanda, is because white water mixes high and low frequencies together, and they say that's the most pleasing sound to the human ear. In Oscar's unmoved silence she heard how less than pleasing to her *own* ear the theory was. How petty it sounded. No, she said, sharply disagreeing with herself. No, the sound of running water must have meant here is somewhere you can live. Here you can drink and eat and cook and plant and grow. That must have made it the best sound on earth.

And because a fountain has no purpose, Oscar replied, unlike everything else. It just is. It just does. That's got to make you happy.

9

In the town of Market Haven the Global Power Forum was meeting at the Metropole. There were no conference hoardings on the rain-lashed front railings. Nor had Reception spelled things out in gold lettering on the purple board.

The Global Power Forum was not a sinister world-take-over bid. It didn't mean power in that way. It meant power as in energy, gas, electricity, and water, their sole supply controlled by a giant multi-utility corporation. It meant power like that. That sort of power. And today at the Metropole, the energy companies and pipeliners were going after the waterworks.

General Electric, Vivendi, Suez Lyonnais des Eaux, RWE, Ethylclad, and Belcatel shared a vision. All the water in the United

States of America. They were going to privatize every drop from Mount Olympus to the Mojave Desert, a suction pod in every aquifer and Cajun swamp. Unprivatized as yet, the US market was estimated at $800 billion. This was the pot of gold at the end of the rainbow. But first they had to come to Market Haven.

Just as a space probe orbits the earth to get a gravitational slingshot to the Martian rustbelt, so these companies must follow the trade winds to this limestone coast by chalk hills in northwest Europe. They were winding up all the energy they would need for the slingshot. The heavier the mass the faster the speed, and so here they came on the slow orbit: loading up. RWE of Germany had bought up Thames Water. Enron Energy had filled its tanks with Wessex Water. Vivendi had filled its ballast with US Filter Corp for six billion dollars. Bouygouynes Construction France had weighted itself with SAUR Water. Ethylclad had printed out water bills in Swahili, Spanish, and Portuguese (and sent form letters of congratulations to the riot-police chiefs), and Belcatel had bought International Waters of London. No one could make themselves heavy enough quickly enough.

And the booster companies had been boosting too. For all the smaller companies had already been once round the globe plumbing the depths of southern hemisphere aquifers. Thames Water had tanked up with Australian Water on its slow orbit, and now RWE circled the planet with both Thames and Australian water cooling its twin jets.

Now that they were at last hitting critical mass, here too came Evan Hatch. For the Global Power Forum was not going to be pulled back down to earth by people who would not understand what their interference might ruin.

You could feel the money in the air. Evan hadn't felt this buzz since the early days of the Multilateral Agreement on Investment. The air's gonna feel different after this goes through, he said to himself this morning. No one was looking around to see if the place was up to their standards, people were all either walking somewhere definite or talking deals with lowered voices and urgent gestures. Intercontinental high-rollers were cracking their knuckles on the blue baize tables. Some looked radiant, others—standing on their own by the coffee urn—looked sick as if like the rest of their career might be decided in the next few hours.

It was a long time since Evan had felt so well. Nothing could stop him now. Not today. If his illness tried anything he'd squash it like a bug. As Evan crossed the sprung floor with a bounce in his step a European commissioner was walking toward him, hand outstretched. Without warning Evan's mouth filled up with blood and his cheeks bullfrogged like Dizzy Gillespie. But Evan just knocked it down in one, before baring his bloody fangs in a smile.

Though it was not yet noon, the sky had darkened so much that the hotel had switched the lights on. Rain kerplunked in pick-up sticks on the roof's art-deco skylight. Evan entered a room with BLUE GOLD written in hasty marker on the door. Lenny from Sawyer Miller was there and Evan congratulated him on the Colombia work.

No, I tell you, it felt weird, that one, Evan. It was like shit through a goose. I was all the time thinking, hold on there's a fairly visible hand helping it along.

Who's that?

The networks themselves. Media companies want to take nervous shareholders into Colombia. There are millions of people watching a sitcom about God over there. Hey, have you been in the other room?

No.

Insane. There's just one guy who has a big sheet of A3 and everybody's yelling ideas like orders for Domino's. Sold, says the guy with the marker pen and writes them down. This isn't a conference, it's like—I don't know what it is . . . outcry trading, maybe.

Evan and Lenny were waiting for the social management working group. The room was filling up now. A couple of *Eurobusiness* centerfolds came in, having delayed their next meeting just to hear this one. Evan, Lenny, and the centerfolds had seats at the table. Soon it was standing room only right around the walls. Except for one chair, the chair. Crowds parted, the room fell silent. Anatole Louis-Rend swept in.

Anatole Louis-Rend was the French-Canadian CEO in charge of the Global Power Forum's social management department. Short, mid-fifties, tanned, and with silver-grey hair, he wore a sharp, silver-grey suit. For some reason he had a dark-green cashmere scarf round his neck and thrown over one shoulder of his shimmery grey suit.

Evan couldn't work out whether this was how scarves were being worn in Paris this year, or whether Charles Aznavour just has to hurry.

Perhaps the green scarf would come off now, wondered Evan, when Anatole sat down smiling to himself, but it didn't. Maybe more Sasha Distel than Aznavour, Evan considered, what with the tanned face, the laughter lines and the air of pickled and preserved handsomeness. The half-moon designer glasses on someone so manicured and elegantly dressed gave him the air of a rich spinster who had once been a leading society beauty. And that was before Evan had noticed that the half-moon glasses were attached to a little gold chain around the French-Canadian's neck.

Nimble and alert, Louis-Rend rapidly introduced everyone to Evan and Lenny and explained their coordination role.

Now I will begin ze meeting myself. OK. First question. What do we do about ze riots? Everyone broke up laughing, and the handsome, tanned fifty-year-old looked up over his half-moons with a twinkle in his eye. Trick question, he added. It depends where, of course. Which countries are likely to wobble first?

Well, it doesn't really matter, began Evan. Everyone looked toward him, grateful to be interrupted before someone else saw a shape in the figures first. Evan simplified: If it's Bolivia? Narco-traffickers. Africa—then it's a tribal thing. India—we're talking about government corruption.

What about the domestic markets? What about at home?

In our countries we just have to depoliticize. We make it a technical question, the great science problem of our time which, as it happens, Company X is closest in the world to solving, so just get out of its way.

And if water bills have regional price splits, said Lenny, we have the astroturf ask why we can't choose where—

No, no, said the severe French-Canadian, while still jotting something down on his pad. He waited till he'd finished what he was writing before going on: No, no, there's a separate coordinating meeting on front groups and two-step communications after lunch.

What room? came a voice.

Iiiii . . . eet doesn't say. But it's hosted by . . . New Policy Foundation. Ah, but who are they really? chimed Evan.

Amid general laughter the Frenchman held the joints of his half-moon glasses between thumb and forefinger, and cast his big brown eyes first at Evan and then warmly over all his clever students. Still resting his elbows on the table, still delicately clasping the joints of his frames between thumb and forefinger, still pursing his lips in an enchanted smile, he went on: Pollution. And new forms of industrial pollution, too. Semi-conductor plants, lead, mercury, hexavelent chromium coming into the water table. It's in the drinking water. Now we know why boys misbehave and grow breasts. Good for Ritalin, bad for everyone else. But what are we saying? What? Job-creation threatened? Or, it's still by far the cleanest water? What do we say?

Well, as it happens, said Evan, there is actually new evidence that's just been published which really gets us out of jail on this one. It's the result of a ten-year study at Oxford University and one of the American universities.

MIT, assisted Lenny.

Yeah, MIT, and this study has come up with this brilliant data. It shows—in controlled experiments—how in humans the trace elements of almost any of these so-called pollutants that you can find in tap water actually encourage and foster our immune systems. You see, they help us create the mild antibodies and antigens needed to deal with the more serious pollutants elsewhere.

Is this true? the Frenchman asked Evan.

No.

Formidable!

The working group moved on to next year's publication of a book called *Cancer in the Water.*

We have a friend at her publisher's, Anatole Louis-Rend was saying, who tells us of all her speaking engagements. It is very nice of him. As soon as we know what TV shows she will be on we get there first and we will demand the interview becomes a debate with one of our independent experts.

I think it's also important, said Evan to everybody, in these situations, to send a legal warning with about half the book marked in yellow highlighter as being definitely litigious. I mean, they have to go through it all. The whole book. That costs. And the TV company has to decide whether it's worth it for three minutes' air-time.

Two hours later it had stopped raining. Evan drove through flooded countryside on the A road from Market Haven.

Flooding feels very peaceable if it's not your house underwater. After high-speed winds there is a sense of violence having been done to nature, of chaos, but the after-effects of flooding spread placidity. Water only ever seeks its own level, after all, and there was, to Evan, a peaceable sense that things had only gone back to how they might have been all along. He noticed how the river, far from chaotically ranging, had merely leaked back along its former course. The water had revealed the real pattern which lay submerged under the hidden faultlines of modern pastoralism. An old stream had been redescribed. And now that the rains had gone, this all seemed to have been achieved logically and patiently.

Fields were underwater but not hedges and trees. Water filled neat oblongs and the square, silver fields looked as if they'd always been that way. If water wanted to play at being a field the trees and hedgerows were happy to oblige, and soberly marked out the field of still water like indulgent grandparents going along with a child's game whose rules they don't understand.

Bright swans drifted on the new, square lakes which had been provided for them. The swans straightened up their necks with a sense that this was really no better than they deserved. (Swan fields. Very good. Not before time.)

The sky darkened. Evan glimpsed a higher slope of chalky seed crop where silver tractor tracks flared like magnesium in the half-light.

Sprays of filthy puddles went over his BMW Z4. The screen cleared itself with one bat of the wiper. Evan enjoyed the feeling of imperviousness. A phone wire coming from his ear, he pretended to be an automaton by pushing his head back against the headrest and letting it wobble robotically when he hit a bump, and by sticking to a pre-programmed, cruise-control forty miles an hour. Man and machine were one. He rotated his head very slowly to look out of the side window like a scanning droid. He soon gave the game up, angry that he was wasting his precious good-health time traveling. Five minutes later he hit a traffic jam. No one was moving. A rural tailback. Here, in the middle of nowhere. Why? Get out of my way, you fucking PEASANTS, he shouted in his sealed car.

The sky went black like an eclipse. He began to feel ill. Cold. He knew very well what was coming next. He turned off, drove up a winding lane and reached the outskirts of some town. Perhaps he'd have time to check into a Travelodge, he thought, until realizing he barely had time to stop the car.

Hands quick and panicky on the wheel, he stopped the car, snatched up his laptop, got out and hurried through a blur of streets, before clambering over a five-bar gate. Three chalky fields brought him to the brow of a hill. He stopped. Looked around. He was far enough away. But maybe a little further just to be safe? No time.

He threw up. The rain began to fall but he couldn't move for vomiting. His hands slipped off his wet knees. The downpour cannonaded on his back. The rain tugged his sodden coat out of shape. His puke was flecked with blood. Rain diluted the scarlet gobbets, sending them running in pinkish traces down the pile.

At last Evan was empty. He stood up. He breathed out and began trembling like a pneumatic drill. He staggered and shook toward a stone barn in the middle of the field, the deluge slapping his face and head.

The barn had no side walls, just two ends. He lay on a stack of fertilizer bags. He waited for it to come. His blood was setting. He could feel its movement through the veins of his arms and forehead, slow and cold as toothpaste.

The attack came. Sandpaper gloves twisted his organs around from the inside. First one way then another. He howled—colon, gut—and moaned—stomach, spine—and screamed—liver, kidney—and sobbed—the chest, the throat. Fresians in the field threw alarmed heads up from the shoulder. The cows walked a few steps toward the storage hut and then a few steps sideways.

Evan roared. He kept trying to twist his body with the organs, only to have to fend off an attack more painful than the last. For the first hour the pain was continuous, and for the next it came in quick staggers with Evan bracing himself for the next delivery.

After two hours Evan dared ask himself, Has it gone? He stayed absolutely still. Was the pain gone? He held his breath like someone who has just sliced himself deeply with a bread knife and must wait a beat before the pain-returns come in. He exhaled—carefully, very carefully—like an abseiler feeding out rope. He took another cautious breath. Was it over? He breathed out gently. Yes, he dared to think at last. It was over.

He stood up, looked around him at the barn and began swearing and shaking his head with a wan smile, like the victim of a practical joke whose friends were all stood around to see how he'd take having the life scared out of him.

Fuckin' *Nora*! Jesus *Christ*!

He took off his fawn crombie with the black velvet collar. The poor old coat had copped all the organo-phosphate swipes, feathers, mud and birdshit he'd been writhing about in. His shirt and trousers were damp with sweat but nothing worse. He took off his trousers. Bless his cotton boxers, they had held the shit. He placed the bundle in a corner of the barn, and put his trousers back on, the damp wool bristly against his buttocks.

The rain stopped. The sky was dazed and the barn roof dripped heavily. He washed his face with wet grass and chomped some more to take the taste away. He arranged his fawn crombie over his arm so that most of the filth was folded out of sight, with only the lining and a clean bit of sleeve on show. Coat over arm, laptop in hand, he wandered down the hill in his black suit.

At the end of the street Evan could see rising brown water closing over the roof of his aerodynamic BMW Z4. A firefighter waded through the high-smelling high water to tie DO NOT CROSS tape to a lamp post.

But it wasn't flooded here when I parked, said Evan.

Been raining all week, she replied austerely.

Evan stood on the corner, looking around in numb bewilderment at the gathered crowd. A pensioner in a short mac and alpine hat had found in Evan what he'd been looking for: someone who'd want his version of events.

The drains burst, all of 'em, and the river's overflowing, I just seen it by the bridge: river's chucking it up on to the road and right up the shop windows! The small, dapper old man was so excited he sounded joyful. The water is *jumping* up in the air. Never seen it so fast when it was in the *river* as it is *now* when it's on the *street*. I say—he said, and looked around hoping other people could get a load of this now that he was in full flow—I say, I've never seen it going so fast when it was a river *in the river* as it is now it's *on the street*. Finding no takers, he returned to Evan. Here's how it happened, cock. I'll tell you now: rain

rain, rain, rain for a fortnight. Solid. Then it stops—oh we're all right now. No! Give it a moment. Brief downfall. Just now. Boom! Up she rises! Heh-heh! I say, that's not your car, is it?

No.

Just as well, eh? Oh-ho!

How do I get to the train station?

Well, ordinarily I'd say *down that street there*!!! But not *today*! Who-hoo! Eh?! Evan looked down at the chuckling alpine hat with its little feather. No!! People are having to go all the way round just to get to the town centre. Whew!! Who knows if *that's* flooded now? Well, I wonder. It's down the hill—it might be! Cheery-bye! Cheery-bye! And the old man beetled away energetically, hoping for the worst.

Evan gazed wistfully down the brown log-flume into town. A man and a woman emerged from a side street in a wooden row boat.

Wanna lift? the woman called out to him.

To the train station? asked Evan

If you like, said the woman. Wherever. Evan glanced up at the pedestrian footbridge. The knot of people he'd been standing with were winding their way up its forlorn stairs. He turned back to the boat and held up his laptop as if to say, will this stay dry? Yeah, you're all right, mate, she replied. All ship-shape here. Evan nodded and compressed the crumple-zones of his mouth into a kind of smile. The boat rowed toward him up the street until its wooden hull scraped the tarmac as slope met water in a kind of spontaneous slipway.

Evan sat erect on a thin plank which had been sawn from a lighter shade of wood than the rest of the boat. He set the laptop carry case upright on his high knees like a wartime evacuee schoolboy gripping his name-labeled cardboard suitcase.

I'm Dom, that's Shannon.

Evan. Do you live here?

Near here. (Ah, thought Evan, *pikies*.)

Shannon rowed the boat through a terraced side street. In the dark water stirred by the oars, Evan saw tilting reflections of net curtains, TV aerials, window frames, house numbers, and stone cladding. Dom stared at Evan, nodding and smiling. He had a small tin on his knees and was rolling tobacco in a single Rizla.

You've got to go sideways first, he said, because the current on the ring road is really strong. That's 'cos it's parallel to the river and, well, it basically is the river. So we're sort of going one up, one across, or one down, one across, if you know what I mean, he said, and licked the skinny rolly one across and one down.

Evan looked at the crew. Dom and Shannon had beads and ribbons in their locks and both wore multiple layers of thick-weave homespun over black drainpipes which disappeared into muddy boots. These two are in their element, thought Evan. This led him to reflect on how his own decision to accept the lift was kind of Darwinian. A risk-taker, a flexible improviser, Evan was not like the bedraggled herd on the footbridge; he was in the ark. His survival instinct had brought him into contact with these two, he considered— as if an earthquake would find him standing next to a seismologist between the RSJs of an underground car park.

The current's stronger here, growled Shannon at the oars. Evan looked up. She was straining just to hold the boat still as the side-street canal they were on crossed a broad stretch of main river. As she struggled with the oars, Evan noticed one pole jammed in the brown liquid, a neat, white fringe of floodwater pooling round it. Dom scanned the current and looked up and down the light brown, fast-flowing street.

Don't try and go straight across, he said. Just aim at the next corner and then we'll have another go.

OK, she gasped, and shipping oars let the boat drift down the main road. As they approached the next canal of terraced houses, she dipped the oars at an angle, using them as rudders to aim toward the junction.

You're gonna miss it, cried Evan. Right hand! Right hand!

Please sit down, mate, said Dom.

I'm slowing it down, sputtered Shannon, heaving the grip of both oars through a slow, forward arc as she resisted the rushing brown water. They were slowing now, but Evan leaned out and grabbed hold of a pelican crossing pole. The rear of the boat swung sharply, tipping them steeply. Fucking let go of it! she shouted at him.

Evan let go, sat back down and watched the side street sail by.

Now we've missed the fucking turning, said Shannon. Now we're going downstream facing the wrong way. We would've made it and all if you hadn't fucked about. Fucking chiseler.

Here y'are, offered Dom. I'll row now I've got me back to it. Jesus.

Nearly capsized us there, she said, staring at Evan while rolling the oars forward to Dom.

Sorry, said Evan.

Which road is this? Dom asked.

Shannon looked ahead of her as the road curved round. Oh bollocks, she replied. Sitting in what was now the front, even Evan recognized the ring road. For this was indeed where the current was strongest and the main course of the swollen river. Dom shipped oars and rested his elbows on his knees. They ran over a floating red-and-white-striped electrician's tent. Shannon sat back in the prow and sang: Hoo-ray! Up she rises! Whe-hey!

Half an hour later, the boat scudded peacefully through open countryside, drifting by trees and hedges, rooks and hills.

We can put you off there if you like, said Shannon.

Evan looked at the beer garden of a dormant pub and nodded in stiff, furious silence.

His fault we missed the fucking turn-off, she added, as if he'd already got out the boat.

Evan laid his laptop on the wet lawn and climbed out of the boat without looking back at them or saying a word. Stomping past the climbing frame, he heard Dom shout after him: Pint of Speckled Hen! Two packets of salt and vinegar!

Two veggie ploughmans! cried Shannon, and a pint of champagne-top for the lady!

As Evan disappeared up the garden path he heard them dissolve into laughter.

The bus shelter had one more wall than the barn. Evan tied his blue silk tie back on. They'd put up a sign or something if it wasn't a bus route any more? he wondered, after standing alone in the pebbledash for twenty minutes. They'd take the timetable down or something, wouldn't they?

Ten minutes later, like an article of faith, a GreenLine appeared. A bus! thought Evan, his hand on the steel rail of the seat in front. A bus! What was it Margaret Thatcher said? Only losers get the bus!

Evan got off the bus at the train station, got on the wrong train and had to get a small stopping train back to another station, then cross over to the other platform. There was no bridge here and he walked across the tracks where a wooden walkway covered the sleepers.

Evan wondered to find a couple of dozen people on the platform of such an obscure branch line. He moved away from them into the sunlight and kept walking to the very end of the platform, the last horizontal square yard before it sloped down to the track. Here he sat down, leaning his back against a square, wooden flower box.

This was, it occurred to him, the first time for years no one had known where he was. Even the weeks he'd spent ill at home while everyone thought he was away on holiday hadn't felt as disconnected as this. For then his home phone would still ring every day leaving him messages for when he "got back." This was different, almost an adventure, a day out.

Evan looked at the hills, breathed in fresh air, tipped his face to the light, closed his eyes and then got angry—because he didn't have time to waste like this. He could be working. He was meant to be using his intervals of health to ready a series of easy pots on the pool-table pockets for when it was his next go. Stuff like the Seattle speech, for example. He switched on his Powerbook.

How could he outflank the other flaks who would speak after him? There was something Anatole Louis-Rend had said in their one-on-one, red laminate lunch meeting which had given him an idea for his Seattle presentation. Evan had glimpsed the inside track from something he'd said. But what was it? His Seattle presentation would be just a couple of months before the World Trade Organization's third ministerial. It was something to do with that, but what? Evan slightly lowered the Powerbook lid as he forced his mind to remember.

I think we've gone as far as we can in saying this system is just nature, Louis-Rend had begun. You know, you can only tell people God put the king in Versailles for so long. So: I think we have to spend less time saying globalization is a force of nature, like rain, like air, and spend more time in making the case for this philosophy as a philosophy.

Why? Evan had asked.

Because, he'd replied after a little pause, at the moment of greatest success you are exposed to greatest risk. Bio patents and water privatization raise the most dangerous of all political questions: philosophical ones. Questions about who owns water. Who owns the land? About the rights of man. Let me paint you a picture of the future. I can see the environmentalists hitting a home run. They shift the argument and say: Look, we can argue about capitalism theoretically, but the fact is that in purely practical terms growth is unsustainable and capitalism cannot survive on this planet. It may work on another planet, but not, they will say, on this one.

Because of global warming? said Evan.

Global warming and water shortages and the wider ecological breakdown—all these things together will mean they will find themselves in a position to say that people have always had the dream of a different way of organizing things but have always put it off for a rainy day.

But now that rainy day has come, said Evan.

But now that rainy day has come, Anatole repeated, gesturing toward the window and nodding admiringly at the exquisite wit needed to point at rain when the word rain has just been said.

The waiter arrived holding two dishes.

Confit de canard? *he asked. Anatole pointed to himself.*

I think, he continued, when the napkin was arranged to his satisfaction, we have to give people a story of dangers we're facing in the future, and then say: Now, here are the custodians—the corporations who are developing sustainable alternatives.

The dangers, thought Evan. It was something to do with the dangers . . . It was on the tip of his tongue, the thing he'd thought of in the lunch meeting which would give him the whole angle for his Seattle presentation. It was . . . It was . . .

Excuse me, said a voice. Evan looked up. A well-dressed woman in her early sixties was smiling down at the well-dressed man in his early thirties. They were both well dressed. That's why she'd picked him out. That was the reason why she had chosen to confer her question upon this particular young man who was, like herself, so well dressed. Or, at least, expensively dressed, for she was dressed like the Queen. She wore a custard-coloured hat with a silver brooch on the front which matched the custard-coloured A-line coat over the rhubarb skirt-and-jersey combo. Do you happen to know, she began, when the next train is coming? Only they haven't made any announcements, of course, have they?

What am I doing?

I'm sorry? she asked, bowing slightly to hear him better, smiling sweetly and convinced she'd misheard him.

Evan gestured toward his screen. What am I doing? he asked, this time in tones clear and slow enough for the simplest person to understand. I'm *working*, said Evan. With upturned hand he gestured at all the other people standing on the platform. And what are they all doing? he asked, with a sweet smile of his own.

Well, I must say . . . ! the woman did declare but Evan had already returned to his screen.

Thank you, he announced as her best shoes clattered back the way she'd come.

During this exchange the unattended screen had reverted to his SmartSlide screen saver which was now flipping through its Activist Gallery slide show. Auto-uploaded in his absence (by subscription to the Public Affairs International database), there were many in the pix-file he'd never seen before. He could measure the length of his last sick leave by the number of new suspects, fresh faces. This stuff was scary. He watched the procession of headshots, each holding the screen for a few seconds with text below: nationality, organization, age, campaign history, arrests, publications. And then he remembered the idea that had come to him at lunch: *fear.*

Evan would just scare the CEOs. All the other flaks would be laid-back and make out they had all the bases covered: *We know how to handle it, we've done this before.* And so what I'll do, thought Evan, is scare them with the dangers, totally new dangers. Fear is the power lever and it's better if I don't give them any solutions or easy answers. Where Louis-Rend is wrong is that he does, and that's a mistake. If you say you have the solution it's offering them consolation. No solution, no consolation—only *then* are they in my power.

And look at them go, Evan chuckled to himself, as the SmartSlide ran G8-summit protesters, crop trashers, and Indian "Cremate Monsanto" farmers. He imagined the powerful effect this would have as a back projection, spooling along, while he told executives their futures. Multimedia, but unfussy, just have it rotating behind him while he spoke. *These are vocal, articulate, well-organized groups,* he would say, *who can cause an emotive reaction that will cost you billions.* What's their nightmare scenario? he thought. Broad alliances; transnational and cross-sectoral activists. NGOs, trade unions, students, and locals all getting it on together.

He watched them go: photos culled from Detroit charge sheet, Birmingham CCTV, Kenyan news clipping, Indian book jacket, Madrid conference, and Kurdish ID card. And none of them, thought Evan, none of them wherever they are, has any idea that their face is right now being looked at by someone on a branch line somewhere in England after a flood.

He rolled the mouse-ball to get a blank page and tried to think of the opening words for his Seattle presentation, but couldn't focus his mind. The agony he'd suffered an hour ago had spooked him and he feared its return. There was something else too. With no one knowing where he was, the blackbird on top of the alder was singing just for him. He gazed at the trees on the skyline while he waited for this nature mood to get boring again, just kind of stared out the hills which rose toward the sly clouds slipping away after their raid, the fast ones sliding over the slow.

He looked back at his screen. It had reverted to SmartSlide again; more faces were looping, looping, looping. He watched the procession of new human faces. All of them extremists, all of them believers. How arbitrary identity is, thought Evan, as he sat on the train platform. Here's a feller called Obasingo and he thinks this and this, and here's a woman called Birnur and she lives there and believes in that.

It is a matter of keen regret to us all that whereas our own political beliefs have been founded on detached observation to arrive at the logical conclusion of common-sense consensus, the beliefs of other people have so obviously been moulded from some sort of *social basis.* We have often had occasion to remark how views unlike our own are invariably the result of some kind of unhappy accident—dusty climate, colonial legacy, historical hangover, religious influence, distant mothers, overbearing fathers, sloppy potty-training, class, race, fatty diet, haphazard education, excitable fundamentalist temperaments, personality disorders, chalky soil, peer pressure, over-exposure to emotionally irresponsible propaganda, the sectarian gene, or just plain bad luck. Ah, if only others, we think, could detach themselves like we have, and, following our example, consider the facts on their merits alone, then they would surely come to the same conclusions we have. But alas, we sigh, they cannot; and therein, we conclude, lies the central tragedy of human affairs!

And still the faces churned and churned. Evan shifted his position on the crumbly asphalt and, riding his shoulder blades up the ridged and varnished wooden flower tub, he became more and more fascinated.

Here's Medha Pakra, read Evan, she's from the Narmada Valley and campaigns against the Narmada Dam. Well, she would wouldn't she, he thought. But she wouldn't if she lived near here. Here is a woman called Adiboya from Ogoni, with the locality's matching frown and headscarf. And here is a man called Mariano Salgado from Mexico, who is also known as Chano.

A face stared out at someone on a branch line somewhere in England after a flood.

10

Finding himself on only his third day in Mexico halfway through his second working day at the docks, Daniel was as unsurprised by this happy turn of events as the English swans his Uncle Evan had just seen taking a turn around the new, waterlogged fields had been. To Daniel getting this job was just a bit more like it. A touch. Excellent. And, now he thought about it, kind of how he'd always known things would turn out.

People who never look before they leap will often believe that a guardian spirit watches over them. This is because they get in situations where only the most extraordinary fluke enables them to live to tell the tale. Thus the mere fact that they are still alive and so able to have any beliefs *at all* confirms them in this one belief. They therefore not only have a belief in a guardian angel, but tend also to have had that belief demonstrated. To the logician's frustration they will, necessarily, have lots of evidence to back up their conviction that a spirit watches over them, and are best left to it.

Villegas was a feeder port ferrying containers on tow-decks to the ACL cranes to the ACL cranes of the main Calderon docks three miles up the coast. There was a cargo terminal, storage yards, and a row of fish-gutting factories.

Oscar had got him this job rebagging the coal, but Daniel reckoned that the man he'd met fixing the motorbike was behind it. Blas. He must have had a word with that woman who worked at the *caseta telefónica*. (To check this theory, Daniel had asked her if she knew him, but she'd said his name so coldly—Blas Mastrangelo—that, what with her forbidding manner and all, Daniel had asked no more questions.) He wondered—for a passing moment—whether there might be more stuff going on than he knew about. Then again, he thought happily, maybe a job just came up and—boom—there I was! On which sunny reflection, Daniel took another clean blue slip-shiny bag from the pallet.

He had to rip open the old sacks and re-bag the coal in the new blue vinyl ones. Years ago, the coal had been neatly stacked, but it had been left out so long the sacking had rotted. In some places, the bags had weathered clean away and chunky coal heaps glinted in the smokeless sun. The dilapidated mound of old grey synthetic sacks was six feet high in the middle and stretched across the whole storage yard.

A chainlink fence separated the coal mounds from the convoy of trucks lining up for customs. Daniel was back where he'd found his ride into Tonalacapan. Charcoal dust was stirred by a truck's diesel down-draft and Daniel dragged another torn and weathered sack upright.

First one, then another, then three, then four, then a procession of tiny children arrived outside the chain-link fence. These were the dock workers' kids bringing their fathers their lunches. The men soon appeared from port-side, walking a clear path along the far edge of Daniel's coal compound. Through the fence's diagonals the children passed their fathers food and drink. One docker pretended to be a zoo animal, opening his mouth wide and rattling the fence as his son handed him his lunch. Daniel looked on hungrily at a burrito tied down with string over a plastic box of something hot.

A small, dusty girl held a large wad of foil, from which a lamb bone stuck out, Daniel noticed. The parcel wouldn't fit through the mesh. Her father walked two steps to his right, looked round, and then lifted the fence where it had been cut. The child stepped through the gap. When the flap fell back you couldn't see the join. Daniel looked back at the quayside buildings. The boss was in his window. Maybe he knows about the gap, Daniel figured, but doesn't mind, just as long they don't make it too obvious or wait until he's looked the other way.

A peal of high-pitched chuckles rang around the empty sheds, bouncing off sagging shale and dead gravel. The peals of laughter came from the seven-year-old girl who had just now entered their cage. Daniel looked on from the highest pile in the coal yard. Her father was ignoring the tin foil, growling and making to eat his daughter as if she was his lunch. He lifted her high and horizontal and tried his teeth on whichever ligaments might best be severed first. His daughter's uncontrollable giggling rose and fell as his teeth tried each joint in turn . . . knee . . . elbow . . . ankle . . . neck. All along, weak with laughter, she kept bopping him full in the face with the lunch, helplessly shrieking: *bolsa . . . la bolsa! . . . en la bolsa!*—the bag! . . . the bag! . . . it's in the bag! At last her father seemed won over to the compromise lamb-for-daughter deal, set her on her feet and formally accepted the tin-foil parcel.

Sitting on the top sack in the middle of the coal yard's mound, Daniel sucked the orange half he'd been saving and gazed at the eating, talking, drinking men. This is what I would have done if I had grown up here, he thought. I would have brought lunch to my dad. Maybe even here on the dock. And we would have had a bit of a wrestle. And I'd have been accepted by the other men and allowed to sit in on their chat.

The tin-foil man sat with his daughter on one leg while he ate his lamb and listened to the other dockers. Maybe, Daniel wondered, one of these men even knew my dad, grew up with him; maybe they all did.

Daniel rubbed coal dust on his hands to take away the stickiness, and began to speculate about the opening in the chainlink fence. I could make myself a den under the bags, he thought. Then tonight I can come back through that gap in the fence, maybe with some blankets or seat cushions I've found, and sleep here.

Daniel had so far slept two nights in an abandoned black Lincoln

Towncar with a cobweb-cracked windshield and flat tires. The Lincoln was in a plot of weeds near a rickety, steel water tower. The first morning he'd woken up asphyxiated in the sealed car's thickly misted windows, groping for the door to break the airlock before his lungs burst. He'd slithered out of the car in a heap to lie on his back on the damp weeds breathing in clear air. After a while, he'd opened his eyes and seen an upside-down man above him. Daniel had recognized the short round man from El Café Fuente, where he'd been standing next to that tall thin woman called Yolanda who worked at the *caseta telefónica*. The man had introduced himself as Oscar and then told him about a job at the docks.

The dockers went back to work and Daniel set about making his den. He clambered up the rotting bags to the very centre of the pile, where the sacking was more sound. Here there was a fissure in the stack. He lowered himself down into this narrow shaft, squeezing and turning his body until his feet were on asphalt. He looked up at a gap of blue sky through the high-stacked turret. The shaft was wider at the bottom than at the top, but not wide enough to lay down in.

He knelt down and slit open the seams of the very lowest sack, then reached in and scooped out the coal, before sliding the flat, empty sacking out to reveal a small patch of concrete. He filled a blue plastic bag with loose coal and pushed it up the shaft and out of the top. He then repeated this operation with all the other ground-level sacks in the shaft (hoping the whole pile wouldn't collapse on top of him into the hollow he was creating): slit the sack, scoop the coal, slide out the flat empty bag, until the floor was large enough for him to lie curled up on. The torn-open empty sacking would do as blankets, he thought.

Building the den, however, had put him behind with his work. At the end of the day, the boss would count how many blue bags he'd filled. But it now occurred to Daniel that there was a brilliant scam to be had. From the top of the turret he pushed a full bag down into the den and climbed down after it. Working his knife between the stitching, he sliced open an old synthetic-weave sack. He emptied it into a new bag in one go, sending an exhalation of coal dust puffing straight up through his new chimney.

Oye! shouted the boss. What are you doing? Daniel rose like a periscope through the dust cloud. Not there! shouted the boss from his window square. Work from the outside in!

Right! called Daniel and, in stages, heaved out the blue plastic bag he'd just filled. He then climbed down the outside of the pile to the very outlying edges of the yard's sprawling coal heap. Here he looked back at his den. Yes, he decided, it looks just like a pile of coal sacks.

Daniel had walked half a mile from the docks when he smelled fried chicken, saw the red flatbed truck parked on a verge and thought: What a strange place to have dinner!

In the back of the truck was a red plastic table and there was Oscar standing at a smoky grill with barbecue tongs in his hand. Yolanda and Alma-Delia sat at the table unwrapping paper plates and Alma-Delia's kids, Iriate and Reyes, were already eating tamales.

Daniel walked up the lane toward them, dropping the shredded pirule leaves from his hands. (Oscar had told him about this lane which led to the shortcut through canola fields which made it only a mile or so from the dock to Tonalacapan.) The engine was off but the truck radio played tinny, lilting *tropicales*. He drew near enough to see the white paper napkin tucked into the collar of Oscar's blue and white sweater with the alpine scene (knitted reindeer, woollen pines). They still hadn't seen him and yet he was close enough to see brush marks in the red house paint with which Oscar had basted his truck. At last Daniel said: *Que onda?*

Hola vatito! replied a king on a cloud.

What's up? asked Daniel.

Spatchcock, Oscar replied matter-of-factly, in preoccupied contentment.

Picnic, said Yolanda airily—or as near as she could get (she was a much less convincing eccentric than her husband). You eaten?

No, he said.

Climb up.

Climb up, swing up, step up, chirped Oscar.

Daniel was good at climbing. He hoped they could all see just how niftily he used back tire and tailboard, brake light and wooden slats to hoist his nimble frame in. But they all seemed happily oblivious and hardly noticed his arrival at all.

He sat down on an empty gallon water drum. Alma-Delia casually handed him some warm and damp tortilla on a paper plate. (How Stefano and the men on the *Jennifer Lopez* would love this tale, thought Daniel, when he told them about these mad Mexicans!)

Jesse James (so called because his real name was Jesus Jaime) strolled by. Jesse James was a docker friend of Oscar's and it was he who'd finagled Daniel's job. He stood at the bottom of the truck, hands in pockets, looking up.

It'll never catch on, Oscar, he observed.

Pues . . . replied Oscar and stood up, still chewing, to separate another plastic chair from the stack.

What's left? asked Jesse James.

You'll have to come up, said Iriate.

Jesse James sighed and, with the whole truck listing as he hauled himself in, grumbled: You'll have to come round to my fork-lift for Christmas.

Daniel piped him aboard by saying: *Oscar el Cretino*'s forgotten where he lives!

Oscar frowned sharply and quietly told Daniel: This is my truck.

That's my husband you're talking about, said Yolanda.

The small, private way Oscar had frowned and the modesty of his grounds for taking exception—this is my truck—made Daniel hot with shame to the roots of his hair. He knew that Oscar's staccato growl was saying: I may get it from everyone else, but not from you. Not in my truck and not when I'm having my dinner (even if those things *do* happen to coincide)!

Indeed Oscar did get it from everyone else on account of his being, as they supposed, not that bright. This tag had caused him three changes of headgear in recent months. At first he'd worn a cap with the cigarette logo Carta Blanca on the front, but having this written across his forehead had caused much too much merriment. Next he'd thought he was pretty safe with a Cemento Monterey cap, but this too had turned out to be a source of immense glee. He now wore a red Unifab cap which had so far drawn no fire.

Standing with his back to the flatbed diners Daniel scrunched his face in a paroxysm of shame. He had only wanted to sound like someone who'd been familiar with Oscar for years. He'd seen all the joking which took place whenever Oscar was around and had simply wanted to feel like he belonged—belonged here so much that he could do that love-disguised-as-rudeness thing he'd seen the others do, had thought this was how men showed love and affection to each other. But now he felt himself cast as the ungrateful free-loader, and saw for the first time how this short, stocky man alone stood between him and obliteration. But how could he make amends? he wondered. How could he show Oscar that what he'd said wasn't what he felt?

The name of our village in Costa Rica, he attempted, is Oscar as well. Just like you. Only it's Oscar Felipe . . . Daniel tailed off. But he'd find a time, he vowed, to show them his gratitude and his worth.

Everyone kidded Oscar for being dumb, except of course Yolanda, the cleverest head in Tonalacapan. Yolanda knew that had she ever tried to tell anyone at El Café Fuente how they had Oscar all wrong, or if she were to speak of her husband's subtle intelligence, they would laugh out loud or humour her or think her sentimental and extravagant with *chicha*. And yet, she thought, passing a chicken leg to Iriate, the fact remained. Oscar knew her silences, the unspoken which frames all words spoken. Whenever she shared any passing thought with Oscar it was always received exactly how she meant it to be. For this reason her many prejudices and pronouncements were an expression of intimacy between them. (And she had many: for instance, People who own or work in *panaderias*, bakeries, will be the first to embrace military rule and secretly wish it . . . Men who aren't members of unions are lost fragments, which is why they are loud . . . They are called *coyotes* because those who live in the desert have a desert for a soul.)

Jesse James tore off a chunk of chicken thigh, took a swig of *chicha* and stared at Oscar, Yola, and Iriate's hands.

How come you've all got paint on your hands? he asked. They inspected their hands. Greasy fingers were flecked with yellow, blue, black and red.

Banners, said Oscar, wiping his mouth with his napkin. For the *manifestación*.

And puppets, said Iriate. And *giganticas*. We're making them up at the Uniones hall.

Coming? Yolanda asked Jesse James, but with an eye on Daniel. Daniel, however, was busy discouraging four-year-old Reyes from climbing the flatbed's wooden slats and so didn't know if she'd included him in that *coming?* He hoped she had.

Though it was still daytime, a single, round wall light burnt over the entrance of the Unión de Uniones hall.

From inside the open doorway came the sound of a ghetto blaster cranking out *disco-merengue.*

As Daniel walked into the crowded hall he saw old men in white shirts and old women in cotton tracksuits. There were info-posters on the wall and a limescaled samovar on a table. A dozen ten-year-olds were sitting on the wooden stage all perched in a row like crows on a power line, and students in a corner were making a large papier-mâché head for a *gigantica.* The students included a woman with a shaved head. Daniel had never seen a woman with her head shaved before. She caught him looking at her; he was worried she'd be angry and was about to turn away when she smiled and waved.

The far side of the hall was dominated by a curious mural covered in thick, clear perspex. Daniel went up to it.

The painting shows a woman who is flying up through the sky in loose, grey, ghost clothes. She has just stepped out from a doorway with no door and no building attached to it. Above this free-standing doorway is a low, full moon. Across a little dirt road from the white doorway is dark, thick forest where three puma-dog-men are lying in wait. Daniel has been looking at the trees for some time without seeing what's lurking there. He gets a jolt when he does. The bared fangs of the beasts at first make Daniel think they're vexed to see their quarry escape by having flown up into the sky. But then he looks at their eyes and sees they are staring straight out of the painting as if they haven't noticed how the woman has already flown or are waiting for whoever's next.

The woman has left a pile of ordinary, everyday clothes by the huge, white, free-standing doorway. These are the worldly clothes from which she has ascended, flying up, eyes wide open as if intrigued by her new adventure in the ghost clothes. Her long black hair flows behind her, already stirred by a breeze from the freer air up there. There's something written too in looping black handwriting whose curling black letters coil about the clothes she's left behind. *Cuando me buscan nunca estoy.* When they look for me—or come for me—there's no one there.

From across the hall Yolanda watched Daniel study the mural. How strange it was. The boy had no idea that he was staring at the key to all the mysteries of his life, even while his face was reflected in the perspex; no way of knowing that he was looking at a representation of his mother's last seconds on earth, and not twenty feet away from the very doorway where she was killed. For Yolanda it was strange in another way too. She and Oscar had lost a boy, and now this boy had come along, a boy about the same age Oscar Jr. would now have been. The boy with the question they couldn't answer.

The puma-dog-man eyes had fixed on Daniel's own with evil intent, and yet somehow the picture gave him a sense that here in this hall he was among friends. And so he wandered over to the students who were making the huge papier-mâché head. When he got closer, however, he saw that the other *giganticas* were being fitted on children quite a few years younger than him. This made him acutely self-conscious and embarrassed, until the shaven-headed woman said: Ah, at last, someone strong for the big one, and smiled with a wide mouth and perfect teeth. Daniel wondered how many years off he was from being considered someone this beautiful woman might consider. He had a fine down on his top lip and was tall for his age, taller in fact than one of the young men she was working with now. They lowered the diving bell of a papier-mâché corn cob on him. It came down to his knees.

Yolanda hadn't noticed them come in, the two strangers who sat with their backs to the wall. Both wore make-up as thick as cosmetics-counter saleswomen in downtown department stores. Yolanda looked around for Oscar, wanting to know if one of these two *cholas* was the woman who'd given Daniel the gold tank top, but he was out of the hall. Holding down a corner of a banner which was being painted, Yolanda thought it possible she might have seen Shellacked Orange Hair with Blas Mastrangelo one time. Then again, she considered, it could just as easily have been the other one, Back-Combed Honey-Blonde Big Hair. *Las cholas* all looked the same to her, same orange lipstick, same birdcage of gold jewellery going on. In their leopard-print, semi-transparent tops, and their cross-strap mini-bags, the women were out of place in the hall and they knew it. They sat on their own and giggled and chatted to each other self-consciously.

In the meantime Daniel had spotted *las cholas* sitting against the wall. He recognized the one with the orange hair as the woman who'd given him the gold tank top which she had said came from Blas, the man with the motorbike who knew people who had known his father. (You're his . . . friend? Daniel had asked her that time. She'd responded with a smirk and a ripple of the chins which had told him he might read as much as he liked into that and still be cold.) The same orange-haired woman in the leopard-skin now tapped her sternum then pointed at him, as if to say, Why aren't you wearing the top? Daniel made to walk toward her, but she just smiled, shook a *de nada* finger, got up quickly and left with her friend.

A little while later, Yolanda was adding figures from receipts on a pocket calculator when a paper cup of coffee appeared by her side. Looking up, she saw that Daniel was holding his own paper cup of coffee. They remained in silence for a bit, him standing, her sitting. And then Yolanda turned in her chair to face him and found herself saying words she used to say to Oscar Jr., even though their meaning was changed in this context.

Never forget, she told the big brown eyes now fixed on her, it's not you but everything else around you that's wrong. If you feel all wrong you have every right to do so. It's not you it's all the rest of it. And if you feel things are weird it's because they are. After all, why else would you feel all wrong, my son? No other reason in the world.

Because this remark had seemed to come out of the blue, Daniel attached a mystic significance to it. This was something, he felt, being slipped to him through that gap between what people see and the limits of what they talk about. If experience was like a line that doubled back on itself either side of a decades-long chainlink fence, Yolanda had palmed this piece of wisdom to him through a gap the boss couldn't see. Yolanda saw his big brown eyes get bigger as he chewed on the rim of his cup, before, with a half-nod, he wandered off again. She smiled, sipped her coffee and went back to working out how many cans of paint the kitty would stretch to.

We've put more foam padding on the shoulders, the shaven-headed student told Daniel. Do you want to try it on again, and see if it's better now?

Wandering around in the giant corn cob, it was exciting and secretive to see and not be seen. It would be fun to go outside like this, he thought, and waddled and bumped through the doorway until he was standing in the dust outside in his papier-mâché yellow and green costume, looking at the sunny world through his mail-slot eye hole. It was weird standing outdoors in vivid disguise and eye-catching invisibility. On a wide turning-circle he shuffled first to the left to see if anyone was coming, and then 'round to his right. He hoped it would be someone he knew. But all he saw was exhaust smoke and dust thrown up by a cherry-red Silverado disappearing into the distance.

The mail-slot peep hole framed his vision like a painting. He looked at the thick trees and bushes across the road from the hall, but there were no puma-dog-men in that particular thicket.

He waddled back to the hall in his corn-on-the-cob costume, not seeing the wasteful round light shining like a full moon above the door.

Part Two

When the *coyote* went in to see the new police chief both men had already heard of each other. Blas Mastrangelo took one look at the new Zone Commander and felt scruffy. This guy was trim and alert like an ad for sparkling, herbal brain drinks. Young and handsome with a short spiky-gel, he looked natty in his Zone Commander threads. Blas saw also that the *comandante* was indeed a new broom: upright and bristling, stiff and clean, the complete definition of himself.

Zone Commander Ilan Cardenas indicated the chair opposite, but before he sat down himself, he went to the door and opened it. Two patrol cops came in, scowled at Blas Mastrangelo and sat in the two chairs against the wall. Blas knew what this was about. Not security, but rectitude. No bribes could be offered this way and none could be taken. It was like the glass-walled offices at immigration. That was meant to stop *mordida* too. Blas sat and smiled indulgently at the sham, like a parent at a school nativity play. This was very well done, he thought. Open door. Sit. Very stylish. Very good.

Ilan retained his cool but the *coyote*'s smile of approval disturbed him. Blas Mastrangelo seemed to be calling upon him to share his enjoyment of a sick joke whose punchline was that all personality is show, that everyone is corrupt and only really in it for themselves.

And this was what Blas believed, with one exception. Blas Mastrangelo. He alone was not pretending. If needs be, Blas *could* pretend along with the best of them. Certainly one theory sounded as good as another. And in the right company and feeling *simpático* it was as pleasant to fall in and tap his toe to the neat symmetries of whichever creed he'd just clinked bottles with. It was as pleasant to describe, say, the pretty patterns of the self-regulating free market as it was to describe a centrally planned state taking care of business for everyone. (Although, it had to be said, that sometimes when a *vato* talked communist, Blas would feel like the sun had gone in on all that made life worthwhile.)

Here in the police station, of course, it was slightly different. In a police station the game for all *cholos* is not to let being there change you any more than you deem politic. Not to let authority have any power over you. You go in there with your own vibe and you leave with your vibe untouched.

Ilan sat behind his big new dark-green desk, fingers and thumbs locked in front of him. There was a stillness about him, thought Blas, like a monk packing a piece. Blas relished being able to sit in front of a man who would have liked to bang him up, for Blas could do a deal here where none seemed possible. Ilan raised his eyes to Blas Mastrangelo, and then his chin a little. Blas, while recognizing that he was being asked to speak, took a small pause just the same, before earnestly opening with: I have a lead on the terrorist case.

Ilan raised his eyebrows a little at this cop-way of putting things. Only a little, though. In these early days Ilan's promotion still had the cellophane on. He felt that his new posting was shrink-wrapped and pristine, and he sought to preserve this agreeable sense with economy of movement. Economy of movement seemed to go with mental tidiness. And so he merely waggled his wrists while keeping his thumbs locked, as a way of suggesting that the *coyote* should go on. The *coyote* smiled, seemed to sprawl a little, and wagged his head side to side in an appreciative imitation of Ilan's wrist wiggle.

Abruptly Ilan now spoke: Whatever arrangement you had with my predecessor you don't have with me. And won't have.

I know that, *comandante,* said Blas. I've heard about you and, of course, I knew before I came here that the old ways are gone. So I offer my information freely.

But again his tone offended Ilan for it suggested that they were both just doing their little dance, an excessively formal dance. The more formal the dance, it seemed to Ilan, the more corrupt the age, like the top hats of the *Porforio,* like periwigs scattered on the courtesan's fetid sheets. The information, he said.

There's a teenage kid—fourteen, fifteen—going around searching for his dad. Thinks he's dead. He's the son of the terrorist you're looking for—Chano Salgado. The boy's name is Daniel. Daniel Salgado. And he hangs round El Café Fuente in Tonalacapan.

Where does he live?

That I don't know.

Where's he from?

A *Tico.*

Costa Rica?

Yeah. Costa Rica.

Ilan looked down at his interlocked hands; this information tallied with his own research into Chano Salgado's personal history. So he waited to hear what Blas Mastrangelo would say next.

Maybe your terrorist comes from there, too, said Blas.

This was exactly what Ilan had wanted to hear Blas say next, for it was the natural—and incorrect—assumption to make on knowing that the boy was from Costa Rica. It therefore proved that Blas wasn't just feeding Ilan pages from a past history he knew about; that he wasn't dealing from the bottom of the deck. Ilan scanned the *coyote*'s eyes for deception and found none. And so, hands still clasped together, he rolled two thumbs forward, slow as snail's horns, to bid Blas continue.

Now I tell you this upfront, said Blas, to show I'm not expecting no deal, no special favours, no trade-off, no plea bargaining, nothing. But, chief, here's the thing. I tell you this now. (Here Blas sat up in his chair.) If you arrest the boy today then I will be revealed as the grass. Clear as day. So I humbly request that you let me get out of town a few days before you pick him up. And maybe, in return, I can help you with other intelligence too.

I know about the *manifestación*.

Which will be the perfect time to pick him up.

For you. Not for me.

You're going to give up your sources?

How will we know him?

I gave this boy, Daniel Salgado, my hundred-dollar Michigan basketball jersey which he liked. It's a gold one. So your spotters will be able to recognize him easy.

Your one?

Yes.

He's a boy.

The kids wear them baggy like *los earringos*, said Blas.

Ilan chuckled austerely to himself, then said: No, you'll have to do better than that. He could wear any other top. No, I think I'll just use you as my spotter—have you right there in the jeep next to me pointing the finger. You wait in the car until we've got him. I mean, he's not even Mexican, this long-lost son you've found me. We'll keep you here in the meantime, he added, looking toward the two patrolmen who began to get up.

Wait, wait, that was just on the way, just along the road, walking along to the next thing. This is it here, right now. *Orale,* what I was getting to is this: the *manifestación.* OK, you know about the *manifestación*—well, all the young kids got a costume right, cardboard heads of wheat, tribal *giganticas* and shit, OK? Check this out: Daniel's a bit older than the others and he's got fitted with his own special carnival costume. Blas left a pause for Ilan to ask him what the costume was. Ilan said nothing so Blas had to join the dots himself. It's corn, he said. The only one. That's what he'll be wearing. There's only one head of corn and it's him!

While one of the patrolmen escorted Blas Mastrangelo off the premises, Ilan asked the other: Do you think the boy is Chano's son?

It's hard to say.

Or will I pull this rope and find myself naked down-river in a whirlpool?

The boy's not even Mexican, sir.

Salgado has a son. A son from Costa Rica.

Does Mastrangelo know that?

I don't think so.

Well, in that case . . . maybe.

Thank you, said Ilan, and the patrolman left.

Ilan hadn't been serious about having the *coyote* with him in the car. Blas Mastrangelo's face was too well known and his presence would only forewarn those who were aiding and abetting Chano Salgado in Tonalacapan. How much face will I lose, Ilan wondered, if it's not the boy or if there's no Daniel Salgado at all?

Ilan knew the snatch would work better on a small scale—by just slipping in a few men undercover—but that would be difficult thanks to the state policy which meant the army had taken over the hunt for the terrorist.

2

To Ilan the whole drama of modern Mexico struggling against the skeletal clutch of the past seemed to be summed up in the response he now gave to the Englishman sitting on the other side of his desk: I regret to tell you that I'm looking for him too: your brother is a wanted terrorist.

Mexico had just joined with Canada and the United States in forming the North American Free Trade Agreement. Mexico (post-NAFTA) stood poised to become a First World country. She was about to free herself from the tentacles of years of unbroken rule by the PRI, known as *el pulpo*, the octopus. Now Mexico had a new, young breed of intelligent economists and politicians who had all studied free trade at the University of Chicago. Now there was a chance of more foreign direct investment: free-marketeers and entrepreneurs who despite everything were willing to invest in Mexico, to believe in her.

It was obvious to Ilan that things should be done in Mexico like they were done in the USA, with business experts and technical specialists running the economy; people who knew about making money, not about giving speeches to grumbling trade unionists and *campesinos*.

He pitied older colleagues who wondered what the point of policing was after years of arresting criminals and seeing crime increase. Now more than ever there was a point, a bigger picture. A new Mexico was emerging, one in which the police had a key political role to play. Ilan Cardenas saw what was needed: a police that could help create the stability needed to attract foreign capital investment; a flexible police, but a tough police; a liberal police, but a powerful police; above all, a police for the many and not just for the few.

Thus it was, then, that to Ilan the whole drama of modern Mexico's struggle against the skeletal clutch of the past was summed up in his telling the European businessman sitting opposite that his Mexican brother was a terrorist.

Evan Hatch knew this already but pretended he didn't. To show foreknowledge would arouse suspicion.

At least this means, said Ilan after a beat, that you're not alone in your search. As of today, in fact, we've got a very, very promising lead on . . . on . . . your brother. And when he is arrested, Ilan continued, he will be much more likely to help you if it means better treatment for him to do so. Not that there's bad treatment—although that still goes on in Mexico like all countries, as you know. But what I mean by better treatment is access to that system of little perks and privileges for prisoners who cooperate and reform and rehabilitate, or, as they say in the US, get with the programme.

While Ilan waited for Evan to mentally regroup, he regretted the fact that breaking this news had kind of ruled out chatting about economics. There was now no chance that they'd meet up for lunch and that Ilan might talk macroeconomics and foreign direct investment, discussions he'd missed since leaving the capital.

What did he do exactly? asked Evan. (All he'd read in the Chano Salgado SmartSlide database file was the name of an anti-water-privatization network in Mexico City and a link to a terrorist info-site.)

The Englishman's Spanish was very good but Ilan kept it slow and even just the same as he told him the story of the Ethylclad pipeline being blown up and about the explosives found in the shack debris, a shack to which only Mariano Salgado had the key.

When Ilan had finished Evan asked: Does my brother have any other family?

No, answered Ilan.

This lead, Evan asked, I mean, how long—roughly—would you guess before you manage to find him?

In life, Ilan answered with a quick smile that showed his small, white teeth, things always take longer than we think. Ilan then took his time before going on, as if to illustrate the philosophical truth of his wise insight that, truly, in this life things always take longer than we think. Finally he spoke again: I can say, however, we're talking days not weeks.

You're not just saying that so as to . . . Evan rephrased what he was about to say. I don't want to be rude, sir, but you're not just saying that to keep me 'round a bit longer in the hope that he'll get in touch.

Ilan leaned right back in his chair. He beamed beatifically so as to show that not only was no offense taken but that he was above such pettiness (which, when the company was so agreeable, he was).

Well, yes, I see what you're saying, Ilan replied, still smiling broadly, but for that matter you could also argue that I might *not* want a rich

English brother around to sign checks for a top-dollar legal team from Mexico City. So, no, I'm not bargaining.

Well, I doubt very much I'd do that, after what he's . . .

Yes, said Ilan, but that might be the deal he offers *you*. No legal team, no bone marrow.

Yeah, but I've worked for—on a contract with Ethylclad, and helped in the NAFTA deal myself.

Ilan glowed. *Did* you? he asked.

What, NAFTA?

Yes.

Yeah.

I have no cigars, Ilan said, wafting his hands either side of his empty desk, as if to say, were I a corrupt libertine instead of an ascetic man of duty what was mine would be yours.

Evan laughed and said: Just on the government relations side. Selling its merits to a lot of stuck thinking.

A lot of stuck thinking, Ilan repeated, nodding his head slowly up and down, his shining eyes locked on to Evan's. Ilan had found a fellow spirit. Stuck thinking and fixed ideas, he continued, a lot of stuck thinking. You know, people here still cling to socialism or anarchism or communism and yet what always amazes me, Mr. Hatch, is that when these people want to make some money, where do they go? *El Norte.* They go to the Evil Empire. The same people. Come back with hard cash, new shirts, Dodge pick-ups and Ricky Martin videos. But do they ever stop to think why? They never think that maybe *trade liberalization* might have something to do with it?

No, said Evan.

And is that how you come to speak Spanish so well, asked Ilan, through working on NAFTA?

Oh no, I never came here I'm afraid. I was solely working from London plus a little bit in Washington and New York. I suppose you could say I should have been here, so as to respond to the environment here on the ground.

Oh no, replied Ilan with a little laugh, that's *my* job!

Ilan would have loved to talk more about trade liberalization—he missed his university friends—but he had a stronger fear of the English Mexican changing the subject back to the terrorist first. Ilan didn't want to appear unprofessional or to confirm stereotypes of the dilatory Latino. He still paused, however, before making his next suggestion. Looking at the desktop, he ran a finger down his forehead a few times—not, this time, to illustrate how in life things always take longer than we think, but because he knew he must be careful here.

The first straight line he drew down his forehead reminded him that he had his own plan for catching Chano Salgado and didn't want the English brother getting in the way. The second line pointed up that this would be a Big Arrest. For the attack, added the third, had made TV. With a fourth crisp line his index finger underscored the fact that this Big Arrest would be all the better for coming so soon after the departmental humiliation of having had the army called in to sort out the mess. A fifth plumb line, however, came back to the potential of this English brother acting as a stalking horse, and found it too promising to renounce.

Ilan came out of conference with himself and announced: You might ask around Tonalacapan and Nahualhuas villages. Although not tomorrow. Tomorrow there's a big march on and it will be chaos. No one will talk to you. Anyone who's shielding Mariano Salgado won't have time to weigh up whether you're for real. No one'll believe you're his brother in that sort of . . . paranoid atmosphere which, our intelligence says, is going to be quite ugly for us. So not tomorrow, but maybe a day or two after.

Today?

If you like. But do tell them you're his brother, though.

What's the protest?

Fear of the modern world, fear of change, fear of technology. *A lot of stuck thinking.* Where are you staying?

Hotel Hernandez.

Very good. Yes. Try El Café Fuente. In Tonalacapan. And let me know if you hear anything, said Ilan, giving Evan his card. It was the first business card he'd given out since coming to Calderon. Evan gave him his.

Alone in his new office, Ilan went over the interview. If Evan Hatch is going to be asking around, he thought, the chief benefit will be to know which people in Tonalacapan say something like: No, never heard of the man but do tell me where you're staying . . .

He walked over to the window blinds. With thumb and forefinger he spindled the cord, swiveling the hanging steel slats ninety degrees. He put his fingertips on the sill and arranged them so they were in as neat a line as was possible. He looked down on to the street and saw Blas Mastrangelo at the bar opposite, ordering a drink and back-slapping an old man reading a paper. Ilan observed how the old man and the couple who ran the café smiled wearily at his bullying bonhomie. *Los cholos*, thought Ilan, always impose their mood on a wide area, aggressively coopting everybody else to celebrate their fantastic life, but the people they cajole are always wary, for they sense how soon a man like Blas Mastrangelo turns violent.

Ilan rested his cuffs on the white windowsill, which smelt of pine-scented spray polish. He looked with distaste on Blas's self-conscious sense of style. *I do this and then I do that and it's neat and it's cool.* They are propagandists, thought Ilan, for their own slick aggression, their own sense of style. He rolled his wrists on the thick white paint of the windowsill's edge. Yet they don't know, he decided, how much they fear they are shit and rubbish.

He turned and stood in the middle of his office staring at the new and perfectly blank whiteboard on the wall.

He was mobilizing an operation on one noncorroborated informer. Was it possible that Blas Mastrangelo was setting him up? Could the whole thing have been designed to divert resources from something else? Ilan re-examined his deduction of the *coyote*'s motives. No, he decided, it cannot be a set-up for the simple reason that I will know who set me up. He doesn't want me to bother his business, that's all.

The snatch would be his first large operation in his new post. And it could result in failure. Especially now that the military had to be called in, so there was no chance of doing it discreetly by just inserting a few plainclothes cops disguised as protesters.

I want prisoners brought here and not taken to the barracks or it's no longer my operation. OK, cell clearance. I'll clear the cells in anticipation of public disorder leading to mass arrests.

Ilan would still have to tell the military about the raid he was planning, of course, but would leave it to the morning. This way it would be *his* raid that *they* were coming in on, rather than a meek handover of an operation he couldn't handle. He would stop just short of requesting assistance. He'd frame it along the lines of notifying them of a stray piece of intelligence which may or may not be of interest to them. Perhaps they'll ignore it, thought Ilan, and I can do this thing as it should be done—low key.

He turned on the smooth and shiny, hard grey linoleum pulled tight to the stone floor like a judo *dojo*. Meantime, if I'm going to do anything more than just hope this English Salgado will get back to me—which he won't of course—I shall need eyes and ears . . . Blas Mastrangelo? Perhaps I can put my *coyote* on a leash. My *coyote* will have to earn his keep. The more Ilan thought about this idea, the more he liked it. For if he was ordering Blas Mastrangelo to a certain place at a certain time, he could cleanse himself of the criminal's impudent, unspoken, suggestive claim of some kind of grubby conspiratorial graft between the two of them.

When the two patrolmen came back in, Ilan was staring out of his window. Without turning his head he told his men to get the *coyote* back in again.

Where is he? one of them asked.

Try the bar across the street, Ilan replied, still not moving a gelled hair of his head but all the time staring down at the café opposite, where Blas Mastrangelo was just then being handed his second beer.

After they'd left, Ilan replayed the scene to himself a few times, savouring how cool he must have looked to his new charges. *Try the bar across the street.* Not batting an eyelid, not moving an inch, just: *Try the bar across the street.* Ilan was well pleased with this. First impressions count. And there was something else to be pleased about as well. How neatly this move would turn the *coyote*'s suggestion of some kind of understanding between them on its head. Ilan would be smiling at him this time. He spindled the blinds shut, closing out the street with a dozen clanging steel rulers.

3

Blas Mastrangelo was the snowflake that didn't melt in hell. So it was with a sense of symbolism, of style, of front, that he'd chosen the bar right across the way from the police station. Sat right out on the sidewalk, too, with a foaming, cold Japanese beer. Blas Mastrangelo in a bar right across the way from the policia, and having just seen the Zone Commander himself! *Orale!* . . . now let's watch the *carmencitas* parade . . .

A businessman was walking along the sidewalk looking at his mobile phone. Blas fell to admiring the man's designer suit. No tie. Just T-shirt. A good look, *compadre*. Suggests you got plenty of suits. And the sandals? Why not? As the businessman passed his bar-stool, Blas was startled to hear him speak to himself in English: No fucking signal!

Blas sat up sharp. *Esta chingon!* A Latino foreign national from an English-speaking country! *Esta padre, man!* That's a fifteen-thousand-dollar passport! That's fifteen thousand dollars right there. That accent . . . it's not American or Canadian. What is it?

Taxi! shouted the foreigner. And now Blas had it: *Inglés. La Unión Europea!*

It was a Calcab taxi. Blas stood up and stepped into the road, shielding his eyes so he could clock the driver behind the windshield. If Blas didn't recognize the driver he knew others who worked out of Calcab. Stay in this lane you bastard so I can describe you to my *hermano*. Good boy. OK, let's see . . . so you're a fat, flabby bastard with slicked-back hair. But what brand's that you're smoking? What's that light-blue cigarette packet peeping out your top pocket? Never mind. Light blue, keeps them in top pocket. Cluttered dash. A hanging saint and a pine-fresh on the rear-view . . . and Two Thousand Dollars in the back still playing with his phone.

The taxi hit the horn. Blas jumped smartly out of the way back toward the bar, where he back-slapped an old man who was reading a paper.

Oye! Another beer! called out Blas and sat back down to reflect upon chance. Whenever a man, he considered, does an intelligent thing—like me seeing the Zone Commander just now—it leads to luck; and in the same way losers are always on a downward spiral because . . . they are losers. Blas took a sip of Japanese beer. Shame the suit wouldn't fit him though.

4

In life things always take longer than we think. A few hours before Ilan was to share this observation with Evan, a chain of events had already begun which would soon prove that his maxim was true, except for those times when things go much faster than we think and before we're ready. And before, as it was to turn out, anyone was ready.

The chain of events had begun when Chano had sawn off the top of a plastic bottle of water with a machete. Five hours before Ilan was to observe how in life things always take longer than we think, Chano was carrying the ribbed-plastic jug he'd just made toward a natural spotlight thrown by a gap in the treetops, all the while being careful not to trip over roots and spill the precious water.

On day one in the *reserva ecológica* he'd shaved off his moustache and all his hair. He'd kept shaving his face but not his head. He was hoping his hair now looked like a normal, bristle-top buzz-cut rather than the cut of a Wackenhut chain-ganger or Reynosa mental patient. He had a baseball cap he was going to wear, but what if he was stopped and the cap taken off? He peered down to study his reflection in the plastic bottle's disc of water. Frames of a normal man flicked up at him now and then. He sipped warm water from the serrated edge and put the sawn-off bottle between two roots. Bending down he felt another hunger shard splinter his belly. Like prenatal contractions they were coming more and more often now. He knew he should try and hold out, but he was so hungry he knew he wouldn't be able to think straight if he left it much longer.

Chano began walking through the forest toward the highway. Ayo had brought him a work permit and identity papers which he'd got from a Guatemalan who worked in the same *finca*. Chano tapped his breast pocket. The papers were there. He repeated his fake Guatemalan name seven times: Nestor Galvan, Nestor Galvan, Nestor Galvan . . . Ayo's masterstroke had been to leave him the machete, so now, as Chano walked toward Nahualhuas, he was just another tired, dirty, hungry-looking *campesino* wending his way home along the highway verge.

One hour and twenty minutes' walking later, he approached a road block. A thick lug of rope lay across the road. Soldiers and police. It doesn't apply to *campesinos,* he reminded himself, walking past the traffic checkpoint, it's just for cars and trucks and—

Oye! shouted the soldier. Chano nodded, changing direction toward him. The soldier finished what he was saying to one of the cops, before turning to Chano. Where are you going? he asked.

Home. Nahualhuas.

Where you been?

Finca.

ID, he said.

Chano handed over Nestor Galvan's Guatemalan worker visa. The soldier jigged his machine gun back on his shoulder a little, before scrutinizing the mouldy scrap of paper. He held it close to his eyes like a betting slip. Chano's mind wobbled like the disc of water in the sawn-off bottle he'd left in his camp. His bristly scalp tingled under his cap.

This is out of date, said the soldier. You gotta go downtown.

He gave the bogus papers to his young friend. Chano felt the handle of his machete being removed from his hand and watched as this, too, was passed to the cop, who wore a dark-blue uniform and paramilitary top-boots.

The car wasn't speeding. Chano was in the back but uncuffed. It would be OK. He stared at the dead-straight, dead-flat, fawn-coloured road, shuttered either side by thick, viewless bio-zone monotony. Maybe they just want an excuse to drive into town, he thought. His mind felt clear and calm. He counted thin strips of black tarmac every twenty-five yards of manila concrete highway.

At the Calderon precinct he isn't put in a cell but pointed into an office and told to sit there. There are three desks in the small office. Only one is taken. At this desk—in the corner—a police officer with a side arm sits writing up a report in a binder. One wall is a floor-to-ceiling, no-bribe-taking window which gives on to a busy corridor infested with cops. The plastic chair Chano has been told to sit in faces this full-frontal window. He tries—by tiny degrees—to turn his chair away from the glass. His aluminium chair leg rasps the floor. The cop-clerk looks up at him, twitching a moustache which seems too small for his top lip. Chano sits stock still. He focuses on the hands he folds in his lap. He can feel the cop staring at him. He daren't look up until he's sure that the cop's eyes have left him. He looks up. The cop is still staring, still twitching his moustache like it's too tight for his face.

5

Two hours before Ilan was to observe how in this life things always take longer than we think, Daniel was walking at a clip along the dock past rows of shut-down gutting factories.

At the far end of the waterfront he saw the *Jennifer Lopez*. He tried to keep his walk casual, but he couldn't wait to see the eyes that had seen the same places he had, to tell them all how he had fallen on his feet and had a job and everything. He was nearer now. They had their backs to him, all busy gutting at the trestle table. The crew still hadn't seen him and a new thought struck Daniel.

Maybe I'll just ask to come home. Maybe there'll be space for me on the boat. I'm a long way from home. I'll ask if there's room. I could wait till the next time. But what if they don't come again? It's strange they still haven't seen me. Perhaps that's a sign. I'll ask if there's room now. Today. And if they'll take me then I'll go. I want to go home.

Hijos de la chingada! shouted Daniel, running backward under a hail of tuna brain-stalks flying through the air like a Pharaoh's curse. The crew had turned as one.

Ayyee vatito! Ay Daniel! they cried and kept the offal flying. *Cabrones!* he laughed, still retreating under the pelting shower of fish guts.

Stefano, Jordi, and the crew wiped their palms on their trousers and came toward him. They stopped. Daniel heard a truck. He looked round, still picking fish from his sweatshirt. The open-topped truck stopped. A dozen men stood up under its bare steel hoops. Daniel didn't know if they were troops or police. The soldier-cops jumped wearily down and dropped the tailgate. Daniel felt a hand on his head and heard Stefano's voice: Don't worry, Danilito, it's just a shakedown. *Mordida*, he added disgustedly, dropping his hand to Daniel's shoulder. It's just payola time.

And with that Stefano walked alone over to the dark-blue uniforms, paramilitary boots, and matte black rifles.

The crew stood and watched him in conference. Then saw him turn and walk back.

What did they say? asked Jordi.

Illegal fishing.

Yeah, yeah.

He says we've got to get in the truck, said Stefano.

But what about the catch? asked Jordi. Did you ask him what about the catch?

He says get in the truck.

The horn sounded. They got in the truck. As the crew were climbing in the horn sounded again. The men looked round to see Daniel standing alone on the quay.

He's not with us, said Stefano.

The soldier-cops stared back blankly and said nothing. Daniel got in the truck.

Each policeman sat with legs apart and a black rifle propped against his instep. Each made a point of not making any room for the prisoners. This meant that the fishermen had to half-crouch, half-kneel or perch on a crewman's knee. Every time the truck turned a corner they fell over, to be pushed back by laughing cops.

6

One hour after Daniel joined the crew of the *Jennifer Lopez* in the truck, and forty-five minutes before Ilan was to observe how in life things always take longer than we think, Oscar and Jesse James were driving through the outskirts of Calderon in the red flatbed truck.

Oscar was flustered. Usually when he drove into Calderon it was to the *comercializadora* district and early in the morning, when the stone floors of the big, open-fronted wholesalers had just been hosed down and were stacked with fresh fruit and vegetables. This was the first time in a long while that he'd driven downtown in the afternoon, right into the crowded town centre. The dusty, gritty sky seemed broody and tetchy as they crossed the Puente del Papa, its three yellow arches like a mutant McDonald's. The bridge spanned a hundred yards of pebbles called Rio Santa Katarina after a broad river that used to flow on this very spot until a couple of years ago. The stranded pebbles, smooth and round, looked hopelessly lost.

No, we're on the wrong side now, said Jesse James.

The dead river divided the town. Here on the east side there were no municipal buildings, no banks, no hotels, no *panaderias*, no air conditioning. Just a shanty town built up the side of a mountain, a *favela* that looked down upon the elegant west bank. It could look but not touch. A white Chevy Tahoe police jeep was parked parallel to the stone-river, guarding the internal border between rich and poor, between downtown Calderon and the hillside *favela*.

How do I get back on to the bridge? asked Oscar.

Left here.

A few blocks into the west bank, however, Calderon's scruffy, grey-walled side streets had the stench of backed-up sewers. The sanitation department was busy paying interest to an alliance of the world's bankers known as the World Bank. Oscar parked the red truck on a crumbling curb. A broken drain by the parking space had made a filthy pond in the street and was about to send a hair salon out of business. Oscar and Jesse James walked past cardboard and blanket in a dry outflow wall-pipe, which was some *descamisado*'s home.

Just remember, the dockworker reminded Oscar as they crossed seven lanes of Calderon traffic, this ain't a local cop shop, it's a big city police station and we'll be here for hours. Patience, patience.

Claro.

The grey-stone, big-city police station took up most of one side of a long, quiet street.

Thirty minutes before Ilan was to say that in life things always take longer than we think, Oscar spotted Blas Mastrangelo trotting down the station steps like it was the aisle of an award ceremony.

At the desk, Oscar and Jesse James presented a Port Authority letter certifying that the boy worked at the docks, then sat down on

bolted plastic chairs and waited. Jesse James nudged flattened cigarette butts with the toe of his boot on the glittery linoleum.

Did you see who that was as we came in? asked Oscar.

What, coming out?

Yeah.

No.

Blas Mastrangelo.

Who?

He's that *coyote*. The *patero*.

Don't know him.

A few minutes later Jesse James nudged Oscar who looked up and
saw the desk cop hand the paper they'd given him to another cop and
mutter something.

It looked like they were deciding to let him go, said Oscar. Jesse
James knew it didn't look like anything. But why stub Oscar's hope
out among the flattened butts? he thought, and so just nodded.

7

Two soldier-cops in navy-blue paramilitary uniforms perch on a
corner of empty desk apiece, one boot each resting on a chair. Tight
Moustache stands in front of the teenager and silently reads his
charge sheet. He twitches his upper lip from side to side and glances
up.

You Daniel? he asks.

Yes, sir.

You a fisherman, Daniel?

No, sir.

No, you work at the docks. That right?

Yes, sir. At Calderon, sir.

And you're Mexican?

Yes I am, sir.

Sit down and wait, he says, and steps out of the office. One of the
Navy Blues drags the chair his boot is resting on nearer the desk,
pulling it back with just his heel. The chair legs screech along the
floor.

Chano gazes dully at the teenager and goes back to studying the heels of his palms. He may not be a fisherman, he thinks, but he's trailing more fishy fumes than Satan.

The door opens. Both Navy Blues slide to their feet and gather their rifles.

Salgado, calls Tight Moustache from the door.

Chano and Daniel both get to their feet. Chano stops himself halfway. Their eyes meet.

Not you, says Tight Moustache irritably, *Salgado*.

Slowly, his unblinking stare never leaving his son's face, Nestor Galvan sits back down.

8

Twenty minutes after Ilan had observed to Evan Hatch how in life things always go much slower than we want, Evan passed a filthy, fish-smelling urchin on the first-floor corridor who was looking for his way out of the police station. He heard the boy kick a chained double-door fire exit. In a little while his nephew overtook him again like a bee searching for the open window.

When Daniel finally found his way out of the police station, Oscar and Jesse James were waiting for him by the door.

We'll take you back to work, said Oscar.

Shouldn't I wait here for the others?

Los Ticos? Your friends have gone already.

Mordida, commented Daniel with a little grin, making the money between fingertips gesture.

Relieved that the boy didn't feel as deserted as he'd feared he would, Oscar's round face broke into an even larger grin. Yes, he replied. That's it!

As they all got into the truck, Oscar saw Daniel looking at the battered, green loudspeaker fixed on its roof. The red truck pulled out from the spreading sewage puddle and into the seven lanes of traffic they had just run across. Changing gear, Oscar followed the movement of Daniel's head, the boy's gaze tracing where the megaphone lead flowed into the hand-set. Oscar waited for him to ask.

Can I use the loudspeaker? asked Daniel.

We've nothing to sell today, said Oscar, nodding his head back toward the empty flatbed.

Is that what it's for? asked Daniel.

That's what it's for. In every town there's trucks with megaphones selling fruit, scrap metal, and a mayor not like the last one.

I'll tell everybody my manifesto, declared Daniel. Everything is free! No more work for nobody! *Vivan los Zapatistas!*

Wait till we're out of town, said Oscar. On a quiet road.

Yes, and you'd better tone down your manifesto, said Jesse James with a gloomy note in his voice.

The truck chundered and rattled. Oscar had long ago given up trying to understand the Calderon one-way system, whose signs sent you first one way and then the other. He ignored them all, navigating solely by landmarks. Right at the ripped awning; left at the crumbling corner of a tenement block whose walls no longer met the sidewalk, leaving a wedge of thin air as if the whole block might tilt. Daniel placed both hands on the dashboard and let out a scream as Oscar swung the truck sharp right and drove straight at the rubber slats of a warehouse door. To his amazement the rubber slats burst apart to reveal open country! Wide, low, sage brush stretched for miles behind the deserted shell (where corn used to be delivered when corn used to be grown). They drove across a white concrete acre which had once been the warehouse floor, and found a slip road with a mohawk of weeds and wild flowers. The slip road brought them out on to the dead-straight Calderon-to-Tonalacapan *libremente*. As the truck drove the plumb-line, viewless, tree-tight road through the dense *reserva ecológica*, Oscar flipped the black mike off its hook and handed it to Daniel.

Hello, said Daniel in a low, robotic voice.

No, you've got to turn it on, said Oscar. Wait. Wait a moment, he added, disentangling the loudspeaker's curly flex from his face and neck. The little truck stopped. Jesse James got down and held the door open. Daniel climbed back from the truck's cab into the wooden pen without touching the road and Oscar passed the mike up from the driver's window.

Don't step back or you'll break the lead, he said as the truck lurched off again.

Right, right, OK, said Daniel, with the extreme earnestness of boys finding their way in the world of men.

Hello! Hello! Is it on? A howl of feedback told him it was.

Oscar beeped the horn in complaint at the noise. He slowed the truck and leaned out: Keep the mike turned away from the speaker or it'll howl.

OK, yes. Sorry. Like this?

Yes. The truck wobbled as Oscar pulled the door shut, then sped up again. Second gear. Third.

My name is Daniel! Can anyone hear me? Oscar, if you can hear me beep the horn. There was no beep. Daniel banged the roof of the cab.

Oscar slowed just enough to lean out and call back: What do you want?

I just said you were a pimp.

Oh, said Oscar, and Daniel immediately felt bad that Oscar hadn't got the joke.

I didn't really.

When it's above second, said Oscar, and doing more than twenty-five, we can't hear you.

Soon they were rattling through the blurry bio-zone with no other cars around.

Hello trees, crackled the speaker. My name is Daniel. I have come back. Come home.

The sound of the wind whooshing by the truck became the cheering of cowed citizens hiding in the trees who now recognized the Deliverer and emerged—not quite into view—to cheer.

Yes, you know me. Tomorrow we march from Calderon! Eleven o'clock we assemble! We march at twelve! Daniel began to worry they could hear him in the cab and so tried to be a bit jokey. Trees! Keep on growing! Good work bush! But this wasn't as sweet to him as before, what with its concessions to the small-scale, teasing reality of adults. And so, once more with feeling, he went on: I am Daniel Salgado. I am returning to the land of my ancestors, Chano and Marisa Salgado. I find this land in turmoil, but do not despair: I am here now. And here I shall stay. I left you once, but never again. Daniel has come back to Mexico! . . . Past one, passes another, he lays it off to . . . no, a dummy! swerves . . . will he shoot, no, no, he goes round the keeper, he must score now . . . GOAL!!!!!!!!!

Oscar started beeping. Daniel's cheeks and neck scalded with embarrassment. Had he been overheard? Oscar, however, had sounded the horn to warn the boy to pipe down now that they were approaching Tonalacapan and passing its bleached billboards advertising faded motels, torn cars, and pale candidates. Oscar's hand came snaking out of the window and he clacked his wedding ring on the roof. Daniel passed the black hand-set through cold breeze into warm hand.

The truck toured once, very slowly, round Tonalacapan. El Café Fuente was shut. The fountain seemed to Oscar more decrepit than he'd ever seen it. Water lurched on its three high ledges like when you use a broom's bristle block to shunt water from a flooded floor. The fountain flipped tiny hummocks of water off the ledge. It shucked, it shucked, it shucked: a cardiograph fighting the flat line.

9

Less than an hour after Ilan had observed how in life things go much slower than we want, he'd ordered the cells emptied to clear the decks for the mass arrests at the *manifestación* swoop tomorrow. It may be we'll have to trawl with a wide net, he had told his staff.

Early the following morning Tight Moustache was on the stairs when this order was passed on to him. He went back up to the processing office and had Nestor Galvan brought up from the cells.

At first light the building was almost empty. Even so, Tight Moustache made sure to stand between Chano and the floor-to-ceiling window before he began his speech: Violating visa requirements brings a criminal charge usually. There's a day in court and . . .

That "usually" was all Chano needed to hear to produce eight hundred sweaty pesos from his shoe.

This is all I have, he said.

That will do.

Do I have to sign any papers or anything?

No, said Tight Moustache, chucking the eight hundred in his desk drawer. You're refused charge on a first misdemeanour. You can go now. But get your papers sorted out, he said twitching his top lip from side to side. A second offense is a different story. These documents are very important. Very important.

Yes. Thank you, sir, said Chano and left the office. He walked down the steps of the police station. The sidewalk was being hosed outside the bar opposite.

Chano had spent his night in the cells wondering whether the police already knew his identity, and whether they'd brought in his son to test how he'd react or just to show him they had him. He'd become convinced that he was being given the night to think about it before being brought up—tenderized—for questioning. But now they'd let him go . . .

Which means they must have let Daniel go as well, he thought. And a fresh hell descended on Chano in the pale light: he'd lost him again.

He came to seven lanes of fast, early-morning traffic. It could not be that once again his son was about to be snatched from him by fate. Everything he knew of the universe militated against this. Chano didn't believe in any kind of gods, still less in ones which single out a particular human for themed suffering. Yet how could it be that his life had once more sharpened to a point where his son was gone and not gone?

They'd asked Daniel if he was Mexican, thought Chano. Now what if Daniel starts telling them details of where he was born, who his father was, so as to prove his bona fides?

Chano passed a bus stop crowded with *maquillas* and cleaners and pulled down the peak of his cap. Daniel won't know I'm in the news and on the police bulletin board, he thought. So—suppose the cops need to talk to him again about whatever it is he was being held for? All it takes is one cop, one informer, asking one lucky question, a single cop to read his unusual surname and ask if he's any relation, for the chance thing to work against us.

Chano knocked on the door of a one-room walk-down under a shuttered newspaper kiosk. He heard shuffling and the door scraped open. Ruiz "Bad Medicine" Gatica squinted up through his filthy glasses a long moment before he recognized Chano.

Chano was a few frantic phrases into telling Ruiz that he'd seen his son, when the old man said: So, you were there at the same time?

The matter-of-fact tone in which he said it stopped Chano in his tracks. You *know* he's here? he asked.

We got him a job, replied Ruiz.

You know him?

Yes, we—

You didn't tell me?

Well, we—

Why?

We didn't know who he was at first but as soon as we found out—

How?

Eh?

How did you find out?

He asked Yolanda if she had ever known you.

Who else knows?

No one. Just me, Yolanda, Oscar, Erik, Alma-Delia, Jesse James. Oh, and little Iriate and Reyes, Alma-Delia's kids. That's all.

Wishing he could shout, the fugitive jerked his arms around instead, and in a gale-force whisper rasped: Then why have they arrested him?

Tranquilo, answered Ruiz, his Bad Medicine face wincing even more. Daniel was picked up at the docks. But Oscar and Jesse James have got him out.

When?

Yesterday. No one else knows, said Ruiz in his cracked and wavering voice. As soon as we found out we tried to get word to you. We waited in the pipeline but when you didn't come we—

Ayo told you about the *pipeline? Pinche!* Chano's eyes bulged as he clenched and unclenched his fingers. Why? What's he do that for?

Because someone else has been asking for you.

What are you saying?

A foreigner.

Who?

He says he's your brother.

Where's he from?

He's English. He just came one afternoon, asked around, but no one trusted him. Because why is he asking now? Why now when you're on the run? But anyway we've found out where he is staying.

Daniel?

No, your brother.

My brother.

Yes.

Do you think he is?

I don't know. But if he is or he isn't there's still a foreigner walking round with lots of cash to give to anyone who knows where you are, or to somone who can name your friends. It's very dangerous.

Ruiz thrust his hands in his pockets and frowned as he tried to recall the name. Ivan? he ventured.

I don't know his name, Chano replied.

Well, this one's called Ivan.

Does Daniel know I'm alive? Chano asked.

No.

Good.

You are dead. There's an end. He doesn't even know that we ever knew you.

Daniel—ha! Daniel! exclaimed Chano, elated to be using his son's name familiarly as if it were Ruiz or Ayo or Yolanda or Oscar. Daniel, he repeated. But you got Daniel a job . . . ?

Bagging coal at Villegas with Jesse James.

Ruiz, thanks. Thanks, *compañero*, said Chano. And thank Jesse James, too. And Oscar, thank Oscar. And now tell me about Daniel, tell me about my son. All about him.

Ruiz put two mugs of hot water before them and scooped out a spoonful of coffee from the large economy jar in the middle of the table.

Well I'll tell you how he got the job first of all, began Ruiz, sitting down at the little table with a chuckle.

Through Oscar?

Through Oscar. It was like this. Once we'd worked out that Daniel was . . . was Daniel, Oscar tells the boy that he knows about a job going at the docks. But we don't want Daniel to think anyone's doing him any kind of special favour. So Oscar says he'll need to give him a job interview, pretends he's the union rep. So Oscar interviews him for the job and it's the easiest job interview in the history of the world: can you stack things on top of each other? Stuff like that. Anyway, so then Oscar says, Very good, phone this number tomorrow and a woman in the office—Yolanda—will let you know if you've got the job and where you've to go.

Now, Oscar has the number for the *caseta telefónica* painted on the inside of the truck door. This is so he can phone Yola from wherever his travels take him. So they're standing by the truck door which is ajar and Oscar's hunting round for a pencil. But then Daniel starts making up a little tune to help him remember the number, you know, kind of setting it to music. And so what does Oscar do? He joins in. *He joins in.* And when they've both got the tune down pat, he only lets the boy walk off singing this twelve digit number song! That night at El Fuente everyone was shouting at him: How could you be so stupid? The boy won't remember! He'll never know which dock now and so he'll run out of money and he'll go into town.

Yolanda takes off Oscar's cap and cuffs his head with it.

And Oscar says: He will remember, he will.

What makes you think that, Oscar? says Erik.

It's a very catchy tune, says Oscar.

And so Yola says, Sing it, then.

Oscar can't remember how it goes. He asks Yola to remind him of the numbers first because then he'll remember the tune. But Yola won't tell him of course. She's just standing there like this—Ruiz sat back arms folded—and everyone except Oscar goes and sits down at the table, and he's left sitting on the fountain in the dark. Oscar's trying to remember the tune. He's got to prove he has not been stupid, see, and he's going: la, la, la, no, no, that's not it, no . . . Da, dum de . . . but the tune keeps changing. Then he tries some numbers, any numbers, just calling them out into the night, hoping they'll form into shapes like breath in cold air. *Uno . . . seis . . . ocho.* And he's looking sadder and sadder. *Quince . . . ochenta . . . cero, cero.* There he is under the Christmas lights on the tree with a wet dog licking his leg. And first he's trying them in a deep voice: *Uno . . . uuuno . . . UUUno . . . UUUUUU!!* Then he tries singing them high: *Veinti-uno! . . . Veinti-uuuno! . . .* Out there by the trees he sounds like a lonely owl: *Ocho! Ocho! UUU-no! . . . Veinti-uuuno! . . . Veinti-uuu-no! Uuuu-no!*

OK. Next morning, first thing, Daniel phones Yola. He's remembered the number. She tries to hide her relief. Yes, she tells him, all formal-like, I believe there is a job, you have to start today and I will take you there myself.

Ruiz took off his thick, brown-plastic glasses and said: I mean we can laugh about it now because it turned out all right, but we were scared. You know we'd been so distant with the boy—for his own safety you understand—but because of this there was absolutely no reason for him to come back to El Café Fuente or Tonalacapan ever again. And so anyway, now Oscar loves him. What a smart kid, he's saying. Very bright kid. Very smart, he is, very clever, says Oscar.

Chano stood up and peered through the cracked and dusty wooden shutters. There was a strange, hollow ache in his face bones. His eyes filled with tears. He heard Ruiz step outside. Chano dried each eye with a swipe of his forefinger. There was, he considered, no need for Ruiz to have stepped out. These were only tears of relief.

His breath was short as he blinked his vision back to normal. Gradually, he saw soldiers in the mini-market opposite. None had any insignia and all wore basic combat gear in dark blue or black. One picked up a gallon water holder; two others were chatting about which bag of Lay's crisps to get. Chano watched a grey-haired soldier in his forties finally plump for a family-sized, light-brown bag of sour cream and chives. Ruiz came back in quickly.

I've seen them too, said Chano.

There's always soldiers in the supermarket, said Ruiz casually. They're just like any other shoppers except they never use a wire basket. They always walk round without one . . . I guess they're trained for situations where there might be a total absence of wire baskets. But I suppose they're just passing through.

The old man stooped noisily and opened the steel door of a small and rusty cupboard, which had once been an oven, to see what other provisions he could find for his friend. He placed a can of tuna, a paper bag of sunflower seeds, and two bell peppers on the cupboard's flat steel top.

It looks like they're loading up for a search patrol, said Chano.

Or the *manifestación* in Calderon, said Ruiz crushing a bell pepper flat between his palm to put in Chano's bag.

Maybe so, said Chano, maybe so.

Here in the old man's room, Chano's mind tried to fuse all the conflicting information and events from the last few hours. Through all his joy and relief he'd had a nagging sense that there was something wrong with the picture. He didn't know what it was that didn't fit, but was aware of some jagged fact struggling into consciousness. He sat back down at the little wooden table, hoping Ruiz wouldn't start chattering again. He wanted to let his mind go blank, to let the silt and sediment settle so that he could see things clearly. He opened and closed his hands around the empty coffee cup. Slowly his lips parted, but it was several seconds before the words emerged in a low, ashen monotone: But you said Daniel's been asking if anyone knew me.

Ruiz froze. Slowly he put a can of beans down on the drainboard. He cocked an ear, waiting for Chano to speak again. But there was only silence. Staring at the worn steel, Ruiz smoothed both palms side to side across the ex-oven's steel lid as if flattening out the map of a whole new battle they could only lose.

Chano knew there was only one way of saving Daniel once his son's identity was known (if it wasn't already); to save him from being arrested by Ilan and held as the magnet which would pull the father into giving himself up. Chano would have to cross the border and send the police captain a photo of himself from the United States.

I won't trust a *coyote*, Chano began at last. And if I rush the road in El Paso I'll just find *La Migra* in the desert.

But if this man is your brother, the one who came to El Fuente . . . ?

10

Inside the old walled garden of the colonial Hotel Hernandez, a woman in a white apron is skimming a fishing net over the still surface of a lozenge-shaped swimming pool. The pool wants to become a pond. Each soft dip and sweep of the long pole nets leaves, weeds, dead beetles, twigs, seeds, spores, and mildew. Thick, tall trees hush the shaded courtyard and creepers climb its high, grey walls. From the open door of a little shed comes a generator's gentle hum. A broom leans against the iron slats of an old patio chair with its mattress off. Now and then an invisible parrot trills sporadic bars, bridges, and middles, practising its Best Of compilation for the foreign currency.

A man with bow legs and a patchy horizontal beard steps through a door inset into the closed wooden gate. His straight black hair sticks up like a crow in a birdbath. He wears a tweedy jacket over grimy black drainpipe jeans and a faded black sweatshirt. He has a small red nylon haversack on his back. He kisses his sister on both cheeks. She lays the long pole on a heap of wet yellow leaves. From one of the big pockets in her white apron she produces a large key with a clump of wood attached.

A hotel loses lots of keys and has replacement copies made. Cleaners find the lost keys later. In a wooden wall cupboard in the generator room where mops and buckets are stored, Ayo's sister keeps all the keys she finds. This one looks like it would open a castle keep.

Ayo emerges at a clip on to the second-floor balcony which runs around the cloister. He twirls a paisley bandana between thumb and forefinger of both hands and slows a second to tie it behind his head. The curtains of the last room—number 12—are still closed. He lets himself in.

Can you come back later? says a man's voice from the bed.

You are looking for Chano?

All in one movement Evan whirls round, sits up, stands up, sees Ayo, sits down again, nods.

Why? asks Ayo.

Are *you* . . . ? asks Evan. The scarved-up man shakes his head slowly, his level brown eyes seeming to stay fixed while the rest of his masked face goes side to side. I'm his brother, says Evan. It's because, because he's my brother . . . that I'm looking for him.

Why now? asks Ayo.

I am dying. I need his bone marrow. And blood.

Ah, says Ayo, so now you drop by. And after so long.

The masked man picks up Evan's small black leather bag and roots through it. Fearing kidnap by terrorist guerrillas, Evan gives a little cough to show that he's in too poor a condition for a forced march to a jungle bivouac. Evan rules out the man's handgun being in his jacket pocket or waistband. Holding up the purple passport he's found, the croaky squawk behind the bandana says: If your story's true then you were born on May 28, 1968. He thumbs the pink pages, then unslings the red backpack from his shoulders. So that must be where the gun is, thinks Evan, of *course*. Ayo drops Evan's bag into his own with the unmistakable nylony noise of a completely empty backpack. Back soon, says Ayo in TV English. He stops in the doorway to remove the bandana, flicking on the room light on his way out. As Ayo crosses past the window, Evan sees only his own reflection standing bewildered and powerless under an overhead light.

The man's shadow returns. The door opens. A ragged beard now frames the face which says: Let's go!

11

In the park at El Refugio El Reparo, on the northern outskirts of Calderon, protesters were gathering around a concrete square. On the stone stage someone was failing to get a PA system working. Oscar parked the red flatbed, which had stopped along the way to pick up other people walking to the demonstration. A cornet played a few practice notes, followed by a little snatch of tune. A carnival drum banged. Three times, rat-tat-tat. Then stopped.

Daniel climbed down from the truck and mingled among the virtuoso banners of the trade unionists who stood around chatting and joking. These men and women have been on so many *manifestaciones*, he thought, that what's exciting for me is just routine to them. To Daniel their easy attitudes seemed to say that radical social change was a cinch when you knew how—like taking down scaffolding or rolling steel. (But their utility belts showed that they'd have to be straight back to work as soon as the march ended.)

Some women were telling kids Daniel's age to take off the paisley bandanas they'd tied round their faces. It isn't that sort of march, they scolded. Deep in the crowd, someone Daniel couldn't see was waving a giant Mexican flag on a tall bamboo pole, an enormous wipe-out of green, red, and white. Here I am, thought Daniel, but I don't belong here, this isn't my protest. I'm in the wrong place.

Half a dozen women from the (now-embattled) Taxco Santos *chicha* co-op all backed away from each other, like folding a sheet in reverse, to open out their banner. It was made of trawler netting with bright, chunky 3-D letters sewn on to it. When the women had right-sided it, Daniel read: *Por la humanidad y contra el neoliberalismo.* Above the legend, a blue river of plastic foam padding flowed in winding curves into a dollar sign before it reached a stranded yellow steeple and brown rooftop.

Daniel turned 'round and everything went dark. The smooth nylon of the giant Mexican flag ran over his face like a blind man's hands but, finding nothing familiar, soon passed on. As the flag left him, Daniel saw the students unloading the *giganticas* and props they'd been making in the Unión de Uniones hall.

They'd customized the huge, papier-mâché corn on the cob for him by adding extra foam to the wooden shoulder struts. It was a relief in all this confusion to be within the enclave of his own echoing breath. Other costumes were handed out. Looking through the eye-hole, Daniel observed the rapid evolution of walking fish, waddling bell peppers and leggy coffee beans. A gaggle of small children became stunted pines, small-brained conifers who didn't know which way to turn.

There came two taps on his domed corn head. He turned round. No one there. Dropping into view there came a beautiful woman in a white taffeta dress, her painted face and extravagant carnival headdress bobbing in front of him. *Que onda?* How's it going, man? she asked, enjoying her cartoonish, carnival glamour just as Daniel was enjoying his own corn-cob disguise.

It was a moment before he recognized the beautiful eyes and mouth of the shaven-headed woman. When he did so he asked: Who are you looking for? And she laughed.

Ay, thought Daniel, I made her laugh! I made her whole body shake! She had to put her hand down on the ground and everything.

We'll be here a while yet, you don't want to get hot, she said and lifted off his costume. She was, he now saw, wearing a big pair of work boots beneath the white taffeta dress. Together they lifted the papier-mâché corn head back on to the stone stage, where they sheathed it tightly in a black treash bag. Consequently Daniel hurried away without saying goodbye.

Oh there you are, said Oscar. Wondered where you'd gone.

I was over with the students.

The students?

From the hall?

Don't know them. Oscar looked around at the gathering crowd. There's not enough people here yet, he said.

It being early there was still room for a few teenagers to be tossing a hollow plastic baseball through the basketball net. The small white ball bounced off the backboard with a weak slapping sound like a wet fish. Daniel watched them, half wanting to join in, but feeling that he was here on business. In Mexico it seemed he wasn't a teenager anyway. His friends were all as adult as the exigencies of his new life.

Did you ever have children? he asked Oscar.

Yes, we had a son but he died.

I'm sorry.

No, no need to be sorry, said Oscar. When a father has a son, then even if that son's taken away, it's still the most special thing that ever happened to him.

Just then Oscar had a startling revelation. It occurred to him that he'd hit upon an ingenious way of both telling and not telling the boy about Chano. And so with great significance he put a hand on Daniel's shoulder and began: You see, Daniel even if, eh, if a son goes away . . . No. No, if the *father* has gone away . . . if he's not there . . . and the son is still . . . that's it, yes—the *son* is . . . eh . . . then . . . then, hold on. No, ah . . . the *father*—he, uh, always thinks . . . eh . . . if . . . the father never . . . uh . . .

Take it easy, Oscar, said Daniel.

What? Oh. Yes.

12

Shards of sun breaking through the *reserva ecológica*'s treetop canopy struck white concrete. The forest's shining tunnel segment was half underground, half aboveground, a concrete hoop arching over the forest floor like a ten-foot-wide folly bridge. The pipeline section was part of a water-supply ring-main project abandoned following the peso crash; an abstract sculpture commemorating the bail-out of New York banks.

Ayo led Evan into the cement tunnel, came out alone and turned his head slowly from side to side, scanning the forest. From out of the trees a crop-headed soldier strode toward him. Ayo ran back a few steps, then recognized Chano.

Que onda güey? asked Chano.

Bueno. Ayo handed over Evan's bag and a litre bottle of water before returning to the pipeline alone.

Looking through Evan's bag Chano read the corporate letter-heads. Agro-Tech, N-Viro, Mauser Forest Products, Belcatel, Crédit-Plus des Eaux. In a zip compartment he found pastel pages of printed manuscript with hand-written corrections in blue ink. He skimmed lines from Evan's Seattle speech. Every now and then Chano looked up, squinting into the bright light of the treetops as he tried to remember the meaning of words like "trenches" and "raid," "rear-guard" and "ranks." He read out loud: *The best issues management you never see, you just notice your opinions slowly changing.*

Chano squatted flatfoot on his haunches and looked around him at the trees he'd been stuck with these last few days. Then back at the documents, the letterheads. Many of these corporations had been involved in one way or another with the desertification of Tamaulipas. But then that wasn't such a coincidence. The story was the same any-where from Alaska to Tierra del Fuego. He opened a little diary, closed it, looked at its cover, looked at a tree trunk. Then he looked back at the last thing he had seen. The cover was embossed with a US company logo. The same one he had seen on Marisa's photocopied files on their table at home. The one she and her *autogestión* had once struck against.

There was no greeting. Chano just dropped into the pipeline holding Evan's bag and stood there silent. His face was filmed with dirt and sweat. His violently cropped hair showed razor nicks and shear stabs. There was a crusty scab above his top lip.

Oh shit, thought Evan. Oh fuck, he's a mad tramp who lives in the woods! A hermit, a mental patient!

In Spanish, Evan began his story.

Ayo, meanwhile, was squatting halfway up the curve of the pipe and halfway between the two brothers. With both feet together in front of him as a brake and upper arms hanging off his raised knees, he looked like a tetchy cormorant, or an officiating macaw.

. . . enlarged digestive tract, Evan was saying, damage to the intes-tines, heart damage . . . Here Chano and the cormorant glanced significantly at each other. Evan hesitated. . . . Distended heart, he went on, uneven heart rate, shooting pains in my arms and legs . . . But even as he continued, Evan became more and more dejected by the utter uselessness of his mission, the pointless absurdity of what he was saying. He remembered he'd gone to the trouble of looking up the Spanish for "distended" before he left. And for this. For this. Here he was: the first time he had been wholly without hope since becoming ill. And so almost to himself he recited the litany: . . . terrible pain right throughout my guts and stomach. Pain generally. Everything hurts . . .

Still he continued his audition piece, staring at the seam of dust in the concrete floor. They thought it was viral, he mumbled, because I have a day, a week or two like that, then it goes away, and I have a few weeks when I'm fine . . . Also fever, tiredness, diarrhoea . . . Out of breath. Vomiting, no appetite . . . Evan didn't so much stop as run out of things to say. He dried up in the pipeline.

And then the apparition, which he had no choice but to believe to be his brother, spoke: It's not leukaemia.

No. I know. *Myelogenous* leukaemia—

Not that either. And it's not a virus. It's no mystery.

You know what it is? asked Evan, his question ringing loudly around the high concrete pipe.

Yes I do. And your illness, brother, is something for which there is no cure. No cure except for everything being done differently. But that will come too late for you. So—

What is it? asked Evan.

So I can't help you, but you—

What is it?

Chagas. So I can't—

Chagas?

Yes.

What's that?

With a sigh like he was finally being forced to confess to something, Chano replied: It's a disease which feeds on the blood of babies round here. It feeds on the blood of the poor. The infection only hatches many years later. When you're an adult.

Evan wondered whether this strange word might be a part of local myth or folklore. This chagas sounded like the allegorical name given to diseases which weren't understood, or the local slang for infant mortality or chance or bad luck. That would explain why he was being lectured not diagnosed.

So I can't help you, Chano now said, but you can help me. You wanted my blood and my bones, I just want your papers.

I know why you need to get out of the country.

No, you don't know why.

The hostile tone of the terrorist madman scared Evan. Yes, yes, of course, yes, sorry, he replied, hasty and placatory. You're right, I don't know why.

It's my son, Chano told Evan.

On his perch Ayo folded his spiky head toward Evan and announced: And you can't have *his* bones either!

Chano said nothing for a while. Then, to Evan's astonishment, the mad hermit of the woods began speaking confident English: I was taken to prison after my wife was assassinated. The people here thought I was dead. They found a home for my son, for Daniel, but, like your home, his home wasn't in Mexico. Now my son, like you, has come looking for me. But for very different reasons. Now the police know he's my son. If you do not help me to cross to the other side, from where I can send a letter to the police chief—a friend of yours, I think—then my son who is fourteen will be held prisoner, will be kept in a special jail indefinitely until I swap myself for him. And if I swap myself for Daniel, if I do that, then I'll never see him again except as a prisoner, in the visitors' room.

Instead *I'll* go to jail, said Evan tapping himself on the chest.

Don't be stupid.

You aren't helping me, so why should—

Perhaps I would have helped you, said Chano in Spanish again, if you had come a year ago. Perhaps I wouldn't.

Why not? asked Evan also in Spanish.

You know why not.

No, I don't know. Why not?

Well, look, this is all just talk now, said Chano, who wondered to find himself—suddenly and strangely after years of isolation—in the middle of a family crisis. I can't help you. First I've got to get across the border and for this I will need my bones—

And a full tank of blood, squawked Ayo from his perch.

And secondly, said Chano. I can't help you because no one can help you. There's no cure for what you've got.

That's not, countered Evan, what the leading experts, the doctors and specialists in Europe say. But if this is a *deal* then all right, yeah, let's cross the border and find a hospital in Houston.

Here Chano paused a beat. Paused then resumed in English: No, Mr. Hatch, it's not a deal. I don't think you have thought about how unjust your words are. Or how they seem. I don't think it's a deal as you call it. I would not bargain. Even if you had come a year ago. I would have said yes or I would have said no. Not everything in this life is a deal, Mr. Hatch. Is money. What I'm saying to you—here Chano paused once more then reverted to Spanish . . . You came to me for help. I cannot help you. But if I could—if you just had this myelogenous leukaemia—then perhaps I would have helped. So. Now I come to you for help. For my son. For his freedom. It so happens that you *can* help. Perhaps you will. I am not bargaining. We are not cutting a deal. Here's what we're doing, what we're doing is this: I am begging and you are listening. So. There it is.

Can I have a drink of water, please? asked Evan.

Yes. And here's your bag, Chano replied, handing it over, and adding a few moments later: I was hoping you weren't going to look in it.

Evan crumpled the corners of his mouth into a quick smile of apology, then put the bag between his feet. Ayo slid down the curve of the pipe and produced a bottle of water from his red haversack. Evan drank the litre in one go, hardly gulping. When he had finished, he looked at Ayo who was staring intently at him like an examining parrot.

And you, said Ayo, you have nothing to lose. Not any more.

13

Walking to his truck, Oscar figures it'll be at least half an hour before everyone has assembled and the march begins to move off. People are still arriving and he'd rather miss all the speeches. He climbs into the red flatbed and sets off into Calderon to buy *chicha*.

He drives past one of the city's huge, dead-as-dust marble fountains, its brass spouts all stuffed with litter. Stopped at the lights, he watches the *La Prensa* kiosk woman chatting to the water man on his orange tricycle. Oscar wonders what they're talking about. Perhaps, he thinks, it's *Have you sold many bottles today?* Or perhaps it's *Have you sold many newspapers today?* Perhaps it's that. Or *How's your sister?* Or maybe *What's in the paper?* No, he reflects, it's impossible to know. A car horn sounds behind him. Oscar looks up. The lights have changed. He lets off the handbrake and holds his hand up in the rear-view.

Three blocks on he passes two grey army trucks parked up a side street. The troops are sitting on the verge smoking, some stand talking or lean against one of the big, grey trucks. He drives on another block until he comes to Plaza de Republica, a quiet square with a small *supermercado*, a bank, a café and a sandbagged machine-gun nest.

The pill-box is a permanent installation. Behind the sandbags is a primitive, breeze-block hutch whose corrugated-iron roof usually shades a few skinny, rural teenagers in olive drab holding thin rifles. But today, as Oscar drives past, he sees instead a lot of soldiers in black. Turning the corner he passes another big grey army lorry standing empty. He wonders if these special troops are on standby, ready to raid the rally or to stop the march from getting to the centre of Calderon. He tours another circuit, then backs into one of the diagonal parking spaces which ring the square. The army truck is parked three spaces away, with one pick-up and a smaller truck between.

Oscar gets out of the truck holding his skate, a carpeted square of wood on four trolley castors. He lies down on the skate and slides under his own chassis. He takes a breath then scuttles under first one then another truck. He stops. Listens. Takes out a screwdriver and puts a slow puncture in the tire.

Soldiers' boots crunch the loose tarmac. Heart knocking, Oscar crabwalks the skate round parallel to the drive shaft to hide his feet. A truck door opens. He turns his head to one side, the skate's carpet bristles his ear. He studies worn creases in shiny, black army boots. Hears more boots. Hears a voice say: Corn. Big and yellow. Even you can't miss it. You've all seen corn in the fields. In the shops.

What if there's more than one, sir?

There's only one.

The army truck's engine explodes into wobbly life. Oscar whacks his head on the chassis then tenses his thighs, timing his escape. He vents a sigh of relief. It's not the engine he's under which has started up. It's the one next to it. Words are still being said but Oscar can't make them out. Doors slam.

He scuttles the skate along until he's back under the chassis of his own truck. Oscar lies still for a few minutes more. He hears first one, then another truck drive off. He stares up at his own truck chassis whose diff shaft needs realigning. He raises a weary hand to it like a baby investigating the mobile above his cot. He sighs then scoots himself out from under the far side of his truck. He won't buy the *chicha*, but will drive straight back to the assembly point of the march to tell the others there's troops in the area.

Again he drives past the dead, municipal fountain with its litter-stuffed brass spouts, where *La Prensa* woman is still talking to the water man who still sits on his orange tricycle. It's incredible, Oscar reflects. Incredible. You see people talking all the time and whatever you guess is wrong. These two, well, they could be talking about pumpkins or cantaloupes. Who would think that soldiers would be talking about corn? Corn. Unless corn is a code word, he considers. Operation Corn. Or maybe corn means a part of town. Corn Sector, Grapefruit Sector, Pomegranate Sector. Or perhaps they're simply going to burn down someone's crops. A field of corn. I should think hard about this, it could be important . . . Maybe the cadets are off to hide in a field on manoeuvres. Or, or, yes, *directions*. It's probably directions: when you get to the corn field turn left.

The crowd has grown. There are now about five hundred people massing for the off. Oscar can't see any of the people he knows. He parks the truck, opens the driver door and stands on the seat. One hand on the roof and the other on top of the door for balance, he scans the crowd, searching for faces he knows.

Can we put our drums in your truck? asks a voice. Oscar looks down.

Eh?

Can we load the drums on here?

Yes, of course.

Thanks.

What's wrong? asks Oscar

Someone just let our tires down.

Oh, says Oscar, too preoccupied with scanning the crowd to pay this remark much attention. Oscar's eyes follow the unhappy drummer as he rejoins the samba band by the little stone stage. Ah! and there's Jesse James talking to some other dockers. A little way away, Oscar spies Daniel too. The boy is backing toward the stage as a costume is being lifted out of its black trash bag and lowered on to his shoulders. He could be a local, thinks Oscar. If you didn't know any better you'd say he'd lived here for years. Oscar watches him being helped into his costume by one of the samba band. Daniel disappears into a giant papier-mâché head. It's so badly done, thinks Oscar, it's hard to tell what it is. What's the boy supposed to be? he wonders. A pistachio? A peanut maybe? A bottle of salad cream? Perhaps a coffee bean? Daniel waddles about, flapping green stalks which are attached on poles. Oscar watches as the green stalks goose Jesse James, who turns and grins.

Suddenly all heads turn like a field of corn. Army trucks, prickly with rifles, speed toward the crowd, grinding in high gear like chainsaws. Soldiers drop from the sides and hit the ground running.

All around Daniel the crowd scatters amid screams and shouts. He starts running, green stalks flapping and the bulky cardboard shell banging his knees. Where's the crowd deepest? That will be safest, he thinks. The wooden struts chop his shoulders. His eye hole is askew. Someone knocks into him. He trips. But keeps running.

Over the noise of engines, over the earth rumble of hundreds of feet, over the din of screams and shouts, over the sound of his own heavy breathing echoing in the papier-mâché dome, Daniel hears an electrostatic howl, the ringing screech of a cheap loudspeaker. Hears a man's deep voice: Daniel. This is Oscar. Daniel, it's you they are after. Daniel, the Corn! Daniel, the soldiers—

A single rifle crack declares itself. Over and above and instead of everything else. One shot. Incontrovertible. Craackaroooom.

The one-second silence which follows the shot is like a gap in time, as though reality has been sliced open with a skinner's knife. In that one-second silence Daniel stumbles, falls on his side; bodies dive to the ground this way and that; a high-pitched scream is announced over the air, and through his rolling, cardboard eye hole, Daniel sees Oscar drop in a straight line from the red truck's door.

Daniel tries to fight his way out of the corn head. He's stuck.

Strong hands grip his ankles. He screams. In one movement he's yanked out. Still screaming he looks up. Jesse James is shouting at him: Run! Daniel hesitates. Looks past the docker. Sees people forming up to block the troops. Sees women walking in front of the soldiers, snatching at arms, hands, tugging their shirts. Go! shouts Jesse James. Daniel looks back at him. Run! he shrieks.

And Daniel runs.

14

Traffic lights on red, the cab driver first glances in his rear-view then looks 'round. Asleep, eh? he asks. Asleep, he concludes, and respectfully turns the music down a touch and winds the window up a little.

When they were standing in the half-submerged pipeline, Evan had told the terrorists that he needed time to think about it and that he needed to phone London to find out what would be the latest that he could arrive in Seattle. He didn't think it'd be a problem, he'd said, and had wandered off to stand outside the tunnel.

When we are lying, Ayo had told Chano, we give two reasons why we can't do something. When we tell the truth we give one. And Chano had nodded while staring at the back of his brother's head which sunlight buffed from black to light brown.

Ayo had led Evan to the high road by the eco theme-park which no one ever visited, and had left him at the bus stop saying he'd come for him in a few hours. Evan had then got off the bus a stop too soon.

Losing his way back to the Hotel Hernandez he'd come out at a deserted café across from a fountain in a dusty square. He recognized this place as El Café Fuente, where the day before he'd asked if anyone knew a Mariano or Chano Salgado.

The café was closed, the street and square empty. Evan had the whole place to himself, the fountain humming and grafting quietly in the silence. He felt a little bilious and sweaty and sat on the fountain's ledge facing the locked and shuttered café. He slid his sandals side-to-side in the dust. Part of him just wanted to topple back into the water and splash about in the bird bath. Perhaps he would another time, he thought. Perhaps there was a whole other side to himself which might bloom here in this strange place which was also, in a way, his home.

For Evan had noticed the look which had passed between his brother and the Indian. He would surprise them, he decided. They think me a time-tabled automaton. I'll show them I'm not the man they think I am. Why not? Yes! Why not do something radical? But then Evan remembered the Indian's words and felt like a captive: he would come for him after dark. Evan was being put in a kind of holding cell it now appeared. The man would be coming for him in an hour or two. It was like: *Don't move until we say you can.* And why had they been so relaxed about him making his mind up? Because they had a *plan.* Evan saw it all clearly now: *what he didn't give, they would take.*

His face and neck felt cold and clammy. He turned and dipped his hand into the fountain and splashed his face with water. Thinking he might vomit, he got up and walked round the back of the fountain and bent over among the trees spitting for a while, but nothing came. The sign said *agua potable* and Evan scooped some fountain water into his mouth and rheumy eyes, swilling the cool, slightly gritty and salty water around his sore, acidic mouth.

A horror took hold of him. To be ill here so far from home, so far from medicine, to die with no dignity amid ignorance. And this isn't my home, is it? he reflected. And suppose it is this chagas like he said it was? If so then the very first thing I've got to do is get to a big-city hotel where they've got an Internet link. Find out about it. See if it exists for a start. See what drugs there are and if there are any specialists. That's what I've got to do.

It was hard for Evan to think clearly because the fountain was making sucking, gargling, retching, sputtering noises. Walking back to the hotel, he felt he was escaping with his life. If he stayed here he would die. And as he stepped into the white-tiled Hernandez lobby, the clarity of the air conditioning seemed somehow to confirm his decision. He ordered a cab at the front desk and went up to his room to pack.

In the superior air of chilled room temperature, Evan didn't feel so bad about the decision itself, but only about not saying goodbye to his brother. But then again, he reasoned, if his brother hadn't made him feel like a captive he wouldn't be needing to sneak out in the first place. He got up and retrieved his credit cards from their hiding place on top of the shaving light.

His garment-bag was on top of the narrow wardrobe. He was very tired now. He lacked the energy to stay on tiptoe for as long as it would have taken him to edge his garment-bag off the top and so he just pulled it noisily down, straps flying. He packed some clothes in slow motion, sliding folded shirts off the wooden shelf. He stumbled over the corner of his bag and fell on to the bed, landing on one knee. He stayed there for a few seconds before he had the strength to stand up. Then he put his shirts in the garment-bag.

The son, he thought and sat down on the bed. Daniel. Suddenly my brother wants to be friends with his son again. No, there was a story. He blinked. A story. The boy has come to look for him, my brother, Chano. His father . . . Evan was so tired he had moments of pure stopped-clock blankness.

. . . Chano was in jail when his son was born, they've never met. And so now it happens—just as he's wanted for a bombing and I'm in town with my crisp peso-coloured passport? Yeah, right. Fuck that for a game of soldiers. He stood up and put his toothbrush and toothpaste back in his shaving bag.

Throughout childhood, boyhood, youth, Evan had now and then fantasized about his blood family. When he did, he'd imagined something a bit like an advert for pasta sauce. He'd pictured a big, extended family all eating under a pergola. There would be much laughter, a lot of accordion and fiddle playing from Mariachi elders . . . That it should come to this instead! A bitter loser in a filthy mustard-coloured jumper in a sewer pipe! An angry man whose own family were scattered. And, hey, said Evan, zipping up and folding over his garment-bag, might there be a little, you know conn-*eck*-tion . . . in these two things, *hermaaano*? So angry at me and the world with his hectoring sense of you must give me, you owe me . . . That's alienating enough, bro'.

Evan paused in his packing. He knew this was beneath him. He knew very well that Chano wasn't angry and bewildered all the time, and even if he was, Evan told himself, did he not have good cause? Ilan had touched upon the death of Chano's wife.

Evan sat down on the bed. To stop himself blacking out he kept the small of his back propped against the garment-bag in a deliberately uncomfortable position. He ran a hand over his face. His mind went blank like a fried egg whitens. What really should I do? he asked himself. He repeated the question out loud to the silent room: What *really* should I do?

He switched off the ceiling propeller fan, whose circular blur tried to resolve itself into three distinct wooden spokes. What should I do? Evan asked himself again.

You do what you can. Evan immediately recognized the wisdom in that everyday English homily. He said it out loud to remind himself, so far from home, of the easy demotic in which it might be said, as if to summon a cloud of witnesses to whom this response was good and proper, and for some reason found that he put on a no-nonsense Yorkshire burr when he said it. You do what you can, he said.

So, what can I do? he asked in his own voice now. What *skills* do I have that he doesn't? Well, I can talk to Ilan. That's something I can do. Call him once I'm back in England, and let him know I'm aware of what's happening, and so bear witness like . . . like Amnesty. That might be all it takes. OK, that's what I *can* do, now what *can't* I do? I *cannot* stay here because I might die—pure and simple. If your very survival is at stake, if it's a matter of your own life and death, your own health and illness and possible recovery—well, what could possibly more define something you can't do than that? I physically *cannot* stay. I *cannot*, however much I may want to. I can't risk my life and it's no sin not to. Only saints risk their lives. No one thinks bad of those who do what they have to do just to survive. And it's wrong to feel guilty for surviving, for not being a saint. I am ill. I am a sick and dying man. Evan looked up at the three propellers of the fan. They were still and defined now, centrifugally separated. And I might not even have come here at all, he thought, and then Mariano Salgado would have just had to find another way anyhow. It's just that I'm the easy option, which is seldom, if ever, the best option.

Each of Evan's statements were in themselves true but he knew that the whole was false, was what Poley Bray called "peripheral processing." A mantra in his work life, "peripheral processing" meant the appeal to association rather than reason. It was an occupational hazard. Peripheral processing had leaked into Evan's own intimate processes. Yes, he thought, but when we are confused we have to rely on instinct, and what is instinct but a kind of association of images anyway? No, he decided, the consideration is itself peripheral.

He would write a letter at least. A letter to be left here. A goodbye. But what if he did stay, he wondered. What if he did stay? The phone rang. Evan jumped. There wasn't time to decide. The phone continued ringing. A 1970s, *Kojak* dring-a-dring. There is time, he told himself. I can just pay the cab off.

He picked up and asked reception to tell the airport taxi to wait ten minutes. He hung up and began thinking faster now: OK, imagine if I stay—it's not as if the doctors in Britain know what they're doing, and if it's a local illness there may be a local homoeopathic cure. And even if Chano's wrong and it is leukaemia then I will need the bones and only his bones will do. I'd better stay.

I will stay.

He lifted the receiver. He put his finger in the number nine to have reception pay off the airport taxi. He dialled. As the dial ran back a figure passed the window. Evan put the phone down and waited for the knock at the door. It didn't come. It wasn't the Indian. But Evan had had such a feeling of dread that it was Ayo's shadow which had passed the window, such a dread that his own powers of choice would be taken from him, that he got straight up and finished packing.

If I'm wrong, well, I was ill and not in my best mind, he said to himself. That sounds like I'm guilty. OK, I feel a bit guilty. I haven't answered all the questions that need answering in my mind.

I can always come back. And once I'm at the Westin Hotel in Seattle I'll be able to think with a clearer head. That's it: *Any decision I make here will be clumsy because rushed.* You do what you can and no one will look after me here. And I'm so tired.

And, in truth, checking out of the Hotel Hernandez, Evan knew a blackout was coming and fought to keep conscious on the way down to the cab. He was bone-tired, tissue-tired, his hanging face rippled like rotten, sodden wood. He lay across the black plastic back seat of the cab with every limb aching. Before he passed out, he barely had time to utter the single word: *aeropuerto.*

The cab takes the elevated ramp on to the highway with signs for Reynosa. On the fast-flowing freeway the driver winds his window all the way up.

Evan's unconscious head trembles against the rear-door under a loose window which rattles in its frame. Evan is leaving Mexico for the second time in his life; and in his sleep like the first.

15

Dusk is closing down the woods near El Refugio El Reparo. Daniel lies belly-down. He listens. Somewhere a soldier whacks into something and swears. A voice, two voices come from another direction. Then others from somewhere else again. The troops are spreading out. Which way to crawl? Daniel asks himself. Am I surrounded?

He hears a word. Can it be? Was that the word? Was that what they shouted? He listens as first one then another soldier calls out: Daniel! Daniel!

Daniel, it's your pappa here . . . It's Chano. I got a skateboard for you! . . . I got tickets for the *Tigres*!

The troops are out of earshot of their officer. Now they're just trying to make each other laugh, seeing who can come up with the thing that'll most spook the kid.

Hey Daniliiii-ito! I've got your daddy here, shouts a voice, smashing rifle butt against tree. Ooof, ow! Please! No more! I beg you. I'll tell you everything!

From elsewhere on his sonic map of the forest Daniel hears suppressed giggling.

Gunshots. Daniel's supine body flies about in the mud. The shots sound so near. Gales of laughter follow. In the far distance, a siren whoops one short call. And then more words. A name? Daniel can't quite make it out.

What's that you say? calls another soldier in response.

Then no voices. No sounds. Why? Are they looking this way? Ten minutes later Daniel hears one soldier calling to another. Further away than before. Daniel shuffles a few centimetres forward on his stomach. Stops. Did he make a noise? Slowly, he raises himself first to all fours, kneels, then lifts one knee. He climbs to his feet as if balancing an apple on his head. His legs are solid. They feel useless. His heart is pumping so hard that his wrists bounce to the heavy pulse. He hears a soft hissing noise. Hot piss courses down his thighs.

He waits, very still. He stays this way until long after his legs have become cold and itchy. A branch of springy twigs is pressing hard against his chest. Holding a sprig between thumb and forefinger, he moves his arm very slowly, pushing the branch away from his body. He concentrates on moving his stone legs, and, trying to remember how it's done, takes a first unsteady step.

16

Evan begins slowly to wake. He is outdoors. He is on a street perhaps. Have I been in an accident? he wonders. He senses someone crouching over him, lifting his heels, taking off his shoes. He feels it would be a bad idea to open his eyes. He is safer like this.

West of the Falcon Dam, a service road runs off Highway 2 between the junctions with Highways 97 and 101. Off the service road, a fire-track leads into the forest. At the end of the fire-track, a black and white mini-cab is parked, engine running. Two doors, front and back, are open. From the highway, baffled by trees, comes the looped din of traffic. Ten yards ahead of the car and thirty below, the Rio Bravo bellows a hue and cry.

Blas Mastrangelo moves around Evan's body as fast as when he's at the pool table. Shoes, belt, trousers, watch, yes, yes, good. Blas darts a look at the man's eyelashes and crinkly eyelids. He grabs both halves of Evan's unbuttoned shirt in one fist and lifts his head off the ground.

Evan opens his eyes. Blas nods to himself. He was right: awake. Evan tries to raise himself. Knuckles press into his chest. He looks into the face of God before He pistol-whips him. Instantly, the Englishman is dead weight again and the shirt pulls through Blas's fingers to the floor.

With the tips of his fingers, Blas rolls the head around on its spindle experimentally. He lifts it by the hair and lets it fall back down. He hears the man breathe irregularly, snorting and snaffling. Blas stands up and looks down at the body. He runs through a mental checklist.

The dark skin will, he figures, make this dead Englishman look like any other wetback who's died trying to cross the river; just another naked brown corpse. No one'll even report it. The thirty-foot drop down the rocky cliff will add more dents and bruises; so too will fifty miles in the stone-polisher. Only if there's a bullet wound will Ilan come after me for a murder charge, Blas reasons. But if there's no bullet wound then by the time this *cabron* is reported as missing, well, it could be that he went missing in Houston or maybe even New York. He could have disappeared anywhere by then. In Europe, in England, anywhere.

But now a snag occurs to Blas. A snag which might mean he'll have to shoot the Englishman after all. The teeth. The teeth.

I think ahead, I think ahead. Every technicality. I'm thorough. Technical expert. He checks inside the European mouth. There's something that looks like a crown, maybe, yes it is a crown. Blas taps at it with the gun muzzle . . . Yes, that's capped. Blas tilts Evan's head back and, while talking speculatively to himself, slides the metal gun sight clacking along the groove of the upper molars.

Now, let's see . . . Little bit of decay back there . . . upper rear molar . . . Little bit of bridgework up at the back here. That does look very natural, though, doesn't it? You've really got to get . . . under it . . . to see . . . nice bit of dentistry . . . but apart from that . . . no, the teeth aren't too good, nothing a wetback wouldn't have. So, just the crown then.

With brisk, deft, workman-like movements Blas props Evan's jaw open, wraps the gun's matted steel grip in Evan's shirt and brings its butt down on the upper right teeth.

Blas quickly strips the rest of the clothes from the man. The passport and flight tickets he puts in his sock. The black suit he lays in the trunk, neatly folded so it'll look like his own.

He returns to the wax-lipped sleeper. Double-checking for tattoos he rolls the body over. The skin is indented with a criss-cross tapestry of pine needles and dusted in a light bricolage of bark chips, pine-cone fragments and grit. The Englishman lets out a groan.

Blas rolls the unconscious Englishman like a carpet until he has him lined up; until feet, knees, shoulders and head are all flush with the edge of the rocky drop. Blas sits down. He looks up-river, he looks down-river, he looks behind him and then across at surveillance-heavy *el norte* (a much longer look this last one). He leans back and raises his knees. With the heels of both boots Blas shunts his most recent past over the long rocky drop into the Rio Bravo.

17

Shadow soldiers stand in the back of army trucks below the silhouette of metal arches. The shapes of kitbags and helmets swing on the crossbar. Nightfall weaves the cat's cradle of wires and power lines criss-crossing Calderon's filthy sky into one black mask. When the army trucks pass a brightly-lit shop front, the young, naive faces of the soldiers can be seen posing with assault rifles over the mighty quake and rumble of the Mercedes engine. Some wear helmets, one wears a green forage cap, another has a green open-face balaclava over a peaked green cap. The truck speeds out on to the main road and once more the soldiers become shadows, spiky with rifles.

Even right up close to the flap in the chainlink fence you can't see the join. Daniel climbs through and lets the flap fall back.

The vinyl bags on top are cold on his bare arms as he lowers himself into the shaft. He wriggles down through the old coal sacks into his den and sleeping quarters. He sits on the floor of his secret chamber, listening to his own breathing. Coal dust works its way into a cut on his back he didn't know about. He winces. The branches, he thinks. He rubs his face with coal dust. He feels a cough coming and places his lips on the curve of a sack: eyes streaming he struggles to cough silently. He's getting cold and puts the empty grey sacking over him like a blanket.

A plan has formed in his head. He tries to resist the plan. Just lay still, he tells himself. Stay here. Safer. He tries to think of some other course of action. It's the last moment for any other ideas that aren't in the plan. Just lie still, he tells himself. Stay here. Maybe, he thinks, the same man who found him his job will shelter him and get him back home. But once more he hears Oscar's dying squeal broadcast sacrilegiously through the loudspeaker.

He comes out of his hole like a marmoset. As many of the unused, slippy vinyl bags as will fit into his worn, leather belt on its widest notch he packs around his waist. There's a blue rope which holds each gate open by day. He undoes the knots which bind each length of blue rope to the two gates. He coils both lengths and slings them across his shoulders. A voice in his head patiently flashes the word *fool* at him like the slowly revolving red harbour light to his right. He goes to the fence and once more searches the chainlink fence for its invisible perforation.

Daniel spies three wizened apricot trees in a smallholding. There is only one light on in the small stone farmhouse, whose tin roof is stacked with an ironmonger's yard of metal objects. He climbs over the dry-stone wall and walks through two dozen dusty rows of pulses guarded by a padded scarecrow. Gently he draws down a branch, reeling it in, twig by twig, to pluck, at last, an apricot. The branches catapult, crashing into the tin roof. Dogs start barking a mile away. Daniel leaps back over the wall. Then runs, cursing and swearing and holding one saggy apricot.

He comes to an outlying barrio and walks through the silent darkness of the sleeping quarter, the seven plastic bags in his belt creaking like a centurion's skirt. He steps over a low wall into a cement yard. Indoor smells seep out through the screen door—rugs, babies, cooking oil. He feels he is desecrating night and the trust of sleep. Clothes lie folded in a plastic laundry basket under a polythene porch. Two steps from the basket he freezes. The dog makes a half-waking, half-sleeping, lip-smacking grunt. Daniel lowers his foot to one side of the sleeping dog. He bends down, hoping his knees won't creak. One by one he removes the plastic clothes pegs lying in the hollow scoop of a worn brick. He picks up the brick. Softly he places his palm on the ground next to the dog's shoulder. He slams the brick into the back of the dog's skull shunting its brains forward over its snout. The dead dog rolls on to his hand which he drags out from under the heavy fur.

The starchy clothes feel brittle and rough against his arm as he walks quickly up the street. He looks at the clothes. They're too small. Three doors down he sees more clothes hanging from a line.

They will fit him better. There is no dog guarding them. He pulls what he needs from the washing line, then sits down on the curb and cries bitter, muffled tears. *Pinche cabron*, he whispers. *Hijo de la gran puta!*

He walks on. Every shout, engine and light switch sends him leaping into a bush or doorway or kneeling between two cars. He hears talking. Stops. A cluster has gathered on the next corner. Still up, they are discussing the raid on the *manifestación* in urgent tones, like power surges buzzing in the pylons between which Daniel used to pick bell peppers. He takes a dog-shit alley away from them all and comes out on to a parallel street.

He hears a motorbike. Two motorbikes, their engines razzing nearer. He leaps into the shadows of a wooden, tin-roofed shack and waits in its creosote intimacy for the motorbikes to pass. From inside the wooden walls comes a lumbering around. Someone's woken up. A heavy object is thrown at the wall. Daniel jolts.

Who's there? shouts a man's voice. What are you doing outside my house?

Daniel steps into the street. Jumps back. Three police bikes have entered the top of the street, each rider shining a hand-held searchlight like a dentist's lamp. Their engines grow louder as they draw near, then quieter, as they slow down outside the shack. Quiet enough for Daniel to hear a heavy drawer being tugged open in the shack. Quiet enough for him now to hear the voice mutter: My gun! My gun! Who's there? Eh? he shouts again. Who's there? Bright lights flood the side of the shack. Daniel drops sideways, slicing his knee open on a nail. From inside the shack he hears a metallic click-clunk-clink. The motorbikes purr to a halt. Daniel sees the weeds at his feet spring into colour. Hears voices from the street. The bikes rev up. The lights move on. It is dark again. The police motorbikes fade into the distance.

Daniel stands up and bangs his fist hard on the wall of the shack, shouting: *Chinga tu madre!* He kicks the troll's hut once, twice with the flat of his shoe trying to knock it clean over, then runs off up the street.

He enters a field of canola laid out in long strips. He can still hear engines in the distance. Fearing that at any moment the field will suddenly light up like a runway, he climbs a steep wooded hill to the top of a copse. His good knee leading, he clambers sideways down the cemetery hill.

From behind scrub, trees, and rubbish, Daniel studies the ground between the fountain and El Café Fuente. The fountain snores in the night, fringes of water waving up and down. Its white stone glows under cold stars.

He emerges from the trees. The fountain snaffles in its even sleep, then sinks back into its regular drone. One by one he drags the mouths of the stiff-sided blue bags through the pool. When each bag is half-full he twists it off and drags it into the scrub, where he pegs it at the top. Daniel sits and rubs a leaf on his stinging knee.

He tries the outside freezer. *Disfruta Coke.* It's locked. Goes through bins at the back of the café. Stuffs a bag with rotten fruit and rock-hard tortilla. Pulls lettuces from the kitchen garden. Breaks into an outhouse store cupboard. Loads canned food into the bag. Finds a cutlery knife. Hopes he'll be able to pierce cans with it. Carries the bags of food and offal back past the heavy-snoring fountain. He has nothing to cut the rope with, so he coils it round the neck of one bag, knots it tightly, then runs the same length of rope round the next. One water bag he leaves behind.

Three bags on each shoulder, two ends of rope in each fist, the slack bracing his forehead, he squats like a clean-and-jerk weightlifter. He stands. Loaded like a migrant farm worker, he walks off through the scrub, until his own heavy breathing replaces the sound of the fountain at the centre of the world.

Through the gap in the coal-yard fence, Daniel bypasses the locked and floodlit gates of the container yard. The security guard in the harbour terminal's Origin Station is watching television, that memory of the campfire. The small set strobes the whole bare office with now blue, now red, now golden flickers of light.

Daniel leaves his bags in a corner of the yard and walks over to where shipper loaded containers are stacked. He sees what he's looking for: a soft-top container. Maersk V00502-North. The voyage number means it has already been inspected by customs and cleared through the port. It will be towed up to the automatic crane lifters and loaded last. A tarpaulin teepee is pulled down around whatever tall structure it shields. Daniel climbs up the container crate and peeks under the tarpaulin through the gap between guy-rope and hook. He speculates how much the load will shift, shunt and slide when swinging in the grab of the automatic container lifter. He unhooks a guy-rope, climbs in and clambers down the silver structure to the bottom of the crate. He has no idea what the strange steel contraption is, but it seems solid enough not to start sliding toward him when they are both in midair.

Ten minutes later, Daniel stands on the rim of the Maersk container, lowering the roped chain of blue bags into it. Scared as he is, Daniel would be more scared had he any idea of the full danger of his plan . . .

Soft-top containers are used for those outsize, extraordinary shipper loads which won't fit into the forty-feet standard containers. They are top-loaded on the vessel, stacked last on top of all the other containers piled high on the hatches. The higher they're top-loaded the more they sway at sea. Top-loaders are "throw overboard" and "total loss." If a vessel's top-heavy in high seas the captain is mandated to dump them into the sea.

Daniel wakes to movement, to sun and shadow on the pale green tarpaulin. He is too scared to climb up and look out. Twenty-eight days. The sheer expanse of time terrifies him, a great reckoning in a single box, too big to get his head around. An enormity incomprehensible in this confined container. Twenty-eight days! How will he survive four weeks in this deep steel tank? How will he endure a day? Where will the ship go? North, said the voyage number. But where north? He starts crying, for his escape now seems a disaster.

Daniel climbs up and peeks through a triangular gap between guy-rope and tarpaulin. Land is a mile away. Everything I do is a failure, he thinks. He remembers the hopes he had on first coming to Mexico, on his arrival there in the land of his mother and father. But then, as he looks at Mexico, he begins to wonder if the coastline will start to look like it does on the map.

18

There was a nun and a Chicano. She was small, Mayan, dressed all in white from her starched cap to her trainers. He was big, wore a checkered cheesecloth shirt and work boots. Always her and the Chicano. The two of them drove around in his Toyota pick-up. Four searchlights on the roof. You never saw them speak. People said that a few years ago the Chicano had sent his daughter a Western Union money order to pay a *coyote* for *pasado*. She'd never arrived and her body had never been found. And so had begun the nightly searches of the Arizona deserts. They'd never found her but they'd found others like her. And so they'd kept on. Two nights a week. Every week. Seeking out dead mojados. They'd found so many. Corpses jammed brokenly in filthy outflow pipes, whose dead bones the Chicano had to break again to work the body loose; whole families who looked as if they were sleeping together on a star-lit campout. All were loaded into the back of the pick-up, another night's mission over.

The nun and the Chicano drive toward a body in the distance which, when the four beams colour in the *piñón* and sage brush, is a bleached cottonwood log.

Here, west of Tamaulipas, tributaries straggle away from Rio Bravo and fan out through the wide limestone reaches of Nuevo Leon.

Nuevo Leon can take the river out of *la frontera*, but can't take *la frontera* out of the river. The river remembers what it did last year: sent north and put to work in the gardens, kitchens, and semi-conductor plants of the rich. It leaned its drunken head against Friday-night urinals in pay-day bars blurry with zero-hour contract workers, and had nothing left to send back to the family smallholding. The following spring Nahualhuas finds the river too fucked up to hide its junk-food addiction, its substance abuse, its sinister hoardings of trophy tampons and women's shoes as it crawls along the ground like an old wasp, a groggy ditch mumbling to itself and breeding jejen mosquitoes. No one blames the river if, when it does at last come back, it goes on a bender and is discovered next morning sitting mildly and peaceably in the ruined crops, a clumsy swirl of its reach describing a broad, haphazard domain while slurring the words *All mine!*

After a heavy rain or a run on the dollar, the tributaries tout corpses. Sometimes a dead woman still crazily searching for one of her old shoes on the riverbed, arms out to stop anyone blocking her light. Sometimes a man floating face-down, the back of his lime-green shirt forming a puffy dome, an air sack sailing slowly down-river and steaming slightly at first light. There's never an investigation unless there's a bullet in them because they're just *pobres mojados*—poor wet-backs. The unlucky ones, the ones who never made it to the strong currency, who went sideways down rivers which spread out and sub-divided and dwindled.

The nun and the Chicano drive toward a shallow of broad pebbles at a bend in the river. The Sister plays the beam of one of the pick-up's detachable searchlights across the surface of the water. She sees an object. It might be a man or it might be a garbage bag.

19

Oscar is dead, said Ayo, but your son got away.

Still holding his hand, Ayo found himself lowering Chano like a mountain climber to the forest floor. Chano sat staring crazily about him while Ayo told how yesterday Oscar was shot and Daniel escaped but no one knew where.

Chano buried his face in his T-shirt and sobbed. For a few minutes Ayo watched the spinal bumps along Chano's bared back. Then Ayo gently kicked him, just as he had once kicked the bag of ammonium he'd brought to Chano's *chicha* shack in Taxco Santos.

From within his T-shirt Chano nodded slowly as if to say yes, I understand, give me a moment. A glazed face emerged from the damp cotton, the eyelashes long and black, like, thought Ayo, when he was young.

But where is Daniel? Chano asked in a clogged voice.

He escaped is all, said Ayo. More than that no one knows.

No one knows. So he could be recaptured by now? asked Chano. Or lost in Calderon or anywhere?

He escaped.

Yes. He escaped, repeated Chano nodding, trying to hold on to it. A fresh sob broke from him. *Ay!* Yolanda! And Yolanda!

Yes, groaned Ayo.

Who's with her now?

Alma-Delia and Iriate, I think. Jesse James went with . . . with the body, with Oscar. More than that we don't know.

Que viva!

Que viva.

And my brother?

Gone.

Of course. Of course.

20

In 1886 a single, wacky US Supreme Court case (*Santa Clara County v. Southern Pacific Railroad*) decided for all time that a private corporation was a natural person. And as modern corporations became transnational they soon enjoyed "the legal right of persons" worldwide. Or rather, what used to be the rights of persons before corporations had them as well.

It is to the great and eternal shame of so-called humanity, however, that for so long corporations were seen as no more than objects of use. Having suffered years of abuse and cruel denial of their civil liberties before 1886, we can perhaps understand the modern corporation if he (or she) is still furious and insistent on getting his (or her) proper respect. And if this means that people now have to fit into a world made by and for these easily offended minorities . . . well, now we know what it feels like. To our credit, conscientious human legislators (acting for us all, impelled by our collective guilt) have done their level best to set right this historic injustice.

Old habits, however, persist. Even in the workplace there is still the bacteria of human contact, of company-time chatter and office friendships—even here where it should be clear who has the legal right of persons and who has not. (And this despite the best efforts of newsreaders reporting the tragic waste of "man-hours," which costs billions each year.) Thus it was that Rosa, who worked in the Nahualhuas Tel-Mex *caseta telefónica* had been phoning her friend Yolanda on the free, op-to-op switchboard line ever since she first heard Oscar had been murdered. Talking and listening to her friend on the company's time, but mainly listening. Rosa's call this morning, however, was on a different subject.

. . . and we're trying get some soup in him, she was saying, and we ask where he's staying. First he says nowhere. Then Tonalacapan.

Is he still with you? asked Yolanda.

Do you know him?

Yes.

He's still here, said Rosa. It was the Chicano and the Sister who found him, the Chicano was still in his thigh-high waders. They found him in the river last night and because he was still alive they brought him to the nearest pueblo . . . So, anyway, a few more spoons of soup, the Englishman looks around, stands up and suddenly he gets possessed, like a devil. All this energy—from nowhere. A fury. And before long I'm putting all these calls through for him. He phones this international number and he gets someone to arrange replacement flight-tickets and then he phones someone else who's sending him an emergency passport to the safe at the Hotel Hernandez. Then he phones this cop, Ilan Cardenas.

What does he tell the cop?

Says Chano Salgado is behind it, says he met Chano in a pipeline and describes the *coyote* who robbed him and tried to kill him—

How?

Like how you'd describe Blas Mastrangelo.

Right.

He tells him where—

The cop?

Yes—except he's not just any cop, he's the Zone Commander—and the Englishman tells him he's here but says he's going straight back to the Hotel Hernandez. OK, now get this, Yolanda. Then, see, he hangs up. Sits down. I'm watching him and—*esta chido*—it was like this: one minute his eyes are bulging, and the next he's collapsed again! Unconscious.

When?

Just now. Just now. Right before I phoned you.

I'm coming right over. Which house?

Mine. I'll go back now.

Vale.

A long phone cord trails under the door into the only four-sided bit of the Tonalacapan *caseta*. Yolanda is sitting in the phone shack's exchange cupboard amidst creakily rotating telecommunication drums and a twisting complex of circuit wire.

Back home, she takes off the blue and white snow-scene sweater she's been living in. The sweater has kept his presence around her in smells and spores. She folds it and places it on the wobbly kitchen table.

This is the first time Yolanda has been in the red flatbed since Jesse James cleaned off the blood which had smeared a phone number painted on the side door's vinyl interior. Yolanda slots key into ignition, then sits with both hands folded in her lap. She looks around at the space which Oscar occupied for so many years. She puts her hand on the rear-view mirror to adjust it, hesitates, and tilts it up, erasing another trace of Oscar's existence forever.

She swings the truck out on to the road. How strange it is to be in a hurry to get somewhere. She is still indifferent to every object, but how many objects now speed by her indifference! She feels reckless and a little mad, like driving with four flat tires on the wrong side of the road.

One hand only on the lowest part of the wheel, she slings the truck through a corner, in unconscious imitation of Oscar's driving style, and the red truck bounces up on to the Nahualhuas road.

21

A short steel bridge three times the width of the chemical trench links Matamoros to the USA. A bridge too short to have a name— more like the steel ramp into an aboveground parking lot. (A fly-blown, stagnant ditch, the blue of chemical toilets, the Rio Bravo only just makes it into Matamoros.) Before daybreak, cleaners and dishwashers walk over this short steel bridge into the United States, and after dark they walk back again.

"The paradox of US-Mexico integration," it's been said, "is that a barricaded border and a borderless economy are being created simultaneously." One academic describes *la línea* as "this bizarre combination of ineffectuality and force at the border". Another argues that the border has, in fact, "never been intended to stop labour from migrating *al otro lado*. On the contrary, it functions like a dam, creating a reservoir of labor-power on the Mexican side of the border that can be tapped on demand via the secret aqueduct managed by *polleros, iguanas,* and *coyotes.*" One of whom, Blas Mastrangelo, had been picked up at the checkpoint on the south side of the short, steel bridge at the very moment when Rosa at the Nahualhuas Tel-Mex was phoning Yolanda at the Tonalacapan *caseta telefónica.*

Ten minutes later, standing in the centre of the grey floor of his clean office, Ilan was trying to work out the shape of what he couldn't see from the shadows of what he could.

First, the English brother's allegation. Did Blas Mastrangelo, Ilan asked himself, steal Evan Hatch's passport on orders from Chano Salgado? How much substance do I give this? Mr. Hatch has deceived me once already: he had been in contact with his brother but only thought to inform me about that small matter when he was double-crossed. I think it's more likely that Blas Mastrangelo was on his way to sell the passport to the Heredia brothers in San Antonio. That's why he was crossing legally under his own name: because he must have been planning to go further than usual into the US. He'd be worried in case he was stopped in *el norte* before he could deliver the passport to the Heredia brothers. But I'll soon have an opportunity to ask him myself. Right now Blas Mastrangelo is in the back of a white Chevy Tahoe on Highway 10, being delivered back to me by Matamoros Seguridad Publica. In the meantime—Evan Hatch.

Mr. Evan Hatch. I need to talk to him again. Easier said than done. He'll be too scared to talk to me once he's calmed down enough to think things through. And he'll have an emergency passport on its way by now, flight tickets too. But they'll take a few days. He says he's going back to Hotel Hernandez, but I don't think so. There's no reason he should. I can still catch him in Nahualhuas, but if I don't . . .

Ilan picked up the phone and ordered a fast patrol car for Nahualhuas. Ilan felt crisp and clear. He searched for which area of light-grey linoleum was the best spot for him to do his best thinking.

The recovered flight tickets and original passport from Matamoros are coming here to me. But if they do, then Evan Hatch, because he has something to hide, will not. It's fighting talk, a threat when someone stands still and says: *Come and get it. Here it is. It's right here. You want it? Come and get it.* So—Evan Hatch will disappear.

Ah! But if Evan Hatch is told his passport and tickets are waiting for him in the hotel safe, then I *help* him come to me, because to open the safe you need two keys. Evan will have one key for the safe-deposit box, but I'll have the other. The monkey will put his hand in the jar.

Yes, that's good and what's more it will be a cool display of clinical efficiency, too. One which might perhaps get me some respect from this Englishman who has shown what he really thought of me. In spite of how well we got on together and the conversation we had he decides to treat me like a *pendejo*.

I can set all this in motion from the car: phone the hotel manager, then radio Matamoros and have them take Mr. Hatch's effects straight to the Hernandez safe.

Ilan looked down from the window and saw the revolving siren of his Nahualhuas car.

22

Rosa pressed her friend to her chest. Then, holding Yolanda's arm and hand in one coiling-trellis grip, she took her in to see the find.

An unconscious, battered man lay wrapped in a blanket. Beside him, Rosa's brothers stood uncomfortably in the room. One of them wondered whether you were supposed to take your baseball cap off when a recent widow walks in. Deciding against it he just readjusted the peak on his head. The way he did so looked just like how Oscar used to readjust his own cap, and for a moment Yola's vision was snagged on the peak of the man's cap, even as the rest of her face turned slowly away to ask: Will he survive being carried to the truck?

Let's see, said Rosa.

The brothers carried Evan Hatch out to the red flatbed truck, propped up the half-dead Englishman in the passenger seat, and came back to join the women on the step.

What do I say when the cops ask where he's gone? asked Rosa.

Yolanda looked from Rosa to her brothers. They all wanted an answer to this one. I'm not sure, she replied.

Tell them he phoned a cab? suggested one of the men.

No, said Yolanda, better say a cab came by and you gave the driver five dollars to take him back to his hotel . . . Only the driver was just passing through. You don't know him.

The men shrugged.

When he comes round, said Rosa, tell him—

If he comes round, said one of her brothers.

Tell him he got another call just before you got here. It was saying they've got him another flight only it's not for three days. She handed Yola a scrap of paper with an international number and a locator reference.

Driving the truck out of Nahualhuas, Yolanda looked across at her unconscious passenger, wrapped in his blanket. The truck hit a pot-hole and Evan sicked up in a single, smooth lurch like a baby on the shoulder. Yolanda drove the next mile with her head leaning out of the window, breathing in the whipped air, which smelt of dry *piñón*, stirred dust, and diesel. As the road forked she drew in her head and double-de-clutched on to the Calderon highway *libremente*. She checked her speed and got it level at forty-nine. Ahead of her an old Toyota pick-up was doing forty-seven. Close enough for the family in the back to see the ancient Cherokee beside her. She lifted a plastic sandal off the gas. Forty-five.

Leaning her elbow on the rubber sill with her arm straight up gave her confidence. She clacked her wedding ring on the roof, like Oscar used to do. A police car sped by in the other direction, its siren wailing so loudly that it was some distance before she could hear her wedding ring clacking on the roof again.

Either side of the highway, *piñón* bushes stretched for miles in a green, hazy bowl ringed by the Sierra de Cruillas. Vast, lush, and untouched, the valley looked as if it was waiting for dinosaurs to pop their heads back over the misty mountains. Yola glanced up at the Sierra's highest peak, its snow cap receding above a headband of mist.

A *Respete Las Señales* road sign. Those with respect for tradition instead had peppered the white tin square with bullets. Each raw dent and grievous hole probed her brain with a filthy trigger finger.

She passed turn-offs for Tonalacapan, Taxco Santos, and Ejido El Refugio El Reparo, and headed straight for Calderon. Her passenger keeled forwards and she put her palm on his chest and pushed him back into his seat, wiping the sick off her hand on his blanket. She will stash the English brother in the Calderon hillside *favela* where she herself grew up. Until Chano can be told of his brother's where-abouts, the Englishman will rest up with her cousins on the hill.

Two hours later the red flatbed pulls up in front of El Café Fuente. Yolanda rattles the café's screen door. Locked. She'll have to wait for Alma-Delia, Erik, or Iriate to come back. Tell them where the English brother is, then hope someone can get word to Chano—and tell him about his brother's call to the cops, too.

She sits on the fountain ledge as if she has been deposited there. The sun heats one side of her, but only in the way it heats a brown canvas bag hanging on a nail, not like it heats crocus, water, dog, burro, soil, algae, woman, man. The fountain plays alone and at half-mast. Yolanda feels that it will soon, without any warning, collapse altogether.

Who am I? she wonders. Here I sit in this spot but it could be any other spot. Here I am looking at things through my eyes but anyone else's eyes would do the job. Anyone else's eyes might look at this fountain, that bit of broken bottle in the dirt, that blue vinyl sack in the trees, and the trail where it has been dragged along from the fountain for some dull reason not worth knowing. I have this thought and I have that thought but they're just other little cave trickles in one head among countless other heads each with their own little cave trickles. There is no point thinking anything.

She stares instead at the thoughtless, brightly sparkling light of the fountain, so busy at its stem, so preoccupied and driven, until she becomes mesmerized by its fixity of purpose.

Oscar always seemed to get a real pleasure out of looking at it. She remembers that look in his eyes whenever he turned away from the fountain. Nothing major. Just a sense of his having been quietly fulfilled; his general-agreement-with-the-world face turning to hers bright from the sun-distilled water before padding back to the café thinking, Now what? What else?

The drop in water level has left a tide mark around the fountain's cansetta stone. Now that the water has sunk a little, she finds she can dangle her feet over the edge without them touching the surface of the pool. She is very anxious for her feet not to be touched by the water. She slips her heels from her sandals but the plastic heels touch the pool. Now she can't relax in case the sandals fall into the water. She takes them off and puts them on the ledge beside her. Her bare feet hang, swing and dangle above the surface of the water which they touch only as shadows. She taps her heels against the reassuringly dry, cansetta surround.

She'll go to Ciudad Victoria to be with her sister and look for work. Fewer and fewer people have been using the independent phone shack as new Tel-Mex *casetas* are opening everywhere. Last year was worse than the year before, though with Oscar's earnings they had between them they just about managed to survive.

Like steel rolling off a press, a smooth sheet of water is always pouring off the fountain's lowest ledge, before it joins the broad pool of the fountain. The deep round still subdues these new, tumbling, churning arrivals to the restrained mores of pond life. The sheety roll, however, shucks a last foaming hem of white water which bounces—with amazing consistency—tiny beads clear as Monterey glass. To and fro the beads are thrown in an arc. Constant pops of glass beads—hoopla—still emerge perfect and round, perfect and round, to disappear into the frothing shuck before Yolanda—much as she tries—can ever see them burst.

Abruptly she tires of the game and looks around her. What a dead, stagnant place, she thinks. She's been thankful for her friends and their help with the body and arrangements, but they get on her nerves, too. They don't know the exact nature of her loss because they never really knew her husband, even though they all think they did. This she hadn't minded when Oscar was alive. In fact, it had been a source of clever pride; the best-kept secret. But now it's galling, their affectionate contempt for him, especially that short-sighted Bad Medicine who thinks he's so clever. So unlike Oscar's honest admission of bafflement with the world. And that stillness at his core which, she reflects, had made him the only one in the noisy crowd to hear what danger the boy was in.

Without him, her many judgemental *dichos* will now, she fears, become banal prejudices, whereas Oscar always knew the many shades of meaning in what was unspoken . . .

Then again, she asks herself, *did* he? No longer swinging her heels, she recalls his terror whenever she'd ask him a call-and-response question like: *And so of course what does she say then . . . ?* Or, *And he's only gone to look for work as what . . . ?* To each of these questions, she remembers, Oscar would become *petrified*, eyes wide open like a fugitive caught in the searchlight's glare, until she answered her own rhetoric. The danger passed, Oscar would then break out in a relieved smile, and begin enjoying her story twice as much, his beaming face really getting into it. As she remembers this she laughs, smiles, and swings her feet once, twice on the fountain wall. And what was once a worry about what the others thought doesn't worry her any more.

A hand on her own is the first she's aware of Iriate sitting beside her on the ledge facing the other way. Yolanda closes her fingers around it.

23

Sometimes, reflected Ilan, it might be less draining to drive myself. He phoned the Hernandez again. No, Mr. Hatch still hadn't shown up.

Ilan took off his shirt and his belt and hung them carefully on a wire hanger dangling from the ceiling's bare pipe. Then he pulled off his boots, took out his yoga mat from the cupboard and knelt.

Ilan observed a personal rule with his thirty-minute Iyengar yoga sessions during office hours. If his mind wanted to go blank he let it, and stayed half an hour later at the end of the day. If, however, yoga helped him think work problems through, he left his office at the fixed time.

Ilan rolled his neck. He exhaled a long hot breath and began the Iyengar Salute to the Sun. He raised both arms in the air until thumb and forefinger of each hand touched.

Exhale. Forward bend.

Ilan had driven over to Nahualhuas or, rather, had had himself driven there (leading to all-over body tension). Evan Hatch had gone.

Right leg lunge.

He didn't believe the story about the passing cab driver and the hundred pesos.

Lower to plank.

He had interviewed them one by one in the passenger seat, asking the same question. Who came and collected the Englishman before I got here? (It was handy that the people in Nahualhuas had had no idea that he didn't use brutal methods, or that it wasn't his style to be oppressive or tyrannical, for they had been in a pliable state of fear.) Yolanda from Tonalacapan. That's who had picked up Evan Hatch. Well, tell her to tell him, he'd said, that his passport and tickets are now in the safe at the Hotel Hernandez.

Left leg lunge.

He didn't know where Evan Hatch was now, where Yolanda Gutierrez had taken him. No matter. He could turn that screw later. He was sure Evan Hatch would get the message. Someone had obviously made contact with him at Hotel Hernandez before. Someone from Nahualhuas or Tonalacapan. Word would get to him. (The galling thing was he may have passed the car or truck or bus carrying Evan Hatch going the other way on the highway.) No matter . . .

Back to standing.

Ilan's back still felt tight and tense. He had saluted the sun—in the modern way of course—but hadn't yet reached his special Iyengar yoga "moment" where transcendence broke like water through rocks. And so he kneeled down into Hare Pose. Head and hands touching the floor—arms at their furthest extension—he sent the pressure all the way down his spine toward his tail. He held this until the pain–pleasure balance shifted to a point where, Ilan evaluated, he might become more tense.

Walking his toes toward where his palms flat-handed the mat, he raised his haunches into Dog Pose. He straightened his head into line with his spine. As if by magic he felt energy electrically transfer from the base of his skull, neck, and shoulders, travel up and over the apex of his butt, deliciously transmitting through his taut hamstrings. He concentrated on sending a second and then a third electrical wave the same route from his shoulders, up the hill and down his hams. He held the position, his bottom high in the air, and breathed. Oh, it was righteous.

A knock on the door. He heard it open.

Chief, Blas Mastrangelo has—Oh sorry, chief, shall I go?

Go on, said Ilan, still holding the Dog Pose, but exhaling heavily now—perhaps to make it seem a bit more like lifting manly weights. Blas Mastrangelo . . . ?

He's here now in the cells. He says he wants to go to an out-of-state penitentiary—Coahuila, not Sonoa. That's his only condition: one prison, not the other. Says he'll be killed in Sonoa. Says he'll give us all we want. I think he means it.

During this speech, Ilan had gone from Dog Pose to Police-Chief Pose. He stood in his socks, hands on hips, flushed and nodding. But in the time it had taken him to get up the sergeant had finished his report, and all Ilan had to say (after nodding some more) was yes, good and thank you. The patrolman left.

Puta madre, thought Ilan. He knew that if his first, big investigation failed then being found with his ass in the air as the whole operation collapsed around him would be a career legend that would never die. His epitaph. *Madre de la chingada.*

24

The forest floor had the dank stench of shuttered places. It smelled like a hobo's hedge where, ducking out of the sun into reeds or bushes, you find hidden dirt paths leading to scorched tinfoil and muddy syringes lying in a stinky clearing. Then again, thought Ayo, the smell could be Chano. Ayo and Ruiz watched him study the passport then close it and put it down.

When's the flight? Chano asked.

We've got ten hours.

What, ten hours till we need to leave here?

No ten hours till the flight, replied Ayo.

Where am I going? asked Chano.

Ruiz slid his thick, brown glasses down his nose, tilted his head back, squinted his permanently squinting face and began turning the thin pages of the ticket. At last he found the word he was looking for and read it out loud: Seattle.

Matamoros Seguridad Publica had retrieved Evan's suit, shoes, shirt and tie from the trunk of Blas Mastrangelo's commandeered cab, and had left them folded and bagged under the front desk at the Hernandez.

Ayo now hung the same suit up on a bouncy branch. From his red nylon haversack he then handed Chano bottled water and tortillas, red cooked sausage and *chicharrones*, green bananas, and dark-brown *chicha*.

Chano rammed food breathlessly into his mouth, gasping even as he packed more *chicharrones* up to the back teeth. Ayo and Ruiz tried to ignore him as he poured in *chicha* to wash it down. Half the beer couldn't find its way through the thicket of jammed pork rinds criss-crossing his gullet like a beaver dam. *Chicha* came out of the sides of his mouth, through his nose, and down his chin.

Take it easy now, said Ruiz when Chano had finished coughing.

Yes, croaked Chano and picked up an orange, hoping the act of peeling would slow him down.

The three men glanced at each other, each sharing versions of the same thought. How impossible it was that from here, far in the depths of the *reserva ecológica*, sitting like primitives on the rank and pulpy ferment of forest floor, one of them could just up and go into the high-tech world of planes and automated check-ins. Just up and go and tomorrow be in a city in *el norte* with all its noise and weather. And yet here they sat like fantasists, dreaming an impossible dream, munching away.

I should never have sat down, groaned Ruiz. I won't be able to get up again.

What do you need? asked Ayo, cutting a sausage.

Pointing at the passport with upheld palm, Ruiz flipped invisible castanets. A little gift from your sister, he said.

Ayo put a knife-load of chorizo in his mouth and handed the passport over to the old man like it was the salt.

Ruiz wiped the grease from both hands on his grey shirt before daintily picking up the purple document between the tips of his fingers. He studied the photo of Evan, looked up at Chano and then back at the passport photo.

Ayo wiped his pocket knife with a folded leaf and said: It's a strange thing, Chano. You don't look like brothers in the flesh, but that photo, well, it could be you.

Ruiz took a careful swig of the communal *chicha* and dabbed his bottom lip with his hand. All the while his eyes, enormous behind square plastic lenses, never left the small full-colour photograph of Evan Hatch.

Yes, you're right, he declared. It's like the two faces meet halfway in the middle, Chano and . . . his brother. Here Ruiz gestured at the empty suit of clothes dangling man-height on the tree behind him. Chano looked up just as a hollow trouser leg flopped down to hang straight. Coming from different directions, Ruiz continued, passing each other going the other way. At this moment in time, right now, they *cross*. They cross.

What do you mean? squawked Ayo.

Still studying the passport photo, Ruiz elaborated: The Englishman was born with a tight soul, but his closed soul expanded with the never-dreamt-of ease of his new life. My friend Chano here was the other way round. A good soul, but one who got tired of oppression as he grew up. So you see, it's like they passed each other going in opposite directions.

What do you *mean*, man? asked Ayo, taunting openly now (not that the old man noticed).

Look at the set of the mouth, said Ruiz. The Englishman perhaps began his adult life with a sloppy mouth—

What do you *mean*, man?

—but as an executive he tightens his mouth: watching his back all the time in the corporation and in . . . in the loneliness of the north. (Here Ruiz underlined something in the photo with a stubby fore-finger.) This explains the ridges under the eyes. Now, Chano here starts off a young student and at this point he has the fixed mouth which you get from . . . from solidarity and political action, but then came . . .

And the ears? asked Ayo, swapping a sly look with Chano.

Oh well, said Ruiz, his free hand waving away such an elementary mistake, as if even laymen like Ayo and Chano could be expected to understand *this point*. Well, the ears are just . . . ears. Always have been. That's in the nature of ears, they're just . . . On saying this, however, he broke off and began intently studying the ears of the close-cropped man in the photo. Ayo looked at his watch.

Yolanda says your brother won't arrive in Seattle until three days later now, he told Chano. She says that was the earliest flight he could get.

How do I get to the airport? asked Chano, in a voice which was much louder than he realized.

There's the single most difficult thing of all right there, announced Ruiz. How to cross a territory when the soldiers and cops are out looking for you.

Maxi-taxi from the Hilton, said Ayo. They've got the name of the hotel right on them. They're never stopped. They only take American and Japanese executives from the lobby to the terminal, terminal to lobby. Best would be if you can get in one that's full of other businessmen.

But how will I pay? asked Chano.

We've been thinking about this, said Ruiz. You make me out a back-dated bill of sale for your house, from way back, from last year. Then we can pay back the collective.

Vale, said Chano. But what if the police are waiting at the airport? What if they've opened the safe and found the tickets and passport have gone?

All three went quiet for a bit before Ayo said: OK, so when you get near the airport call the Hernandez. We'll tell you if the cops have opened the safe.

Who will?

Ask for Room 12. That's where my sister watches TV between shifts.

Then they'll know the room is empty.

OK, someone will have to take one of the eight-dollar rooms, which are 1 to 7 on the street level.

Which one?

Ask for Signor . . . Alfonso.

Fuente. Easier to remember, said the old man.

Fuente, repeated Chano loudly. As they set to working this out his skin prickled with dread, his breaths came shallow and fast and his eyes zipped up, down and all around. (Ayo studied Chano and chewed his lip.) All the time we're talking, thought Chano, it could all be in vain. Daniel could already have been picked up. He could be being arrested right now, at this very moment that we sit here discussing plans. Might be in a cell this minute. A crowded cell.

Yes. OK. A Signor Fuente, said Ayo. And if they've opened the safe and found the playing cards and menu in the envelope then my sister will know, and she'll tell me or whoever's sitting in the room—Mr. Fuente—when you call.

Not you, said Ruiz. It shouldn't be you.

OK. You're right. Well, I'll find someone.

And I just ask "Is everything all right?" asked Chano. And then Signor or Signora Fuente just says no or just says yes. Right?

Yes, said Ayo. And if it's OK then you know you're safe. You hang up and then you just walk through Immigration speaking English and holding a *USA Today*.

Right, right, said Chano. So, no balaclava, no pipe, and no Mayan harvest songs?

Ayo laughed two, short flute notes, relieved to see how composed Chano really was, never realizing the brainstorm which had given rise to Chano's levity, even as he was infected by its electrical field himself.

25

Evan sat alone on a concrete ledge high up in the hillside *favela*. A warm wind ruffled his hair. Getting no more rise out of him than that, the wind went huffing and puffing against cement, wood, or plastic-sheet houses all built higgledy-piggledy up the mountain.

The mountain wore a headdress of radio masts, telecom aerials, and giant logo billboards. A line of grey scaffolding poles was slung crazily up its side like the handrail of the gods. The scaffolding poles were the neighbourhood's water pipes. Joined end to end, they ran water down from the head pressure tank to the hillside *favela*. From each grey steel pipe branched green plastic hose pipes, which themselves subdivided into a thousand hose pipes filling sinks and saucepans, pot plants, and plastic bottles, and where, spilling from overflowing tubs of grey laundry, water trickled down a mazy casbah of steep white steps, trickled through the dizzy *pueblo*'s sheer cement

drops, and trickled into fast-flowing gutters to grow muddy and slower
way down below, where cars were parked with rocks under their back
tires.

This was the first day Evan had been able to get out of bed since
he'd been deposited here. He was mildly bemused by everything, too
washed out and detergent-smelling to care. It was pleasant to sit here
in the stone stillness of perfect fatigue. His strength and vital irri-
tability would probably return soon enough. Or maybe, he fantasized,
they never would and he'd stay here, drained and glad, sitting on a
ledge a few feet from his new front door.

The two-room shack had been empty when he'd woken up. By the
side of the bed was a note he hadn't read yet and the folded clothes
he now wore: a quilted brown anorak, shiny red Monterey *Tigres* football shorts and a purple sweatshirt that was too small.

He looked down. These football shorts are a piece of work, he
thought. The red, satiny things were covered in ads, script, and logos
slanting this way and that.

Evan sat hands together, forearms resting on knees. He sniffed
the lemony chemical smell from some laundry hung out to dry, one
up and one diagonal away. He looked over to where the mambo-rap
was coming from: a big, blue concrete hacienda two hundred yards
across and thirty down; the *caudillo* of the hill, providing a kind of
local radio for a community who were hosts to many giant radio masts
but guests of none.

Mira eso, Alejandro! *Mira!* A couple of boys flew kites made of polythene bin liners, which soared above the whole city of Calderon. *Epa!*
Epa!

Evan looked straight across to the distant west bank of Calderon,
where hotels and office blocks stood a mile away across the valley. The
valley floor was a wide, pebbled, ex-river called Santa Katarina. Cars
were moving along the crosstown highway down in the grimy, dusty
air. But neither the traffic nor anything from that humid, steaming,
gleaming necropolis could be heard up here in the cool sky of Mount
Shanty.

Atop his eyrie, Evan tried to remember how he came to be here. He
put the violence from his mind, only touching lightly on his cuts and
pressing gently against his busted mouth. (Each day he could press a
little harder before it hurt.) He didn't remember much about the

river. He remembered the disgusting intimacy of an industrial out-flow pipe. Remembered a shelf of thin water sliding over fat, white pebbles. Remembered trying to lift his neck before he passed out. Then a man's hands lifting him. And . . . some kind of impossible nurse standing above him all in white. Am I broken? he'd thought, ter-rified to see operating-theater lights behind her, before he saw that she was, in fact, holding a full moon in her hands, one so bright he could not look at it as she played its beam this way and that as the man's hands had lifted him out of the river. And then . . . then nothing.

Until waking up in some other place—a village?—waking up and being fed a strange greasy soup. Pork fat or pork skin, very hot. On his feet, feeling insane. Energy burning him. He recalled how he'd been winding up a tirade, ready to let fly the second the Tel-Mex woman didn't let him use the phone without paying. But—she did. She did. Evan had been momentarily stunned by her receptivity, by how she'd simply accepted the idea of him being able to just use the phone with no cash on him. Perhaps, he considered, looking out over the distant towers, perhaps she just knew her place in the economic peck-ing order. Or had word got around these strange villages? Did some people know who he was?

A different woman had driven him here. Green and white head-scarf. Big glasses. The truck had smelt of sick. He remembered a hand on his chest pushing him back into his seat. He'd seen her before in El Café Fuente, this woman. Spoken to her even. *No, not from 'round here,* she'd told him that earlier time. *Chano you say? No, I'd remember a name like that. Mariano? No, never a Mariano either. There's more than one Tonalacapan* pueblo *in Mexico, you know. And this isn't even the largest.* He wished she were here now so he could ask her all about his past.

Evan closed his eyes and raised his face to the sun. He listened to the kites flicking, snapping, and fluttering. Silent when their balance was hover-perfect, washboard-skiffle when they ripped upwards or nose-dived on to concrete; wooden when they knocked into each other midair.

Alejandro, shouted a high thin voice in the high thin air. *Mira esto!* Their voices as they called to each other had that ozone-timbre of children on a beach. Alejandro! Check out how high my kite is now! *Epa!*

The older boy looked up and nodded in polite respect, then walked backward up a rubble-strewn ledge to get his own kite to go still higher. Keep yours away from mine!

Evan looked again at the silent city opposite, at the hotels and finance towers half a mile away as the kite flies. Between the ledge he sat on and those Evan-friendly interiors lay hundreds of casbah steps he must soon prepare himself to walk. One last effort, he thought, but not yet, not yet. He leaned back on the palms of his hands and watched the kites.

The seven-year-old's kite was made of clear, dingy, rubbish-tip polythene, the twelve-year-old's—Alejandro?—flew higher and was made of a black binbag. Both kites were prettily constructed with blue plastic butterfly knots tied to their long, plastic tails and tracers. The frames were made from sticks. When the kites changed altitude their polythene skin rippled and bubbled like plastic on a fire, but once hovering on the level again, they sat with the cushioned stability of fighter planes. Snappy and authoritative they looked, so high above the busy, silent city down below. Ahead there was nothing higher for a thousand miles. There were higher things behind them, of course, the radio masts and hoardings, but not out in front, where the money was, and over which the polythene *basura* kites rose and carved.

How fresh and good the world seems, thought Evan. A chicken nervously inspected him, as if Evan had just been in a terrible temper and the chicken were wary of setting him off again. Perched on his clean ledge high in the air, hundreds of feet above the silent city, Evan thought: It's like I've died and gone to structurally adjusted heaven. Soon, he imagined, a shame-faced and harassed-looking small bald brown God would come out of one of the *favela*'s mazy alleys and start complaining about the IMF: "I know it's not exactly, ah, heavenly," He'd begin, adjusting the tie of His cheap suit and clutching His bulging delegate's briefcase. "Far from it, of course. And I know it's not what you had in mind. Not what you thought heaven would be like. But you must understand that I've been forced to make severe cuts in basic infrastructure and social spending if I am to have any hope of qualifying for a loan . . . to, ah . . . pay off the last one. I've had to gear the whole Divine Economy toward exports," He'd mutter, "so as to generate foreign exchange. They've got My balls in a vice, here. What can I do?" Having said this, He'd look about the place hoping—but failing—to see evidence of a successful local project with which to appease the new arrival. "We're gonna clean up those human turds up by the radio masts and aerials," He'd add, "just as soon as we can. That I can promise you. Don't worry about *that*. And the tampons and nappies and old bottles. You have My Word. Anyway, thanks for coming. Have you been in the store, yet? It's quite good. They sell, uh, cold drinks and stuff."

The seven-year-old Polythene Kite Boy began to draw down his kite, an arm-length of twine at a time, and quickly glanced at the older boy to check he wasn't looking. He wasn't and so the younger one was free to pretend that he was climbing up the string to join it in the air. Boy and kite thus landed together, as it were, on the cement ledge.

Maybe, however, this is my heaven, thought Evan. The one I've deserved. Maybe this is just how high I got, he wondered, little realizing that with this very reflection he was already preparing himself to come down from the mountain top; his spirit banking before a diving re-entry into all he really deserved.

I'm going to make it go higher now, said Polythene Kite Boy in a confiding tone. Sitting next to Evan, he put the kite on his knee and took some more string out of his pocket.

Evan could usually count on not being bothered. His leave-me-alone look was recognized in over a million outlets worldwide. So much so that it was unconscious and without effort, this expression of his that said "no" to all comers. This was one fare with whom no London cabbie, however talkative, ever chatted. It was a quick "Which way do you wanna go, guv?" in the rear-view and straight back into their tax-return face. But though his surroundings may have seemed very alien to Evan, he himself evidently didn't seem very alien to the little boy. To Polythene Kite Boy, Evan was just another *barrio* denizen sitting on a ledge. A somewhat eccentric fool on the hill, perhaps (with his brown jacket, red shorts and fucked-up face), but, the boy may have supposed, all the more receptive to the joys of kite flying for that very reason, more so than you might usually expect an adult to be. Evan was so startled at being spoken to that his reply came after a long enough delay for him even to have thought about what he *would've* said (Yes. Good.) if he *had've* responded to the boy when he spoke to him.

Yes. Good, he said at last.

The boy's face turned frankly toward him. When I tie on all this extra string, he said, it'll go that much more high.

Looking into the boy's face, Evan was suddenly aware of something he'd been unconsciously registering ever since he'd arrived in Mexico a week ago. The place was full of children who all looked like he did in his primary school photos. Same jet-black, dead-straight hair in a fringe above the same slightly oriental eyes he'd had when young. Same tiny milk teeth. The same hopeful, open expression of his childhood photos, too.

Hope . . . Expectancy . . . He knew why they'd lose theirs, but why had he lost his? Because I'm dying, he thought. But he knew that wasn't the answer: it had been going on for much longer than that.

Do you want to try? Polythene Kite Boy asked, only half-serious. Alejandro, the older boy, now joined them, decahedron under arm, and Evan saw his Gateway Comprehensive First Year photo beaming down on him generously and *simpático*.

No thanks, he replied, smiling politely.

You sure? asked the older boy. You can if you want. It's no problem.

Well that's very kind, replied Evan. Another time.

Vale, OK, man, said Alejandro.

Okay, *vale, hasta luego,* said Polythene Kite Boy, trying to copy his elder brother's casual tone. They smiled at Evan, then disappeared down the steep cement steps into one of the cement-box shacks somewhere on the cement hill.

Evan sat still and perfectly thoughtless for a moment like a kite balanced on a thermal current. Slowly he screwed up his face. Hot, spicy tears filled his eyes. He clamped a hand over his face and clenched his teeth to keep his crying silent. Sobs heaved and bounced his back. What sort of person doesn't want to fly a kite? he asked himself. He rocked to and fro, face sore and gasping. What sort of person?

Half an hour later he stopped and wiped his wet face. What was all that about? he asked himself (in that Yorkshire burr again). Five minutes more and he thought: How long have I been here?

He went back inside his new front door and read the note. It seemed to be the dingo-took-missing-baby defence. A *coyote* had stolen his passport, he read, and not his brother. But his brother, he learned, was now borrowing it. Well, that's all right, then, thought Evan. Now, what the fuck am I doing halfway up a mountain in a fucking slum?

He began the long walk off the hill, down the steep, concrete stairway. Step by step by step, turn, a little concrete walkway, turn, step by step by step. Evan couldn't get a rhythm going; each step was just that bit longer than it was high. (The builder's focus had been on getting *up*.)

At last steps became the steep streets. Here it was busier too and people looked at him curiously. At the bottom of the hill, where the road flattened altogether, Evan passed derelict factories and gutted warehouses. He walked through a settlement of multicoloured tarpaulin market stalls selling mainly broken stuff: splintered digital watches, headphones with the foam bits missing, cracked plastic radios and CD players with no lids. It was as if, at a single moment in the 1980s, every consumer in Tokyo had suddenly dropped what they were holding and stampeded toward Sega World's opening. This debris was what they'd trampled over and left in their wake.

A stationary white Chevy Tahoe police patrol jeep guarded the border between the *favela* and downtown Calderon and in a few strides Evan was on its good side. He limped across Puente del Pappa over a collection of stones as wide as the Thames. On the bridge he passed a *No tire basura* sign. For some reason this don't throw litter order made Evan start angrily swearing, fuck you and your tin-pot shithole.

Entering the cool, air-conditioned logic of a Chase Manhattan bank, he sat down at the big empty desk in the middle of the marble floor and stretched out his legs. He began to smile, put his hands behind his head, then smiled even wider. Home, he said.

But not quite.

Only when he was safe in the Brownsville Sheraton across the border was Evan able to remember the full horror of having been a naked, brown helpless body that had been tossed in the river to die. A special horror of this state was having been robbed of all identity, and being safe at last only compounded Evan's sense of loss. For only once he was safe were the conditions of his safety revealed in all their insignificance. When he'd been naked, brown, and left to die, there'd been no essential difference between him and the most destitute *descamisados* living in a Calderon overflow pipe. Even so he had expected a difference to be recognized and, indeed, it had been. But on what was that recognition based? That if allowed to use the courtesy phone for an unspecified period of time, he could more or less prove that he had once opened a bank account in a high street on the other side of the world? Or that he happened to be in the address book of several people who weren't themselves destitute? But was that enough on which to lay a claim for human uniqueness and his right to live? Not only was it enough, it seemed, nothing else would do. But not for Evan. It didn't answer his questions. It left him, for a time, feeling like a bag of flesh and bone, who happened to be called one name and not another purely for reasons of administrative continuity.

26

The Westin Hotel might have been designed as an asylum seekers' welcome centre. The still bewildered and scared refugee expects only suspicion and hostility but how friendly the airport limo driver who ushers him from the confusing crowds! How welcoming the receptionist who gives him his key card and asks no questions! Even if the Westin had known exactly what the refugee has been through they could not have been more thoughtful. Walking into his air-conditioned room he is greeted by soothing music and an on-screen waterfall. A chilled bottle of water awaits him on the table. A personal letter from the manager hopes he will have a relaxing stay after what has been a long and tiring journey (the manager here favouring discreet generalization as being less likely to excite post-traumatic stress). And only an extremely picky asylum seeker would care that the manager has got his name wrong.

Chano opened a cupboard. His brother's spare suits, flown in from England, hung in the wardrobe. The manager's general letter reminded him of the particular one the receptionist had handed him as he checked in. Chano opened the envelope and read it. He would be picked up on Thursday to give his presentation to the Washington Board of Trade.

Yes, from the Westin Hotel the refugee is chauffeured within days to a conference hall, where he reports on the latest problems facing the poor to an audience of international business leaders, some of whom will have flown from as far away as Europe just to hear his testimony!

27

Ilan opens a zip-lock US airmail courier packet. He takes out a letter. A photo and the top half of a newspaper front page fall to the floor. The unread letter in his hand, he crouches down to pick them up. The newspaper is the *Seattle Times* with the date circled. Yesterday's. The snapshot shows a short-haired man in his thirties standing in front of the Space Needle holding up the same newspaper. Neither smiling nor frowning, the man's brown eyes look out with the frank intensity of silent communication, like a Mayan in a 1920s anthropology book. Even though there's not much family resemblance, even without the moustache and thick hair and the *pobre* clothes, and even without reading the letter, Ilan knows that it's Mariano a.k.a. Chano Salgado.

A red light winks on his answering machine. He puts down the letter. He'll read it later. Ilan plays the message. He plays it again. Then he walks around in silence for a bit. He plays the message once more.

Ilan is not to worry because Evan's recorded voice is now at the Brownsville Sheraton, where it will be for two nights while an emergency passport is Fed-Ex'd from the UK consulate in DF.

Yesterday Ilan had driven to Tonalacapan. Yolanda Gutierrez had gone. To Ciudad Victoria, they said. His officers had had the safe opened at Hotel Hernandez. Evan Hatch's passport and ticket were gone, so too his suit from under the front desk. The incarcerated Blas Mastrangelo, meanwhile, had fleshed out the links which Chano Salgado had with the Fuente crowd. The boy had been working at the docks, he'd said, in a job which the Fuente crowd had got him. (Again

Blas Mastrangelo's only condition had been not to be remanded to Sonoa penitentiary. Certain death, he'd claimed, awaited him in Sonoa.)

The passport, the hotel, the docks, the Fuente, the safe: Ilan sees he is up against a whole network of grassroots, community subversion. This is an organized terrorist cell and has to be combatted as such. In which context it may after all, he thinks, be best value to work with the military. New policing means a pragmatic application of what works rather than sticking to worn-out dogma. New policing, by definition, means being continually receptive to new ideas. (And, since the newest idea to come to Ilan is closer cooperation with the army, it must therefore be new policing.)

Ilan sits down at his desk with Blas Mastrangelo's transfer sheet in front of him. If Blas Mastrangelo hadn't been in such a hurry, he thinks, then he'd have realized how much more valuable Evan Hatch could have been than a stolen passport and a suit of clothes. Mr. Hatch would've paid Blas Mastrangelo a Colombian ransom to bring his brother to him. But Blas Mastrangelo was like the greedy workers: a short-term pay-raise rather than long-term economic prosperity. He was old Mexico. Indeed, he had even tried to murder a wealth-creator.

Sonoa.

Part Three

1

Housekeeping, said a Latino voice.

Chano hung up. Again he read the hotel-information instructions for dialing long distance, again he dialled Mexico.

Housekeeping, said the same weary Latino. Chano hung up and remembered a conversation he'd overheard on the plane. Two US businessmen were comparing notes on Mexico: It's like a country run by the help, one had said. Except, replied the second, you'd think it'd be tidier! *Real* tidy, chuckled the first, *spotless!*

You dial Mexico, thought Chano, and get housekeeping. That's globalization. (Indeed, in the words of the IMF, Mexico was "integrating with the global economy," suggesting a space pod docking with the mother ship. Through shiny sliding doors a small group of Mexicans come aboard. Still marvelling at the miles of gleaming space-age corridor, they're shown to a cupboard full of mops and Jeyes fluid.)

Wearing his brother's suit over his trainers Chano searched for a pay phone on Fifth Avenue. Fine drizzle stuck to the black suit like fluff. He walked slowly, scared that when he phoned Yolanda at the *caseta telefónica* she'd tell him that Daniel was still missing, scared that she'd tell him he was dead.

Life gives only to take, thought Chano, and just when you think life has taken everything it takes a bit more. Life had sat hope down a few feet away in the Calderon police precinct, only to snatch Daniel from him again. His hopes dashed, Chano was not simply back as he was before he had any hope, either. It was worse than before because a slice of hope had reopened the wound.

Chano stood under the grey overhang of an AT&T pay phone in the sea mist of the Pacific Rim. He already hated this pay phone. It was the diving bell under which he'd lived his adult life. He looked at the gun-metal punch numbers. Tragedy, which had always known where to find him, was about to finger him again. The receiver was greasy in his hand. His legs shook and his guts ached. He looked at the LCD flashing double zeros . . . then hooked the receiver back in its cradle. He put his two silver dollars in his brother's pocket and walked back into the crowds and drizzle.

2

Here's our guy! said a tall, lean man, about sixty-five in Rich Years. He clenched Chano's hand in a large, dry mitt and brought his face up close, leering with gamy intimacy as if last night he'd lent his trophy wife to Our Guy. The tall man then moved on from the lobby. A crush of delegates stood in an anteroom having finger snacks. Passing through the anteroom, the tall man called out a jokey greeting to a few of them on his way into the conference hall.

Standing alone in the lobby of the Bell Harbor Convention Center, Chano listened to the talk and laughter coming from the anteroom. He unbuttoned the jacket of his brother's black suit and took a few steps toward them. A Filipina servant, dressed in black skirt, white apron, and carrying a tray of canapés, stared at him. He turned back. Found another oak door and pushed it open.

Chano had never imagined toilets could be like this. The floor was marble, the taps were gold and the stalls were made of oak. Dulcet classical music played from invisible speakers. He washed his hands with lavender soap and dried them on a folded, white flannel. He looked at his cleanshaven face in the mirror with its cropped, gelled hair.

Just leave now, he thought. This is madness. If I stay I'll be arrested. And then they'll find out I'm illegal. I'll go to prison and then be handed over in handcuffs, bound at wrist and ankle, trussed up and delivered to Ilan Zone Commander at the border. Chano refolded the clean flannel and put it in his side pocket. He looked back at his face in the mirror. Just walk away Chano, he told himself. Just walk away.

He held his gaze a moment longer and tried out the following words: Speak truth to power. No sooner had he said them than he knew, once and for all, that he was going to do no such thing. He filled the pockets of his brother's black suit with little boxes of soap and walked away.

He came out into the now-empty anteroom. On the four-colour display board he studied the register. Dresdner Bank AG, British Invisibles, ROBECO Group, Alcatel, Bank of Tokyo-Mitsubishi, Chase Manhattan, Citigroup, Agro-Tech, Balfour Beatty, Burson-Marsteller, N-Viro, Hill & Knowlton, Bechtel, Ethylclad, MFP, USA Engage, Royal Bank of Canada.

If ever he believed in speaking truth to power then this was the time and this was the place. Power was certainly here. And yet here he was walking away. Had any of his beliefs ever been true beliefs? he wondered. Or had they just been something he'd always said when discussions had got to this point or that? He'd thought that by walking away he'd escape, but he now saw it wasn't going to be so simple.

For there was something else as well. Ever since his escape, Chano had hungered to be able to do something to help Daniel and, once he'd mailed the proof to Ilan, had known the frustration of being unable to. At any given moment he never knew whether Daniel was safe or in danger and there was nothing to be done, nothing he could do.

The father's numb suspension had brought visions of his son's unrestrained despair. Once, in monogrammed terry-cloth robe, Chano had slid open the window and listened to the crushing and grinding city. He'd heard in this crushing and grinding all the world's blind, brute force and violence, through which his skinny son walked alone in a thin T-shirt.

And yet if his beliefs now proved suspect, then what of this yearning to help his son? After all, he asked himself, had he not made much of his hotel room's hot bath and lain there for hours in the pine-smelling suds? If even his belief in speaking truth to power was not, now he was put to it, solid, then was there anything at his core? Did he really love his son? Did he really believe in anything? Were all his beliefs and convictions and emotions no different from a borrowed set of clothes like the black suit he stood up in? Clothes which say the right thing about you; clothes which present a selected version of yourself to others; clothes which, when you wear them, you get to thinking *are* you. And if, thought Chano, it turns out that I'm not convinced by my own convictions—not enough to act on them—then who am I? And who was I all along? What have I been playing at?

This is my chance to speak truth to power, he tried saying to himself again, but already the words sounded less convincing than they had when he'd spoken them in the mirror of the paradisal toilet.

Still here? a PA asked him, a walkie-talkie sliding down the shelf of her clipboard. You've missed drinks.

She dropped her eyes from his face to scan his laminate, to find out precisely how much love he merited in a sane and ordered world. OK Mr. Hatch, she said, smiling like a courtesan. They're all in, I'll show you to your seat. I'll try and get you front row because you're speaking third . . . no . . . *second*! Oooh! Follow me!

Chano followed her. The woman's reaction to his laminate—the way she'd taken a reading off the chip for the man—made him momentarily more secure in his imposture. She had done exactly what the tall man had done when he'd said Here's our guy!

Through the open door he glimpsed seated delegates in the packed auditorium. Soon, thought Chano, I will speak truth to power. But it was no good. The words were weaker than ever, as weak as he felt himself as he followed her into the conference hall. Ground floor, he told himself, fire escape routes, security controlling entry not exit, lots of windows.

The tall lean sixty-five-year-old who had shaken his hand was speaking. The triangular sign in front of the table mike told Chano that the man was called Desmond Gearey and that he was president of the Washington Board of Trade and Development.

Desmond Gearey welcomed the delegates with an amused, laid-back voice. His fingers doodled on the white linen tablecloth as if he were not, in fact, speaking himself but was instead listening to someone who he was far too crafty to believe.

It occurred to Chano that he could get up as if he was going to the toilet and then flee. He looked at the doors. The PA was standing there and she had seen him coming out of the toilet. What else? Left his notes? Glasses?

The first speaker was introduced and climbed the stage to stand at a lectern next to Gearey's white table.

Gaze locked into the middle distance, Chano seemed only to be able to attend to what didn't matter—the plastic flowers in a tub on the stage, the hinge of the speaker's glasses—and this weird detachment made what was coming seem, in another part of Chano's mind, much more terrible. He couldn't concentrate on the words being spoken. Quite lucidly he heard himself thinking: Soon I will have to get up and speak, but here I am right now with absolutely no idea what this man is saying.

Somehow the speaker had finished and Desmond Gearey was talking again. The moment was coming. Chano was trapped. In the hollow of his bones he knew a catastrophe was coming. What form the catastrophe would take—that alone he didn't know. He was set upon a course and there was nothing left to do.

But Chano knew all about there being nothing he could do. High-tension powerlessness was all he'd lived and breathed these last few days and nights in Seattle. That being his emotional home turf, all fear seemed to evaporate, leaving him a residue of numb apathy. In this remote gloom, Chano suddenly found himself able to take in the words that were being said. He was able to concentrate as if he was watching the whole thing on television, and not as if he himself were about to be called upon to talk within minutes, even while he knew that this remote dejection was itself another confirmation of the impending disaster.

The WTO is the place, Desmond Gearey was saying, where governments can get together against their domestic pressure groups. Quite often, for example, we invite the Japanese to appeal against one of our laws as trade restrictive, and they in turn often invite us to appeal one of their laws as a trade barrier, too.

Desmond Gearey grinned a craggy, well-weathered smile. He crossed his arms and leaned over them. The desk light which now shone on his glasses was like a public-address system for the twinkle in his eye. He spoke slowly and levelly. His amused tone, Chano noted, was that of a benevolent, kindly brother who patiently and magnanimously corrects the crises of democracy caused by his two younger brothers: government (the adolescent) and citizens (the toddler) . . . And as with Japan, he continued, so with the EU. Speaking just at the state level here in Washington, we were very encouraged to find our EU colleagues were just as enraged by the statist interventionism of some of the acts coming out of Brussels as we were. They were just as angry in the ERT as we were in NAM—that's, uh, the National Association of Manufacturers by the way, not the Asian war [laughter]. And so, through the WTO, we've found we're able to work very successfully together toward harmonization on a whole raft of issues: pollution, financial services, and trade liberalization in general. OK. So. How does this bring us on to the next speaker?

Chano's guts sank, his heart pumped furiously as if making up for the lost time when he'd been in a daze.

Well, said Desmond Gearey, the nub of this whole plenary, what comes up again and again is the absolute centrality of—well, call it strategic communications, call it knowledge management, public affairs, or active agenda setting, whatever—creating the right environment and the right business climate. Now we've only got one speaker on these issues, but let me tell you about his bona fides.

Forearms crossed like a lion, he read out the following: *Evan Hatch, O'Dwyer's issues management man to watch, a key thinker on regulatory rollback whose firm Poley Bray is expert in controlling the debate surrounding contentious regulatory and legislative issues*—I'm reading from their literature now, said Gearey, so who knows how much of this we can ah ... [laughter]. Sorry Evan! *Their approach to issues management mirrors that of a political campaign.* Gearey pushed the paper away from him and sat back in his chair. Well, he said, since the landscape's changed and we can solve many legislative problems, rather amicably as it turns out, at treetops level, is there a correspondingly changing role in public affairs and social relations? And Evan is going to tell us, I guess—is this right, Evan?—why we need to still pay close attention to the source of these ongoing hostilities when we allocate our war chests.

There had been no round of applause for the previous speaker but there was for this one. Chano walked to the podium at the right of the speaker's table, suffering the tightness of his brother's shoes.

He stood at the lectern in black suit, azure cotton shirt and blue silk tie, small boxes of soap in his jacket pocket.

Business heads studied the dark, unhealthy-looking speaker who placed a single sheet of paper on the lectern. Chano waited for the applause to end. Five long seconds later he still hadn't spoken. What looked like stage-craft, however, was simply the placid detachment of total fear. It occurred to him—in this peculiar, out-of-body state—that he had forgotten the opening words. Yes, he thought, that's what the problem is—I can't remember the opening words. He looked down at his sheet of paper and for a moment was intrigued to see his dear, old, familiar handwriting in so strange a place. He found the opening sentence written there in blue ink on the Westin notepaper. His thoughts strayed to the hotel room, its clever lighting system and its complimentary blue pen. He looked up and promptly forgot the opening words he'd just read. He read the opening sentence to himself again. He looked up, opened his mouth and, after a while, was surprised to hear sound emerge.

Imagine I am not Evan Hatch, he began, but a humble Mexican *campesino* standing before you. Would you be able to agree with what I say? Are your interests and those of the poor really the same? What do we—the poor—want? What do you want? Well, we want to get the blood-sucking government off our back.

The very last reaction Chano expected now happened. Gleeful cheers broke out from the assembled business leaders. In nervous response, Chano gave a weak, wan, sickly smile whilst still having no idea why they cheered.

None of the wealth, he continued, goes to us, even though we're the ones who've put in all the work. And why? Because the money is taken away from us by these foreign governments.

This was met by even stronger and more sustained applause.

Here's our guy! Desmond Gearey broke in happily from the table mike.

Either you have democracy or you have private power—you can't have both.

A cloud passed over the business heads. Chano expected his next words to be greeted by stony, chastened silence. The penny had dropped and cold reality was unmasking itself.

Democracy, Chano declared, is fine in theory but not when it affects business interests!

The laughter was so loud it seemed to bounce off the back of the room. The ironic cheering at this was terrific. Now they'd twigged that he was serious the sound had discovered a new depth. Bewildered by bellowing roars of approval, Chano could do nothing except carry on even more stridently.

Well, it's good that you can laugh but there are some, many, who cannot. The one-fifth of Mexican children who are malnourished as the result of bankers telling us to import corn and grow cash-crops.

The lectern was too high for him to rest his hands on and too low for him to lean on.

Until a bad corn harvest here in the United States left corn to spare and . . .

He tried to slide the paper a little higher up the lectern so it would-n't be so far to look down.

. . . and, so, as I say . . . one-fifth of Mexican children suddenly have malnutrition. That was two years ago.

This brought a temporary cessation of mirth. Exploiting the silence, Chano began reading from his notes again: One world dom-inated by totalitarian structures, every economic policy the same . . .

He didn't get very far before he was interrupted by a point-of-clar-ification heckle.

I think, came the assist from the floor, the polemic is more effective if you give each topic a general heading. Otherwise it's a bit confus-ing.

The heckler's overly helpful tone—like a friendly training-course facilitator—cracked open another full-bodied audience laugh. Chano felt his atoms detonate to the four winds. He would never be whole again. His legs were wobbling, setting cement. He was running out of places to rest his eyes. He couldn't look at any of the audience. The black spaces between them were too perilously close to the heads either side.

It was a rare type of isolation which he now experienced. The fact that he'd violated deep codes of tribal assembly freed the assembly to dispense, in turn, with all ancient hospitality codes. It seemed entirely possible to Chano that at any given moment they might all climb to their feet, descend the raked seating and methodically kick him to death.

. . . in every nation the same extremes of rich and poor . . .

He was alarmed by his every second in this uncharted taboo terri-tory. The stowaway had been discovered but the crew had decided—ominously—to keep their quarry before them.

. . . We want control of drinking water and so do you. What we want and what you want is the same thing—but . . . (here Chano tried and failed to remember the English for the Spanish word: *irreconcilable*) . . . but different. Perhaps. But perhaps they are not different. But things that can't be had at the same time. Although they sometimes are.

The laughter grew to hilarity. For the assembled business leaders could now sense that even *he*, the speaker, didn't truly believe his own words. Even he—they saw—even he found what he was saying over-pious and clunky. The room relaxed palpably, seats creaking, legs stretching, necks swivelling and paper wallets being rapped exultantly. Before their very eyes he was losing faith in his own cranky worldview! A miracle! Having begun his speech full of certainty this engorged Latino activist was ending it full of doubt.

This speech which had begun oh-so-cleverly by *pretending* to be reifying their positions might—the crowd sensed—end up by *actually* reifying their position! As the speaker stammered in confusion, there was a real possibility that he might come full circle and conclude that only increased private power could save the world! Even if this was not what he'd believe, how sweet to hear him say it all the same. Really it was glorious! And still he kept at it, white flecks silting the corners of his mouth, drying at the throat, Catastrophe's child: Well, you will react this way because you must—but your time is over. There is a global uprising, millions of . . .

And so, alas, is yours, spake Desmond Gearey. The applause which now thundered was malevolent. In an impassioned yell Chano Salgado gave his real name but couldn't be heard for malicious cheering. He raised a weak fist salute and left the platform to now lazy, sardonic applause and slow hand-claps.

Thank you, said Gearey, whoever you were.

3

Evan sat under the cement ledge outside the airport's revolving doors. Ground level seemed underground. What scant sky he glimpsed behind the overhanging car park's grey ramps and dingy concrete levels was dark and rainy. Recorded voices in mild English and genial Japanese made threats of punishment. All the faces at Passport Control and Immigration had been oriental. It's like *Blade Runner,* thought Evan.

He'd missed by half a day his whole reason for being here in Seattle. Too late for the conference and too soon for the Millennium

Round ministerial. He had missed his connection. His initial reason for being here gone, Seattle was now an entirely arbitrary city to Evan and it seemed like he'd been teleported in from another time. His hold on the present shaky, Evan felt like he was in the future, the future, that is, in which he had no place. He was seeing the world as it would soon look without him. Unless, of course, Evan could disprove his brother's gnomic utterances about blood-sucking beetles and a disease with no cure.

The City of Seattle has traditionally been the place where olde-tyme sci-fi goes to die. It is the white elephant's graveyard of retro-futurism. The monorail. The Space Needle. And as Evan climbed into the back of a yellow cab, Seattle was just a few short months away from completing its hat-trick of sad, futuristic fantasies by hosting the Millennium Round of the World Trade Organization. "The WTO is writing a constitution for the global economy," its president had declared. "Each Member [nation]," stated this constitution, "shall ensure the conformity of its laws with WTO objectives."

Evan settled back in the leather seats. Having been so far from all he knew, he once more inhaled the delicious alpha-benzine, full-colour print tang of *Business Week* before cracking open the *Herald Tribune*. Sensuously he traced a theme which seemed to be running from one story to another. A connection. In *Business Week* was the headline "Thanks Goodbye—Amid Record Profits Companies Continue to Lay Off Employees." And now, on the *Herald Tribune*'s front page, Evan read "Rise in Jobless Delights Markets." There was a linkage here. It might come to him soon, nose to rag he'd soon pick up the scent. Interest rates. Ah, yes, it was probably all to do with keeping inflation low because—

What happened to your face there? asked the Bengali cabbie. If you don't mind me asking . . .

Evan pretended he hadn't heard. To do with interest rates and—

Your face, said the cabbie. You have an accident or something like that?

Evan lowered the paper. A little. Just enough to ask: What am I doing?

What's that?

What am I doing?

After a pause Evan decided to give him a clue, a simple, *Sesame Street*–type clue that anyone could understand. Catching the cabbie's eye in the rear-view mirror, Evan rattled the pages like maracas. He then raised his eyebrows and lowered his head to check that the message was received and understood.

The cabbie said nothing but after a while reached for a stack of full-colour leaflets on the passenger seat. I don't know how long you're here for, he said. But take one of these . . . Here. He held his arm back until Evan took it. Back inside the *Herald Tribune* he read the leaflet: CITY-WIDE WALK-OUT. N30. ONE-DAY TAXI STRIKE IN SOLIDARITY WITH ANTI-WTO PROTEST.

Evan found out which hotel room Mr. Evan Hatch had been staying in for the last three nights. He knocked on the door hoping to find his old life in. He was badly missing his connection with it all. He heard his old life fiddle with the chain-lock. His brother opened the door, wearing a white vest under an unbuttoned shirt and trousers too short for him: all Evan's clothes. Their eyes met. My brother has become the "stand-in," thought Evan. Chano suddenly bent at the knees to catch a heavy falling object. As he blacked out, Evan's last consciousness was of strong arms in pristine white cotton catching him beneath the armpits.

Several hours later Evan opened his eyes and looked at his feet in their Ben and Jerry cow-print socks. He was sitting propped up on a twin bed. He looked at his brother who sat on the edge of the other twin bed. Chano had, Evan observed, changed back into migrant costume, faded green jogging pants tucked into brown boots. Over these was a pair of baggy purple shorts (which had themselves been cut down from an even baggier pair of tracksuit pants). He wore a thickly padded zip-coat over a grimy hooded top, with a cuboid baseball cap on his head. Outside it was dark and quiet with a pale orange light coming from an invisible store sign.

How long was I out? asked Evan with a fixed, artificial smile.

A few hours.

Have you been here the whole time?

I went for a walk a couple of hours ago.

Chano had been planning on leaving without a word as soon as Evan awoke. He was going to wait till Evan came round and then, without a word, just drop the passport in his lap on his way out of the door. Vigil over. Make my point. Go. But now they'd spoken Chano wasn't going anywhere. From the moment those few words passed between them both brothers knew they were going to talk. And here in the room. (Chano feared ejection from the communal area, and Evan feared looks from people who might know him.) It would happen here.

I'll wake myself up, said Evan.

For the next hour Chano heard Evan shower, vomit, clean his teeth, crack pills from a blister pack. He saw him return in shorts and a Fidelity Investments T-shirt. Chano winced at the raw-hamburger wounds on Evan's legs, knees, wrists, and elbows.

The river?

The river.

In Evan's absence the room service he'd ordered had arrived. Now, together, the two brothers ate sandwiches, chips, cakes, and cookies, eating in silence but looking up at each other now and then.

Evan crossed his ankles. Chano leaned back against the radiator and raised his knees. Each on his single bed. Two brothers sharing a bedroom.

A trolley rattled in the corridor. A fire door closed. They sipped their fresh coffee. Still neither of them spoke. Words crossed their minds about what they might say to each other—"How do you feel now?" . . . "So tell me . . . ?"—but they seemed wrong. And they seemed wrong for a reason, but they neither of them knew what that reason was. And so they sat and waited, each letting his own mind go blank while hoping the other would figure out the reason why their beginnings seemed false in their own heads.

A cake crumb in the back of his throat sent Chano on a short but violent coughing fit. When it had passed, he coughed once more to settle his throat. It was one of those muted, formal coughs—hmm, hmm, hmmm—like a stranger sharing an elevator. And immediately, in the very formality of that cough, both knew exactly what it was that had so far kept them silent: this would be the last time they would ever talk together. And so both started at once.

How do you feel now?

So tell me—

After you, said Chano.

No, go on, said Evan.

No, you. Please, invited Chano.

Evan paused, nodded, said: What did you mean when you said there was no cure for my illness?

Oh, I'm not a doctor.

No, no, said Evan, scratching his cheek. You were very definite when you said it.

What do the doctors say?

They've no idea.

Well, you're probably too old for what I was thinking about anyway, said Chano.

What? Is it something in our history?

No.

What is it then?

It's something in our geography.

What is it?

Or maybe not. It could be anything, said Chano. I don't know.

Chagas, said Evan.

It sounded like chagas, yes. From what you told me.

Did my parents know, do you think?

Which ones?

English.

No. The point was to get you somewhere nice where you could have a life. They wouldn't have been told. If the nurses had said "this baby is a time-bomb of sickness and disease," then who would've adopted you? And it may be they hoped that in Europe you'd have the drugs to treat chagas, said Chano (knowing all the while that there were no drugs for chagas because it was a disease of the poor).

So, you knew.

We feared. They feared.

Why? Was I bitten by the beetle?

It killed our mother. She was bitten by a *vinchuca* when she was carrying you. You were born with it.

She died of chagas?

Yes.

So if it was in her blood it might be in mine?

But it might not be, said Chano.

Did I show symptoms? What are the symptoms? (Evan had already looked them up—on the Brownsville Sheraton's in-room Internet—but wanted to check they were the same.)

Well I don't remember you showing symptoms, I was four and if you were ill I was probably kept away from you. I don't remember. I should but I don't.

Evan balanced cup and saucer on his lap, looked across at his brother and asked: Aren't you boiling in that coat?

Not yet, answered Chano. Even when you're by a radiator the cold here doesn't take its claws out of you. It's a cold mist that gets in your bones and your blood. It leaves its hook inside you even when you're in a warm room, like it'll never go.

What's it like out?

I just said. Cold.

How like two teenage brothers sharing a room we are, thought Chano. Or how like an older brother I'm behaving. How like the way a fourteen-year-old answers his younger brother's questions: acting haggard with the weight of every grim reality the youngest doesn't yet know. It's cold out there, kid. Putting on a show of taciturnity but letting him have it all the same. He glanced at Evan who was wiggling his toes in their patterned socks. And how like the baby of the family he looks, thought Chano. The pampered favourite. The one who doesn't know how many battles were fought on his behalf. The one who assumes it must have been as easy for everyone else as it is for him. Except, no, reflected Chano, because he's *not* the one who gets away with what the eldest never did. No. He gets away with nothing; of the two of us he is the more punished.

Well, you should take it off for when you have to go back outside again, said Evan maturely.

Yes, in a minute or two.

Evan readjusted the pillows behind his back and flexed the stiffness out of his knees.

What do you know about our parents? he asked.

Only what I heard. He was a seafarer. Had been. Came from El Salvador. They say he walked all the way. He was working in construction. He was older than our mother.

How did our father die?

Building site.

After our mother?

Just before. They were both younger than we are now.

Evan sipped his coffee then asked: What was my name?

José-Maria.

Evan noticed how the name came instantly to his brother's lips and was glad. For he knew by this quick reply that José-Maria had been part of the family story in some Mexican town, had been remembered, wondered about and hoped for by people for whom he was a living presence. He had existed.

José-Maria, said Evan. José-Maria! Ha! he chuckled, wondering how different his whole attitude to life might have been if his name had always been José-Maria. José-Maria living for the day and the next dance, eating in the street on his way home in the morning. José-Maria strolling with a loose-hipped walk and returning the flirtatious cat-calls of *carmencitas*. José-Maria Salgado.

Tell me about your life, asked Chano.

Evan Hatch began not at the beginning but by describing his transition from youthful radicalism to the first flush of love for his present career.

Chano interrupted him to ask: Tell me about your job. I can't picture quite what you do.

Shorn of the dialect of buzzwords, it seemed to Evan that this was the first time that he'd actually looked at what he did. As he began to describe his job he seemed, to Chano, like someone sitting under a tree and wondering if it has started to spot with rain.

I help my, our, clients fight their corner in a hostile environment, I help them find ways to communicate with the public and the media, helping to ensure there's a favourable business climate. I monitor changes in the . . . All the while Evan spoke, however, he was thinking of something else . . .

Many of the things he loved about Poley Bray he considered more personal than professional. He loved the dispassionate appraisal with which his peers spoke of someone when evaluating his or her capabilities (to see if they were suited or unsuited to this role or that). This clear-minded awareness of each individual's character flaws and strengths allowed one to resonate in one's full individuality. It was a tone or an attitude which had inspired in Evan the realization that all those things he'd formerly felt as somehow apart from work—what you did in your spare time, the music you listened to, the way you drove—were relevant. He was incorporated. Maturity was about how awake one was, how removed from fantasy, how in the real world one was. Outsiders always thought of corporations as faceless monoliths, cold and robotic and full of drones, but to Evan each firm seemed just the opposite. If anything, he felt, they were more like some kind of group-therapy battalion.

He was just trying to think of a way of beginning to communicate all this to his brother, when Chano said: You must hate yourself.

How's that? asked Evan.

When you spend all your time tricking other people because you have contempt for their intelligence, giving them not the real message but one a baby can understand, then, *hermano*, you must end up with contempt for your work, for what you do, and you will end up hating yourself.

No, said Evan, his head on one side. No, I love what I do. I have a talent.

In their exchanges there was a strange neutrality. Words which in any other conversation would have been fighting talk weren't loud or aggressive here. They were like two actors reading through a hammer-and-tongs fight scene just to check that each knew what they were doing. This was in spite of—or perhaps because of—the fact that they were speaking from the heart more than either of them was in the habit of doing, and because they were two brothers speaking for what both knew would be the last time.

Evan looked at his brother and leaned forward from the waist with one leg bent underneath him. The fact is, Chano, the plain, brutal, hard, cold, unpretty, but real honest truth is pure democracy would never work.

Chano's faith in speaking truth to power had, of course, been but recently destroyed. (Not that, as Ayo had suspected, faith was ever the word for it.) The upshot was that Chano now rode his words less hard, and when he spoke was not so wild-eyed with five hundred years of exploitation as the man in the pipeline or the One Dollar Diner had been.

I don't think so, he said. No elite can ever run things well—only everybody altogether.

People *are* stupid. Some people *are* brighter than others. You *have* to have leaders.

But you know it's rotten, it's lies, it's for the powerful against the powerless, it's anti-democracy.

Ha! Democracy! said Evan, with his head on one side as if trying to guess a familiar song from its opening bars, a song whose title was on the tip of his tongue.

It's corporate rule, said Chano.

Well, "elites" is a dirty word, of course, but there's always been rulers and ruled from the beginning of time, Evan declared. All through history.

And we were always living in caves and hunting mammoths. And if there was a bad harvest we knew the Sun-god was angry with us because we hadn't killed enough spastics.

Yes. *Until* we got leaders and a bit of organization and some long-term planning.

You're right. We're not clever enough, said Chano. None of us. That's why it's impossible for one human or a few humans to lead lots of other people. *Only* the people can run their own lives. One leader makes everyone else less human. Chano found there was something about talking to his younger brother which lent him fluency and clarity. He was surer of certain beliefs than he'd thought, not in the sense of being sure those beliefs were right, but of being sure they were his. Although the Bell Harbor Convention Center debacle was too recent and too raw for him to be convinced that these beliefs possessed any sort of irreducible core, they did now at least ring true. Where are those brains so big and so powerful, he now said, big enough to understand a million hopes, wishes, needs? No one. No one head, no one leader. But only everybody together, equally.

It's beautiful, brotherman, but it's a pipe dream. You're off to never-never land, it's a utopia.

I don't think it is, Evan, Chano replied.

Well, said Evan, I don't see the masses out on the streets calling for the revolution that you want. I see them buying Air Nikes, queuing for the multiplex and buying the free-trade coffee with Big Mac and fries.

Quetzlcoatl comes back as a white man to destroy the land!

To bring investment and CDs that rock. Because what they really,

really want is the satellite dish, the air-conditioned hatchback and a funny programme on the TV, Chano.

But look at who you work for.

Who do you mean?

You work for the corporations, not us.

It's the market and it's the only game in town.

If globalization is natural like you pretend then there's no need to do that job you do. "It's the market." Fuck the market. Why not society for humans?

Because the market's the only thing humans have ever found that works—

Who for?

—not perfectly, but it works. Planned economies didn't work, don't work. Free trade does.

If it's not a planned economy, why are they having a big summit here next month?

To make sure there's no planning, replied Evan with a smile. To make sure everyone is playing by the same rules. To make sure no one fucks with the market mechanism. To get more things out of the way.

Things.

Obstacles.

People.

Governments.

A coup . . . ?

Social change.

Chano laughed and Evan laughed at his older brother laughing at him. It's like they say, said Evan chuckling, it's the worst system apart from every other one!

But listen to your laugh when you say that! It's the laugh of someone getting away with something.

No. Go on. I'm still here. Let's have it . . .

What a waste of human potential, said Chano. What a waste of time! Don't your knees buckle at the thought of the billions of people whose lives might have had meaning and dignity—if this coercion and control of the public mind hadn't shut down all oppositions to its one idea?

In a word, no. I used to feel the same way once but there're new realities out there now.

Out there?

Yes, out there.

But how much self-disgust lies behind a philosophy which is new and the opposite of what you used to think?

No, it was disgust at the old ways not at me. That's what I was gonna say . . . Here's you . . . well, I think you've had to, you've . . . you need to believe there's an inherently evil system so as to give meaning and dignity to the murder of your wife. But suppose it wasn't capitalism which killed her, but just, you know . . . some *goons.*

No, Evan, said Chano gently. We always thought, both of us, there was a tyranny and it had to be fought. I've always thought that.

Why is it a virtue never to change your mind?

You say that and yet the only way of doing things in the whole world is what a few Wall Street economists have decided. There is no other way, they say. And they've got the tanks and troops behind them. *Orale, man!* What a waste. The things humans could do if everything, *everything,* was not in the service of profit. But for that we might create thousands of other ways of organizing our lives. I mean, how can you not feel we've been defrauded out of our birthright as human beings?

Well, I feel like I've been defrauded out of my birthright of being human for much longer, said Evan, but that's nothing to do with anything except bad luck.

We've both had bad luck.

It must run in the family.

I hope not.

Any word from your son, from Daniel?

No.

Good luck.

And good luck to you. But you give things up too soon, said Chano (echoing Dona, his foster mother), and then still hope to know what your own nature is.

No, I'm a sticker.

The older brother thought about this for a while and saw it was true. He nodded his head and his reply when it came was gently spoken: Yes. Yes, you are. And you have the scars to prove it.

Gracias, said Evan.

Two drunks stumbled up the corridor, coat fabric whining against wallpaper in high-pitched friction. Then silence.

What will you do now? Evan asked.

In Seattle? I'll look for work, a place to stay.

What sort of work?

I don't know.

Chano stood up, put on his coat and walked over to Evan. Here's your passport, he said.

Evan looked at the passport without touching it. He looked up at his brother. I know it wasn't you, he said. For a moment I thought it was, and I'm sorry I accused you to the cops. But I was in a state.

I wish I *had* stolen it in the first place, said Chano.

Evan took the passport. Hold on, he said. He got up painfully and took a clip of money from the sealed plastic Bureau de Change pouch. He handed Chano the five-hundred-dollar clip without counting it.

Chano took the money without counting it either. Thanks.

De nada. Well, I'm gonna be back here in a few weeks for the WTO. Maybe I'll see you then. I'll be staying here.

Maybe so.

Yes, maybe so.

4

A noise penetrated his fever, an ugly screeching. Daniel raised his heavy head. Seagulls.

Seagulls were inspecting the soft-top container. It was the shit and rotting food which had attracted them. Seagulls were broadcasting his position over and over with their codger shrieks of discovery, all competing to get a peek at the find.

Daniel stared at the neat triangle of sky between canvas and steel-crate. White herring gulls. There they were in impossible detail, so clear and defined, wing-fringe and tail-feathers transparent against the blue sky. They hovered with their yellow legs stuck out in front. Each gull eye had a machine-tooled, black bead dead centre of a perfect, bright, yellow circle. Their straight, yellow beaks were hooked at the very tip, a fat pinky-red circle on each stem.

Daniel could hear shouting down below. He knew it wouldn't take long for the hovering, cawing seagulls to be replaced by peering, grizzled human heads. It would be better for him to come out. Better to reveal himself than be found at the bottom of this metal gully like a netted rabbit.

In a daze of fear he was climbing down the wind-whipped outside wall of the high and swaying stack of container crates. Seized before he got to the deck, he was hit round the head. He got the gist of the first words: *Kuckin sin Meksicki!* He was grabbed by the hair at the back of his head. It was a big fist that clasped him, pulling him this way and that.

Pseto malo! This way, that way his head was yanked. Horse-eyed, Daniel tried to find what meaning he could in these faces, voices, hatches, waves, coats, bibs, clouds, boots, as his head was wrenched to and fro on the swaying ship.

Sta cemo sad? said a man. Daniel couldn't see the face but heard its tone of malevolent dejection. The rumour had started up a week ago among the Bosnian crew; a muttering speculation and the vague, unconfirmed sense that they'd got stowaways. Now that it was confirmed at last, the crewman who'd been the rumour's strongest advocate was vindicated: *Rek'o samti!* he declaimed. *Jesam to rek'o da imam slijep putuika, jesam! Rek'o samti?* Looking at the others while his boots stamped the fact into the moulded steel deck, he stabbed a finger toward the boy. *Sta samti rek'o!*

Daniel was stood still now by the hand that controlled his movements.

Kucksin Mecksicki! Hard as a donkey he kicked Daniel in the ass. The boy lurched his lower body forward with the blow but the man's fist tugged him back by the hair. Daniel screamed as the fist twisted eye-stalks at the roots. Soon, he felt, his stinging, watering eyes must pop out.

Dobro je ba, a voice behind him said. The voice threw open a hatch door with his free hand. The hatch door flung back on its hinges. The voice kicked it open again before it could close. *Uzlazi unutra,* the voice told Daniel.

Daniel was in a small, empty, steel hatch. Two pipes. One hot, one cold. He had been here for two days. They had given him a blanket.

Now and then they gave him food and water. Daniel wished they didn't, for there was something in the way they did this which made him more nervous still. A man—always a different one—brought him, in turn, water, then bread, then a piss bucket, a plastic flask of coffee and a singed, green padded coat, leaking kapok like the lagging of a boiler. None ever spoke. Each tried not to look at him.

Inside the steel hatch Daniel couldn't hear any voices, but he knew by their silence when they came in, that he was the topic of grim and continual debate.

Daniel didn't know how long it was since his sickness had begun. His eyes shimmered open. Someone was squeezing a yellow sponge on to his forehead, but as soon as his eyes opened the man left. Daniel had—he now saw—been put in a new place. A bunk. A window. Sheets. A pillow. Cold soup on a chair next to him.

Another time the soup was hot. He was getting better.

The fever broke at last. He pretended he was still unconscious.

Instinctively, Daniel knew that things were all right so long as the situation was one in which the crew knew what to do. He knew things would get dangerous when they didn't. He was safe if he was sick.

Every now and then he scanned the room, careful just to open his lids a little and do it a flicker at a time. Two men were looking at him. He shut his eyes. But it was too late. He was put back in the small steel hatch. Again the two pipes, one hot, one cold. Again the routine. Door opens, shield eyes from daylight, single crewman takes four paces in, averts eyes, deposits mug of soup or bread, exits, door closes. But there was a difference, too. Daniel sensed anger now, lingering like the smell of whichever crewman had just left.

On what Daniel guesses to be the fifth day since his fever broke, he sits with his back to the wall facing the door, one arm coiled around the hot pipe. The door opens. No one enters. The door is left open.

The sky is white as Daniel emerges blinking. The air is clear. Not long ago, however, it must have rained for raindrops judder on the grip bumps of the steel deck. The crew stand in a horseshoe at the far end of the ship. They seem laid back as if assembled for a routine fire drill. No one is nearby to grab him. He's free and not free. This is the scariest part of all. He knows he must go to them. There's no choice.

He walks slowly toward the men. The ship tips a little. Daniel lurches, falls over. The crewmen don't move at all. He gets to his feet, remembering tumbling about in the soldiers' truck with the Costa Rican crew from the *Jennifer Lopez*. He walks slowly toward the men.

A big man puts his arm round Daniel's shoulder and chats matily to him in his nightmare seagull dialect. The other men follow Daniel and the big man's slow progress toward the taff-rail.

What can I do? thinks Daniel, looking at the man's face. I know what he's going to do. The man halts in what he's about to do, in what is coming next. He is, thinks Daniel, waiting for something or someone. Daniel's eyes dart from face to face, trying to glean information—though he knows that whatever he learns will be bad. Another crewman returns from below with a yellow flare gun, hollow and plastic like a big toy. With a show of great care he puts it in Daniel's hand, then explains its function in seagull language and human mime.

A clattering sound on metal. The crewmen look down. Daniel has dropped the big yellow flare gun on the deck. They put it back in his shaking hand thinking the boy has dropped it by accident.

Again the clatter of plastic flare gun on steel deck. This time the crew gives a cheer. *Bravo Meksicki!*

Another Bosnian comes forward and points at far-distant, brass-coloured lights scattered like grit.

Nije daleka.

Daniel turns round to look. How far?

Hands on his back and legs. A hoist. Flying. Screaming. Falling.

The sea punches him in head, knee and ribs. Dropping, dropping through sea as heavy and black as oil, he fears being sucked under the rusty hull into churning propellers.

Air.

The ship, it seems, has sprinted away. In the flattened, spreading, triangle of its wake Daniel sees an object floating on the unzipped foam.

Half an hour's swimming and he's no nearer the yellow plastic flare gun. Perhaps it is bobbing away at exactly the same speed that he's swimming. Death is in every one of the colossal water's hisses, rattles, snaps, trills, gurgles.

Solid and hollow in his palm, the flare gun makes swimming more difficult. He stuffs it in his belt and slips under the waves doing so, shipping salt water into his throat and nose. He breaks the surface retching, coughing.

Daniel scans the tilting disc of the horizon this way and that. He can't see the tiny lights any more. Can't remember where they were. He waits. Here it comes. A large wave lifts him. Lifts him high. He looks. He sees the lights.

There are many world records, daily, for which humanity keeps no statistics, has no measure. For example, on any given day there must be one person who is at, let's say, noon GMT the single person most in love or most full of hate in the whole world. Luckiest or unluckiest or most in physical pain. There must be each day the person who's been up for longest in the whole world. The big wave lifts Daniel high. He sees the lights. A sound escapes him. And with the single, loneliest groan in the world that night Daniel sees for the first time how impossibly far away are the lights. In Shacklewell, Kladno, Krosno, and Grozny were people who, at this exact moment, uttered loud groans of total despair. But whatever their time zones, none, for a full hour, uttered a cry as lonely as this boy in these waters at this time.

A flare gun will only fire once. He must get nearer the tiny lights before he fires into the air. He swims, treads water, swims, treads water, swims for an hour more. He fires the flare gun.

The damp squib flies up. Nothing happens. He utters a wild, little whimper. It bursts yellow and streams vivid and huge through the sky like a miracle. Daniel is sucked down into the sea. When he resurfaces there is no sign that the flare ever happened. The night has reached out a black glove and snatched it from the sky.

5

Driftwood, a forty-seven-foot boat and Market Haven's last working trawler, is fifteen miles out to sea. By the cabin's black windscreen, two wristwatches, a wedding ring and a mobile phone are laid out on a bar towel. On another stand cans of beer, a packet of cookies, and some blue rolling papers. The coastguard's radio channel, which overrides all other signals and silences, bursts into the cabin in conversation with a distant Norwegian vessel. The coastguard's voice flutters about noisily for a few seconds like a trapped moth, before finding its way back out into the night.

This is *Driftwood*'s last working night, the final put-out before they oxyacetalene the boat for scrap. Knocker and Pockets aren't bothered about that so much now. They've dropped some acid which hasn't worked very well, and snorted some speed which has. They've got a compilation tape with groggy bluebeat ska interrupted by urgent flashes of 100-mph gabba-techno.

Out on the wind-pummelled deck, still hot in their T-shirts, Knocker and Pockets stagger about tying a rope around the neck of a giant inflatable alligator. They then stumble about cutting the tangle net's guide-rope free of its ten-pound iron weight and its coloured float. They lurch and list about attaching tangle net to the alligator's dog collar. This done, they throw the inflatable alligator over the aft, watching the fifty yards of carefully laid tangle net follow it out to sea. The tangle net flies zig-zagging out of its crate like, thinks Pockets, a snake rising from a snake charmer's basket. Or lots of snakes. Flowing snakes. A nest of flowing snakes.

They fumble with the UtilityLite searchlight which stands as tall as a short man. A metallic clunk bursts a quarter-mile beam into the sea. Each holding a can of beer and an air pistol, they begin shooting at the inflatable alligator tied with a long leash to stern.

Oh fuck, said Knocker, reloading. Can you remember where we shot the nets?

What, the actual nets?

Yeah, the ones for fishing.

No!

Falling and laughing, they shoot at the inflatable alligator which is desperately trying to catch up. Now ducking into the darkness, now twisting into the light, rolling and plunging in their wake.

Back in the cabin, Pockets is building a spliff. They're still buzzing . . . for the last couple of hours they've been swapping radio insults with the crew of a Spanish trawler.

A voice breaks into the cabin through the speaker: Beckham takes Posh Spice cock up his ass!

We agree, replies Knocker, and puts the hand-set back in its ceiling rack. Knocker then immediately unhooks the receiver again and steadies himself in his wellies before broadcasting as follows: Fuck off out of our fucking water! How can this be your fucking water? I can see my fucking house from here! (He can't.)

Driftwood, like other British ships, flies the red maple leaf of Canada from its flagpole, in commemoration of when Spanish trawler boats tried to enter Canadian waters a few years before and were run out by warships.

No time for 'em, says Knocker, who speaks like a controlled explosion. His deep and staccato West Country growl sounds as if each terse phrase is letting a bit more nitrogen seep out safely and that he's been told always to use short sentences on doctor's advice. I'll turn off their jabber now. Unlike them to be on the radio, anyway, innit? Never *usually* answer, you know? When you try and warn 'em they're too near yer nets. I've got no time for 'em, me. No time for 'em.

Pockets passes the spliff and Knocker, slowly exhaling the powerful skunk, says: One time, right, I was out with Spike. Went right alongside them. Stood on the rail, I was. Holding the hand-set in my hand. Held it up even, pointing at it. But it's no use. Still won't use it, will they? Still go right over your markers and all. Got no time for 'em.

Pockets presses the hand-set again. We've got guns. State your position. Over. He turns the radio off before the Spaniards can come back at them. Knocker chuckles grimly, his thoughts elsewhere. I'll turn it off now before they can get back at us, says Pockets.

Yeah. I saw you do it.

Oh, I wasn't sure I did.

Pumping water into the kettle, Knocker says: So I go down Housing—Petherdene Road, right?—and the kiddie behind the glass and that, he goes there still ain't nothing down for you. And I goes why not? And he gets this list out and shows me, right. The actual list. And he goes, he goes—See all these people, right? These are all the people that the local authority's told us to put before you. And I read it, this list, and it's refugees right at the top, asylum seekers and that, and then he's showing me all these different categories. This category's for ones that has just come in, this category's for ones being resettled from somewhere else in the country.

But he could have showed you the list when you first came in, innit?

There's that, said Knocker, slightly pissed off that Pockets hadn't quite got the point he was making.

Pockets is nodding out, sitting with his back against the cabin's plywood. Shall we turn the radio on again? he asks.

Minutes later Knocker replies: Yeah.

Yeah, says Pockets a few minutes later still.

Neither moves.

Pockets, though . . . if we don't get up we'll just nod out. Lively up yourself.

Right.

Neither moves.

Over the last few hours Pockets has woken up for a few moments every now and then. Each time he's told himself that the sea lion sitting opposite him will be gone when next he wakes. But here it is again. Blubbery and black. Wet and slimy. Whiskery and tusked. There's one good thing, though. It appears that each time he awakes a different detail or two has gone from the sea lion. This time there are no flippers and it's less chatty. With which happy reflection Pockets goes back to sleep for another lysergic hour. When next he wakes, the sea lion is still there. Less whiskered and slimy. More silent.

But there. Oh still there. Pockets lets his heavy eyelids fall and leans back against the cabin's plywood.

The sound of Knocker hammering conger eels up on deck wakes Pockets up for good. He opens his eyes. Closes them. Slowly he opens his eyes again. The sea lion has assumed human form. A boy drinking soup. Wearing Pockets' black puffa jacket, a dark-grey blanket wrapped tight around round his legs, and drinking soup from a pewter tusk.

He remembers now. Remembers hauling the boy in.

Pockets lifts his back off the wall a few inches and inclines his head to ask, ever so politely: English? Speaky de English?

Pockets looks up as Knocker steps heavily down the step into the cabin. He watches him press buttons and turn the wheel with the vengeful alacrity of someone trying to get their shit together while still fucked up. He don't speak English, does he?

No, Pockets, says Knocker testily. He *don't* speak English.

Pockets, taking the hint, gets up and gets busy.

Daniel could smell rotten fish heads, damp towels, and alcohol. He was still shivering but his teeth had stopped chattering. He was sitting on an old bus driver's seat bracketed to a wooden box, the grey blanket over his legs hanging to the floor. The coastguard's voice broke in for a moment through the black speaker mesh.

Oh my fucking Christ, said Knocker to himself. To Daniel the man's voice sounded as if it too had been strained through the speaker mesh of a two-way radio, and was coming from far away where conditions were unpredictable. The man sat on a high seat at the wheel, one foot resting on the floor. Yellow foam gaped through the seat's busted seams. He wore battered and cracked day-glo orange dungarees with silver reflector flashes up the sides. Under the dirty orange bib and braces was a faded blue turtleneck. Humming tunelessly, Knocker's voice was a murmuring growl as he stared out the black windscreen across which a little wiper wiped even though it wasn't raining.

Daniel studied the high-tech navigational equipment bolted to the otherwise condemned ship. Radar screens, number displays and electronic maps. Were they soldiers? He looked at Pockets again. Probably not.

Suddenly a flow of Spanish entered the room, too distorted to make out. Daniel watched Knocker unhook the hand-set and pat the smooth, black oval into his big palm like a lucky pebble.

This is TWO-SEVEN-SEVEN-TWO-THREE-EIGHT-NINE-EIGHT-ZERO. MOTOR VESSEL: "DRIFTWOOD." CALL-SIGN: OSCAR PAPA ECHO DELTA, said Knocker, POSITION, er . . .

He reached over with his free hand and touched a button on the Lottery Box, as Knocker and Pockets called the Global Positioning System. (They called it the Lottery Box partly because it looked like the corner-shop ticket machines and partly because it was rubbish. A bottom-of-the-range, bottom-of-the-sea GPS-90 which Knocker's dad had bought from a salvage sale. Brought up by a wreck-diver it was, his father had cackled. Similarly, the cheap but first-hand Neptune Fish Plot 12 trackplotter was called the Black Box.)

Knocker pressed a button over and over but it kept going back to a computer-graphic map of the world. He whacked the Lottery Box with the flat of his hand. Now it flashed the numbers he wanted but too quick to read. Like the mother ship on Space Invaders the numbers seemed programmed to disappear before he could react. He pressed the button and thumped the Lottery Box again. At fucking last, rumbled an explosion from inside a mountain tunnel. POSITION: SIX-TWO-ONE-ONE DEGREES NORTH, ZERO-ZERO-SEVEN-FOUR-FOUR DEGREES EAST. I need someone who can *hablay ingles* on the *San Sebastian.* Over.

Immediately more voices came howling through the speaker: *Malvinas. Malvinas para Argentiiiiiiiii-naaaa!* Fuck the Queen!

Inglese, por favor, please, said Knocker. Important. *Importantay.* Very. Over.

Daniel listened to the Spanish which now came through the radio: I can speak English but I don't want to, whereas your mother cannot speak English because she has so many cocks in her mouth. Over.

What did he say? Knocker asked Daniel. The boy looked at him helplessly. O'course, sorry mate, said Knocker correcting himself. But . . . er, can you *mime* it with your hands, he asked, miming miming with his hands. Daniel understood what he was being asked to do. He thought a long moment, and then, very slowly, shrugged.

In English now the voice whirled and sieved through the speaker mesh, slowly announcing each heavily accented word like a speaking clock: Your. Mother. Sucks. Much. Cock. In. Piccadilly. Over.

Yes, yes, yes, said Knocker, I know, I know. *Correcto.* Many cocks. But, please—do you speak any *more* English? Over.

No me da la real gana!

Listen. Serious, we have *amigo español* . . . Over. But there was only static and crackle.

Daniel saw the man in the cracked orange bib hold out the handset to him, then point at the Spanish-speaking display panel. Daniel knelt up with a painful bending of aching thighs and calves. *Hola?* said Daniel.

Press that, said Knocker. Good. Keep it pressed while you, uh, *hablay.* Daniel was about to speak but stopped to stare in curious fascination at Knocker who was miming vomiting copiously yet casually. Speak, said Knocker, Goo on!

Hola, San Sebastian. My name is Daniel. I was rescued from the sea by these two good men. I was thrown overboard from a container ship.

I stowed away in Mexico where soldiers tried to kill me. I don't know why they were shooting. I think it was something to do . . . I don't know why, why they were trying to catch me. I was protesting. I am fourteen. I am, I was, like you and like the two kind Englishmen, a fisherman. I was a fisherman in Costa Rica and in Mexico. These two men need you to help them talk to me and understand. Please tell them what I have just told you. I don't feel well and may need medicine when I get to England.

Daniel waved the hand-set in the man's direction. Knocker took it and said: Over.

They heard a hum and buzz of conferring and clanking, and then, in English: Please wait. Over.

A new voice spoke. I am Javier, I speak English and Spanish. This he then repeated in English, adding: But what are *your* names on the *Driftwood?* Over.

Knocker and Pockets. Over.

In a little while they had a three-way conversation going, a bilingual conference call.

Pockets then took the hand-set. Javier, hello mate. Ask him please why he left his country?

Five miles of black sea away the Spanish trawlerman translated this for Daniel, and Pockets handed Daniel the hand-set. Daniel spoke to the radio. And then Pockets and Knocker learned in broken, crackly, five-mile-away English that Daniel had worked on a fishing smack but that it was impossible for small boats to make a living in Costa Rica.

Well, now you know why we don't like *your* mob in our water, Javier. That's how we feel about *you*, said Knocker. Over.

No, said the trawlerman, wrong, wrong. It's the same for us. That's why we come here. Over.

We gotta live, said Knocker, and you're stopping us living, my friend. *We* don't go to the Bay of Biscay. Over.

Yes. British factory ships go there.

Alarmed to be out of the loop, and deducing that he'd rekindled the feud with the *San Sebastian,* Daniel looked from Knocker to Pockets.

Knocker now spoke into the hand-set looking into Daniel's eyes the whole time. Tell him, he told Javier, we can't take him ashore 'cos lorry drivers are being fined tens of thousands of pounds for bringing in, uh, illegal immigrants. The term illegal immigrant sounded embarrassing now that Knocker and Pockets were actually with one.

As Javier's Spanish translation came through the radio, Knocker and Pockets saw the alarm on the boy's face when the bad news finally arrived from the *San Sebastian.* Between the two crews and the boy a three-way plan was worked out for when *Driftwood* docked at Market Haven.

Knocker and Pockets walked up a long, steep, narrow metal ramp with railings either side. It felt strange to dock and not offload a catch.

We'll find the nets tomorrow, said Knocker.

Don't matter if we don't. It was just tangle nets. I remember that.

Was it? asked Knocker, pressing the electronic gate-release button six feet from the top of the walkway. Well in that case we might have been on Hunter's Point.

Silent on its rollers, the electronic gate slid sideways before the weary men reached it.

Daniel still asleep?

Fast akip under my sleeping bag. I chucked your duvet on him and all.

The Help the Aged had still to open for the day. As Knocker and Pockets drew near, two lads were tearing through the bin liners left on its doorstep, hurriedly sorting out what they needed and chucking to one side what they didn't. Pockets made to approach them but Knocker held his arm and said: Nah, they'll just leg it with all the bags.

And so the trawlermen leaned their hangovers against the street railings until the lads had walked off with a pair of trainers, a kettle, and a leather jacket.

Knocker and Pockets gathered up all four ripped bin liners from outside the shop, picked up three fried-egg sandwiches from the café, two Beefeater Bloody Marys from the 7–11 and went back to *Driftwood*.

6

When they'd said goodbye, Pockets had taken out two fivers but they were both in bits, shredded by seawater. Knocker had found a better tenner in his wallet and given it to the boy; Pockets had given Daniel his black puffa jacket which now hung unzipped about his knees.

Daniel walked alone through Market Haven, wearing his charity-shop selection: black lace-up shoes too big for him, shiny tracksuit bottoms rolled up at the hems, a patterned cardigan and a T-shirt bearing a screen-print school photo of a Punjabi girl.

Daniel thought he'd better buy food now before the shops closed for the afternoon. He went into a shop and bought a plastic-wrapped ham and tomato sandwich and a Sprite. The man handed Daniel his change. Daniel looked into his palm then looked up. An awareness of the full horror of what had just happened shocked him. The price was round about what he guessed it might be, the food he'd bought had taken roughly the bite out of his ten that he'd expected. But this was another feeling. He was shocked not by the change, but by the exchange, by what exactly had just happened. Ten pounds was all I had in the world, he thought, yet this shopkeeper casually takes away

a piece of all that stands between me and death . . . He wants to anni-
hilate me. *Qué barbaridad!*

Abstracted by routine, the shopkeeper was listening to the radio
playing attenuated pop and twitter. Daniel stared at his lazy face and
the shopkeeper turned to the dumbstruck boy. Yes, mate. That's right,
mate. Seven pounds and forty-two pence change, mate. Tapping the
electronic price display, he added: Two fifty-eight, mate.

Daniel left the shop and stood on the curb while the shopkeeper
watched him from behind a stack of one-litre cartons of orange juice.
To Daniel, not having understood a word, it was as if the shopkeeper
had said: Yes, that's right, that'll be a night sleeping under a hedge.
That'll be you trying to steal a samosa from here next week, mate.
That'll be selling yourself in a subway toilet. That's right, this is how
we'll kill you. Seven pounds and forty-two *centavos* change.

Suddenly illiterate, Daniel stared at the writing on shops and signs.
Across the street he saw an emperor: head erect and walking fast, a
long, flowing, purple robe cloaked his shoulders. The young emperor,
not much older than Daniel, clasped his gorgeous train together with
one hand at the collar. Only when the young emperor swept by did
Daniel notice the quilted stitching of a purple sleeping bag.

And then it began to rain. Grey sleety rain coming at an angle to
him. The beggars—all young—got up and disappeared. Daniel
zipped up his puffa jacket and started trembling.

He crossed a footbridge over four lanes of traffic all going the
wrong way. The sleet didn't so much stop as get itself jammed or
wedged up in the sky. At the end of the footbridge he looked down
over a wall on to a train platform. What he saw scared him. As he
stared down at the people on the platform he knew that he'd chosen
the wrong time to arrive. He'd come at a time of bad news, he now
saw, and would be blamed for it. Something must have happened.
Something big. A national tragedy. Everyone stood singly, each fixed
on a midair focal point a foot from the end of their noses.
Occasionally these people darted reproachful looks at one another
when no one was looking. On the road under the footbridge, the lone
drivers in sealed cars were in mourning too.

Weak and slow-moving, sockless in shoes three sizes too big, Daniel
knew he was dwindling down and down. Seven dollars and forty-two
centavos.

He tried ducking into shops for warmth but was chased out of one and finessed out of another. (Can I help you? asked a young man whose smile was enough to tell Daniel that the question was just cruel pantomime.) In the shopping mall boys his own age chased him, throwing stones until he was out of range.

A woman came up and asked him if he was all right. Daniel looked into her kind face, nodded and walked quickly away. Speeding up, his legs began to wobble and he felt sick and hot and sweaty.

He searched for somewhere he could sit down, a park, a bench, a fountain. He found a quiet, scrappy side street and sat down on a green milk crate across from a skip. At last there was no one around.

He hears a rattling from round the corner. A shopping trolley appears full of gas pipes, gaskets, sprockets, springs, tin cans and torn copper wiring, pushed by a wiry, old man who leans into it with his whole body, muttering and gnashing away. He wears a thin and filthy grey coat, and slopped like soup over one eye are many of the ingredients for a hat. His eye is blue and manic with effort. At least eighty, a stroke has winched one side of his face into a ferocious wince. Unless, Daniel wonders, the wince is his actual face and the other side the stroke. His chalk-white hands and forearms are corded with thick blue veins.

The *pobre viejo* pushes his shopping trolley up to a yellow skip. He lifts a tottering knee on to the trolley. Surely he's not going to try and climb in, thinks Daniel, and looks up and down the street hoping someone coming by might stop him. The old man grips the rim of the clattering cart trying to get purchase, his forearms shaking. And then, exhaling a vicious snarl, the old man is, to Daniel's complete amazement, standing in the wire cart on both laceless baseball boots. The *viejo* hauls himself from cart on to skip ledge and disappears into skip.

From inside the yellow skip come metal shelving slats, spark plugs and radiator pipes. Daniel waits. He hears grinding and shunting and watches for the old man's reappearance. There arises instead, by inches, a long white radiator. The old man slides the radiator, like an up-and-over garage door, out of the skip and into the trolley.

The forbidding *viejo* begins climbing out of the skip. Daniel watches in horror as a leg attempts to become the bridgehead from skip to cart. The old man is very quiet and concentrated, his blue eyes gentle now. A wavering baseball boot finds the rim of the wire trolley. It takes a while for the foot's discovery of the trolley to be transmitted to the old man, whose sunken face steams in the cold air. One foot on the rim of the trolley, one foot on the ledge of the skip. He is ready to take his moon walk. The old man puts out a hand and steadies himself with the radiator which sticks up from the trolley like a metal sail.

Daniel stands and begins to step forward. The old man swings his weight from skip to trolley. The cart scoots out from under him, but, as if this has never happened, he takes a slow step back toward the ledge. Misses. His foot slides into skip. He falls head first, overturning the trolley which crash-lands, tolling and chiming.

The old man lies on his back surrounded by scattered gaskets and pipes. Blood flees from greasy, grey-white hair. Daniel kneels by the man, whose rasping breath comes in noisy heaves and whose blue eyes flash the boy some urgent signal.

Has someone called for an ambulance? the cop asked the woman who was pressing a wad of mini-hankies on to the head wound. She pointed at a man with a mobile who nodded and pointed at the ear-piece in his ear. Squatting down the cop asked who found him.

I think he did, she replied, and pointed at the boy.

The squatting cop bounced round on his haunches to face Daniel. You saw him fall? he asked the boy.

No English, Daniel replied. The cop stood up. Daniel faced him. His arms hung by his sides in exactly the same way they had when he'd stood on the steel deck of the container ship: hapless and ready to meet whatever would come next.

The cop didn't like this defiant gesture one bit. None at all? he asked. Daniel couldn't understand the question and gave an ambiguous shrug.

It's on its way, said the man with the phone, pulling out the ear-piece wire and walking to the newsagents for another pack of hankies. The cop turned back to Daniel. He knew there was something illegal about this teenager. His face had a look which crossed all borders. It was transnationally identifiable: he had that look of the international poor (and would've had even in brand-new clothes).

Market Haven had made national news with its asylum seekers. Or, more accurately, national news location hunters had scouted Market Haven and found its streets telegenically suited to wind-up vox-pops asking if Britain was being flooded with a wave of immigrants so serious as to have brought the *BBC News* camera van all the way to their unremarkable town. Here—if the TV crew was patient— were rare sightings of Albanian headscarves holding up the Tesco checkout with Sodexo vouchers. Here, journalistic experiments had concluded, you could compile excellent montages of humble lions slowly rising from slumber—once you'd edited out your own questions. The humblest he and the most preoccupied she slowly coming to, visibly awakening to the, yes, severity and the, yes, extremity of the, yes, *crisis.*

Where do you live? asked the cop, cannily.

7

The night was close and still as Yolanda walked her slow picking walk through Ciudad Victoria's Parque Democracia. As yet she didn't know how long she'd stay in the city, which was a whole day's bus ride away from Tonalacapan. She had come to be with her sister (who was working a late shift, sitting in a toll booth on Highway 80) but also to look for work. She wanted to stay. There was nothing for her to go back to. Perhaps she'd soon find a job here, too.

Palm trees and narrow strips of lawn surrounded Parque Democracia's central square. A rough twenty-foot-high wall in the park was a noisy fountain. Water appeared from nowhere at the top of this free-standing wall, cascading in torrents. She tried to work out how this municipal fountain worked, then dismissed it abruptly as impressive but gimmicky.

A few others sat here and there on the bleachers, where Yolanda now sat, watching an evening pasadoble class in the square. The class was taken by a man and a woman in their late thirties, not much older than Yolanda, but the dancers were seven elderly couples. The women had well-worn walnut faces and wore long floral pasadoble skirts over their jeans.

Uno . . . Dos . . . Uno . . . Dos . . . Uno . . . Dos, announced the instructor in a clear, ringing voice. *Uno . . . Dos . . . Uno . . . Dos*.

Yolanda found herself wondering which old couple she and Oscar would have made, which soon became trying to figure out which old man Oscar would have become.

Not Straw Hat, she thought. Not that life-in-the-old-dog joker with his proud, white moustache and the string vest steaming through his shirt. But maybe Blue Trousers . . . in his baseball cap and dingy white shirt, and whose paced steps matched his partner's. When Straw Hat, that young-as-you-feel codger, spun his wife, his feisty, hold-me-back-ma steps left him hopping up and down and out of time in the eternity it took for his *pareja* to come out her stately revolve. But Blue Trousers' modest little shuffle had nothing to prove. Yolanda watched him twirl his old lady, step once, step twice, and clap hands in time to meet her unsteady return on the beat.

Imagining what a future with her husband might've been like left Yolanda with a familiar feeling. The folds in her brain had been carved by a river of the same shape. For so often had she imagined her son at eleven, at fourteen, at sixteen. And so, watching the dancers, she was reminded of what she never forgot, and reminded, too, of that other sudden absence: Daniel. She knew the police wanted to talk to her, maybe the army too; it was safer to stay here. But the boy might try and get in touch, might get to a phone. And if he did, there was only her. Must I go back? she asked herself. Being in Ciudad Victoria, away from everyone, gave her space to grieve. Except that it didn't feel like grief. It felt much lazier, looser-strung. Must I go back?

The dancers broke up and the women untied their long flowery skirts at the waist. Signora Blue Trousers leaned against her husband's shoulder while she delicately lifted first one wavering jeans-leg out of her flouncy skirt then the other.

Yolanda took off her glasses and folded the arms flat. Clip-clip. There was no rush. She still had a couple of minutes, she figured. She got up and wandered over to stand in front of the torrential wall.

8

A.A., B.A., C.A., D.A., E.A., F.A., H.A., J.A., I.A., and K.A. were leased light-industrial units on the Harmondsworth Industrial Estate. D.A. and J.A., however, were different from the other buildings in the crumbling, four-acre business park. D.A. and J.A. were surrounded by high steel fences topped by coils of razor wire. D.A. and J.A. were secured by electronic gates, uniformed guards and a kennel full of dogs.

Before Sodexo's refugee mega-prison opened at Harmondsworth (that families might be all locked up together for the first time since the Poor Law), and before Sodexo's dividends started City analysts wondering whether refugees might be bigger than dot.com, there was D.A. and J.A.

D.A. was a cramped 1920s building which had once been council offices. No one stayed in D.A. longer than it took to tape a crayon drawing of the last Queen of Estonia to the wall (next to Ogoni village, Albanian boyfriend, and red Ferrari). From here you would be ghosted to Belmarsh or Rochester, Campsfield, or Oakington, and then back again to Harmondsworth D.A., before Wackenhut took you to Heathrow. British Airways, whose tinted-glass offices overlooked the Harmondsworth Industrial Estate, had the monopoly on this lucrative human traffic; flying you out on a snake-head return to Kinshasa, Istanbul, Teheran, Ankara, or Bogota and delivering you safe into the hands of the security services in your country of origin. (From whom you had nothing to fear because we sold arms to them, so they couldn't be all bad.)

J.A. was a long, thin, pre-fabricated hut. If you went from D.A. to J.A. you might be here for a bit longer. (There was a small exercise yard in J.A.) But then again you might not. You never knew. Some men and women spent less time in J.A. than D.A. Five months or five minutes. You never knew. But usually a transfer across the light-industrial estate from D.A. to J.A. meant you'd be in detention for a bit longer.

Daniel watched a tall, blond, lone Ukrainian with a mighty scar on his forehead playing basketball in the sagging nets with a foam ball.

Daniel stood in front of the photocopied picture menu. Halal. Traditional British. Afro-Caribbean. Salad. It was still two hours before dinner.

Daniel bounced a tennis ball he had found. The tennis ball had a phone number written on it.

Daniel plucked and shredded leaves of bramble and chickweed and saw himself doing it.

A Boeing stormed out of Heathrow.

Daniel climbed on to the windowsill in his tiny room and looked at a cornfield through the bars. Fish stew and dumplings, he thought.

In Market Haven's police station parking lot Daniel had sat in the back of a Sodexo van, a Peugeot Boxer. He was in a cage. There was a bolted grille of bonded mesh between him and the rear doors, and another between him and the front seats. There were no side doors and the small windows were blacked out, too. After three hours he'd been joined in the cage by a Colombian. They didn't greet each other, didn't look at each other and didn't speak. Twenty miles later, the Colombian began out of nowhere: Every week I go to the police station and I sign the register of aliens. Every week for six months I do this. For six months! Today I go in and they tell me my application has been turned down, then they put me in handcuffs and throw me in this van. They don't let me go home and pack and collect my clothes, my money, my toothbrush, my soap, my address book, nothing. No, it's: "In the van! Now!"

He'd said nothing more for the rest of the ride.

Daniel looked in on the blacked-out, empty TV room. Azuma—his Angolan friend—must be in his room, thought Daniel. Yesterday his one other friend—a Colombian woman—had been ghosted to another prison. He would never see her again. He bounced his tennis ball in the hall. Azuma had told him that the tennis balls with writing on came from the demonstration last month . . .

They were climbing the walls—he'd explained to Daniel in "Spanugese"—and shouting out "What's your name?" And they were kicking the steel fence with their backs to it, making a big noise. We got a drum and marched in the corridor. Then they threw tennis balls with phone numbers and "What is your name?" written in many languages. I climbed up the fence far enough to shout out my name so they could visit. Then when they came I told them I was being removed without having seen a solicitor. No one had even heard my story. I told them they say I'm refused right to seek asylum because I've been in a safe, third country, just because the plane stopped in Germany.

Daniel had then broken a rule among the inmates and asked: Why did you have to leave?

Azuma had looked at him for a moment, but, seeming to allow the boy's age as an extenuating circumstance, had replied: It's never two sides fighting in a revolution, but three. I was fighting for the rebels but they were just as bad as the government . . . So the protesters get me a solicitor, but it's too late and I'm put on the plane. Last time they put me on a plane I took all my clothes off and so they had to bring me back. But this time I have two security men either side of me and chains on my wrists. The plane is all businessmen. But then, twenty rows ahead of me, this young man stands up. In a suit but he is not a businessman, just pretending. You can tell. He calls the steward over and says something. It looks like he's apologizing. She goes away to get another man. And then the young man makes a speech to all the passengers. He says he's making a protest because there is someone called Azuma Rambo on the plane who is being forcibly deported and he won't sit down until I'm taken off the plane. He looks round for me and our eyes meet. Me and this total stranger. He has big, beautiful eyes. And I see the stewardess tell him to sit down. But he stays on his feet. He stays on his feet! Then a male steward tells him to sit down. Then the pilot. He stays there with his hands behind his back quietly and politely telling them he won't. And then—*oh then!*—the captain says he can't fly the plane if someone is standing up. And so . . . and so I'm back here. But now I have the judicial review in six weeks.

Bueno! Daniel had said.

No, because soon they'll move me from here.

Why?

Because I tell people they have a right to a solicitor, a *right*. I give them phone numbers.

Daniel Salgado! called a guard from the office in the hall. Daniel went into the little office. The guard had a grey quiff and a black packet of Pall Malls in the chest pocket of his light-blue Burns Security shirt. Daniel tried to decipher the faded-blue tattoos on his forearms. The guard squinted through his cigarette smoke while he found the page he was looking for. He flattened the book out on the table top like it was never going to be used again, then met Daniel's eyes and said: Here.

Daniel read the Spanish phrase a sovereign-ringed finger was pointing at: Your removal order is for tomorrow.

At eight A.M. said the guard, holding up all the fingers not holding a fag. That's when you're removed. Eight.

Mexico?

The guard flipped over a page for the phrase he was looking for. Daniel read: Country of origin.

Daniel had five pounds forty left (there'd been a soda dispenser back in D.A.). He wondered who he had to phone. He only knew one person on the phone.

He walked around the exercise yard humming in broken snatches. Da, dum de . . . but the tune kept changing. He pictured the heavy-footed jig Oscar had danced in accompaniment to the phone-number song and remembered an ardent, forceful knee-bend and clicking of both thumbs which Oscar had done on the number twenty-one. *Veinti-uno . . . seis.* Daniel sang Oscar's little tune to himself. *Veinti-uno . . . tres, seis, ochenta, ocho, cero . . .*

He stood under the hooded pay phone in the dark hall.

Hola?

Yolanda?

Daniel! Daniel!

Yes.

Daniel, where are you?

England, but I'm going to be deported tomorrow.

Where to?

I don't know. Probably Mexico City.

Daniel, your father is still alive. He's in Seattle and he . . .

Yolanda tried to tell Daniel all the things she never had, but as Daniel listened to her voice all he could think about was that his arrival in Tonalacapan had killed Oscar.

I'm so sorry, I'm so sorry, Daniel sobbed. I'm so sorry, I'm so sorry! And crying ever louder, he hung up.

9

There's nothing you can take from me that's not been taken already. My feet and hands, maybe. That's about it.

You haven't answered my question, said Ilan coolly.

Yolanda examined the spotless grey linoleum and decided to ignore the question again. (It being: Who else helped Chano Salgado?)

I don't think you're going to arrest me, she said.

No? Ilan replied lazily.

At the trial you'll have to describe exactly what my role was and that will look bad on you.

What trial? Ilan let that hang for a few moments. Then he added: Plus I could just arrest you for anything.

You won't do that.

Why not? he asked.

Yolanda ignored the question. You won't do that . . . yet, she said. But you will do it later. To someone else.

How so? asked Ilan amused.

In time you will but not yet. Not now. If you did that sort of thing now you'd feel like you were doing wrong. But every day you stay in the job you will make a thousand little rationalizations. You only get to the head of an institution as much as the institution gets into your head. How much a part of it you become depends on how much a part of you it becomes. Whether it's the police or the PRI or—

Or the Frente Auténtico Trabaja—

—or PEMEX or the World Bank. One day you will tell yourself that you have to live in the real world.

I have to be flexible, yes. Flexibility, fluidity, the ability to respond to change—well, it just so happens that I think these are good things. And not being married to dogma, that's a good thing too—a necessity, in fact, in times of change.

Ah. But you can't be a bit pregnant and you can't be a bit flexible. There's one place where you are totally inflexible, and all your other little flexibilities will have to go the long way around it.

The law.

Ambition, said Yolanda and let *that* hang for a few moments. You want to get on in the world.

Again—a bad thing in your communist utopia. And also, interestingly enough, among goats. Does it not occur to you that I might want position so I can institute reform?

I know that's what you tell yourself. The next day you will talk about having to make unpopular decisions.

I can't imagine.

Or pragmatic decisions.

When will *that* day be?

And the day after that someone will be assassinated but you know they're guilty anyway, and the day after that day you will order them shot yourself.

We shall see.

We shall see. This is a process which will go on every day. But it can't be rushed.

In life things always take much longer than we think? Ilan asked her.

Yes.

You are wrong again.

Yolanda gets off the bus by the long straight road which leads from the highway to Tonalacapan. The Mayan woman and her cold-drink stall aren't here today.

Yolanda's slow picking steps stir puffs of white dust from the long road. Her green headscarf is folded back on her head and tucked into the arms of her large plastic glasses. For thirty minutes she walks her erect, impassive walk. Thirty yards from the phone shack, however, she hears the ringing and breaks into a sprint.

Daniel, *aiee* Daniel! Daniel, my love, she gasps. Don't hang up this time. Give me the number where you are. Stay there! I'll call you back.

On the Lower Clapton Road a phone rings in a cold, late-night phone box.

Hola, says Daniel.

Hola. At last. *Ay!*

I'm not going to be deported, Yola.

How? she asks, still gasping for breath.

There was a protest outside the prison-camp at the same time as a riot inside. And I escaped.

Are you safe?

Yes, yes.

Daniel, says Yolanda, listen. Your father is in Seattle . . . Watching the numbers click round on the meter, the phone operator keeps a mental running inventory of all the things she will have to do without to pay for this call, as she tells him all he needs to hear about his father, his mother, the pipeline and the past. Are they looking for you? she asks.

No.

But you escaped?

Yes, yes.

How did you escape?

Ay Yola, estuvo padre! Padrisimo! There's a demonstration outside so the guards start to lock us down. No phone calls . . .

Yolanda watches the numbers clicking round on the meter [bus fare, morning coffee].

. . . But my friend Azuma's only just got through to his lawyer after hours of trying. He's my friend and he's on the phone and it's his last hour to get a lawyer. If he doesn't he goes back to Angola.

Right, says Yola [return bus fare, electricity].

And then we see the guards dragging him off the phone. They've got him in a choke-hold and he's shouting that he can't breathe and then he can't shout at all. A little later we see ambulances and everyone says he's dead. And then everyone starts smashing up their rooms.

Did you?

Yes, and trying to get out into the exercise yard, and outside the protesters are drumming and climbing up on this fence where it dips forward over the camp. They're calling out "What's your name? What's your name?"

[washing powder, kerosene]

And they're kicking the fence like donkeys, and some of us scramble up on the roof, and I look out at this cornfield and our eyes meet—me and this woman—and we smile and she holds up a pair of bolt croppers and nods with her head which way to go and I drop down and follow her along, still on the inside . . .

[marigolds for Oscar's cross, beans, eggs]

Meanwhile the big chain fence collapses. A few prisoners run and the security guards chase them and they're soon caught. But where I've followed the woman, there's a huge crowd of people on top of a fence that hasn't collapsed and I go through the bottom where she cuts a hole and I get swallowed up in this crowd. Someone gives me a banner to hold, a backpack, sunglasses and a hat.

[next month's electricity]

And then this older protester with silver hair shouts to all the kids on the fence that it's two P.M. and the demonstration has to stop now because it's visiting time for the prisoners. And suddenly all the drums and whistles go quiet. Everyone quietly climbs off the fence, the guards are still running through the cornfield but I'm in this crowd of people just walking back through the fields and past the police.

[my job]

Will you phone me again? asks Yolanda.

Yes, yes.

I will tell your father you called next time he phones.

Yes.

Where are you now?

In London. In a school.

10

Built in 1899, Clapton Priory-Cavell Primary School had church windows, separate entrances for BOYS and GIRLS, and a carved-stone, open book on the lintel.

When, four months previously, the school had been closed down, local parents had occupied it for two weeks. Hackney Council had said: OK, we won't close it down. The parents had de-camped and Hackney Council had said: Tell a lie, we *are* going to close it down.

Schools, playgrounds, and nurseries were being handed over (with money) to the market. The crisis in state-run education had gone on too long and the private sector was charging to the rescue like the Seventh Cavalry to Wounded Knee.

Thanks to the private sector, exciting educational changes were afoot. Where state schools had once been drafty noisy places full of demoralized teachers and Ritalin kids, free-market school build-ings were dynamic centres of excellence where, in place of chilly assembly halls, leaky classrooms, and crumbling playgrounds, there now arose new facilities more suited to the high-tech age: IT con-sultants, video distributors, a model agency, a design warehouse, digital printers, loading bay, receptionists, and, best of all, no shriek-ing kids.

For a fortnight, the security contractor's modish designer hoard-ing had hung on the chainlink fence to announce just who'd be doing the bricking in and the boarding up (and also to suggest that this bricking in and boarding up would be performed with a certain flair). Then Monica and a dozen locals had occupied the school full time, and so had begun four months of eating at tiny tables while sitting on tiny plastic chairs. The *Hackney Gazette* called them squatters, but it was an occupation: they ran a nonprofit day-care centre, cyber-café, youth club, nursery, samba classes and held a jumble sale.

Four months on, however, the final eviction order had come. Monica was weary of moving on again. She was tired of living in squats (even though it was an occupation). Plus it was all coming on top of another problem for Monica: she worked as a care assistant for Down's adults, but expected to be getting laid off any week now.

Monica and Ramona were setting up the sound system and the turntables. A benefit for the Legal Defence Monitoring Group for June 18 prisoners.

I got my compo, said Monica. From when I was knocked off my bike?

How much?

Four hundred pounds, said Monica.

They settled?

They always settle when they find out you're on legal aid, 'cos they know you can go on for ever.

What you gonna spend it on?

Lorraine's keeping a room for me. In Hebden Bridge.

What, PGA Lorraine?

No, Used-to-Live-in-Manchester Lorraine.

What, Gasboard Lorraine?

Autonomous Centre Lorraine . . .

Oh, you mean CAGE Lorraine?

Yeah, Lorraine.

Oh, *Lorraine* Lorraine!

Yeah, Lorraine. But I can't go yet because Bridgeway's just been given another few months.

How come?

They shut down another Special Needs instead. So we've got, like, three months more they reckon.

What's gonna happen with the residents after?

They'll be welcomed home by their loving families.

It was to the Clapton Priory Occupation that Monica had taken Daniel. Ramona (who if there'd been another Ramona might have been called Bilbao Ramona, but as there wasn't was just Ramona) was staying here.

Daniel had been helping with the lights. But there was nothing left for him to do and he was just wandering about on his own. Watching Daniel look at noticeboards he couldn't read, the women saw the shadow hanging over him.

Does he want to go home? asked Monica quietly.

He says his dad's in Seattle, said Ramona.

Not Mexico?

Well, I'm not even sure Daniel's from Mexico.

Why?

Just when I asked him where he was from he kind of thought about what answer to give.

But his dad's in Seattle?

Yeah.

Does he know where?

Where in Seattle?

Yeah.

I don't know.

Daniel! Monica called out. You dancing later?

Will you have a dance? Ramona translated.

No.

Why not?

I can't dance.

Everyone can dance.

Not me.

We'll teach you, said Monica.

She says we'll teach you, said Ramona.

But I don't want to dance if I can't dance well.

He don't wanna dance bad, translated Ramona.

Tell him he'll be dancing good style, said Monica.

But Daniel had already sped away into an office where, relieved to be ignored, he watched someone trying to fix the motherboard of a donated computer.

One evening a week later, Monica and Ramona took Daniel to the attic of an end terrace in a narrow dusty side street in Aldgate. The three of them arrived halfway through the meeting. Copying what the women did, Daniel placed a sample square of carpet on top of a milk crate and sat down.

On a horizontal plane, where once there'd been a ceiling, hung a midair relay of strip lights. There were narrow, arched windows and a dormant fireplace. A triangular road sign, also balanced on milk crates, made a low table. Steam rose from a battered kettle over a tin tray holding veggie cakes, a damp bag of clumpy sugar, chamomile and Somerfield tea bags.

The (non-smoking) meeting was being addressed by two Colombians from a touring delegation, trying to coordinate an international, grassroots resistance against Plan Colombia. Both Colombians were exhausted by ten European capitals in four weeks, sleeping on sofas, bus-station benches and train seats. Having finished speaking, the Colombians sprawled on a dingy futon, leaned their backs against a rickety banister and fondly remembered the coffee they'd had in Milan.

Daniel hadn't known why he'd been brought along until he'd heard the Colombians speak his language. He was looking forward to talking with his fellow Americans after the meeting. A few minutes later, however, both Colombians got up, made their farewells and left. Daniel looked at Ramona, but she was looking over the minutes of what she'd missed. He wondered if he'd see the two Colombians again. He hoped they'd come back later. Meanwhile the meeting continued (as meetings do).

He sat on the futon just vacated and nudged the two-bar electric heater toward him with his feet. Now the meeting wasn't being trans-lated into Spanish, he was bored and cast his mind back to that . . .

He'd been sitting in Monica's windowless room in Clapton Priory, while she and Ramona practised mixing on two turntables. Monica had slid down everything except the bass and had pulled Daniel to his feet by the hands. Ramona had stood up too, saying: We all stand in a line, side by side. OK. Don't move, no one move anything. Don't move at all Daniel.

Daniel was pleased not to move.

This is the hips, Ramona had said, bahm bahm bahm bahm bahm. Just the hips, don't move anything else. No feet, no shoulders. Just the hips. Daniel had swayed his arms by his side like a tranquillized long-term patient. Just the hips, Daniel, nothing else. Yes, better.

This wasn't too bad, he'd thought, just moving your hips. Not too bad. But then the women had started swaying their arms around and Daniel had got embarrassed.

No, no I don't want to learn, he'd said, wishing they'd turn the music off.

OK, Ramona had said. That's all for today.

Later, alone in Monica's room (she was sleeping in with Ramona to give him space), he'd put a gabba-techno cassette in her sausage-shaped ghetto blaster. He had done hips, done shoulders and had tried—and failed—to copy a little heel-shuffle thing he'd seen a man do at the benefit the night before. Then there'd come a knock at the door and he'd been brought here. He'd have another go at that heel shuffle tonight, he thought.

Meanwhile the meeting continued (as meetings do).

We could take something from the benefit for the flight ticket.

How much is it?

A few hundred.

Do you know about this thing where if you check in at Dublin you don't have to go through US Immigration . . . ?

Yeah, but you still go through US Immigration, you just do it in Ireland, said Monica. I think it's best to fly to Vancouver straight from London.

Why isn't Daniel being included in this discussion?

Hearing his own name mentioned Daniel looked at Ramona, who leaned toward him and said: What we're talking about is that quite a few of us are going to Seattle, and we're trying to work out a way to get you there, too. If that's what you want . . .

That's what I want, said Daniel, nodding vigorously like a boxer assuring the referee he can go on.

And we think, Ramona told him, it's gonna be safest to go to Canada first.

The meeting continued. Every now and then, if they got ahead of her, Ramona held up the right-angled thumb-and-forefinger translation sign. As Daniel listened to Ramona, he watched the different speakers.

I've got a passport for Jack, said Tessa. He's almost thirteen but the picture was taken when he was nine. And he's dark.

Is it still valid? asked Monica.

Till next year, said Tessa.

But we'd need you to go, too, said Monica. It'd look more likely.

I can't go into the US, said Tessa.

Why not?

M42.

But you're all right for Canada?

Oh yeah.

So you don't have to get into the US, said Monica. You could just have a few days in Vancouver and then come back again. Ramona held up her thumb and forefinger while Daniel whispered in her ear. She nodded and told the group: Daniel's worried that it would mean her leaving her son on his own.

Can't you leave him with someone? asked Monica.

Not at the moment, said Tessa.

OK.

Well, I can leave Jack with someone for, like one night. I mean, he wouldn't mind if I was just gone for the day. I mean, if I went to Canada for the day and came straight back . . .

A day return? asked Monica.

Yeah, he'll be all right with that.

But would you want to?

Yeah. Fuck it. Just so long as I ain't paying.

Best thing then is, began Monica, if we all get tourist-looking return tickets, like three weeks, and Tessa changes hers for the flight back. You sure?

Yeah, said Tessa.

All right, said Monica. So, Tessa gets to go on a day return to Canada!

11

Chano sat down on the stoop of the Yesler Way hostel next to Baker, a cranky addict with tired movements and an energetic, blown-gasket voice.

Hey, brotherman, said Baker, his black leather box-jacket creaking as he turned, you living on Skid Row now.

Yeah, I know.

No, no, I mean this is really Skid Row. The *original* Skid Row. Used to be its actual name on the street signs: Skid Row. Written.

No, no, there's lots of Skid Rows.

But, you see, this was the first, the *original* Skid Row.

How come?

Skid Row? Time was they'd slide the tree trunks, logs and shit down from the forest, keep this road sluiced and slippy so they'd slide down easy. Plus you'd be poor anyway and drinking. You couldn't cross the street for falling over, you be covered in shit and shit and people took one look at you and said: That man living on Skid *Row!*

Thank you for letting me know about that.

Yeah-heh! This be where you is now, *hermano*. Skeeed Row! Skid *Row!* And when you reach the bottom the only one way you going is *down!* Ha ha! Down, my friend, down. Vvooosh!! And you know that!

I hear you.

You ain't a hunnert per cent safe till you get to Canada, hermano. Not a hunnert percentile, you ain't.

Chano got up and walked back down the steps. He shared the Yesler Way basement room with three other illegals from Guatemala. One of the Guatemalans spoke very bad English but insisted on the conversational practice, which limited all of their words to Old Testament proverbialism or Mexican *dichos*.

A dollar goes fast from the hand in Seattle.

When they know you're illegal they cut wages in half.

The free extra coffee at the Turf Bar is worth a kettle in the room.

Any fool can spend money, but it takes a wise man to send it home.

This oddly formalized dialect amused Chano and he joined in happily. You are not a hunnert per cent safe until you get to Canada, he announced.

Working *again*? asked Baker when Chano reemerged in his coat. What you doing *this* time?

Washing up at Virginia Mason.

Later, *hombre*, said Baker.

Later Baker.

Washing up at Virginia Mason. And scraping the leftovers (that don't look too forked) into his own doggie bag and hoping they don't have SIDA. Filling the glass-washing machine. Hand-washing pots and pans, plates and cutlery. Mopping the floor. Getting the stainless steel sink and counters all shiny and dry just in time for one of the waiters to find another few dirty glasses and ashtrays which means it'll have to be wiped down and polished all over again, just because of those few bubbles like standing mercury which the boss goes on about. (Unless, of course, Chano simply carries the glasses and ashtrays out to the alley dumpster.)

Three days a week at the Virginia Mason and two at a diner on Broadway. So here I am again, he thought, among steam and steel.

The Virginia Mason on "Pill Hill" was half-hospital half-hotel. The hotel bit was for relatives visiting patients. The two halves of the building were joined at the restaurant.

Chano looked through the serve hatch while he waited for Luis whose shift was next. He watched a couple eating blueberry muffins. They were both in wheelchairs with tall steel poles like bumper cars, from which each had a blood-plasma bag hanging.

A hand on his back, Chano looked round. Luis joined him at the hatch, studied the scene and said: Just put the blueberry muffins in the drip-feed. Cut out the middle man. Put the muffins in the blender and then just pour that blueberry shit straight down the veins, man.

Chano grinned. Now Luis was here he could go.

A mile from the steel kitchen a lemon-greasy smell still haunted Chano right up to the door of the Turf Bar in Pike Place Market. The door opened on to the smells of cigarette smoke, fried sausages, coffee, eggs, ketchup, damp clothes, newspapers, and corn hash. It was as warm and smoky inside as it was cold and sea-misty out.

A wide corridor with a pay phone led to the toilets at the back of the Turf Bar. The corridor had an independent existence from the café. One wall of it was the tinted glass of the pawn-shop jewellers next door. The corridor was, to different people, a walk-in office, a shelter, a meeting place, a bazaar, a money mart, and a needle exchange. Its muddy squares of cardboard soaked up the street life.

The Turf Bar itself was busy, its fat, bright-red leatherette bench seats all taken. Drinking his coffee on a stool by the bare-brick wall, Chano watched the patient Filipina waitress attempt to reason with a three-hour coffee hobo. She looked back toward the kitchen and pulled a hopeless face. At which appeal, a small, hassled, bald man with glasses came out from the kitchen in apron and shirt sleeves.

Chano listened to the Filipino's reluctant pleading. Three hours you been here now, the cook reminded the hobo.

The hobo said nothing.

D'ya wanna 'nother coffee?

[Nothing.]

It's lunchtime now. We need the tables.

The bearded hobo gave a growl-grunt which could have meant anything: leave me alone / I'll just be five minutes / I've haven't quite finished / OK, OK, I'm going / I'll buy another one / all of the above / something else.

The cook hesitated, wondering for a second whether the man could speak. Do you wanna 'nother coffee?

[Nothing.]

The short, bald cook gave up and disappeared inside the kitchen.

Chano crossed to the pay phone in the corridor to try once again to get hold of his cousin in New Mexico. The cousin had once lived in

Seattle and Chano was hoping he might still know someone here or in Yakima who could get him a decent job. Chano didn't recognize the Spanish-speaking voice on the machine as his cousin's but left a message saying he'd call again. He still had some credits left. He clinked the quarters in his palm and felt the silver dollars through his pocket. Should I phone Yola now? he wondered. Do I want to get bad news here? Turning his back on the busy corridor Chano gazed at all the numbers scrawled on the wall in hasty pencil and ink. They'd all risked it. Why shouldn't he? He put in all his coins and dialled the *caseta telefónica.*

Hola? asked Yolanda.

Hola, compadre.

Chano! Daniel is in London.

He phoned you?

Yes. He's in school!

How did he know the number?

Oscar's tune!

Oscar's tune, repeated Chano. Oscar's tune.

He's phoned twice. I was praying you'd phone last week. But now I'm glad you didn't—well, not at first—because the first time he called he said he was being deported.

But not now?

No. He's not being deported. He's in school!

He's in school?

Yes!

Is he legal?

He must be—

He's not being deported?

No, Chano, it really sounds like he can stay because— [loud pips were followed by the callous landlady of AT&T].

And you? Chano continued after the recorded interruption.

I was arrested but no charge. Not yet.

Will you stay?

I'm going to my sister's in Ciudad Victoria. She's having a baby. I'll get her job on the toll booth.

Suerte.

Cuidado.

The connection ended, Chano listened awhile to what was left; a silence deep as the sleep of underground cables told him how far he was from home.

Standing in the Turf Bar's one toilet cubicle, Chano took off a brown boot and lifted the groggy insole. He prised out and unfolded the damp cash, then counted how much he had left from what Evan had given him. You ain't a hunnert per cent safe till you gets to Canada, hermano. Daniel was in England now. In London. It might be safe now to risk moving through *el norte*. Canada was not far, but he still felt he'd be safer with his cousins in New Mexico.

Chano walked back to his stool by the wall in time to see the small, bald cook come out of the kitchen again.

D'you wanna 'nother coffee? the cook demanded, this time with a tone of real ultimatum. Conversation fell in the café. Everyone was watching. The short, bald cook placed both hands on the table top and brought his face close to the hobo's. D'you wanna 'nother coffee? he repeated louder still.

The hobo fiddled in his filthy clothes, searching his pockets or perhaps just scratching himself. But then he opened a filthy hand to reveal a filthy dollar. Aggrrugger . . . ccoggfffah! he said.

The cook smiled and nodded, as pleased and polite as if the tramp had said: Why, my good man, I think I *will* have that extra coffee since this *is* my wedding day! With relief in his voice he shouted out: Coffee table two! At which the Turf Bar resumed its contented hum and whir.

One Sunday a week and a half later, Chano was sitting in the Washington State Trade and Convention Center. Above the high windows was a blank Seattle sky the colour of wax paper. Roller shutters sealed the weekday sandwich shops. Homeless Chicanos, mute and solitary as monks, were dotted around the first two floors of the Convention Center. Each sat on his own. Not wanting to get done for vagrancy, each had his blanket rolled tight and neat like a kit inspection.

In a few days' time this same building would become one of the most expensively defended, highest-security places on earth, when it would host the Third Ministerial of the World Trade Organization. It would be full of loud trade delegates (all of whom were experts on the complexities of global economics). But on this damp Sunday it sheltered lone, silent migrants (none of whom knew anything about the complexities of global economics). For Chano and the others on this damp, sea-misty Sunday, however, the Washington State Trade and Convention Center was simply somewhere dry where you could sit down for a few hours.

Chano was still debating which way to go. He hadn't so far been able to get his New Mexico cousin on the phone. So maybe San Francisco . . . I'll try my cousin once more, Chano thought. Failing that I could just get on a bus to San Francisco. Once I'm down in the Mission, someone on Caesar Chavez Street will know someone who knows someone, or who just knows where to go . . .

Chano's eyes rested on the escalator's blind, relentless teeth meshing and meshing and meshing and meshing . . .

12

They'd taken a bus from Vancouver International down Highway 99 to White Rock. In darkness they now walked across the big lawns of Peace Arch Park. A full moon was moored out at sea. They could hear the Pacific groaning, pinned down by Point Roberts and San Juan Island. Daniel smelled sea air stirring the dark maples and ferns. He was dressed for *pasado al otro lado* as a rich kid: baggy skate pants with a long chain looping from front to back pocket, black Marilyn Manson T-shirt under an open tartan shirt, spiky hair, eyeliner and a studded wristband.

There's the Peace Arch, said Ramona. The huge, free-standing doorway in the middle of nowhere troubled Daniel. The Peace Arch was bottom-lit and its white stone appeared to glow. Two flags—US and Canadian—flew from its roof. It's best we stay in the light under the arch for a while like tourists, she added, in case someone's looking.

The Peace Arch is a monument to the longest, unguarded border in the world (from the Bay of Fundy to the Strait of Juan de Fuca).

Chiselled into its portico is the legend May These Gates Never Close, after an 1817 agreement between Britain and President Monroe. (He who closed the gate on Mexico so the USA could steal half its land and plunder the rest.)

Ramona sat on the open, black iron gate under the white arch. In hokey symbolism the cement-fixed gate was impossible to close, the hanging chains impossible to lift and a giant open padlock impossible to lock.

Blaine's just through those trees, said Monica.

How far? asked Ramona,

Well, I think Peace Arch Park sort of *is* Blaine. It's like a city park.

Monica grinned at Daniel, who looked away and frowned. He'd worked out what was troubling him. The Peace Arch Memorial reminded him of the free-standing doorway in the mural in the Uniones hall. The boy looked at dark, rustling bushes and trees, where the puma-dog-men of law and order were lying in wait.

OK, let's walk slowly, said Ramona, sliding down from the black gate, but walk straight toward Blaine as if we're just going home.

They began sauntering south and out of the light. As he stepped on to the tingling turf of Estados Unidos, Daniel feared that at any moment he might, without warning, find himself flying up into the night in loose, ghost clothes, leaving no sign of his existence save a pile of everyday clothes, which were never his anyway, next to an ornamental flower bed which he'd never seen in the light, and whose colours he'd never known.

13

Friday morning, riding the downtown Metro trolley bus Chano's head drummed gently on the misty window. He wondered if the young woman at the back would ever stop ranting. He was trying to think. New Mexico direct? Or San Francisco? He had one more shift to do at the Broadway diner before he collected his pay, before he got on the Greyhound. But sitting back-seat centre was twenty-year-old Wyconda Holcomb from Mobile, Alabama. (Though her name was unknown to Chano Salgado, she was to become a local public figure over the next few days . . . For Wyconda, who was working her way through Seattle Central Community College by doing late and earlies at Taco Time, had taken it upon herself to testify about the World Trade Organization to the captive tram audience every ride.) As she sat on the back seat this morning, she was in mid-flow—she was always in mid-flow—loudly testifying: Who suffers from it? The water suffers, the air suffers, the earth suffers! Who benefits? The WTO! They're all about money!

Chano smudged a circle of mist and filth with the flat of his hand. The window became even more opaque—the exact opposite of what he'd intended. San Francisco and then maybe on to New Mexico? People got on and got off, but Wyconda ran on as charged and incessant as the blue-sparking overhead tram cables.

They giving us genetically engineered foods and using us like guinea pigs! You been had! You been took! You don't how much of what you're eating is already contaminated with GM. Why not? Why don't you know? The WTO! They won't let you know what's in the can! They won't let the label say GM. That's outlawed. Who says so? WTO!

Chano got off at the end of the line—the Transit Station on Ninth and Pine. He checked the bus times south. He'd go to San Francisco, and from there maybe on to New Mexico. Yes . . .

Walking from Transit Station to Broadway, and knowing that he was soon to leave this city, Chano experienced a profound sense of disconnection, just as his brother had in the Seattle Airport cab line. Except that where Evan had seen the future as it would soon look without him, Chano experienced the invisibility of the paperless, spectral migrant and saw the present as it looked without him.

At his industrial-sized sink in the Broadway diner, Chano heard rumours of a sudden sunny day and kept craning his head to look out of the window.

A five-minute break. Chano emerged into warm, bright sunlight in his white apron and white hygienic cap. He'd been looking forward to this brief, snatched moment for now he could think. Standing outside the diner, he set himself to decide between New Mexico or San

Francisco. He scratched his moustache which, though it had grown back, still itched at its repotting in a new country and was not as broad as before.

He sipped his coffee and felt the sun on his face. Broadway was, he noticed, closed to traffic. Chano was just wondering why this should be when he heard a samba band playing. He looked up and down the deserted street but couldn't see where the music was coming from. What he saw next, however, made his jaw drop: coming over the brow of the hill was a troop of Mexican Day of the Dead puppets. White skeletons rose on towering poles. Bare white skulls brushed traffic-light cables above the street. In the warm breeze black crepe blew back from stovepipe hats. Hinged jaw bones swung as if they were talking or laughing or singing or chanting.

Chano stepped back onto the sidewalk to avoid a police motorbike. Behind the Day of the Dead *giganticas,* a procession was filling the street. A forest of triangular, light-green cardboard conifers passed the diner followed by an army of coral-blue sea turtles. A stiltwalker in humbug trousers bowed elaborately to Chano and handed him a leaflet. Male and female Radical Cheerleaders in conscious pompoms and red ra-ra skirts chanted:

Wake up!
Rise up!
Wake up!
Rise up!
Wake up!
Rise up!

A butterfly boy with hinged wings of tasseled yellow silk was overtaken by the Naked Lesbian Avengers with black duct tape criss-crossing their nipples and slogans written on their bare flesh, which Chano found himself too shy to read. Followed the Rap Wagon, a white van with a sound system blasting hip-hop breakbeats and two rappers walking behind its open back doors, holding mikes and heaping lyrical dozens on the rigged economy. Followed swirling flags in yellow, red, or green, each with a single word on them. Insurrection. Imagine. Revolution. Followed the drums and the black and green flags of the Anti-Fascist Marching Band. In face masks and furry black fezzes they drilled in four straight lines, pounding their samba behind windmilling semaphore flags.

Chano looked over the leaflet which the humbug stiltwalker had handed down to him:

CITY-WIDE WALKOUT
of workers and students against the World Trade Organization

[to get involved in the organizing of this walkout call 706-6250 or go to http://walkoutlist.com and sign up]

Join workers and students in shutting down the city during the WTO's meeting of 3,000 unelected, unaccountable, corporate-backed delegates November 29 to December 3, 1999, in downtown Seattle. The WTO has the authority to overrule any national law and community standard anywhere in the world in the name of profits, and is using it. If you don't want minimum-wage laws destroyed, your right to organize taken away, child labor to return to this nation or your school to be completely run by corporations; then call in sick, walkout, refuse to show up, or strike!

WE ARE THE CITY WE CAN SHUT IT DOWN !
NOVEMBER 30, 1999

[then join the mass demonstration and direct action downtown from 8 A.M. until it's over]

Please copy and re-distribute

The old activist didn't read the leaflet as if it were in any way addressed to him. Instead Chano set to working out the politics of those who had written it, first by critiquing the type of language used, next by judging the analysis of the WTO. At length he decided that it was, all in all, a good leaflet produced by a large, non-hierarchical, autonomous grouping with reformist leanings. And with that he had no further use for it whatsoever.

One of the chefs came out to see what was going on. Chano handed him the leaflet, emptied the dregs of his coffee into the gutter and went back to work, with the air of someone who's seen something mildly diverting on his coffee break, like a good argument between two drivers.

14

Daniel stood in front of a giant map and warmed his hands on a smooth paper cup of steaming rosehip tea. The map had been stuck to three trestle tables standing on their hind legs and was drawn large enough to make sense to a few hundred people sitting on the floor. This early in the day, however, Daniel had the map all to himself.

Seattle had been divided into thirteen different pie slices—one slice for each cluster of affinity groups. But for now, Daniel was just trying to fix the street plan in his head. He blew on his rosehip tea, took one step back and studied the giant map. Downtown Seattle was, he figured, a box. The sides of the box were the waterfront to the left and Interstate 5 to the right. This way up, the top of the box was Denny Way. Bottom of the box (he crouched, his finger dropping after him) was Yesler Way. He blew on his rosehip tea again.

Despite having come so far to be in Seattle, he was not searching for his father, or at least not yet. Daniel found he had to keep giving himself reasons why this should be so, why he was deferring his search. He told himself that an army has to dig in and secure its position. Or he told himself that he was like someone cracking a code who first of all has to let the numbers gather in all their confusion before the next step, that of finding a pattern, can begin. There was, however, another reason why he was delaying his search, but one for which the boy had no words and no analogies. To begin the search now was to admit how lost he was because it would mean leaving Monica and Ramona. It was to face the moment, before he had to, when either they would go back to London and leave him here, or— if his search failed—perhaps take him back to London with them, which would mean he'd never find his father.

No longer studying the map, Daniel's eyes strayed to all the streets outside of the downtown box. They were legion. Riding the Metro with his English friends his spirit had quailed at the size and sprawl of this city where millions upon millions lived, and he knew in his soul that he had no more chance of finding his father here than in that other city, London. He sipped his rosehip and wandered off around the Convergence Center.

The Convergence Center at 420 East Denny Way had at different times in its history been factory, nightclub, storage depot and warehouse. Now it was headquarters of the Direct Action Network. Different training sessions were going on in little rooms off the main warehouse: blockades, first aid, communication, and how to get arrested. (Daniel glimpsed two rows paired off like a *pasodoble.*)

He passed through a dense crush of bodies in the tight corridor which led from the main warehouse to the front room. Damp coats, muddy boots, and salvage couches gave the front room a musty, thrift-store tang, which mingled with the smell of spicy veggie-burgers. Steam rose from samovar and rosehip tea tureen, its giant steel ladle clanging dully against the sides. Two blue busts of Elvis stood on a ledge, under the legend ELVIS SEZ—PRAY FOR REVOLUTION. The walls of the action station were covered in printed briefings, city-maps and handwritten notices. A big, bold, printed, laminated hoarding greeted everyone who came in through the front door:

NO DRINK
NO SMOKING
NO DRUGS
NO GUNS

Thus safe from the attentions of Puff Daddy, several hundred sleeping bags were unrolled on the concrete floor each night.

We, uh, ideally want to have one trained legal observer for every cluster of affinity groups, said a woman with short blonde hair.

In the meetings, announcements tended to be flat and practical, speakers were offhand, informal, and downbeat. (This is a feature of direct action groups which distinguishes them from the "organized left": the speech is not the be all and end all.)

Um . . . oh, and . . . and there's a sheet here, put together with the legal team . . . uh, oh Mani, can you . . . you'd better . . .

She tailed off, there was some confused muttering and the mike was passed through a few hands to an El Salvadorean in a knitted rasta hat. He half rose, took the mike, sank down on one knee and began speaking in Spanish. This is a sheet, he said, flagging a piece of paper.

It's called (he turned it toward him and translated) "Legal Rights and Immigration Consequences Concerning Participation in Direct Action." It's written in English but come see me at the end if you are a non-US citizen and worried about your legal status.

After the meeting Daniel waited until the Latino with the rasta hat was on his own.

Que onda . . . ? Daniel greeted him.

Jesus! How old are *you?*

I'm not legal.

Hi, I'm Mani. A paint-can lid was being hammered down a few yards away.

I wanted to know about what you were talking about . . . ?

Eh?

I wanted—

Let's go somewhere quieter, said Mani.

Five minutes later, Daniel stood watching his new friend get fitted for the lockdown. Mani's arms were encased up to the elbow in PVC pipes which were then wrapped in silver duct tape. He rested one pipe-arm on an oil drum and, while the silver duct tape was coated in tar, translated for Daniel the words which were painted on a board leaning against a steel pillar: JAIL SOLIDARITY—TACTICS—STAY IN CUSTODY BY REFUSING TO GIVE YOUR NAME / ADDRESS AND BY REFUSING TO SIGN A CITATION.

15

Monica was leaning over a leaflet-strewn table reading a pamphlet which Ramona's black bloc had produced. Ramona hovered impatiently on the other side of the table.

The leaflet argued that while the cops were busy clearing non-violent blockaders from strategic intersections, the streets would be free for fluid black-bloc formations to take direct action against property, and rejected the last of the Direct Action Network's four-point guidelines. To Ramona the other three were all harmless enough, stuff like "We will use no violence, verbal or physical against any person," but not point 4, which read: "We will not destroy property." As Monica looked up, Ramona said: This had already been called for as a day of action long before DAN were involved.

Yeah, but they're the ones who have done all the organizing, all the work, all the teach-ins—

But they don't have the right, said Ramona, to say *you can't do this, you have to do that*. Who are they to say no property damage?

For *one day*!!! Only for one day!

Yeah, but it's a pretty crucial fucking day!

For one day only. We've got the numbers. That's the particular strategy agreed on—

Who by?

—for this particular day.

So, OK—some of us happen to share the view that passive resistance isn't enough.

Yeah, but they've agreed—

Not with us.

It's just the more effective tactic on the day.

Effective for what?

Peacefully blockading the streets with masses and masses of people, said Monica, is just going to be a more effective way of shutting down the WTO.

And then what? asked Ramona. What's the WTO? It's just one head of the hydra. And as long as this is just about the WTO, then it's just reformist.

Well, all in good time, you know! This ain't that day yet, and if you were really serious about revolution—

Sssshhh!!! ordered a woman in a floppy beany hat. There's a meeting going on here!

Monica and Ramona ceased their debate, and, for want of anything else to do, listened to the meeting.

The City of Seattle, Beany Hat was now saying to a group seated on the floor, has always had a long tradition of mass arrests. Mass actions always equal mass arrests. So the aim is to clog up the courts and prisons system so they just can't process us all. Now, this civil disobedience workshop is to show how to go limp when dragged away—

I think it's important, suggested Monica, to have something about de-arresting as well.

Will you just *sit down* and *shut up!* shouted Beany Hat.

Monica looked round to find Ramona smirking at her as if to say I told you so.

Just shy of the drizzle, Monica and Ramona sat outside the Convergence Center on the hand rail of the porch.

I dunno, said Monica, maybe it's just how they do things here. A different country, cops with guns, you know, and this is the protest culture that has emerged here.

Will you just *sit down* and *shut up!* said Ramona.

16

Couldn't you get none?

No, said Allotment Mark.

What's that? asked Monica joining the group.

Campden powder.

You couldn't get none? she asked.

No, said Mark.

Fuck.

I went to like ten chemists and there's none on the shelves anywhere. I know someone who's got some maddox and she's gonna let me have some. Maddox is pretty effective against tear gas but I don't know if it works with pepper spray.

But it's not Campden powder, though, said Monica.

I know, said Mark.

They were sitting at a long, off-peak table in the Church of Elvis Café next door to the Convergence: Bookfair Helga, Allotment Mark, Pete Pete, Twenty-Minute Dean, Birmingham Sarah, Ramona, Mexico Daniel, his new friend Mani, and Tat-List Monica.

What's Campden powder? asked Mani.

It's the bollocks, said Mark. It's sodium metabisulphite mixed with five parts water.

But you couldn't get none?

No.

And so they discussed instead the relative, anti-teargas merits of vinegar, baking soda, Visine, Optrex, and milk.

They've taken all the gas masks off the shelves, said Monica, but there was a fella giving out swimming goggles to everyone at the Mickey D's action today, so I picked up seven. And I got nail clippers for those plastic Kwik-cuffs.

We need a call sign for if we get split up, said Mark.

Palace Pier? Twenty-Minute Dean suggested. But will that be all right with Daniel? Ask him if he wants us to say something Spanish instead and we'll all have a go.

Ramona went into conference with Daniel and when their heads parted, he said: Palliss Peeyah! Everybody clapped and cheered and Daniel grinned.

The next day, Tuesday, November 30, the World Trade Organization would begin its week-long Millennium Round. The same day would also be the culmination of all the *StopWTOround* printouts left in pub-function rooms and community centres, and of every WTO teach-in, and every workshop on nonviolent direct action in every town hall and every squatted space. All had come to converge on one strategy in one place and at one time.

The strategy was this. On Tuesday morning five thousand delegates would be leaving their hotels on their way to the Washington State Trade and Convention Center. Blockades by fifty thousand people—helped by processions all starting from different points in the city—would try to stop them getting there and so shut down the World Trade Organization.

17

El Mexicano! called a voice.

Hi Baker, Chano replied, and joined him sitting on a doorstep next to the Turf Bar.

You not working today? asked Baker, his words fleeing before a coughing fit.

No, said Chano when Baker had stopped coughing. Not today.

Together they watched the Pike Place Market passersby. Two young men and a woman walked by in hooded tops and NO WTO button badges. One wore a yellow rainproof poncho with Seattle 99—Protest of the Century printed on the front. Baker took it badly, the sight of these hopeful youths who thought the world could be changed; took it very badly.

Someone, said Baker in a loud voice they could hear, better tell these protesters to *stay off my block*—'cos I don't want to go to the *trouble* of *raising my arm* to *shoot* you!

The unfixable hopelessness of all he'd ever seen had made Baker choose addiction. It seemed a good way of, if not killing time, then at least blunting its edge. But what if there were nothing in nature which said things were for ever and always hopeless? What then of the choices Baker and Chano had made?

It was two weeks since Chano had sat in the Convention Center, two weeks since he'd checked the bus times and ticket prices to New Mexico at the Transit Station. But still he hadn't left, and still he worked at the Virginia Mason.

He was in a strange limbo. Every time he'd phoned his cousin Hector in Abiquiu, New Mexico he'd only gotten the answering machine. He could just get on a bus anyway, he told himself. But there was something so forlorn about making a two-day bus trip to nowhere definite that it would, he secretly feared, crush him and break his heart. He didn't consciously admit this fear. Instead he told himself that he was curious about this so-called Protest of the Century. He would leave after the protests. But herein was another, yet darker secret he kept from himself. He was hoping to see this Protest of the Century fail. Its failure would confirm a view of universal hopelessness. And if hopelessness were universal then that would make his blind bus journey less heartbreaking, less crushing, because it would be just another routine event in the common lot of humankind; no more, no less forlorn or lost than what anyone else was doing in this dispensation.

In his political thinking, therefore, Chano had achieved the double: pessimism of the intellect and pessimism of the will. Gramsci would now be slapping that high-domed forehead of his, and Dona, his foster mother, would be wanting words as well. Except . . .

Hope might have survived even his own experience, had it just been his own. But the same things were going on in too many other places that he'd heard about. Was he not then, in Dona's own regimen, just adapting what he already knew? Chano and Marisa had, for example, named their son after Daniel Ortega, in topical, hopeful homage to Nicaragua's Sandanistas. In the year of Marisa's assassination, the Imperium had reached a new impunity in its terrorizing of Nicaragua, when it had simply vetoed the United Nations resolution calling upon all countries to uphold international law. And Chano knew why. Just as everyone knew why. No point being the Roman Empire if you were gonna let the Carthaginians set up their own little tribunals here and there. You had the shield technology, they didn't.

Chano had also seen how, whenever things came to a head, capitalism could always coopt a movement's reformists and isolate its radicals. Or else it could just start a foreign war. Yes, he could keep telling himself that the billions spent on corporate propaganda and repression were testament to the power people had. It was even true. But still the tyranny prevailed. And all he'd seen in his own life had convinced him that private power was something for which people as yet had no strategy to overthrow.

And so Chano would stay to watch the defeat of the protest. He knew it would be a massive defeat, one that would crush a generation. He would stay, he might even join in and—once the protest had collapsed—then he could get on the bus.

Part Four
The Battle of Seattle

Day 1: Tuesday, November 30

1

Under a sky as wet and black as a dog's nose, small groups, here and there, tread silently.

At a crossroads, Pike and Fifth, a voice coos: No cops! Oil drums filled with cement are rolled into place quiet and slow enough to hear each tiny chip of gravel crunch under steel. The chains set into the cement are laid out chinkle-chankle across the street.

A mile away, two thousand stand in Victor Steinbreuk park. Daniel can smell the sea. He can't hear the ocean, but in the pre-traffic darkness he listens to it stir the wet trees and its salty drops tap-tap-tapping on the fat elm leaves. Colour-coded flags for high and low arrestibility are all shades of grey in the black rain. The procession begins to move. A strange silhouette shuffles and swears: a swaying, twelve-legged, two-handed monster. As the megalosaurus passes under a park light it becomes six people walking side by side, arms linked together by hefty steel tubes covered in silver duct tape. Between each person walks another supporting the weight of their arms. Daniel holds up his part of the sagging chain solemn as an altar boy, as the procession exits the park.

In the empty Washington State Convention Center, three rockery fountain jets spurt weakly into life, trickling their pitter-patter into black marble troughs. With a shunt and a lurch, the escalators begin meshing and meshing and meshing . . .

Interstate 5 is greasy with rain. Stationary squad cars, doors open, red sirens silently revolving, are blocking the highway exits by the

Convention Center. The police have been praying for rain. (The FBI estimates six cops shot today, warns of biological weapons.) A cop looks up at a steel-mist sky. The rain stops.

Early commuters slide by on a slate highway. In-car FM breakfast shows swing like manic depressives from chirpy joy to a solemn rosary of road closures in the downtown area: . . . *Union Street off ramp from I-5; Pike Street closed between Seventh and Boren; Convention Place under the Convention Center; Eighth Avenue between Seneca and Pine; Seventh, Pine and Union* . . .

All the downtown cab ranks are empty, striking taxi drivers are only doing their non-emergency ambulance service. On Pill Hill a single yellow cab putters across an intersection.

Buzzing like a soggy fly, a helicopter with a gun turret disappears, small and black, behind distant towers.

Two bike scouts memorize strength and location of a lockdown at Eighth and Union, then cycle away to the next intersection. At Seventh and Union they find a man dressed as a Chiquita banana standing between two steel security fences, through which gap delegates are to be given a police escort. Chiquita Banana lifts one fence out of its cement mooring until it clangs against the other, closing the gap, then D-locks his neck to both fences.

The helicopter passes over a small cluster of protesters blockading the freeway exit at Sixth and Seneca.

On each floor of the Convention Center, lone Sheriff's Department flatfoots, in their light-blue trousers and elasticated leather jackets, listen to their boots squeak with each turn on marble. On the first floor the first metal shutter lifts with a swift rattle on the first coffee and muffin franchise of the day. The cops smell the food warmer.

They don't know when their next Maple-Frosted Butternut Cruller will be.

The bike-scout arrives at Sixth and Olive, where hundreds are blockading the twin cylindrical towers of the Westin Hotel. They are chained together around banners which read Resist Corporate Tyranny Here!

Wyconda, who's been talking it up on the Metro for days, now has a bus load of activists to cheer her on: I said to my boss I ain't coming into work today and if you don't like it you can fuckin' fire me!

Thousands of Koreans, Filipinos, and Native Americans from the one group denied a march permit, the People's Assembly, are all heading up Fourth, while the Family Farmers Rally leaves Pike Place Market.

Lockdown at Ninth and Union. Threading his arms through steel tubes Mani finds his neighbours' wiggling fingers and holds hands. The cylinders are padlocked each to the other with a smooth click. The first black stretch limo is turned back from Ninth and Union. It reverses, thinks Daniel, as if pulled by the black boomerang mounted on the trunk. Daniel waits with Mani until a hundred or so students from Seattle Community College join the lockdown and sit down in a cluster of large cardboard ears of corn. Daniel sets off for Sixth and Union, looking back just once to frown at the hopeful field of cardboard maize.

2

Up ahead Daniel sees the modernist curve of the Plymouth Congregational, white as a Latino church. A street sign says University. He knows his way from here. But as he reaches the corner rows and rows of Robocops block the way.

Old and young, women and men sit before the police lines, filling the street from curb to curb and fifty bodies deep from front line to rear. They link arms, wedged into a clinch with those on either side.

We don't have a vote,
So they won't either.
We don't have a vote
So they won't either.

The riot cops have trained for riots, for standoffs, for crowds that might charge or retreat. But these here are sitting folk, hymn-singing folk, praying, locked-on, non-retreating folk. Behind their visors and gas masks the cops flash urgent, heated, panicky, angry looks at one another—are we ready? yes? no? are we all going as one? is it now? not yet? . . . now? They come on. First in small, stamping steps and shuffles. One. One, two. Each loud shuffle of boots building in resolution. One. One, two.

A thud. A scream. A foot kicks a smoking canister skittering back toward black-steel shinpads. Another deep, pump-thud. Then another and another.

The patience of the low and spreading smoke is its evil. Silence falls over the seated protesters as the lazily uncoiling tear gas sidles toward them. All are cowering. Except one. A young man, not sitting but standing, hands together, praying as the pure white chemical clouds rise all around him, and he disappears into the fumes like a sinner.

Daniel runs back from the grey smoke's slow, even advance, its inevitable progress. His arm is grabbed, hung on to, pulled down.

Don't fucking run, a voice calls up to him. Stay here! Hold!

Daniel struggles with the arm which clutches him, then feels the grasp fall away. Once free of the bodies he's stepped over, trodden on, stumbled through to escape, he turns back.

Swinging varnished wooden staves, the riot cops wade into the crowd, jabbing, clubbing, kicking. Body armour makes their violence appear deliberate and slow like jaded sadists. High-stepping horses wheel chaotically through the crowd.

Hurrying away Daniel thinks: Where are the mass arrests Mani talked about? What's the plan now? Leaving the chaos behind him, he tries to square escape with conscience. This isn't his battle. Not yet. Not his pitch. He's part of another affinity group. Somewhere else.

But he's dismayed by his fear and panic. What a day to find out I'm a coward, he thinks. He's always seen himself as brave, has been secretly looking forward to showing Mani and everyone just how controlled he'd be in the midst of chaos. He'd been shot at, arrested, stowed away, chucked overboard, flown in a plane, and crossed the US border illegally. These experiences had, he'd told himself, made him stronger. But now he finds they've made him weaker. Now he finds that he is more panicky and nervous than he's ever been. Nor does Daniel see his fear as the natural consequence of his experiences, but more like a disease he's caught.

He climbs on to the wall by Freeway Park, then drops back down on to Sixth. He can't remember if Union was above University or below it. A whizz-bang explodes in the air behind him. Daniel screams, cringes, and runs.

3

On the fourth floor of the Washington State Convention and Trade Center, Evan found the blue-curtained booth he was looking for. Pinned to the curtain like a dry-cleaner's bill was a sheet of A4 which read: European Service Leaders Group. The ESLG had hired PB to work on GATS, and Evan's first task of the day was to check the setting up of an electronic system enabling European negotiators to conduct high-speed consultation with ERI business leaders.

The system was a closed-user, secure-pipe, peer-to-peer group server (he'd been told). But Evan wasn't meant to be operating the fucking thing. That was meant to be done by EU people. Only there were none about. All over Europe—in Philips, Vivendi, Belcatel—the screens would be dead. And, conjectured Evan, his mobile would be red hot in the pocket of the man who'd tried to kill him on the banks of the Rio Bravo.

Evan followed the simple list of step-by-step instructions lying in the crisp moulded foam of a bulky flightcase. After a while he had it up and working, as far as he could tell, but it would be useless until he found some EU delegates to man it. The flat earthers' blockade had so far kept them out. Evan knew, however, that it wouldn't hold.

Maybe delegates were already getting through. He set off to find them.

He pushed the weighted door to a conference room: empty. He searched the fourth-floor lobby. Nothing but a Texan delegate saying, Somebody should get out there and explain things to those protesters—tell 'em about what the World Trade Organization does! His remarks were addressed to another haggard refugee, who was sitting on his briefcase eating a sandwich.

The architecture of the Convention Center celebrated the harmony of civic and natural. Giant bay trees rose from stone tubs, suspended by wires from the glass ceiling. Outside the mezzanine's two-storey window, ivy and trellis denied that the garden hung in midair over the I-5 highway.

Evan left the Convention Center through a plywood construction tunnel and made for the Paramount. His fawn crombie had had an uneventful flight from London Gatwick via Houston. He turned up its black velvet collar and clutched coat lapels together to hide his shirt and tie. He was hoping to look like any other Seattle-ite collecting his mom, say, from a hospital on Pill Hill. That's what he would say if some protester tried to stop him. He passed under the shadow of an entire block still under construction. Boarded up on its ground floor, the block rose in hollow, scaffolded squares of cement throwing a pall of neglect and ruin on to the expensive real estate. Orange nylon mesh sagged against bare girders. Generators, duckboards, and wheelbarrows littered the ruin: already today one hubristic leviathan had been abandoned to the wind and rain.

Keen not to waste his up-time, he walked fast to the Paramount opening ceremony. His legs ached a little but Evan felt good and strong. His will had triumphed, he told himself. He had *refused* to be ill; like an athlete he had risen to the big occasion. Let those protesters chant their songs, let them waddle about with their pissy, pathetic little cardboard signs. Let them have their thirty-second prime-time news segment, their feel-good rally in the stadium; let them all hear how right they are in the Lutheran Gethsemane Church Teach-In on Debt Cancellation and then go home happy. Fuck *them*—Evan was here with the big boys, the grown-ups, and he was making the *future*!

Police bikes straddled a cleared crossroads. Evan walked on a block until he came to a row of riot cops strung out across the next intersection. One of the state troopers levelled an awesome wooden baton against him: Go right back the way you came, sir! Evan's eyes became fixed on the long and heavy wooden stave. Small, neat serial numbers indented the wood at the end nearest Evan's nose. The club was thickly varnished like a toffee apple and too wide for the black leather gloves to close around. The state trooper, meanwhile, never took his eyes off Evan's face.

Evan fumbled inside his shirt for his delegate pass. The laminate hung on a cord from his neck but proved tricky to extricate. As he winched it up the cord snagged on a button. He freed it, then it snagged against the pen in his inside pocket. Finally he produced the delegate pass. Having done so, Robocop's entire expression changed, as if his circuits were saying: On you I bestow my happy face. I must help the special people. (The others I must hit with my club.) Smiling as he sent him on his way, the cop extended an arm, like Willie Wonka welcoming children to the chocolate factory, and Evan passed through.

It was kind of embarrassing for Evan to have class lines made so explicit. But was it class lines? Or was that Chano talking? Maybe it's possible, he said to himself (although in the exact tone he'd have used if he was in fact arguing with his brother), just possible that this cop is human, too. All day and half the night he has to do the stern face. So maybe it's a relief for him to be able to show a friendly face once in a while. Maybe that's all it is. All the same, Evan had his delegate pass out good and ready before he got to the next police line.

He could hear chanting now—*Hey, hey! ho, ho! WTO has got to go!*—and smiled inwardly for he knew that this was a battle between those clear-minded rationalists who see the world as it is, and those who are projecting personality problems into the air, lost in a world of fantasy, myth, and ideology.

At Ninth and Pine, ten bumper-to-bumper Metro buses commandeered by the cops ran a ring of steel around the Paramount Theatre, the venue for the WTO opening ceremony, and where hundreds of protesters were blockading the entrance. Evan stood next to the raincoat shoulders of a couple of US delegates. One turned amber tortoiseshell frames toward him and said mildly: This looks like one for the bad guys. It ain't happening.

How long you been stood here? asked Evan.

About a half-hour. Oh, there goes Arnold.

Who's that? asked Evan.

Arnold Shwez? German delegate.

Let me zroo! I haff come a lonk vay!

Go home! the Yankees chanted.

At every point the German delegate tried to enter, the crowd seared shut with flat hands and shoulders. In the jostle Arnold's hair was mussed up and his shoulders spun round until he dropped some folders and retreated.

Go home! they chanted. TV cameras joined the crush. In the surge Evan felt his shoulder being used as a rest for a microphone and shook it off.

This is what democracy looks like! chanted the crowd. *This is what democracy looks like!*

Over the chant the shrill German delegate decried the scene to the cameras: Zeez people do not understant ze benefits of vree trate to ze develpink neeshuns!

The two US delegates Evan had been talking to a moment before were now themselves trying to force a way in, pushing angrily at the crowd of young men and women. One riot cop began stuffing a protester into the wheel arch of a Metro bus and the rest seized the moment and sprang into action, kicking, body slamming, punching and clubbing. And it was then that Evan saw his opening . . .

Where the Robocops were bundling into the shouting, screaming protesters a large space had cleared, like wheat flattened by a sluice of heavy rain. Evan could see the glass door and the stern-faced female cop in blue-grey shirtsleeves behind it. Seizing his chance, he clambered at speed over bodies and slapped his laminate flat against the glass. His hand on the door felt the vibration as a chain was sleeved off the push bar inside. She was too slow. Shouts found him. Hands grabbed him. He was jostled, clutched, pulled, jerked. Then he heard a heavy clunk of wood hit something less heavy, heard a scream and then the door slammed behind him. He was in!

He knelt down and rested his hands on his hips. He was breathing very hard. He put one hand on the carpet.

After a count of four, the stern-faced cop who'd helped him in said: This way, sir.

Yes, said Evan, beating the ten count on nine.

Once he'd got inside the Paramount Evan wished he hadn't. He scanned row upon row of vacant flip-up seats. Each seat had a card taped to the grey padding telling which country where to sit. Only about twenty delegates had got in. A lone Cameroonian in an elegant, dark-green suit sat in the front row. Head propped on fist, his long legs sprawled like late shadows on a lawn. His face had a look peculiar to someone who's just realizing that he's read *Trade-Related Aspects of Investment Measures* for kicks.

Evan checked the video suite where the corporate representatives could watch the opening ceremony. There'd be people there. US trade representative and WTO chair Charlene Barshevsky had five hundred corporate advisers alone. He walked into an empty room with a jumbo screen transmitting a shot of the room he'd just left. Back in the auditorium Evan saw Mayor Shell and Charlene Barshevsky conferring in a corner by the stage, while police wrestled with two NGO activists who were trying to get to the mike. And now, thought Evan, I've got to get *out* of this fucking place!

4

At Sixth and Union, a block and a half down from the white church, Daniel found two neat piles of props stacked on the curb: placards, banners, and costumes left by people who'd peeled off the procession when it reached their pie slice. Two hundred people were sitting in the road. Daniel scanned the faces and saw Monica and the rest of Palace Pier in the middle of the crowd. He mimed saying Palace Pier but was too inhibited—even in the upsurge of his relief—to shout these English words out loud.

He'd just begun to pick out a route through the tightly packed seated bodies when someone shouted: They're getting ready!

State patrol troopers were putting on gas masks. A short woman with long purple hair and a straw cowboy hat walked in the gap between police line and seated blockaders. She spoke through a megaphone: This is a peaceful protest. Sit down and stay sitting. We will not move and we will not be provoked!

Just in front of Daniel a bearded, slim young man with a yellow backpack sat down. Sitting cross-legged, a woman in thick-framed black glasses motioned Daniel to sit down as well. Daniel knelt in the last square of concrete left. Only now did he realize how close he was to the police lines: a few strides, maybe ten bodies away. He fumbled for his swimming goggles, his arms clogged and heavy with fear. He heard a megaphone calling out some urgent plea: *This is a peaceful protest!*

The swimming goggles were tight on his head, pushing back hard against his nose and skull. There was no time to adjust them now. In green light Daniel saw the riot police tusked like wild boars in their double-cylinder gas masks. He felt his arms being linked on one side by Black Glasses and on the other by Yellow Backpack. A green cop was re-jigging the green club in his green gloves like a baseball bat, the gloves opening and closing on the wood to get a good green grip. Behind them a green humvee pulled up. Green violence was coming.

Two concussion grenades exploded overhead, not tear gas, just whizz-bangs. Daniel's whole body jerked. He cursed himself.

Uh do you, uh, *no hablay ingles*? asked Backpack. *Vale*, listen, uh, *cinque minuteh*. That's all. *Solo*. OK? But don't touch your skin—he mimed it then shook his finger—no touch, no, no, bad. OK. It'll be OK. Daniel was just registering the man's vinegar smell when a tear gas fusillade volleyed into the air—chunk—chunk—chunk—the canisters trailing short tails of smoke.

Fuck you! Black Glasses shouted.

No violence! shouted someone else.

Backpack turned his head away to cry out: Where are the fucking union guys? Then put his nose and mouth under a bandana and braced himself for the onslaught.

Daniel heard the gas hissing. Every nerve and synapse in his body had a direct line to his brain and all said the same thing: Take your arms out of the link. Get up and run. Run away and sit in a park. Sit in the Convergence. Sit in Freeway Park. Be somewhere else. Now! He wrenched an arm free and put a pair of old tights soaked in maddox and baking soda to his mouth and nostrils. Thick green smoke surrounded him. Daniel closed his eyes in their pea pods.

Tear gas seared his skin, scorching every pore and blood vessel. He screamed out. Acid hooks pulled at the roots of his tongue, burning

his throat and mouth. Screams broke all around him, bodies were
heaving and tipping this way and that. He tore off his molten goggles
and thrashed around on his back, legs lashing out. The pain grew
worse by the breath. (Like missing the moment you snatch your
scalded hand away from a pan. Instead your hand stays there, only it's
your whole body, and the burning gas is everywhere.) Lava dribbled
down his chin. He grabbed at his scalded eyes with scalding hands. He
whimpered in terror and panic and tried to breathe but seized up,
convulsed in a paroxysm of strangled airless retching.

A short, thick-set man in a brown tin hat with an electricians' union
sticker on the front hauled Daniel upright.

OK Mac? asked the electrician. Daniel took his first tottering steps
and cuffed away the snot, tears and spit, frantically rubbing his burning skin. He felt other hands pull his own away.

Try not to touch your skin, said a woman's voice in Spanish.

And so Daniel stood there with his face screwed up and let his skin
burn, both hands in midair either side of his head, pressing against
the force field of his will.

In a harsh, het-up voice the tin-hatted electrician said: They should
realize if we wanted to raise hell we could! He bent down to pick up
the back of some placard or hoarding lying in the street. He brushed
the dirt off with his sleeve, and in red marker pen wrote in large, looping letters: *Hi honey, I just gassed some peaceful protesters. What did you do
at work today?* The electrician held the card up to the Robocops, who
were now standing across the reclaimed street, staves at the ready.

Palace Pier reassembled further along Union at Fourth and sat down
in the street, Daniel resting a hand on his legs to cover their shaking.
All the time his friends were talking and checking the map he wondered why he'd lost all his courage. Why had it happened now? Could
the others see it on his face? Every time someone looked at him, he
smiled, dreading that they'd ask if he was all right. As they studied the
map, he hoped they'd decide the battle was lost and all troop back to
the Convergence Center for rosehip tea. Instead, they fell in with a
procession of blue turtles as cover to their next point.

The march passed through Pine, and a turtle made a peace sign up at police marksmen on the roof of a hotel. One of the silhouetted marksmen gave the silhouette of a peace sign back.

Oh, that's so beautiful, a Californian woman said.

No it's not, said Monica. If someone says the word down his little ear-piece, he's gotta shoot you, innit?

5

The WTO opening ceremony had been canceled but it was nearly two hours before Evan could get out of the Paramount. I shouldn't, he thought, pounding down Ninth toward Pike, have even fucking been fucking here anyfuckingway!

Laminate in hand, he found himself alone on a cleared intersection behind a line of riot police and next to an armored humvee "Peacekeeper." In front of the black capes of the riot squad were fifty yards of empty street. On the other side of this unoccupied zone was a primary-colour patchwork of seated protesters, their chants echoing up the ten-storey avenue.

Evan flinched at a noise so loud that he didn't know if it had come from ahead, behind, beside or above. Police had fired a concussion grenade followed by a tear-gas fusillade. The Robocops rapidly fell back either side of him and Evan found himself standing level with their line.

He stared in awe at the scene ahead of him. Where there had been banners, costumes, placards, now there were none. Where there had been noise there was now total silence. No sound, no colour, nothing. Nothing except thick rolls of chemical cloud.

The cops waited at the ready, one boot forward, sticks raised. Visors studied the rolling mist fifty yards of bare street away.

The cloud wasn't lifting but with each roll seemed to grow more cumulus, bellying out denser clouds, compact as cauliflower heads. So silent was the street, Evan thought it quite possible that when the cloud lifted, the demonstrators would all have vanished in the puff of sulphur. Had they done so it would have shocked him less than what did happen.

Evan heard police boots adjust minutely in response to something. From out of the tear-gas smoke there emerged first a leg, then an outline, and then Chano Salgado walking calmly and collectedly out of the cloud. For a moment, it seemed to Evan as though his brother was looking straight at him across the unoccupied zone. Chano slowly brought a hand up to thumb and forefinger his eyes, looked up, reoriented himself, put hands behind back, and sauntered on down the middle of the empty street. Just before the line of riot cops, he turned right. Women blockading the alley parted wordlessly to let him through. They closed over him again and he was gone, Evan staring after.

The fraying chemical smoke, meanwhile, was developing arms, legs and heaving bodies, was lifting the lid off crying and howling, spluttering and screaming. The riot cops advanced with raised clubs and pepper spray. Out of range of the tear gas, the young women blockading the alley began to chant.

You! You! The whole world's watching!
You! You! The whole world's watching!

Evan set off toward the Seattle Hilton. A block away he could still hear the chants echoing behind him.

Whose streets?
Our streets!
Whose streets?
Our streets!

He quickened his step and put his mind to the task ahead. At the Hilton, the EU's toxic waste proposals would be traded for the US Clean Air Act and the link buried. I'll suggest, thought Evan, we talk up the EU's power to curb US law as setting precedents for Kyoto . . .

6

Monica was in the front row of the blockade which but a moment ago had disappeared before Evan's eyes. The gas began to thin. Through the eye holes of her black rubber gas mask Monica saw police holding small, red canisters of pepper spray which looked like in-car fire extinguishers. She heard her breathing getting louder in the full-face gas

mask. The slow deliberation with which the police sprayed the heads
of those sitting next to and behind her looked bizarrely careful, like
front-of-stage festival security chucking water over the mosh-pit in
case the kids overheat.

A padded-torso cop swung his gauntlet at her head, punching a cut
to her nose, dislodging her gas mask. He wrenched it off, exposing
her hot, sweating face to the sudden cold which became—just as suddenly—red hot. She tried to get to her feet.

Dragged behind police lines, she felt a knee on her chest and a
hand pressing her shoulder down. She looked up. The cop had a
little red can of pepper spray in his free hand. She clamped her eyes
shut. Cold plastic gloves prised apart the skin above and below her left
eye. Monica writhed in agony as acidic spray soldered her eyeballs,
burning a broad swath over cheeks, nose, nostrils, lips. They turned
her over. She fought to get out from under the cops. A steel knee on
her back, her left arm yanked behind her. She heard a cop's heavy
breathing. Her inner wrists felt the tickle of dangling plastic cuffs.
Opening her good eye she saw a tatty trainer. Was a de-arrest on? Her
eye sizzled shut in the pepper mist. The cop's weight shifted on her
back. Knee lifted off shoulder blade to grab at her tatty-trainered
friend. In that split second Monica rolled and wrenched herself out
from under, got to all fours, stood up and staggered blind. She
opened her eyes a nanosecond. Screaming with the pain rushing in,
she ran into the ten yards of clear street of which she had a fiery, reti-
nal snapshot.

7

At the far side of the blockaded alley Chano emerged into the street.
Turning the corner at the next intersection, he left a brown footprint on a white cardboard sign lying in the road whose red ink read:
*Hi honey, I just gassed some peaceful protesters. What did you do at work
today?* A cop riding on the side of a humvee sprayed some of the hot,
spicy stuff at him. Chano squinted at him through the vapour. As the
truck disappeared down the street, the riot trooper stared back at the
Chicano, unable to believe his non-reaction to the spray.

In the moments before Evan had seen him, Chano had made an astonishing discovery. Alone among the fifty thousand protesters Chano's long years of marination in sodium metabisulphite had rendered him immune to tear gas. Both the oleoresin-capsicum of pepper spray and the orthochloro-benzalmalononitrile of tear gas had been neutralized by the sodium metabisulphite. Every pore and every cell in Chano's body was saturated with the stuff. Had been for years. Now and then he coughed in the gas and his eyes stang a little, but only as much as someone standing downwind of a bonfire. He walked up Seventh on to Pine.

8

Daniel, meanwhile, had made a smaller discovery. He'd noticed that the concussion grenades or whizz-bangs were not gas. They only made a loud noise and left a bit of firework smoke. In his realizing that they were *meant* to scare him, they no longer did. Up ahead distant riot cops clink-clink-clinked into place, the hoof scrapes of horses behind them. The brakes of an armored water cannon squeaked at the corner.

The intersection at Fifth and Pine was rammed. There came a double boom in the air—gas—and Daniel was in a mass stampede running down Pine toward Seventh. There were screams from the intersection behind him, where Nordstrom's vertical sign rose triumphantly out of the smoke to stand proud of the gas clouds under which bodies disappeared.

Daniel's clothes, which had been cold and damp from the water cannon, grew hot as he ran. Odd flashes and burns stung him now and then, where bits of clothing, still coated in tear gas or pepper spray, touched his skin. A concussion grenade bounced off the street, gashing and singeing his forehead. He kept running and the blood which flowed into his eye awoke him to his core. The tall, broad avenue became, he felt, a canyon. Stampeding through this canyon floor the sounds of running rumbled up sheer limestone rockface. Massed shouts echoed between the towers, bouncing off granite and marble. Plywood and pine replaced glass, which lay in scattered crystallized silica on the damp and shady valley floor. In his exhilaration, it was as if a glacier had scooped away all the usual impedimenta of cars and shoppers to quarry out this flat-bottomed valley through which they now ran.

As the stampede flowed around her, a woman standing in the street shouted: Don't run! Don't run! There's people locked on here! You'll break their arms! Don't run!

Not understanding what was being shouted Daniel kept on running. He came to a stop on his own at Seventh and found he'd lost touch with his group. He cursed himself with bitter reproaches for having failed in his duty to look after Monica. He hunted round for them, shouting out Palace Pier loud and clear.

Keep moving! Stay calm! someone was shouting.

9

Chano was walking up Pine toward the crowds at Fifth when a star-burst of tear gas exploded in midair. The white curtain of gas fell and thickened. Chano stood still until the crowd had charged past him on either side.

Hands behind his back Chano now strolled along the broad, occluded avenue which had been emptied in large haste. It felt strange to have sudden individual possession of streets which, a few seconds before, had been packed. He walked the smoky ghost town block, craning his neck as he walked further into the thickening chemical cloud, peering through the mist like a short-sighted academic in some foggy botanical gardens.

Voices grew fainter behind him.

Don't run! There's people locked on here! You'll break their arms! Don't run!

Palliss Peeyah! Pallis Peeyah!

Keep moving, stay calm!

Chano's ears and upper palate were prickly with a vinegary kind of chili tang. Visibility was now down to a few inches. He stood still. He heard boots shift on grit. He took one blind step further and found himself face to face with a pair of black-rubber, port-hole eyes. The gas-masked riot cop was startled to be disturbed in his gaseous no man's land, like a lobster in its coral cave. Trying to turn back the way he came, Chano instead found himself inspecting a row of black shower ponchos, wooden clubs, helmets, and more startled port-holes in the mist. Looking at the ground before his feet, he walked to the side of the street, found the curb and bumped into a trash can. He leaned back against a building and heard the riot cops clink-clink-clink past him as they advanced to the next intersection.

10

Daniel's hearing still rang from the whizz-bang which had exploded on him and singed his forehead. He stopped to rub his buzzing ears. Smoke milled about at the intersection at Seventh. Daniel heard someone calling his name. He looked around.

Daniel! he heard again.

He scanned the crowd for the voice.

Daniel!

At last his rambling gaze found the de-arrested Monica.

Over here, she called. We're over here!

11

It was noon and the sky was clearing over the Memorial Stadium union rally. Chano watched a groggy sun try to rouse itself behind layers of mist. A shimmery, worn-out rainbow tried to make good on an old promise. Steam rose from the blue plastic ponchos of a group of steel workers stepping heavily down the bleachers.

It's like a revivalist meeting! one was saying. Chano translated this to an Ecuadorean called Ruben who he'd seen carrying a cardboard sign which read Unidos Sin Fronteras. His new friend had lived here four years but spoke only broken English through a missing front tooth.

They say there's thirty thousand here, said Ruben. But it looks more, doesn't it?

The stadium's field was packed and its bleachers full all around. Chano and Ruben were near the front by a covered stage with festival amps and a speaker's rostrum.

Under this system, said a tiny Trinidadian from the stage, her head just peeping over the podium, the world has become a race to the bottom: Who will accept the most miserable working conditions?

Chano translated her words to Unidos Sin Fronteras who, still looking toward the speaker, nodded his head like Castro listening to Nkrumah at the UN.

Now came the main event: John Sweeney, the boss of the AFL-CIO, and Chano felt the stirring of an old antagonism. For even though he'd never heard of Sweeney, he knew what he was.

Sweeney's shiny blue nylon jacket was zipped tight all the way up. From this round carapace poked a pale, bald tortoise head. The side pockets of a suit were piled up under the elasticated hem of his cere-monial trade-union dress. The AFL-CIO union boss had small features in a big face with pursed lips. Sweeney's voice rang around the sta-dium, deadpan but with a braying note in it. Chano hated everything about him.

We are walking into the pages of history, Sweeney read from his printout.

Through every roar of the crowd, Sweeney never once lifted his listless head, but merely waited each time for the noise to die back like cut grass.

As he neared the end of his speech, Sweeney proclaimed: We will have a place at the table of the WTO, or we will shut it down! At this Chano turned away, left Ruben without a word and kept walking as Sweeney's untranslated words lingered in the PA static of the Memorial Stadium amid whistling and wild applause.

Climbing the bleachers that led to the exits, Chano realized this was exactly the sellout he'd been expecting. He'd been waiting for this and now he had it. It was twenty years since he'd last heard a union-boss speak and nothing had changed! It was a strange sort of glad fury, a fury of confirmation, of release from obligation. But a fury nonetheless.

Ruben looked around in bewilderment, wondering what English words had caused his new friend to stop translating midsentence and turn his back on the whole thing. What had Chano heard?

What he'd heard was the sellout, the muffle-shuffle, the flim-flam. First the flim, then the flam: the second half of the sentence is always the most uncompromising and rabble-rousing of the entire speech. Five short words punched out like a fist: we will shut it down. And for good reason—the flam always comes right after the flim, the most compromised words in the whole speech: We will have a place at the table of the WTO.

This was an extraordinary and frank betrayal. What Sweeney was really saying was: We're not going to shut down the WTO today after all. But he'd made this betrayal sound like a formality that everyone had agreed upon. And it was the very ineffability of all this, the subtlety of it, which made Chano leave Ruben without an explanation. For how could he have described it? How to describe in one language the linguistic chicanery in another? Sweeney's tortoise head knew, for example, that in a stadium packed with rain-soaked workers who'd been on their feet for hours, the sellout would sound like an ultimatum. And Chano knew in his bones that Sweeney had betrayed everyone, knew that some kind of deal had been done, even though he didn't know its precise form.

Walking out of the Memorial Stadium, Chano heard Sweeney in the ball park commanding thirty thousand workers to do no more than a one-minute sit-down in *symbolic* solidarity with the protests. (This was the trade-off for which Sweeney had been promised a Wednesday morning sit-down with the president of the United States.)

It was a trade-off which meant that at some point in his speech Sweeney's pursed lips would have to say: We will have a place at the table of the WTO, or we will shut it down! A trade-off which meant that Chano, without having translated these words for his Unidos Sin Fronteras friend, would already be on Fourth Avenue by the time Sweet Honey in the Rock's gospel singers sang *Movin' Out*. But, above all, it was a trade-off which meant that at some geographical point in the city, the contradictions in Sweeney's flim-flam would have to be physically fought out.

At a crossroads. At Eighth and Pine. At 1.30 P.M.

12

On Fourth Avenue all the many different marches were converging into one and flowing into Sweeney's Citizens' March for Fair Trade which followed the Memorial Stadium rally. This Teamsters' march was cross-pollinated all along Fourth by a motley swarm ... The embroidered placards and feather boas of the Raging Grannies in their bonnets, bloomers and half-moon glasses; a giant green dirigible shaped like an inflated condom painted with the words Safe Trade; the banners of Via Campesina, Rural Family Farmers of America, Frente Zapatista; the red ra-ra skirts and pigtails of the Radical Cheerleaders; the stiltwalker with long, humbug trousers; flags and whistles and, borne on a litter, a cigar-smoking, big bad wolf reclining in a star-spangled top hat and tails, a silver dollar-sign sceptre in his paw.

The Teamsters' march first wobbled at Fifth and Pine, where they were met with the urgent shouts of people standing on opposite sides of the street, each telling them to go in a different direction.

Go this way! hollered an orange-capped union marshal, his traffic-cop arm directing them along the official route along Pine.

Go *this* way! cried a hoarse Chicano woman, standing on a low wall and pointing down Fifth.

No, straight on.

We need your help! the Chicano shouted. There's about fifty people down there on Fifth. Some people have been gassed, clubbed, pepper-sprayed and shot at with rubber bullets for *five* hours!

Go this way! shouted the testy marshal, louder and shriller now. Ignore them! Go this way. *This* is the route of the march!

No, this way, go this way. There's Cavanagh's! We're right down there, linking arms in front of police lines to stop delegates getting in. But we need reinforcements!

Marchers slowed, stopped, milled. They could hear the ruckus and see the mounted riot cops and police barricades far below in the dip of the hill on Fifth. But up ahead three blocks away they could also hear Hendrix booming from the Local 17 rig on Pine at Eighth. A few ILWU Oakland dockers responded to the call and only the march's own momentum, it seemed, kept it on Pine as far as the next intersection.

Eighth and Pine was the last intersection before the march would turn right. The last crossroads before the trade unionists would begin heading *away* from the Convention Center. The marchers were confused. In all the handouts (printed before Sweeney did his deal) the Teamsters had read the following: Procession from Memorial Stadium to the WTO meeting at the Seattle Trade and Convention Center. But now the route was taking them *away* from the Convention Center.

Chano Salgado was standing in a vacant lot on the corner watching the march pass by the gleaming silver rig pumping out Hendrix. *All Along The Watchtower* began to blast from the big quad speakers running off the show truck's generator. The intro's six chunky power chords—one-two, one-two-three-four; one-two, one-two-three-four—followed by that rattlesnake noise, and then Jimi's lead spiralling high, like a severed power line sparking perilously into the sky, as a thicket of mass-produced Fair Trade Not Free Trade placards turned the corner from Pine on to Eighth.

One of the steelworkers stepped out of the march carrying a megaphone. He had a neat, sandy beard and wore his hard hat back to front. He walked a few yards and then crouched down on the sidewalk while the march flowed past him along Eighth. Chano lost sight of him but heard his megaphone chant:

Shut it down!
Stay downtown!
Shut it down!
Stay downtown!
Shut it down!
Stay downtown!
We need to stay downtown people. There's the Convention Center down there, down Eighth! Go that way! We need to hold these intersections. We can take Pike and 9. Pike and 9. Stay downtown! Go that way!

There must be some kinda way outta here . . . sang Jimi.

Local 9 Oakland dockers and District 11 steelworkers peeled off from the main march, splitting up into twos and threes to slip past the union marshals.

. . . said the joker to the thief . . .

The marshals in their orange caps spread their arms like ranchers herding cattle. Another orange-cap was standing on a low wall, pointing the way up Eighth.

They're just splitting us up, he told the marchers with worldly-wise maturity. This is a peaceful march. We're not here to take on a fight.

The fuck is that? exploded a steelworker in a black baseball cap. What the fuck are we here for then . . . a walk!? And with that he pushed straight past the marshal staring him out all the while. More Teamsters followed, skipping over the little chain fence surrounding the corner lot.

. . . There's too much confusion . . . sang Jimi.

Still more union members peeled off, some running, some trying to look as if they were just going to the rig for refreshments; and then a load more charging through in one block. Chano stepped over the chain link and joined the renegades heading down Eighth toward the Convention Center. A union marshal put his walkie-talkie to his mouth, calling for reinforcements to plug the gap between toe and line.

. . . I can't get no relief . . . sang the son of Seattle.

A hundred yards down the street, heading up Pine from the Paramount, Daniel heard the loud rock music, and walked against the flow of the march to find out where it was coming from.

Businessman they drink my wine . . .

At fifty paces he could just make out a silver *doble semi remolque* with an amp stack.

None will level on the line . . .
Nobody under this world!
Hey! Hey!

Coming the other way Daniel met a small group holding a Maquilladora Justicia Allianza banner and Mexican flags. Perhaps they knew Mexicans in Seattle, Daniel wondered. Perhaps they knew his father. Should he ask them? He stopped to chat. A broad *maquilla* with a headband smiled and made a fuss of this strangely independent boy while the march flowed either side of them. Just then a hard shove in the back sent him flying into the *maquilla* and both went sprawling.

No reason to get excited . . .

A little winded, Daniel had only just helped her up again when another burly orange-bib charged past in a violent fury. Daniel found himself lying on top of the *maquilla* who, with her arms still around him, lifted her head to scream after the marshal: *Chingaaaaatuuumadreyyy*!! As they both clambered to their feet, more marshals in pristine orange bibs and caps ran toward the corner with the pompous urgency of men in uniform.

What's going on? exclaimed Daniel, and set off after them to find out.

Kick him in the ass from me! called the *maquilla*.

For five hours the direct action network had been in desperate need of reinforcements from the Teamsters' march. Now, at last, the union movement came running. To Eighth and Pine. To keep everyone on the official route march.

So let us stop talking bullshit now. The hour's getting late!

Daniel tried to push through the solid wall of marshals blocking the way down Eighth toward the Convention Center, but there were more now than when his father had hopped the low chain fence. Daniel couldn't get through and had to go the long way round. Back the way he'd come and once round the block. He ran.

13

Evan span through the heavily guarded revolving door of the Sheraton, reeling from the noise of choppers, chants, stampedes, whistles, whizz-bangs, screams, and the firework wheeze and sigh of an OC artillery launch. Rubbing his eyes, which stung from residual gas, he sidestepped Seattle's police chief and flopped into a big, comfy chair opposite his old friend Patrick Gajer.

Hello old mate, exhaled Evan.

Hi yourself, said Patrick, and smiled.

Evan wiped a hand down over his face, thumb and forefingered his eyelids, looked up, half-smiled and asked: So, what angle are you taking?

Here, instead of laughing at Evan's little drollery, Patrick sat up, and, stressing the key words (which, it turned out, were nearly all of them), he replied in a tone of canny calculation: I'm talking to Byers tomorrow, and I'm gonna be trying to drive a wedge between him and the EU position on milk.

Evan looked at him, dazed and blank, blinked, then burst out laughing. Patrick flicked the self-standing snacks menu over. Evan, who'd been unable to get anywhere near his meeting at the Hilton, carried on laughing so hard that the police dogs stood up on all fours.

Patrick Gajer presented in-depth, outside broadcasts for *Channel 4 News*. He also wrote a thrice-weekly column in the *Independent*.

What happened to your face anyway? asked Patrick to wipe the smile off it.

Oh, that was months ago, replied Evan. I was run over. Had to take a week off work.

Well, said Patrick, at least you're a bit more relaxed than last time.

That did it. Last time they'd met up had been an uncomfortable occasion. Evan had gone to the Commonwealth Club intending to tell Patrick about his illness. But he couldn't do it. And the more he couldn't say what he had come to say, the more irritating Patrick had become.

In the Sheraton lobby the Seattle police chief was assuring a crowd of delegates that it wouldn't be long before they could get to their meetings.

Anyway, what angle would *you* take on all this then? Patrick asked Evan. Mr I'm So Fucking Clever?

To which Evan dryly suggested: Oh, I don't know . . . the irresistible force of corporate power meets the immovable object of democracy?

Don't be absurd, replied Patrick, as, in one form or another, Evan had known he would. For there was only ever one qualification Evan really needed from a political journalist: mental hemophilia.

After Queen Victoria's son Leopold was born, and for about the next hundred years, a haemophiliac disposition was the *sine qua non* of a royal career, proof that you were fitted for exalted social position, the blood-line qualification for a royal career. Leopold died of hemophilia, his sisters Alice and Beatrice were obligate carriers, as was his daughter, also called Beatrice (as, by this point, they'd decided to match initial to blood group in case of emergency). She passed it on to the tsar's son, Alexis, and there it remained until it was drained off in Moscow in 1918.

The haemophiliac's platelets can never usefully combine in response to what the text books call an external topical crisis. Instead, disconnected platelets just taxi about in the bloodstream and can never stanch a cut.

The mental haemophiliac can never synthesize Fact A with Fact B. It is the *sine qua non* qualification for the political news class.

A full-blown case would catch Evan's eye. He was, for example, already planning to work with a particular *Newsnight* presenter, ever since he'd heard him begin a radio broadcast with these words: American foreign policy has always been a moral affair. Evan guessed the man was sincere *in the moment*. That is, that when he'd said those words he'd believed them. Evan also supposed that he might also *at other moments* have heard tell of one or even possibly more events to the contrary. But the fact that this *Newsnight* presenter was unable to connect what the glossy literature from the Washington Institute of Foreign Affairs told him with the blood bath showed he was the blood elite; the right stuff.

And mental haemophilia was in demand. From time to time, for example, Britain and the US might fancy a war. In such topical crises the news professional has to be able to distinguish between good terrorism and bad; between unimaginable loss of life and unimportant loss of life; between an outrage on civilized values and unavoidable civilian casualties. He or she mustn't let these things stick together and get into any sort of a bind that might impede the free flow. While Evan held these professionals in contempt, he also respected their acquired ability.

Not everyone can do this kind of thing. If a non-obligate carrier or ordinary punter were asked to extol, say, the benefits of market competition they might—catastrophically—offset this with the observation that all corporations own bits of each other. Not so the obligate carrier, not so the mental haemophiliac who could both celebrate and deny the very existence of private power at the same time. And, as the single greatest heresy of these times was that wealth-for-some-was-linked-to-the-creation-of-poverty-elsewhere, the acquired inability to see complex systems was a blue-chip intellectual property.

A curious side effect of mental haemophilia, however, was that the tone of journalists around the world became a queer hybrid of courtesan and commissar.

Don't be absurd, replied Patrick, as, in one form or another, Evan had known he would. Oh yes, he added, *very good*. That's that sorted.

The executive producer of *Channel 4 News* slumped down next to Patrick on the big comfy leather couch, looking fed up. I wanted to go shopping in Nike Town, she moaned, but there's all these *protesters* outside!

14

Secretary of State Madeleine Albright is looking down from her Sheraton window. She sees a young woman sitting on top of the FAO Schwarz toy shop sign holding what appears to be a . . . yes, it is . . . it's a fishing rod. Hanging off the line, a doughnut dangles over the heads of a phalanx of riot police. Fishing for cops, the young woman jerks it away from them when they reach up to grab it.

Told it's still not safe for her to go out, Madeleine has been left alone with her self-hate. She hates hotel rooms as well. During the Rambouillet talks, when she entered the Kosovar delegation's suite, they told her to come back later as they were rather busy and the room didn't need anything doing just now.

Her hooded eyes stare out from the dressing-table mirror. She swivels slightly on the stool to find her face's strong angle, to remind herself of her power. She reruns in her mind a segment of last week's interview for CBS's *60 Minutes* about Iraqi sanctions.

Interviewer: We have heard that half a million children have died. That is more than died in Hiroshima—and, you know, is the price worth it?

Secretary of State Madeleine Albright: I think this was a very hard choice. But the price? We think the price is worth it.

She who had let those ragheads know that the United States was far above their pissy little UN bleatings; she who would act "multilaterally when she could and unilaterally when she must"; she who is wearing her big-time, vermilion dress-suit that she wore on the cover of *Time*; she who holds the fate of nations in her small, pale, chunkily bejeweled fingers (she has always had nice hands); there is *no way* she can be kept in her room by soul-sickening bullies, who want to replace democracy and diplomacy with mob rule and threats.

She has powdered in anticipation of a full day, of the air skimming her scent in the fast walk to the car, of meetings and cameras, formal greetings and quiet asides. The lilac powder hangs oppressively in her chamber. Blowback.

At 3:20 P.M. she dials Mayor Paul Shell.

At 3:25 P.M., on mature reflection and having analysed all the available data, Mayor Shell decides, on the balance of things, to ask the governor of Washington State to declare a state of emergency and call out the National Guard, Special Forces, and the Domestic Military Support Group.

But Madeleine will have to stay in her hotel suite for a little longer: the cops have run out of OC gas. Now comes, therefore, an afternoon lull in police violence. Meanwhile a National Guard helicopter picks up the first of three emergency tear gas and pepper-spray shipments from DefTech (Defense Technology), and a supply plane flies to Malmstrom Air Force Base.

15

Palace Pier squatted and knelt in a huddle. All changed clothes to throw off the continual multi-camera surveillance (Seattle Police Department, NBC, ITN, CBS, AP, BBC, KOMO, KTV).

Is everyone all right? asked Monica. Palace Pier nodded, peeled oranges or drank water.

Ramona came by with her black bloc crew. *Qué tal?*—how are you?—she asked Daniel.

He was no longer frightened of the question, but found, in fact, that he was bursting with impressions he had to share. He told her how strange it was to go one minute from an area of danger, and then a block away there'd be someone singing a folk song, and now here they all were sitting and eating oranges and planning what to do next with a feeling that everything had fizzled out, even though that's all it was, just a feeling, because in half an hour or round the next corner would be something unimaginable! And—

Hold on, said Ramona, staying this puppy with her hand. What are they saying there?

A large cluster had formed where a woman brought a cell-phone down from her ear and said: OK, please repeat!

OK, PLEASE REPEAT! echoed the crowd so that her announcement could be heard by everyone.

Police are controling the area directly around the Convention Center, she said.

POLICE ARE CONTROLING THE AREA DIRECTLY AROUND THE CONVENTION CENTER, they said.

. . . And are trying to clear the streets and push outwards . . .

. . . AND ARE TRYING TO CLEAR THE STREETS AND PUSH OUTWARDS . . .

. . . from there.

. . . FROM THERE.

And we need support at Pike and Fifth.

AND WE NEED SUPPORT AT PIKE AND FIFTH.

Standing near where Palace Pier was sitting, a small samba band considered their response. A slim man who, with little Gettysburg ribbons in his Afro, looked like a younger, untroubled Hendrix, leaned back against the weight of the snare drum on his belly, held both drumsticks in one hand and asked the rest of the small samba band: Well, where do we want to go? This way? he suggested, turning the sticks east like a weather vane, or that way? After muttered discussion, the samba band set off drumsticks-south toward the Convention Center, with about thirty people following simply because the samba band looked like they knew where they were going.

Palace Pier studied their map.

We can probably take this intersection if we skirt round here, said Monica, her Pacman finger traveling up and around two photocopied blocks to Fourth and Pike. And that, she added, will give us all this.

Except we need numbers and the samba band's just gone off somewhere else.

All right. That's quite near us.

That's where we've just been.

No, that was Pine and Fifth.

Oh, right.

Pike and Fifth?

The group packed orange peel in crinkly see-through bags. Daniel tightened the cap on his bottled water, rattled it, then dropped it in his backpack.

After walking along with his *compadres* for a few minutes, however, Daniel had a better idea and gave them the slip.

16

A young, headscarved Chicana with a round, beaming face was standing on a dumpster.

Heads up. FYI. Please repeat, she said. We have a message.

WE HAVE A MESSAGE, repeated the fifty or so gathered around.

They've just announced that the opening day has been called off.

THEY'VE JUST ANNOUNCED THAT THE OPENING DAY HAS BEEN CALLED OFF.

We have shut down the WTO!

WE HAVE SHUT DOWN THE WTO! cried the crowd.

There will be no business as usual today!

THERE WILL BE NO BUSINESS AS USUAL TODAY!

Over wild cheering, the Chicana led the chant (again):

Ain't no power like the people's power
'Cos the people's power don't stop!
Ain't no power like the people's power
'Cos the people's power don't stop!

17

What clothes he couldn't carry Daniel put on over the ones he was wearing. He then put Pockets' black puffa jacket over his new acquisitions: tracksuit bottoms, long cotton-print dress and turtleneck.

Outside the shop, a teenager Daniel's age, bangs plastered in a coiled swipe over her forehead and a paisley bandana around her neck, was lazily flapping her wrist eenie-meeny-miney-mo: Chantelle, you need to go home and get changed. And Troy, you need to go home. Sheboah, you too . . .

At this moment Daniel stepped through a broken window with an unfeasibly high pile of folded clothes.

The girl paused midsentence, arched her back and gave Daniel a sardonic look, like: *Are you sure?* She vogued a moment, then laughed out loud and put a hand over her mouth. She picked up where she'd left off: OK, Sheboah, you need to go home and get changed.

Cold air rushed into Daniel's sore lungs as he ran down the street, the cotton-print dress shortening his strides. Only now did he experience Seattle as a city, as a living thing. Before it had been an overwhelming and random collection of houses and garbage cans, of shops and buildings without a centre. The big lie, the front, he felt, was smashed. Some spell had been broken; a spell, which the shops were somehow part of, had been shattered. The city had come alive. Daniel knew what every tag on every wall and prime frontage window was saying. He could now read the cryptic, arabesque ciphers as the high-visibility tags of the city's invisible inhabitants. *We are here!* said the illegible script. *Tomorrow we won't be, but we leave you this to tell you we exist! You share the city with invisible ghosts. Well, today we are here, in name and in person and in power, and we'll be back!*

Today the city is shaped and styled by those it excludes. Decisions on how things look and how they work are—for one day only—open. Those who have no place—no *business*—downtown have staked a claim. This is what democracy looks like. In stores where a few days earlier Daniel had been followed round by security guards, he now cleared the racks. Today clothes are free. Halfway up Pike, however, he passed Global Citizen "Peace Police" linking arms, like a cut-out row of paper figures, to defend Nike Town's windows. A few peace police detached themselves and tried to stop Daniel. In the tussle he dropped all the sweatshirts he'd piked, and ran off in his long skirt and tracksuit bottoms.

18

As it got dark, riot police walked ten abreast along Pine, clubs at the diagonal, long black Darth Vader capes swinging over the top of their high black boots. They took up position at Fourth, the intersection's yellow street lights reflected on the tops of their black helmets. National Guard soldiers hit the ground running and began clearing the streets and sealing off the whole downtown area.

Chano was on his way home. A mile of Fourth would take him to Yesler Way. But Fourth was blocked at Pine. Chano walked up to the police line strung across the intersection.

This road is closed, said a riot cop through a strange little speaker in his gas mask.

I'm just going home, said Chano.

The road's closed, the distorted voice repeated.

Not fifty yards behind the police line Chano could see a crowd of protesters standing and chatting on Fourth. Turning back to the cop, his glance was momentarily snagged by the sight of a teenage boy wearing a full-length cotton dress. Look, they're all down there, he said, raising an upturned palm. So why can't I go down there?

The road's closed, sir, crackled the transistor voice. Now step back two paces!

Chano cast a last longing look at the straight way home. As he did so, the teenager in the dress turned his head, and the fish-smelling boy from the Calderon police station lifted a bottle of water to his lips.

The end of a wooden club jabbed Chano in the chest. Slowly he turned first his head and then his eyes back to the policeman. He looked at the policeman distractedly. How strange the riot cops' preoccupation seemed to him, whatever it was. He was saying something, the voice crackling away again. A stronger jab in the chest staggered Chano back a few paces. He stared at the full-face visor in bewilderment, then turned about and sprinted to the corner. If he ran he could get round the block on Third before Daniel moved.

At Pine and Third there was a cordon of troops in combat fatigues. Chano turned tail and ran straight up Third to Olive. But as he did so another line of soldiers began to fill the intersection ahead of him. Chano stopped and looked about him. He was in what riot police call the kettle. Boiling in impotent fury, back in sterile steam and mist, Chano's gas-resistant eyes filled with hot tears.

19

Legs apart, taking careful aim, a lone state trooper stood on the hood of an armoured humvee firing rubber bullets. From the Peacekeeper's open back doors more cops fired rounds of tear gas. From a distance the cop on the hood had been a metronome: one controled headshot every three seconds. Crack. Crack. Crack. But as the truck brought him ever closer, Daniel saw the hectic eyes behind his breath-misted visor.

Daniel had run from Fourth up Pike ahead of Monica and the rest of them when he'd heard the commotion, and was now among several hundred protesters being pushed back from Boren along the misty Interstate 5 bridge. A gas canister skittered along the gutter. Feet skipped out of the way left and right, clearing a wide space around it. Pulling his sweater over his fingers Daniel picked up the smoking tube. It burnt through his sleeve as he threw it back at the cops. He smacked his singed palm in a water-cannon puddle. *Chingada!*

At last Monica caught up with Daniel, intending to grab him and tell him off for running away from everyone like that. Still breathless, however, she saw at once the imperative of knocking the cop off the hood before he killed or maimed someone. Scooping up a wooden plank, she ran crouching alongside the humvee, overtook it, one stride, two strides, turned and threw the plank sideways. The plank caught the cop's leg. He wobbled, lifted a boot but kept his footing. The humvee's open back doors came past her. She scrabbled frantically after a still-smoking gas canister to lob back through the doors. A gloved hand grabbed her wrist.

No violence! said a man in a leather biker jacket.

Fuck off! said Monica, and tugged her arm free.

20

A kid came staggering toward him, blood streaming over his face. Would I recognize Daniel, thought Chano, if his face was covered in blood? No sooner had he pondered this than he became convinced that the youth stumbling blindly toward him was indeed his son. Chano ran across the street to the kid who he saw in an instant was not Daniel. He was, however, now Chano's responsibility. He helped the shivering youth to a store front and sat him down, wiping the blood from his face with a greasy coat sleeve.

He called over to some students. One had some bandages, another some water. They'd heard of the boy's affinity group and had a rough idea of where they'd seen them last.

Chano! shouted a Latino voice. He looked round and saw Ruben, his Unidos Sin Fronteras friend from this morning. Get off the hill, man! said the Ecuadorean, walking up to him. We got to get off the street you and me. Seven! It's curfew! C'mon man, it's time!

Curfew? asked Chano, watching the group around the staggering lad disappear.

You don't know?

No.

They declared it earlier this afternoon. Seven P.M. curfew.

Ya basta!

No, man. We've got to *go* you and me! We've got to go!

But what's going on up there? On the hill?

I tell you in a moment. This way now.

Is it seven now?

It's seven! Come on!

Chano looked up toward Capitol Hill from where he could hear shouting, then followed Ruben down Boren toward Seneca. A single siren whooped. Chano was now terrified that he'd be picked up, snatched from his son, deported. Just keep walking man, hissed Ruben. They cut through the back garden of a detached house and walked down a steep hill toward Skid Row.

21

Daniel and Ramona were telling Mani all they'd experienced up on Capitol Hill after curfew, where—no cameras at last—the Sheriff's Department had been trying out their whole "asymmetrical warfare" arsenal. Daniel was still fired up: You know Broadway? *Pues,* no attempt to disperse people, cops just kept firing volley after volley of rubber and wood bullets. (Here Daniel produced a wooden shell and Mani's face muscles twitched with the thought of Daniel being up there copping the payload.)

And outside the Egyptian theatre, said Ramona, the locals all built barricades from stuff in their homes and garages!

If people were alive they got gassed, said Daniel. When all the residents came out in their pyjamas? They got gassed. I saw a curry restaurant with a big fish tank in the window. That was gassed! All the diners were spluttering into white napkins, like they were holding their breath in the fish tank.

And if the cops had succeeded, Ramona told Mani, if people had been driven back, we'd have all ended up in the Convention Center!

Qué jodido, said Mani—what a fucked-up situation.

So, asked Daniel, what are we doing tomorrow?

Day 2: Wednesday, December 1

1

Inside the Four Seasons Hotel, the president of the United States of America was telling the cameras of the world's biggest media corporations: I wanna hear the views of those protesters. Outside the Four Seasons Hotel, there was a fifty-block No Protest Zone, lock-down of all public meetings, suspension of civil liberties, martial law declared, and troops and tanks on the streets. In bullet-proof vests, Washington State Patrol held blue AR-15 assault rifles.

The same two questions had been repeated over and over at Tuesday's police press conference: *Why didn't you arrest more people? Why so restrained?*

The order of the day was mass arrests. On Tuesday there'd been fewer than a dozen. By today's five P.M. press conference there would be five hundred.

2

Chano sat on a back pew of the Plymouth Congregational Church, drinking stewed coffee from a paper cup. He sat sideways, putting his feet up on the empty wooden pew. He was footsore and very tired.

A few hours earlier he had seen his son again. Daniel had been standing on the edge of a group discussing directions, and this time Chano had recognized him at once. He'd walked toward him, heart beating fast, and was only a stride away from touching the black puffa jacket when his son's head of jet-black hair had turned toward him and Chano had found himself staring into the face of a thirty-year-old Filipino with a goatee. Chano had walked on by, faster than before, for he had to find his son today.

The No Protest Zone meant Chano had to pace a wide circuit all day, steering wide of the soldiers. Once when he'd risked entering the Zone, he'd passed a man handing out photocopies of the Bill of

Rights and only seconds later saw him being arrested by a cluster of police who might, he knew, have arrested him too if he'd taken one.

Smoke haze from a burning dumpster had been corrugating the air when, pounding up Third Avenue, he'd heard a round of applause. A teenager in a hooded top had shinned up a lamp post and cut down a plastic pennant which read: Seattle Welcomes WTO. As the pennant fell, the youth had turned his head a moment to look down, and Chano had had to wait for him to shin slowly down the lamp post before he could rule him out. This had wasted precious minutes and he'd taken off again double-quick to make up for lost time.

After seven and a half hours spent like this, it was sweet release for Chano to ease his aching legs along the smooth wooden pew. He wasn't following the Plymouth's teach-in (a workshop on bio-technology and the global economy), but just sipping his stewed coffee and warming his hands on the polystyrene cup.

He'd picked up a leaflet on the way in: Seattle Steel Party, 2:30 P.M., Pier 62–63. The rally, said the leaflet, was to be followed by a march into the No Protest Zone. His mind slow and his face cold, he started to think about this while a Hindu woman was talking about the patenting of life forms and genetic identity.

That is where Daniel will be, thought Chano, because it's where I would've been when I was his age. Where else but the one action happening today? Daniel seemed in his element yesterday, so he'll be at the sharp end today. Plus it will be easier to find him there, because only a few thousand will risk marching into the No Protest Zone.

He looked at his watch. Three P.M. He'd have to run. Run and not get sidetracked by anyone, no matter how much they looked like Daniel. He left the meeting and ran down Union toward the sea.

It was a lucky escape. Five minutes later a speaker was interrupted by the chair to announce that the meeting had been locked down. The downtown suspension of all public meetings meant that no one could leave. There followed an instant change in mood. The audience was no longer a voluntary association but a holding pen, and the meeting was abandoned. People stood up, walked around the church hall, used the toilets, got some coffee, then climbed on to chairs and radiators to look out of stained-glass windows at the free world.

3

On the waterfront, George Becker, head of the United Steelworkers, was at a small podium covered from the drizzle by plastic sheeting.

It's just amazing, he declared, how people can get together for a common cause.

Swaying from side to side in the crowd, one minute lowering his hood as the rain stopped spitting, and the next flipping it back up as the sky dribbled a last shake more, Daniel was thinking how much the speaker looked like Detective Columbo. He had of course no idea what the tuneful rhythm of his words might mean.

This is unbelievable, cried Columbo. When we work together—human rights groups, environmental activists, civic groups, our community coalitions—and we ally this to the trade union movements, there is no force in America that can turn us back!

From two blocks away, through a gap in the cross-wire of two cluttered alleys, Chano, gasping for breath, saw the march. About a thousand kids and steelworkers from the Pier 62–63 waterfront steel rally, all marching up First toward Pike Place Market. Chano ran round the block to head them off at Pike Place.

The quiet march trudged along in the rain with an escort of only six cops. They passed under the shadow of Pike Tower and into the valley of the No Protest Zone. A side street erupted with riot police, all banging three-foot wooden staves on their shields. Peacekeeper trucks careered round the corner, National Guard dropping from its sides. They raised rifles and fired rubber bullets into the crowd. All around Daniel people were screaming, falling, ducking, and scattering under the rattle and clatter of rubber bullets. Steel boots charged the ambushed protesters. The black-clad, padded-torso cops clubbed, kicked, and punched their way into the mass of bodies, from which they snatched legal observers in lime-green bibs, like a fruit particularly delicious to the gorilla.

Chano arrived on Pike Place and ran along the rain-slick street. Here and there, back to back in handcuffs, pairs of seated protesters were stacked. Chano weaved through these sheaves toward two yellow

Metro buses loaded with prisoners. He ran along the windows looking for Daniel. As he hopped up to each window, prisoners held up scraps of paper to him, banging on the glass.

He ran on past the Turf Bar to the fish-market buildings. Here the dispersed marchers had reassembled and were linking arms. Now, twenty abreast and fifty deep, they began marching rapidly back toward the police. Chano scoured these tightly packed, moving bodies, searching for Daniel among large women and students, steelworkers and longshoremen, among showerproofs, duffel coats, rain-capes, and woollen ponchos. No Daniel . . . no Daniel . . . no Daniel . . .

Peaceful protest!

Peaceful protest!

The chant sounded as if they hoped the outcome might be different if the cops could only hear them. Surely they can't think that, thought Chano, fear rising in his throat.

Peaceful protest!

Peaceful protest!

But still a collective tone of indignant, offended propriety rose from the massed chorus. It's as if, thought Chano, they believe that there's been some kind of mistake. They sound *surprised* by injustice, as if they think the police aren't supposed to do that sort of thing. In that moment he despised the marching, chanting protesters. For their chant was the sound of speaking truth to power. And he despised them for the chaos which he knew was about to come. A chaos which would take his last chance of finding Daniel away for ever.

Peaceful protest!

Peace—

Gas shells exploded at their feet; toxic oleoresin-capsicum clouds rising. More shots were fired into the air, the gas clouds now falling.

The air is pure white.

Chano stands alone in a perfect cloud. For a moment everything is invisible. There are no more streets, no shops, no banks, no cops. Only hanging white curtains of gas cloud falling softly, thickening like snow.

All is quiet inside this perfect whiteness. Chano takes a few tentative steps further into its pure silence.

He finds that the cloud hosts a museum miscellany from that other world, the world outside the thick, white gas fog. How odd it is, he thinks, to come across a dark-blue mailbox here, like a symbol in a dream!

He walks on through silent blank suspension. Not quite silent: he eavesdrops on coughing, spluttering, crying, the private scrabbling of bodies on intimate concrete. Two people with their arms still linked appear out of the mist, stagger into him and go by. All is sheer blank again, and then in the cloud—a sapling. Here, thinks Chano, a little tree, here! And yet it could be on a winter field in Peru. Passing the sapling, he touches a branch and plucks a leaf from its bendy twig.

Chano stands over a curled-up body in the mist at his feet. A billow rolls between them. He crumples the leaf in his palm. He breathes heavily, gas singeing his nostrils, its spiky air scraping his throat. He crouches. Lower down the smoke is less thick. He can see him clearly now.

Here in this strange other world, in the calm centre of chaos, in this place where it seems he alone can walk, time has bent and warped. For so much does his son now look like he looked once before: steam all around him, curled up, crying, coughing, spluttering, wailing, and as if abandoned.

Chano strokes the damp hair.

My baby, he says in a slow, quiet voice. Daniel.

Daniel forces an eye half-open. Pain blurs a petrochemical haze. He sees a face floating above him. The lips smile. The voice says: What have they been doing to my boy?

The apparition flies from Daniel's view, the side of its head clubbed. A soldier's leg steps over the crumpled figure who stroked his hair and called him Daniel. The boy screams as a gloved hand seizes neck and jaw, dragging him forward on to his knees.

In green goggles Monica throws herself forward, rolling into the steel shin guards and tumbling on top of Daniel in a heap. The grunt brings down the butt of his stave on her ribs, then turns away.

A long-distance swimmer dragging herself out of the sea, she stands. She reels, at first away and then toward Daniel. She drags him along the ground until she's holding more sleeve than arm. She hauls him up into a three-legged race until both fall into the recessed doorway of a bank, where Monica cradles Daniel's head in her lap.

A bespectacled medic in a green bib pours water from a one-gallon bottle over their faces to sluice the oleoresin-capsicum. Daniel splutters, hawks, heaves. The crudely drawn red cross swims before his vision a moment before she presses a wad of cotton to his eyes, clamping Daniel's own fingers over it. The medic stands up holding the plastic gallon jug. A shot rings out. In one smooth movement, as if she's pushed herself over with the heel of her palm, she clutches her head and falls. Another shot booms. A rubber bullet hits the medic's back but she still clutches her eyes with both hands. The gallon jug rolls into the street.

Monica bends over Daniel's body as a rubber bullet ricochets around the three-walled doorway like a supersonic, rock-hard squash ball, cracking the glass door to land, spent, in the frozen crook of Monica's arm. Slowly she puts out a hand to the quarter-inch hard-nosed shell.

Robocop marches toward the prostrate medic. Stands over her, takes aim and shoots her twice more in the neck. Robocop turns, picks up the gallon jug and empties the water on to the street. Robocop stamps it flat with a big black boot. Robocop turns his plexi visor toward Monica and Daniel. Studies them. Thinks about it. Sets off to protect some place else.

4

Chano hears a woman's voice. He's been hearing it for some time. He opens his eyes. A blurry outline asks: Do you speak English? Blink yes.

Chano's chin is in her hand. He blinks. He's sitting on the floor with his back against a wall. His eyesight clears a little.

You were concussed, says the woman's voice. *Concussione?* Here y'are, drink this, she says, and puts a paper cup into his hand.

Chano gives a loud groan. From the sharp pain in his head on looking down at the paper cup. From remembering how close he was to Daniel. He sips the rosehip tea. Feeling her concerned, patient breath on his forehead, he tells her: It's all right. I'm OK. No problem.

That's great. Now you hold this, she says, and guides his hand up to the lint she's pressing against the side of his head. He presses for a few seconds more then examines the lint. Lots of blood. But not too much.

I'm OK now, he says. Thank you. No problem. Thank you.

What's your name?

He struggles his head up to meet her gaze. She has a kind strong face and light-brown frizzy hair.

Chano.

OK, Chano. Look at that sign ahead of you? The big black letters?

Yeah.

What does it say?

He cranes his neck a little, like a mini abdominal crunch, blinks, puts the bandage in his lap, breathes out and in a dull monotone reads: JAIL SOLIDARITY—TACTICS—STAY IN CUSTODY BY REFUSING TO GIVE YOUR NAME/ADDRESS AND BY REFUSING TO SIGN A CITATION.

Bueno, señor!

De nada, he replies, forcing a smile.

Stay sitting for a while.

Vale.

Chano folds the bandage and reapplies it to his head wound. He looks around the big empty room—a factory? an aircraft hangar? a warehouse? a squat? Nausea comes in waves. He sips the rosehip tea and rests the cup on his thigh.

Propped against a steel pillar ahead of him sits a young woman with a blood-stained bandage over her eyes, her legs shaking. Either side of this woman are two more; one holds her hand, the other talks in a low, sibilant murmur. What happened to her? asks Chano.

That's Carmel. She's a medic, too. Fragments in both eyes from where a rubber bullet smashed her glasses.

Pinche.

Fuckin' A, she says. Then, pointing at Chano's leg, she adds: Oh, and take care when you go outside. The cops sprayed you with marker paint. You got pink dye all down your right side.

He wipes his face. His hand comes back pink.

Pink, thinks Chano. Daniel will be coated in pink dye, too. He inspects the bandage. The wound is stanching.

5

They're sitting on a cement planter in the Westlake Plaza. Monica has an arm round Daniel's shoulders. She has brought him away from Pike Place, along Olive, to this glum, triangular shopping plaza, with its glum, triangular, white plastic Christmas trees. The heated entrances of store fronts wheedle tinny jingles. Under tarpaulin wraps, a merry-go-round refuses to leave its tent. Christmas carollers are singing beneath a lantern suspended from a bough of holly.

We three kings of orient are
Bearing gifts we travel afar . . .

The effects of tear gas are a cover for Daniel silently to cry. After a while Monica feels his sobs through her arm but, with a wise and subtle kindness, pretends she hasn't so that the boy can keep crying.

Daniel is going over and over in his mind the strange meeting he only half saw.

Yolanda said his father was in Seattle. But he knows he mustn't confuse reality with hopes and wishes and fantasies. That's what Arlinda was always trying to tell him. And she was right. Right. He knew that she was right. Daniel wipes his eyes and face.

. . . Field and fountain
Moor and mountain . . .

A few, unwinding protesters gather here or there, some sit on other cement planters, sharing sandwiches, chocolate and bottled water.

Following yonder star . . .

'Ere, they've got you with marker dye, says Monica.

Daniel looks up. What's she saying? he wonders.

It's on your back, she says, pointing at his black puffa jacket.

He looks at her encouragingly, uncomprehendingly. She rubs a

hand down his back then shows him the pink paint on her palm.
Daniel takes off his jacket to look at the damage.

Chano enters the plaza at a jog-trot. Blood flows wetly into an ear. He
scans the milling coats, sleeves, trousers, shoes for a pink flash.

. . . *Oh, star of wonder, star of light* . . .

A Peacekeeper noses out from the corner. Daniel looks up.

Nah, look, says Monica, indicating the shoppers and carollers to
Daniel, who grins, aware that he's been caught out being paranoid.

He goes back to rubbing the pink dye on his coat and trying to
remember . . . What did the man look like? What did he say? He looks
at the goose pimples on his cold bare arms and recalls glimpses of the
face, the eyes . . . What was he *saying*?

. . . *Star with royal beauty bright* . . .

Clink-clink-clink. Daniel looks up. Cops deploying. The clink-clink of
the jogging cops' hinged knee pads and jointed ankle mouldings.

. . . *Field and fountain*
Moor and mountain . . .

They're having a laugh, aren't they? says Monica, but getting to her
feet all the same. Daniel stands up, too. Beeee-*have*! she shouts at
the police.

. . . *Following yonder star* . . .

A canister bounces into the shopping plaza. Nothing happens. It
hasn't exploded! thinks Daniel. Next moment all the oxygen in the
Westlake has gone.

Chano runs confidently into the hissing mist, but then doubles over,
retching and stumbling in the airless plaza. For this is the new gas, the

CN gas, the Malmstrom Air Force Base Classic Reserve, the vintage ethylated chloride. Every orifice on fire, Chano tries to keep running. His legs stiffen, then buckle, and he's on his back, gasping and spluttering, his eyes, ears, lungs, throat, penis, anus, nostrils, ears, fingernails—burning, burning, burning.

Daniel staggers. The air is full of rancid, brown smoke which tastes like metal. The gas is inside his clothes! He can't see Monica. Sees an arm. Not hers. His eyes boil in their sockets. Which way to run? Daniel runs blind, burning, coughing, breathing in liquid fire. He's knocked over. A middle-aged woman's head vibrates on the tarmac, eyes and mouth wide open. A Chinese man on his back dry-heaves, his shoulders twitch uncontrollably, eyes and mouth wide open. Daniel's eyes sear shut, his skin scalding, as he crawls on hands and knees, anywhere but out.

They're sitting on some kind of electrical box by the traffic lights on Olive Way. Monica swings her legs to try and stop them shaking. It's past curfew. She closes her eyes and all unbidden an image comes into her mind.

Sprung from its hydrant, above ground for the first time in centuries, the unleashed River Walbrook has become a fountain, jetting high and strong; sunlight recycles the shivered glass of the LIFFE building; the sound system on the flatbed truck under Cannon Street Bridge pumps gabba-techno to a bouncing, sweating crush of thousands; City of London cops exit both ways, Monica is dancing under the spray of the world's newest fountain, the techno builds to a climax and the crowd roars as one.

She opens her eyes. Ready? she asks Daniel. It's past curfew so let's go home . . . ? Er, *vamos en el Convergence?*

Los otros?

Er, sorry . . . ?

Palliss Peeyah?

The others?

Si, Daniel nods, wiping shredded privet from his palms.

OK, we'll go find the others.

6

Chano lies on his hostel bed curled up on one side, palms together between his legs. He groans and climbs off. He staggers down the landing and pisses blood in the cold communal toilet bowl. (As he did fourteen years ago, in a Tamaulipas police cell, when Daniel was first lost.)

It has taken Chano an hour to hobble all the way down Fourth to Skid Row, his joints stiff as if every last drop of synovial fluid had been vapourised. Poison roiling in his sulphurous guts each hard, uneven step of the way, he'd puked in a bush on leafy Madison and again on Jefferson.

On framing the US Constitution, Madison himself declared: *the prime responsibility of government is to protect the minority of the opulent from the majority.* It was a contradiction that would have to be fought out o'er field and fountain, Eighth and Pine, forest and plaza.

7

Daniel perched on a radiator in the Filipino Center. He pressed a palm against his side where his liver ached like a stitch. He'd been short of breath since the Westlake. He took a deep breath and felt a stabbing pain in his back.

The streets had become scary after dark. Daniel had experienced that special, raw lawlessness which exists when riot cops control the streets and there're no witnesses about; a unique, skin-prickling realization that the cops are now an untouchable gang, tingling with power and impunity in the dark abandoned streets of their own patch. Daniel had felt that anything could happen. The others had, too. Palace Pier had split up in different directions, most taking the long way round to the Convergence, but Daniel and Mani had gone to the Filipino Center.

The teach-in, hosted by Voces de la Frontera, was called Building Cross-Border Resistance to the WTO. Chicanos and Latinos outnumbered Filipinos in the hall, three to one.

Looking around the hall Daniel was reminded of the Uniones hall near Tonalacapan, and yet he couldn't pin down a single thing which was the same. Everyone was speaking Spanish but it wasn't that. Nor was it the shape of the room, nor the colour of the walls, nor the texture of the floor.

The second speaker at the mike this evening was a Mexican woman with long black hair. If the Cold War was the Third World War, she was saying, then this is the Fourth. And it's a war being fought between private power and civil society, between corporations and people.

The more that everything else was changing, the less uprooted Daniel felt. Everything in his life was as new and unfamiliar as the bright pink blood he'd coughed up into the toilet paper which was now scrunched up in his pink and black puffa jacket. And only a new reality—call it the Fourth World War—could, he felt, make sense of his own radically changing experience. It was the golden thread through the maze, the global maze he'd entered on first seeing Beto in a field no longer his own.

The more revolutionary the social transformation contemplated, the more Daniel could make sense of the radically unrecognizable in his own life. Neither the long-haired Mexican woman nor anyone else here was suggesting a shorter gun barrel on the tank and rubber tires instead of metal tracks. No one here was suggesting speaking truth to power. Instead the bold strokes the Mexican woman used emboldened him. As she spoke of cross-border organizing, the borders Daniel himself had crossed became part of a common atlas. He was part of the same process which involved all the other people in the hall, none of whom were where they'd started life either. In fact Daniel became so stirred by what the Mexican woman was saying that he soon was unable to listen, and lost himself in thought.

And yet the more I've changed, he reflected, the more it seems I've become myself. Because it's as if all this was waiting for me. I wonder if Mani would understand that? Shall I tell him? Or Ramona? She might. They both might. Except now that I've made this clearer to myself, I don't feel the need to tell anyone any more.

Mani became aware of Daniel staring vaguely at him, and raised his eyebrows, waiting for Daniel to say something. Nothing coming from the boy, Mani then nodded toward the stage as if to say Pay attention, *chavo.*

Day 3: Thursday, December 2

1

Patrick Gajer went up to a neat, fifty-year-old man in silver glasses. His baseball cap bore the insignia of a US naval ship. Patrick was sure this conservative-looking gent was not a protester.

Are you one of the protesters? Patrick asked.

No, I own a business here. I'm just on my lunch break.

May we interview you?

Well, I'm in a *slight* hurry but, uh, OK . . .

Thank you. Patrick got a raised thumb from his cameraman. What, asked Patrick, do you think of all the violence and property damage?

Well, all the protesters I've seen have been so far peaceful, the man replied in a resigned, hey-ho kind of voice.

But what of the small minority who *have* been intent on violence?

Well, seems most every time the kids try to have a peaceful protest these people just turn up with their uniforms, riot shields and tear gas . . . But what can you do? There ain't no law against it.

Patrick frowned. They couldn't use it. (The shots they had were dramatic and a flippant vox-pop wouldn't fit.) He next approached a young man who had butterfly wings on his back and held two wooden poles wrapped in silver foil, by means of which he was able to flap said butterfly wings. His hair in pigtails, he wore goggles made from two tea strainers which gave him bulbous insect eyes.

Do you mind if we talk to you?

You're from England? Yeah, sure.

Thanks, said Patrick. OK . . .

Oh, do you want I should keep the wings flapping while we talk?

Er, uh, no, that's fine.

It's the Monarch. The Red Monarch.

Of course it is. Oh, and wait till I put the microphone to your mouth before you start talking.

Microphone to mouth. Do I look at you?

Yep, Patrick replied in a clipped undertone. Ready? The cameraman gave Patrick the thumbs up. Patrick held the camera a beat then began: There's a lot of young people here, many . . .

He stopped and turned back to the Butterfly Boy. Don't flap your wings.

Oh, sorry. Habit. Forgot. No flapping. Got it. OK.

Ready? (Thumbs up.) Patrick began again to camera: There's a lot of young kids here—many protesting quite different issues—but how many of them really understand the finer, technical points of trade negotiations?

As Patrick turned, the cameraman pulled back to reveal Butterfly Boy. Can I ask you why you're here today? asked Patrick.

Well, said the Butterfly Boy, like, listening to what you said? I think all the different issues *are* all part of the one issue. I mean if you look at Kaiser, right? Kaiser Aluminium? They're owned by this guy Hurwitz, OK? Real bad guy, and he's locked out Spokane steel-workers for over a year. Now, same guy, this Hurwitz, same guy owns Pacific Lumber, and *they're* behind the global free-logging agreement. So that's why there was that sign which said Teamsters and Turtles Together At Last—because people have found, you know, common cause.

That was very good, but a bit shorter please. It's a news show. If you can.

Okey-dokey.

Ready? (Thumbs up.) Can I ask you, said Patrick with on-screen formality, what you *personally* are protesting against?

The World Trade Organization.

Why?

It sets a limit on what governments can or can't do. It's anti-democratic, laws we have . . .

So you're in favour of the government, then?

Ah. Well, that's an interesting question. Maybe I'll say—best just say, uh, *one step at a time!*

Oh Patrick, interrupted the producer, who was standing just out of shot. She came forward and, with a brief smile at Butterfly Boy, said to Patrick: It's all getting a bit theoretical, isn't it? Just keep it punchy. Remember we've got to talk to lots of other people. So just do the to-camera intro and then one pithy question. She went back to the camera from where she held up her index finger. Just the one, she called.

OK, replied Patrick. Sorry to hold you up, he said to Butterfly Boy. That's cool.

Great. Are we ready? Patrick waited for the nod. No flapping, he hissed at Butterfly Boy.

Fuck, sorry! Right, right.

The producer was looking at the cameraman's fold-out viewfinder. She stuck up a thumb.

There's a lot of young kids here, Patrick began, many protesting quite different issues. But how many of them really understand the finer, technical points of trade negotiations? (Turns, camera pulls back.) Why the butterfly wings?

Oh these? Well the Red Monarch butterfly is being made extinct by GM crops. And it's an important butterfly, the Monarch, you know? A very important butterfly.

Thank you very much.

2

Charlene Barshevsky, the chair of the whole Seattle WTO ministerial, stamped down the escalator, trailing a shoulder throw and a load of delegates behind her. On the up escalator Evan turned like a music-box figurine to watch her go.

The signs were bad wherever you looked, Evan reflected, but at least GATS was safe—it was part of the "built-in agenda." No, his real worry now was TRIPS and TRIMS. But particularly TRIPS (Trade-Related Aspects of Intellectual Property Rights), because he'd worked on TRIPS; because he'd put in so many hours, days, weeks, of his up-time on TRIPS; because the year before in Geneva his last months of full health had been spent on TRIPS. Evan reminded himself of how Monsanto's James Enyart—the working group's chair—had praised their achievements. "Together," he'd said, "we have identified a problem facing world commerce, crafted a solution, reduced it to a concrete proposal and sold it to our own and other governments. We have played the role of the patients, the diagnosticians and the physicians." Ironic that, thought Evan crossing the lobby, since my first major collapse was just after I got home.

On the fourth floor he passed a cluster of TV cameras and hand-held mikes around some furious African or other. On the fifth he found the room he was looking for. It was curtained off against the glare and arc lights of the television cameras. Luckily no one important though, he thought, just Burundi TV and Uganda Plus, Indy Media and Hindi Update. Evan sat at the back, legs crossed, hands linked together over one knee, his body language small.

The Like-Minded Group of Developing Countries had evolved since Monday. (Evan wondered how people could make a virtue out of being *like-*minded.) The small room was rammed with high-ranking Southern delegates. Whenever Evan tried to think of an African, Caribbean or South-East Asian WTO-member country which *wasn't* represented, he'd turn his head, or someone would step aside for someone else crowding in, and a pendant name tag would say Ethiopia, Kenya, India, St Lucia, Nigeria . . .

Behind the briefing table sat a Malaysian and an Indian from Third World Network. Evan thought he knew their names but didn't know which was which, and so referred to them in his mind as the Malaysian and the Indian.

The Malaysian was talking now, wire glasses perched on his broad nose, his hand gestures quick, his undulating, quick-quick-slow Indochinese accent chiming heavy on the last syllables. Now, he said, the patenting of life comes under Article 27.3b of TRIPS. We're very proud that the African group of countries has put forward a proposal that something is wrong in 27.3b, that something has been changed from the draft agreement. The Malaysian waved the draft TRIPS agreement in the air. Article 27, he said, originally read: "intellectual property is to be defined in such a way as to protect indigenous traditional knowledge and products including animal, plant life and micro-organisms." But now we have a new, modified article called Article 27.3b. This now says animal and plant life are still to be exempted as before, but *not* micro-organisms. You *can* patent micro-organisms, it says.

He laid the paper down. He looked up. Rapidly adjusting the square wire frames on his nose, he expounded: This is a clever trick. You see. It's clever. When you patent a gene, it is a micro-organism. Where do you find micro-organisms? Only place you find a micro-organism is in plants and animals. Then, when you *inject* a patented micro-organism into a plant or animal—to genetically modify it—that plant or animal is patentable. You now own the patent on that plant or animal.

The Malaysian was in his element, Evan thought bitterly, as he listened to him extemporizing with rapid-fire confidence: So the group of African countries is saying: "Allow us also to prohibit patenting of micro-organisms which are also life forms in order to get out of the trick—the *trick*—that you have to patent micro-organisms and those micro-organisms if injected into plants and animals—if genetically modified—will also make the plants and animals patentable." This is the reason they force us to allow patenting of micro-organisms. And this leaves the intellectual property rights of traditional knowledge systems and indigenous products protected in the area of stones. The vital area of stones! Stones and non-crystalline rocks! (A laugh rolled from the front to the back of the room—until it reached Evan, with whom it collided head on and was killed stone dead.) Article 27.3b, he repeated, anger and relish competing as his nimble finger drummed the document twice and the drumming echoed up through the table mike. This is the sop they throw to the developing countries!

Evan quietly stood up, shuffled sideways along the back wall to the door. He had to stand aside while a few more crowded in (Tanzania, Trinidad . . .), before he could get out of the room.

He stood alone in the corridor and rested his hands on his knees.

It wasn't just anyone's clever trick, it was *his* clever trick. The problem they had diagnosed in Geneva, the solution they had crafted, the concrete proposal they had reduced it to . . . But all this was now being reduced to rubble, to the vital area of stones. Moth-er-*fuck-er*!

At the far end of the corridor Evan heard raised voices: Africans contesting Caucasians. Hands still resting on knees—for he had a slight stomach cramp coming on—Evan turned his head to hear the fallout. Before he heard the argument he already knew it would be like all the other spats erupting, and for the same reason: the dissent on the streets had created the conditions for the Third World delegates to get cocky inside the hall. In the past, the Washington Consensus had always steamrollered through *precisely because* it could always present itself as a consensus. Corporate-managed trade was the only game in town. But not here, not today.

One of the Africans he knew from his files: Noko, a Namibian delegate. Evan remembered the impossible youth of the man—late twenties?—the tiny Kierkegaard glasses with extremely thick lenses, the dapper goatee and tie pin. Next to Noko was someone called Teffeh Something or other. Evan knew he was Tanzanian, but couldn't remember either his surname or which pan-African NGO he was from. (Evan had been too hot in the stuffy room and was now very cold in the corridor.) Between the two stood the chief negotiator of the Caribbean with his bushy, grey mutton-chops. Governments and NGOs lining up together, thought Evan, that's always a bad sign.

Teffeh Something was haranguing a US delegate (one of Charlene's corporate placemen from Sunwell or I-Net, as Evan remembered) and an English EU delegate.

In Uruguay, Teffeh cried, his voice ringing out along the corridor, the major powers gave us a thirteenth-hour declaration to sign, a declaration we had never seen, which we had to sign blind. In Uruguay you promised us it would never happen again, we would never have to sign blind again. "Just sign it this once for us," they said, "just to keep the process alive, and next time, we promise you, next time all will be different." Well, now is the next time, now here we are again and it's exactly the same!

The grand chief negotiator beamed like Samuel Johnson as he took in the EU and US delegates' discomfort.

We have spent a lot of money to get here, began Noku, hands behind his back, and speaking in the clipped, sharp tones of an angry ectomorph. Evan found himself standing up in unconscious imitation of this neat man's sharp bearing. And for what? Noko asked, enunciating every consonant like an elocution teacher. To be spectators. To be bit-part actors. To lend a spurious unanimity to an agreement over which we have not once been consulted. Not once. Threatened, yes. Consulted, no. We don't know what goes on in your Green Room or Green Rooms, we don't even know where they are. We have been sitting in a room talking to each other like a debating club and—worse, worse—when Quad members have found themselves in a room with us (here his voice began to rise) they have immediately walked out again to discuss it in the corridor or the Green Room! Or the Sheraton or the Westin! Or at the Whites Only Drinking Fountain!

The turtlenecked secret servicemen drew closer; the Sheriff's

Department cops, too. A black man was shouting and getting all fired up. But police and secret service were hamstrung and confused here.

They knew what they'd do most places, but what was the line in this place? Were they *allowed* to shout? A secret serviceman touched his ear-piece and awaited instructions.

Well, yes, replied the US delegate, we need to remind people that this is about dialogue, because, you know, we wanna remind people that trade disputes led to two world wars, and that GATT was set up after World War Two so that these disputes could be settled amicably instead.

Two shots rang up from the streets below. The high-resolution magnified eyes of Noku in his tiny Kierkegaard specs held both the Quad members for a moment. A third shot rang out. Away down the corridor the issues-management expert rested the back of his head against the wall, closed his eyes and laughed. A twisting in his liver brought him up short.

I agree with everything you say, the EU delegate told Noko. Of course, it's deplorable, and we do want to hear all your comments, because the whole *point* of the WTO and the message we should be getting across should be all about how the WTO contributes to a more just society, where people can solve their disagreements peacefully.

KER-RR-AA-BAAANGGG! A thudding double explosion caroomed in the distance, its volleying blast echoing up canyon walls. The US delegate turned away irritably, saying: What are the flat-earthers up to out there *now?*

Black jacket folded over white shirt sleeve, Evan re-entered the crowded briefing room. There was a cameraman standing on the chair where he'd been sitting. Evan stood at the back not able to see for all the Southern delegates and hacks. He heard an elderly Indian voice shouting now: We were cheated out of development by the globalization process in the nineteenth century. We will not be cheated out of this one! We were de-industrialized once before, we will not be de-industrialized again!

Perhaps this means, mused Evan, they've moved on to TRIMS.

The problem of the powerful, continued the Indian, has always been how to bleed the poor—both of your own countries and elsewhere—without it looking like that is what you are doing! Once you had your Cold War and now you have your new world order—and it's just the same old robbery!

Yes, thought Evan with a heavy heart, it's *definitely* Trade Related Investment Measures. He left the room once more, ducking under a furry boom mike on his way out.

Down three floors on the mezzanine, Evan stood on his own with a white cup and saucer of coffee in his hand. He listened to the hum of all the delegates and missions, the flaks and hacks, the ministers and briefings. Under the high ceiling all this talk seemed to form one solid, homogeneous, cigarette-smoky wedge. It was all one voice, a vain, sick, hyper, wretched din. A repellent, dense chunk of stodgy sound. He felt removed, an odd singularity. Tiny ceiling spotlights were reflected on high black windows, mingling with the stars and the lights of the cityscape. He wondered if he'd see his brother again.

Up two floors, he sat in the blue-curtained ESLG booth and did some flack work on a GATS press release for European consumption. Then he wrote a very differently worded one on exactly the same premise for the US. The technical concentration of this, the purity of it, was like a lemon sorbet after a greasy meal. He regained equilibrium.

Walking to the Four Seasons an hour later, however, Evan was troubled by a strange sense of having been, as it were, found out. He felt as if he had been found out by his illness. Tapped and found hollow. (His carotid artery was throbbing and his armpits ached.) This notion had been planted in his mind, he supposed, by his brother; by the mystical way in which Chano had described his illness—with its assassin bugs who sucked on the blood of poor babies in the night. Now had the streets been peaceful, Evan would not have given this notion much headroom. But his sense of having been somehow found out in his own body was mirrored on the streets by the way these obscure trade talks had been found out. The WTO of all things! The WTO had always been strictly page seven of the pink papers. *Newsnight* hadn't even bothered sending a reporter. And why should they? It was entirely reasonable not to have sent a crew here. Just as it had been entirely the right thing to do not to send a film crew to Davos or Uruguay or Marrakesh or Geneva either.

Not a good night to go shopping, deadpanned a soldier as Evan passed through the green capes and helmets of a National Guard cordon.

Evan walked to his meeting, rescheduled from this morning's abandoned attempt. For a couple of blocks the streets were eerily deserted. The white lights of squat Christmas trees were twinkling incongruously on the porches of retail stores as he passed the boarded-up windows of Nike Town, Bon Marche and Banana Republic. He dropped a clutch of folders. Bending down to pick them up, he found that he couldn't grip. His hands and fingers were purple and bloated. Standing up again, his vision was mottled. Three giant brass teddy bears revolved on the toy-shop porch. He began to shake.

He tried walking, his shoulder bounced and slid along the plywood store fronts. Crossing the intersection he stumbled over a bonfire and rolled to the ground with the embers of old placards falling around him. Grey-haired with ash, he crawled clear.

A lone female protester was standing in the middle of the next intersection waving a Mexican flag. Back on his feet, Evan tried to focus on this blurry figure. He took several steps closer, then jack-knifed as puma's teeth tore at his intestines. He screamed out. At the same moment up ahead on the intersection, rubber bullets crackled and flag and flag-waver collapsed in a crumpled heap.

Are you OK? asked a stranger's voice. Were you hit? Evan rested a hand on the man's shoulder while he got his breath back.

When the pain had subsided, he looked up and gasped a reply: Fuck off!

A low-flying firework whizzed through the crossroads. He was, he now saw, among people running about. Skimming sideways, a hooded water beetle sprayed urgent words on a wall. Evan's staggering steps hammered over a sheet of corrugated iron, he tripped and crashed into a burning dumpster, sending up a scatter of sparks and a belch of black smoke.

Peace on the streets! a far-off voice shouted angrily at this anarchist. No violence! At the end of the street, its lights off, a humvee began to follow Evan.

Evan turned the corner and had to stop. Both palms flat on a window, he tried not to scream with the pain. He head-butted the glass, slowly and repeatedly. The humvee, cruising after the man who'd tried to overturn an iron dumpster, rounded the corner just as he kicked in Starbucks' last window. Gear change.

Blind head slumped and nodding on chest and shoulder, every dozen steps Evan forced his heavy eyes open. He saw the red carpet rising up the steps of the Four Seasons. He had made it. There was an armed guard under the green awning. A police dog stared at Evan, unrolling its long tongue and snapping it up again to hang over its lower teeth as he barked. Slowly, amidst the sound of barking and a siren's whoop behind him, Evan heard drums and chanting. He was going to have to pass a blockade.

He began walking up the police dog's long red tongue. But if the dog would just stop barking, the carpet would stop moving and it would be easier for him to climb the steps.

Evan tripped up the busy tongue, fighting his way through the crowd to the top of the steps. A protester's hand grabbed the crook of his arm. Evan span round and threw a wild hook, reeling back on to hardened body armour under the awning.

I saw you! cried a woman. You punched him!

Let me see that name tag, sir, said the cop, taking it between gloved fingers.

Feeling the cord being tugged on his neck, Evan swung a punch at the cop but his legs gave way. He blacked out, spinning, falling.

Police dogs dragged the body which lay face down at the foot of the steps this way and that on the concrete.

Day 4: Friday, December 3

1

Sitting on the road, Chano hugged the underside of his thighs and grinned. He'd decamped with the rest of the vigil outside King County Jail, after a few hours watching silhouettes of prisoners raising fists in high cell windows. A crowd of four hundred or so were now occupying Fifth at Virginia, blockading the steps of the Westin Hotel, where US delegates were in discussion with corporate representatives. Others stood or sat in the road. The blockade's mood was kept up by deliveries of food, every now and then, from Seattle longshoremen and local residents, and by a series of announcements.

Dusk was shading into evening. It was quieter here than at the jail blockade with its loudspeaker speeches and samba drums and Chano could think more clearly.

There is my son, my Daniel, alive, crisscrossing the Atlantic seemingly at will. And with friends. Our Daniel. His mother's son, yes, his mother's son. What would Marisa have given just for this moment? Many parents, thought Chano, sacrifice their lives but die happy in the hope that their child will live freer than they did. Like Daniel. *Ay*, Marisa, and our boy so like a young man now, so capable. He would have made you proud. Very proud.

Marisa's sudden execution, the brutal cutting off of her life, of a story that was just beginning and which was all about beginnings, that had been the worst, most violent thing about it. That had been its evil. Still was. But this was good. This was very good. One of them had seen the boy safe and well. And Chano felt this gave not just his own but Marisa's life new meaning now as well. Hands clasped together under his thighs, Chano rocked his heels to and fro, wiggling the toes of his trainers. Forward and back he swayed, smiling.

A few yards away, Monica had D-locked her neck to the Westin's revolving door, with Ramona standing by her to make sure no one tried to force the door open. Monica was wishing she'd chosen one of the other doors. Neck and revolving door, she rebuked herself, words that should never go together! The door wasn't completely immobilized either and the tinted glass didn't help. Twice she'd felt her ass slide back a terrifying couple of rubber-tread inches before everyone had piled in to jam the door. She was glad of Ramona being so loud and kick-ass, glad Ramona was someone she'd buddied up with a lot on past actions. (Then again, she reflected, it was Ramona she'd been with when she'd broken her arm on an oil-truck's crankshaft, locked on at Coniston BP refinery!) Neck and revolving door! But here she sat, munching chocolate and swallowing with difficulty.

Her neck stuck at its forty-five-degree angle, Monica now saw a man in a white headband sitting on his own in the road. She recognized him but couldn't recall where from. Just a glimpse she had of him, before legs and bodies on the hotel steps blocked her D-locked view. Just a glimpse: a man sitting on the street, rocking backward and forwards, a moustache . . . A spasm of cramp seized her. She rubbed her leg but couldn't reach below the knee.

Movement in the crowd revealed the man again. Yes it was him. Him with the moustache who'd crouched down and said something to Daniel, the one she'd seen stroking the boy's hair. And it wasn't a headband, she now saw, but a bandage. Yes, he'd got clubbed on the head by the soldier from whom she'd de-arrested Daniel. She'd felt the same wooden club in the ribs after her forward somersault over the boy.

A fresh group came and sat on the top step and Monica lost sight of him again. But with a tingling, sickly foreboding, a presentiment, a hunch was already beginning to form in her mind.

Chano rocked some more, rolling his heels, wiggling his toes. He kept going over and over the memory of the moment he'd seen his son. He tried leaving the memory alone in case inspecting it over and over would perish the thought. But each time he reran the memory, he found the opposite was true: he could remember more details, could more fully experience Daniel in his memory again. One thing, however, which he kept trying to convince himself of, he knew had never happened and would never happen, no matter how many times he reran the moment. But that didn't stop him trying. This chimera was that Daniel had been able to see him for a moment longer. If only Daniel's eyes had opened just a bit more. But in his memory he saw them as they had been: like steamed mussels, red-peppered. But Daniel did definitely see me for an instant, though, yes, and he even *tried* to see me more clearly, for a second or two more, but he wasn't able to. He couldn't. There. There's an end to it. And that's OK. That goes well. There I can draw a line. A limit to happiness. (Which, thus contained, was to Chano an air bubble of joy pushing against the marrows of his face bones.) He rocked back and forward again, his feet like flippers, and listened to the assembly's call-and-response litanies.

An announcement was made that a pizza delivery boy had been sent to the satellite van of FOX TV, but that on seeing what was going down, he'd just now distributed his pizzas free to the locked-on activists. Cheers and applause rose from the crowd, who chanted:

Ain't no power like the power of the pizza,
'Cos the power of the pizza don't stop.

The monorail train went by on its fluffy, dirt-clogged slide and the driver gave a honk-honk in solidarity. As always on picket lines, a cheer went up from the crowd. Chano unhooked a hand from under his legs to wave back at the honk-honk monorail. He couldn't believe in the WTO protests for himself. But he *could* believe in them for his son and himself. This change was, he knew, a loss as much as it was a cause for celebration. But the concern was lost in the cheering, as it were.

Someone got up on the steps and said: We've just had a message from someone in the jail . . .

WE'VE JUST HAD A MESSAGE FROM SOMEONE IN THE JAIL . . . repeated the crowd.

A stout young woman then came to the head of the line and stood on the steps. Around her were seated protesters but as she spoke she looked at the cluster of standing bodies in front.

This is difficult for me to say, OK, she began, her voice thick and slightly tremulous.

THIS IS DIFFICULT FOR ME TO SAY, OK . . . repeated two hundred voices. With each sentence shared and embodied by the crowd, she told how prisoners had been denied medication, water, and access to lawyers, how the police had sexually assaulted female prisoners, had threatened to rape one woman.

It seemed to Chano as though the multitude's voice was a more subtle register of each different emotion than the individual's. To Monica's ears—on the other side of the crowd—each repeated phrase sounded like bearing witness, and everything seemed to stop still.

A male prisoner was stripped naked in his cell and beaten up, held down and pepper-sprayed in the eyes. The cops were throwing people against the wall and shouting: Who are the leaders? Who are the leaders?

WHO ARE THE LEADERS? WHO ARE THE LEADERS? repeated the crowd. And it being the end of her message, they continued, more loudly: WHO ARE THE LEADERS? WHO ARE THE LEADERS? (For leaders were there none.)

Under this chant another announcement had begun, but it was a while before the crowd realized.

. . . From the Indy Media Center.

FROM THE INDY MEDIA CENTER, responded two hundred voices.

And now came wild cheering and shouts: REPEAT! SAY IT AGAIN!

Silence fell save for a hum of expectancy and muttering. Was it true? A bad rumour? A cyclist came up and said something, nodded and grinned. A woman on a cell phone shrieked, waved the phone in the air, then handed it on to someone else before walking to the front of the steps.

The talks have collapsed! she announced.

THE TALKS HAVE COLLAPSED!

Not even a declaration. Nothing.

NOT EVEN A DECLARATION. NOTHING.

We've won. The talks have collapsed. This is confirmed.

WE'VE WON. THE TALKS HAVE COLLAPSED. THIS IS CONFIRMED.

Under the cheering, under the standing up of everyone who'd been sitting, under the jumping up and down, under the hugging and whooping, under drumming and singing and dancing, Monica was unlocked from the revolving door. Her legs had set rigid after three hours' lock-down.

It was me! I did it! she said, as they pulled her to her feet. I won it! She fell forward into Ramona's arms.

Lurching on solidified Legs of the Mummy, Monica began searching the jubilant crowd for a moustache and bandaged head. When she got to where he'd been sitting he was gone.

He was sitting on the curb. Monica went over and sat down next to him.

Hello, she said. Do you speak English?

Yes.

I saw you yesterday. When we were gassed? You were talking to my friend. At least I thought you were.

Chano looked at the woman's face. He opened his mouth to speak, but then waited a moment before asking: Are you from England? With this one question—are you from England?—Chano had not only told Monica he was Daniel's father but also that he knew the rough outline of Daniel's story since leaving Mexico.

Yeah, she replied with a relieved chuckle.

From London?

She nodded. Tentative and slow, he continued: And you brought Daniel here? Because you knew his father was here?

Yeah, we did. He phoned someone in Mexico when he was in London—I forget the name—a woman—on the phone in Mexico.

Yolanda.

Could be. I don't know.

Yolanda.

And that's—yeah—and that's why. When we heard and that.

Thank you.

But . . . I've forgotten your name.

Chano.

Chano, yes. Monica.

Chano didn't dare ask the next question because he had a foreboding. Monica, having guessed what he wanted to know, found a roundabout way of telling him, by beginning somewhere else altogether.

He's not in King County. And he's not in Sandpoint, she began. Monica then told Chano how Daniel had been in a police van following a commandeered Metro bus to Sandpoint (the naval academy being used as a brig now that King County was full). About ten miles out into the countryside, the cops had told them all to get out and lay face-down on the verge, and then had driven off laughing. Everyone had walked home together, got a lift after a mile or so and they were back in the city by Thursday evening.

And where is Daniel now? asked the father, emboldened by the evasion he'd heard in Monica's report.

He met some Bolivians at the Voces de la Frontera teach-in on Wednesday night. They were going to Fresno with the FZLN. In a mini bus.

He's gone? asked Chano.

Monica looked at him and said: This morning.

They sat in silence for a bit. Monica waved away a couple of people she knew who were coming over to celebrate.

Did he say goodbye? asked the father at length.

Yes, she said.

But when he gets in touch with you, he asked, you will get in touch with me?

Problem is I'm homeless when I get back to London.

I'm . . . in transit, too.

I could give you my work number in England, 'cept I don't know if I'll still have a job when I get back . . . Daniel had a friend called Mani, but Mani's in King County right now.

Do you know his second name?

No, replied Monica, just Mani. But everyone in King County's giving their name as Jack or Jill WTO, anyway. So it wouldn't be much help if I did.

Chano gave her the number of the Tonalacapan *caseta telefónica*. They sat on the curb as the crowd milled before them.

Monica told Chano about Daniel, about Harmondsworth, Clapton Priory, the Peace Arch crossing, about trying to teach him to dance; told him how Daniel knew some of the story of his father and mother from the phone call he'd made; and described the excitement on his face when he'd come back from the phone box after that call.

Monica then tried to tell Chano what Daniel was like. Each time she began one tack, however, she interrupted herself to say "No that's not it, I'm not explaining it right, that doesn't give you a picture of him at all." Then she'd try another tack, only to interrupt herself once more and say "No, that's not him. He's coming out all wrong. You're not getting him right," all the while feeling she was failing miserably. But what Chano heard in the exactitude she strove for were those qualities in Daniel which had inspired it. He saw that the real picture was the one which she felt he *had to have* because no other would so delight him; and he was, in this, delighted. When Monica said "No, that doesn't give you a picture of him at all," Chano understood that Daniel was someone you couldn't let come out all wrong because he was worth getting right. He put his hand on her arm. She grinned and nodded and stopped.

They sat for a bit more, but Chano wanted to go now. When they'd first spoken he'd felt that he could've listened for ever to her or to anyone who'd spent even one day with Daniel. Now he felt inundated. He was also worried by Monica's look of receptivity and openness, by the fact that she seemed to be creating a space for him if he needed her. This scared him for good reason. (For it would be a very confident exile who could cry on the shoulder of a stranger in the crowded street of a foreign city.) Formal as a Spanish duke, he stood up and thanked her.

And then Chano did a strange thing, a thing which someone who knew Monica would not have done. He put his palm on the dome of her forehead and held it there a moment, before walking away down Fifth Avenue.

She touched the place where his hand had been. It was warm. She set off up Stewart Street, her legs aching as she climbed the hill. She found, at last, an alley, wedged herself in between a dumpster and a broken fridge and sobbed. For Chano, for Daniel, for the strain of having been responsible for that otherwise unaccompanied minor so long, for the release of letting him go, for the pain of letting him go. She thought of Chano and sobbed some more. That this meek, wounded man could be happy with such crumbs, with so little. Not knowing, as she could not know, that for him it was no small thing at all.

2

An eerie, sparse, Santiago traffic silts the late streets. Only federal vehicles and the surreys of private power enjoy road privileges tonight—stretch Lincolns, patrol cars, humvees, and low-loaders carrying helicopter spy cameras. The state of emergency still stands. Here and there a single siren whoop or blinding bright light flushes out a curfew violator.

On Fifth, a private ambulance mini bus crosses Pine and Pike, Union and University, its silent red siren revolving in the night. The ambulance turns on to Seneca and up through the second-gear, leafy steeps of "Pill Hill" toward the Virginia Mason Hospital. Swaying in the back, a medic adds serial vital signs to a flow sheet balanced on his knee. The flow sheet's scrawl reads: 30 *y/o male c/o* 8/10 *substernal chest pressure radiating to back. Asso. with diaphoresis, nausea and SOB. Onset* 23.55. *Exam: diaphoretic, pale, anxious, BP*170/198 *P*112 *irreg. RR*27. *Lungs clear. NTG x* 2 *with complete relief, IV, O*2, *monitor EKG, no acute ischemia. Transport to VM for evaluation. Hatch Evan.*

Part Five

In a consulting room of the Tropical Diseases Hospital, King's Cross, London, a minute had elapsed since the doctor last spoke. Now to break the silence he asked: How did you know it was chagas?

My brother.

How much do you know about the disease?

Transmitted by a beetle, mumbled Evan, the words crawling beetle-time out of his mouth. He knew more but couldn't say another word. Something else occupied him. It was here. This was the place. He had known it from the moment he walked in. Because a tropical diseases hospital could only apply to his beginnings, he knew he'd come to the end. A tropical diseases hospital was so disconnected from the every-day experience of his life, he knew that here was where he would be, too.

Yes, the doctor replied, the vinchuca beetle. Chagas is a disease of the blood. It's only treatable in the first year of infection. After which there is no cure, no vaccine. People usually take between fifteen and twenty years after infection to show symptoms.

With an effort Evan raised his eyes to the doctor and said: But I'm thirty-three . . .

Good nutrition, a healthy environment, fresh air have all given you—or gave you—a stronger immune system than most chagas victims. And so you've been able to fight chagas for a few more years than would have been possible if you'd grown up in Mexico. In this respect you could say it's like measles. Measles hasn't been fatal in Britain since the nineteenth century, but, as you know, it's still a big killer in the southern hemisphere.

But that's because drugs were invented.

Well, actually, that's not how it was eradicated here because—

But for chagas . . . ? Evan asked.

If chagas disease is caught at the first stage a cure is possible. A simple vaccine which works right after infection. *If* it had been diagnosed when you were a baby. But it wasn't. And if it isn't spotted at first infection, then there's no cure. There are no drugs for chagas. I should make that clear. I think it's important that you know this. There is no cure for chagas.

It vexed Evan that the doctor seemed to be following some training-course module called Disabusing the Patient of False Hope. How hopeful do I fucking look now? he thought. He believed that he'd already accepted that he was going to die and was annoyed with the doctor for not being able to see this. In his own mind Evan had come here with the express and sole purpose of rooting out false hope. He was here, he told himself, only to find out how long he had left and what it would be like. He'd accepted for some time he might die—certainly since he'd begun to investigate chagas and, in a way perhaps, ever since he'd listened to his brother in the pipeline. What acceptance Evan had reached, however, had been based on hopes that there'd be some sort of exemption or luck or discovery or escape. Evan thought he was aggravated by the doctor's presumption that he was disabusing him of false hope. But the real reason for his agitation was that he did in fact have many secret hopes and was being disabused of them all. And it felt like a robbery or physical assault.

What's going to happen now? he asked.

The doctor told him how, eventually, his nervous system, heart rate, in fact all his smooth muscle activity, would become unresponsive to external factors and he would have no control over them.

Smooth muscle, he explained, that's the stuff we take for granted, all the stuff we do automatically: digestion, changing our heart rate to respond to external situations. Your body will no longer be able to respond to its environment. It will start with aspirating—

What's that?

Waking up with undigested food blocking your airways; panic attacks as you aspirate—

But there must have been signs when I was a baby, said Evan.

How old were you when you were adopted? asked the doctor, in what seemed to Evan an oddly speculative tone of inquiry, as if he were merely advising him on a small tax matter or the value of an old book.

Twelve weeks.

Well, there'd be no symptoms by then. They'd have been and gone. What were the signs? I mean, supposing it had been spotted sooner.

The most common is swelling of the eye on one side of the face, usually on the side where the infection entered the body through a bite or wound or eye-rubbing. That tends to be the side of the baby's crib next to the wall of the house. After eight weeks there's no symptoms at all. It comes, it goes, it's gone. Except it hasn't. Hasn't gone. All it's done is it's just entered what's called the intermediate stage. Although that's a *very* long so-called intermediate stage.

My whole life.

Indeed. Yes. Yes . . . Then carriers develop irreversible heart and intestine damage. And once that happens, once this stage is reached, the average life expectancy is nine years.

It's definitely chagas?

Yes.

It can't be anything else?

No.

There must be *some* drugs—it's a disease that's known about. Just to hold it in remission.

It's a disease of the poor, I'm afraid.

But it's not a poor man's disease. I've got it!

The consultant looked up at him through wide gold-framed glasses, wondering if he'd made a joke, but then, on realizing he hadn't, changed his smile to one of non-specific benevolence before saying: I mean, yes, anti-inflammatories, steroids, anti-bacterials, antigens, and eventually morphine—we can give you all these—but it's important for you to know these are just palliatives. Painkillers essentially. There's no treatment in the sense of a *cure*.

Why don't they just plaster their fucking walls?

I don't know.

If they know about it . . . Evan fell silent.

A shortage of lime? Or whatever they use locally for whitewash? Plaster costs money. Perhaps there hadn't been a recent awareness programme . . . it very seldom is spotted in areas which are new to it. And it may be that you were born in a part of Mexico with no history of chagas. If you'd been born in Bolivia, say—

But if I've beaten it for this long?

I'm afraid that's just a longer-than-usual intermediate stage. But that ended quite a while ago, didn't it?

So now I'm going to die?

The doctor was silent for a while.

Evan too. Until in a different voice he asked: How long?

It could be a year, or two years, or more.

Less than a year?

Or less than a year.

Most likely?

Well, the fact is there are no statistics for Europeans getting the disease, so we don't really know.

Evan emerged from Grafton Way on to the Euston Road. At the traffic lights, all the cars were about to be released from their petty, timed delay, from lights that always change. Six lanes of traffic all got away and Evan wandered in the other direction toward King's Cross.

Euston Road's big buildings, its filthy sky and its broad-leaved, mighty horse chestnuts were all still there. And all suggested a large-scale scheme of things.

Grey and occluded as the sky above him, a sense formed in Evan that there was still something he could do. There remained something still in his power to change. A change which would stop this verdict from having complete dominion, would stop his life from being obliterated by this nonsense word chagas. A sense that seemed to draw nearer and nearer but stayed just invisible like the dots of grit in the King's Cross sky.

Waiting at the pedestrian crossing opposite St. Pancras, Evan remembered another train station, that obscure siding when no one had known he was there and where there'd seemed so much sky above him; a place he might never have come to in his whole life. On that rural platform he had felt as if he was meeting himself for the first time in ages. And here on the Euston Road, in the shock of knowing he was going to die, there was the same feeling. A sense of meeting himself out of time, in a haphazard and entirely contingent landscape, but one from which he was free to go in any direction.

The green man was beeping. Evan crossed.

Wide, scruffy Pancras Road grew quieter and emptier the further he walked. Its faded, red brick arches sequestered frame fitters, carpenters, prop-makers, mechanics and taxi spares. The discreet, artisanal reserve was interrupted halfway up the street. Here, above a prop-makers, a giant woman's naked torso—the massive figurehead of a wooden ship—rose magnificently above a barn door. Her white-painted, rock-hard breasts jutted forward. Her arms were thrust deep in the timber roots of varnished yellow hair which flew back in the memory of Atlantic gales. She hung in rigid suspense and her wide eyes and open mouth had a fixed expression of anger or horror, depending on how near you were to where the blue eyes had been dotted.

As Evan Hatch passed under her looming figure, blue-overalled mechanics stirred themselves and went back to work, emptying cold tea in the street.

2

A woman stood up with her arm in a sling.

My name is Barbara Liberace. I am sixty years old. On Wednesday I was walking downtown for chemotherapy treatment. My doctor so happens to have an office inside the area which the police had cor-doned off as this No Protest Zone. OK, no problem, I'm not protesting. I look ahead and there's plenty of people going about their business within that area that I need to get to. Fine. I go through. A police officer blocks my way and orders me back. I try to explain and he yells "Bitch, when I tell you to move, you will move." And then he hits me with a baton. He broke my wrist and injured my rotator cuff. Now, for me, what is devastating about this is I'm working toward a degree and my dream had been to graduate this spring with my daughter. But now my studies have got to be put back because they say I need surgery.

And I want to ask the council members for their advice here whether there's anything I can do, and to know what action they think appropriate.

Sue the city! shouted a woman in the audience. Sue the city! called another voice, and then another. Then all the other voices. Sue the city! Sue the city! The chant rose and fell and rose again. Sue the city! Sue the city!

The city councillors tried to find different facial expressions to match the volume of the chants. Solemn *know-how-you-feels* were followed by the polite, cold, nervy smiles of *you've-had-your-little-fun-but-now-let's-get-on-with-it-shall-we?* But then, as the chants grew even louder, these were followed in turn by the judicious, grave nodding of *we-are-fully-cognizant-of-the-terrible-injustice-and-are-your-faithful-tribunes-in-this-matter.*

Next, a skinny young man with ash-white spiky hair stood up in the audience. I was on Capitol Hill between midnight and two A.M. on December first, he said. The police used a stronger gas there, a gas you couldn't see and couldn't smell. We'd been gassed other times by the regular gas, but this wasn't that. People have been saying that it was a nerve gas that's like one down from Sarin? What I wanna know is what was it?

A tall man with a long chin, sandy hair and round gold specs half stood up, clutching a black ring-file in his lap. When he saw someone else was standing up, he sat back down, after an indecisive little bobbing action, to let the Latino speak first.

I also had experience of what this man had, said Chano. A gas you couldn't see or smell on Westlake Plaza at six P.M. I have been short of breath for, well, it's a week now. I've had pain in my middle back near the kidneys and liver, and mouth ulcers. So, what was it and what will happen in the long term?

The tall, sandy-haired man with the gold specs and the black ring-file stood up again. He took in Chano and the skeletal man as he began: Hi, I'm from the National Lawyers Guild and I was an NLG observer on the day. These here are Material Safety Data Sheets which ourselves and the Washington Toxics Coalition subpoenaed from the SPD. The gas used on December first was CN gas. Here's what it says about it: *50 per cent of Liquid Agent CN is methylene chloride—a powerful solvent used in paint strippers and varnish removers. It's listed as an anticipated human carcinogen by the National Toxicology Program.*

And leads to such symptoms as spontaneous abortions and birth defects when it reaches egg or sperm cells.

The man looked up from his reading and said: Now, Article 2 of the Chemical Weapons Convention outlaws the use of any gas made from industrial agents. So we took testimony from people who experienced this CN gas thinking we'd sue the Police Department and the city here. But I'm afraid we can't sue. You see, there's a little legal loophole. While Article 2 of the Chemical Weapons Convention does ban this chemical from *international* conflicts, it specifically excludes *domestic* situations. You *can* use chemical weapons on your *own* people. (At these words there was a short oxygen deficit in the hall itself.) That's a specific exemption in Article 2, the lawyer added. The one thing all nations agree on is that the real threat's you.

Chano and Ruben walked down a steep hill. The sidewalk was thick with wet leaves. Chano leaned back and carefully shuffled his feet in choo-choo-train steps so as not to skid on the mulch, while Ruben took long, toe-flapping strides. They came to a flat cross street, and began discussing the meeting.

Ruben was of the view that this was a revolutionary moment. People had seen that there was not one of their puny civil liberties which power wouldn't stomp all over if the moneyed order were threatened. And once people have seen that, he argued, nothing is ever quite the same again—even though the glass is swept up, the traffic starts moving and the sweatshirts are folded and bagged at the cash desk just as before. Because, he maintained, people have sensed their power.

Chano, however, wasn't so sure. No, he said, it was just a pro-democracy protest. It was even a pro-state protest, a protest in defence of the state. These are *our* laws the people were saying. *Our* constitution, even *our cops*!

Yes, said Ruben, but they were defending it against big business.

But still in defence of the state, Chano replied. Half those union guys in the stadium just want to keep their perks. They don't want one of those trucks with a big hoarding saying Mexico Transfer Job parked outside their plant if they try to organize.

But didn't you feel something special in the air?

Yes, Ruben, I didn't know what it was at first, it was a mysterious something, but now I do. I felt a lot of CN gas! I felt a lot of that, Ruben, a lot of that!

3

Evan jerks awake. He cannot breathe. His airways are choked. Aspirated food has floated up in the night. With a desperate scrabbling hand he tries to unblock his throat. He breaks the seal and unleashes a vacuum-sucking, rasping sound. All at once, he gags, splutters, coughs, heaves, chokes, sobs . . . then breathes.

When he tries to walk fast on his way to the bathroom, his heart cannot speed up as the movement demands and he has to slow down again. Red eyes streaming, he looks ahead at the bathroom and measures how many more seconds it will take to reach the sink.

Chagas has begun its attack on his nervous system. The smooth muscle function is starting to go. When it is cold his skin and blood vessels cannot contract, and when it is hot, his skin cannot open its pores. *Lack of response to environment.* Solid phrases from Grafton Way stick in his mind like the food lodged in his craw.

He is getting used to aspiration. He is getting used to a claggy feel in his soft palate, like a second epiglottis made from pastry crust. The shape of his throat is often not his own but clogged with hard rinds which will neither come up nor go down. When they get to his mouth then at least he can pull out what he can't swallow.

He sits on the bed sweating, trembling. He doesn't want to fall back to sleep before it's time for work.

He is standing in his kitchen, holding a cup of coffee in his hand, dressed in a blue shirt, listening to Radio 4: *And we hear from an environmental statistician who says that implementing the Kyoto agreement would be a complete waste of money.* The corners of his mouth exude a gas-leak smile. All his own work.

Evan Hatch has left Poley Bray to consult freelance on fixed-term special contracts—his latest a Big Oil one. Another has seen him become a kind of showbiz agent for the TV and radio careers of climate-change sceptics and laissez-faire economists. Under the rubric of "securing support for bilateral trade and investment agreements", he also does one-day-a-week consultancy on water privatization.

Word has got around about how he was bitten by a tropical death beetle on a recent trip to Mexico or something, or has got some kind of fatal disease, and either way has only a year or two to go.

He rubs his inflamed eyes. Not quite a dark-glasses day today but he puts the shades in his jacket just in case. He feels the lumps under his armpits. Not bigger than they were yesterday but harder, definitely harder. Pebbles.

Evan's car arrives. On account. Every day it's a different car, different chauffeur.

All my life, he reflects as the black Ford Scorpio winds through Skinner Street, I've been a biological time bomb ticking away. Nature is blind, chaotic violence; but my work is for a human-created mechanism—the financial markets, efficiency, growth—which is not.

The perfect impartiality of the market has added appeal for Evan the more impartial nature gets. Time to dish out some perfect impartiality of his own, you might say. But Evan sees it another way . . . Unlike the Bay Area protesters in their Nikes, he's actually *been* to Mexico, seen the poverty for himself. And not just from some hotel or conference suite either. Has he not heard from the lips of Mexicans, such as Ilan, that trade liberalization and market access is what *they themselves* want?

The *Economist*'s front cover shows a starving naked African child over the caption "The Real Loser In Seattle." Retelling the globalization story has become a growth market. Evan has co-produced *A Briefing Booklet on Globalization and Its Enemies* for Overseas Development ministers.

Evan is sitting in the Old Shell Building, in what is now an office of the Independent Science Unit. It's his ten o'clock with Stella (also ex of Poley Bray).

Actually, the environmentalists are right, Evan tells her, they *themselves* are saying it's too late to do anything about global warming anyway! So if even *they* are saying that, then why change the way we do things now?!

Stella looks at him in puzzlement, a momentary crossed wire perhaps? And then, Jesus, she thinks, he's serious.

Why change? asks Evan. I mean, seriously . . . If it's too late, then why?

Who's saying it's too late?

The Gaia guy—he's saying the planet is like a truck speeding downhill and even if tomorrow all carbon emissions were cut to zero it'd only be like taking our foot off the truck's accelerator! So what's he bothered about? Too late for lies, Stella. I mean, what do the ecologists wanna *do?* What's their alternative? Try to repair the damage and meet the apocalypse in some shack made from recycled pallets? Fuck that. Keep on trucking!

You're not very nihilistic today, she says, thinking his illness has made him feverish.

No, it's the *opposite* of nihilism. Look at a portrait of someone from the Renaissance. They look proud, you know, they're the highest achievement of creation, each an individual human being, as good as it gets. But the ecologists have made us like those schizophrenics who daren't step on the ground because they think they'll actually crack the world, that they'll destroy the earth's crust with their flip flops.

The reason for Evan's stridency this morning is that he hears Stella being a bit tentative on her flip flops, as it were, and it's annoying him. Stella keeps talking up the positive initiatives the oil company is taking. All well and good, of course, except she's spoken these homilies for *his* and *her* benefit, and *not* as possible copy for their clients. She seems to want to justify their brief as being a little wrong for a larger good. And it just isn't like that. To Evan there's no dignity in their work unless they see the truth of the matter, in spite of—or rather because of—the fact that they are to distort said truth for their clients. They have therefore got themselves into an argument about the purpose of "corporate ads," those non-product-specific ones.

It definitely needs text, says Stella, looking at a mock-up of the oil company's full-colour broadsheet centre spread. (A leopard in a waterfall wearing Maori beads.)

Why?

To talk about how we're taking sustainability seriously.

No text.

Or how increased prosperity in the Middle East is good for international stability. And that's also a very good way of preempting the whole global-warming debate.

No text.

It looks defensive if there's no text, if we're not making the case.

But it's not greenwash, says Evan.

Well, not if we do it your way, it's not!

It's not for the readers, it's for the owners. The message says *We are your largest advertisers. We giveth and we taketh away.* And that's all. The more profligate you are with the space the stronger that message comes across.

So, suddenly space is more important than the content.

When it's leverage . . . then, yeah. Anything to take up a double page. A leopard or kitten—

That's so naff.

Well, a dead canary or a pigeon, then.

If we've got a case why not make it?

'Cos revenue's the spike for the bad stuff.

Yes, but not everything's two-step. Sometimes route one is simply better.

It's about creating a financial dependency is what it is. Why won't you see that? And it's good, Stella. It's all good stuff. That's the truth.

4

This being a half-day, and Evan's smooth muscle so far behaving itself, he stands now in a thick black overcoat (warmer than the crombie) on Kite Hill, Hampstead Heath. Remission Day: mid-winter spring is the perfect weather for his unresponsive body.

Evan unwinds another yard of stretch-memory-line from his foam-padded Sky Claws (he loves this jargon). All in the wrist action, his handles pull a back flip to axles with edge work. Hoo-hoo, he chuckles secretly. It's silly but brilliant. Hoo-hoo!

He chose this kite carefully. Not the ballet kite which, he'd been told, was "slippery" and extremely sensitive to "pilot input." He's gone instead for the "rail-like tracking" of a precision kite, slightly heavier pulling, but more "responsive bridling" with no wobbles. (And less fetch and carry in the long grass.) Soaring and swooping, the silk kite seems even to make its own *oohs* and *aahs*.

Most kite flyers face the trees on Kite Hill, but Evan likes to watch his black kite soar and play over the eastern city skyline, over its three outstanding monuments to folly, deception, and greed—the round, the pyramid, the rectangle. He snaps the black kite through ninety degrees and it does indeed settle like tracks on a rail, its red streamer irons flat. *Epa! Epa!*

He sits on a bench overlooking the anonymous city. He drinks his medicine. The kite lifts and stirs on his lap like an unsettled cat.

Evan doesn't believe in genetic theories of inherited characteristics and personality, but he has begun to feel very much his father's son. At least, he often finds himself thinking about his father walking all the way from El Salvador to the northeast of Mexico. Evan has even memorized the route from his atlas. He likes to recite his itinerary: Over the Sierra Madre, Baja Verapaz, Alta Verapaz, cross Rio Motagua, follow Rio Usumacinta along Sierra del Lacandon and then across the Sierra Madre Oriental. On a windy, grassy hill in north London, one extraordinarily brave and headstrong Salgado recalls the hard, lonely, desperate walk another made before him.

Have you got a cigarette, mate?

Evan looks up at an eleven-year-old boy with a London-Irish face. Skiving? he asks him.

You?

I work half-days.

Me too, says the kid, sliding his jaw sideways and grinning. Half-days. Nodding down at the kite, he asks: Giss a go?

Sorry! oh sorry! I'm really sorry, mate, says the lad, looking properly distraught. Oh *no* . . . he adds through gritted teeth, cursing himself quietly, intensely, in a way which makes Evan wonder whether he's *always* fucking up like this, or, rather, always being *told* he is. The stricken kite is struggling to lift itself off the clumpy grass after its high-speed nose dive. The boy runs off to retrieve the kite, but when he brings it back the man has gone.

5

The glass-fronted Day of the Dead puppet theatre cost so much that Evan reflected it was just as well he wouldn't be needing his life savings. Back home he put it on the sycamore kitchen table. He found a two-point adaptor in his laptop case and plugged in the brown, plaited lead. He sat down in a steel chair and studied the case.

There were no strings. The gang of white, cast-iron skeletons held rocks in their hands and looked like the not very hard locals of a small town. Evan flicked an ancient brass switch. Valves heated, the base glowed, nothing happened. He waited. Footlights shone up. Seconds passed. He heard a whirr, a creak, and the tarnished, white figures began to move.

The grinning Day of the Dead puppets enacted their gross parody of the living: humaning around in the clothes we wear, doing the things we do, jiving, eating, drinking, greeting. Every few seconds one of the skeletons lifted his trilby and bowed, lifted his trilby and bowed. Welcome to our arbitrary violence, said the silent puppet. Welcome to our arbitrary violence.

Yes Slim, said Evan, but I can do stuff that is not haphazard. *And* I won't do that violence to my own nature that they call "change" or, cancerously, "growth."

Evan had once heard of someone beating some kind of cancer by eating only red grapes and concentrating on nothing but their breathing for six weeks. I'd rather die, he thought, than let myself become a neurotic little bag of shite like that. Truly, I'd rather die than lose dignity in that way: spitting out the seeds and inhaling, exhaling all day, like an appendage of the disease itself. Why die a stranger to myself? Down at the morgue they'll be painting a lipstick smile on me soon enough and combing my hair into a side parting. But let them wait.

He refused to let death dehumanize him before it actually had. All death could do was its one thing: termination. He could do many things and he would not be cowed or intimidated. He wasn't going to meet it halfway.

Evan had come to despise the hawkers of slow degrees of accommodation and grubby compacts with death. He despised their pathetically diminished paper bargains: "If I can just live to see the New Year / my son's marriage / next week's *Eastenders* omnibus, then I'll go happy." What did it matter *how* you go? thought Evan. You're going! What does it matter if you're up or down at the end? It's *just the end*. Why dignify the arbitrary? Why dress it up in those ceremonial clothes? Give it a funny hat. Dress it in the random, everyday clothes of the living just like my puppets in their glass-fronted high street, with a bar, shops, and a bell tower in the background. The Mexicans, he said out loud, have the right idea about death. And though he said this much as a Greek, Somali, or Chilean might have, the manner of his leaving was to be the most Mexican thing he ever did. He flicked the ancient brass switch off, on, off, on, off, on. The skeletons stopped and started as if they were losing confidence in their power to scare. Death, thought Evan, isn't even the worst thing that can happen to you.

The final stage of chagas is ever wider cycles of disease, each more debilitating than the last. Over the past year, whenever a new cycle had announced itself, Evan had been staggered by dismay and demoralization. On this path he was choosing, that demoralization, when it came, would be worse. But to change, thought Evan, would be a rejection of all my old life. And, what's more, a fetish for change is just a fake way to control my fear at being lost and helpless against destruction. Death has the power to effect a pretty radical alteration anyway. To change is just claiming that power for my own so that I can feel I'm controlling events, that it's my decision.

He wasn't seeking terms and couldn't accept nature's violent robbery as some kind of deity. Not in *that* hat.

He flicked the worn brass switch again. The skeletons fidgeted in their glass case like randy lizards. If you want to knock me off my own path, he told them, you'll get no help from me. I'll keep to my own tracks. Even if I'm sick for two weeks out of three, for twenty-nine days out of thirty, I'll keep my own way for the other one. This was the path he chose.

Thinking about this path, however, his courage quailed . . . If he chose this way, all the cackling Juarez skeletons would be hurling rocks from the roadside, rocks which would hit him harder for as long as he tried to keep to his old path. There would be humiliations—he would collapse in public from time to time. At work.

Strangers would see him weak, soiled, and helpless; everyone would know about his illness. He would have to tell each new (freelance and fixed-term-contract) employer his limitations beforehand. This would sometimes mean rejection. And when he did get the job, he would sometimes let people down. They'd be angry with him. And now and then he'd fail altogether because the rocks would catch him off-guard, fuck him up and make a show of him. He knew he'd collapse at just the wrong time, at a high-powered moment key to months of work. It would mean, he saw, convulsing and screaming on the prickly carpet floor of air-conditioned, design-award, open-plan, riverside office frontage.

But Evan also knew that the alternative was a lie. For there was only one path he could walk and still be himself. The rocks may strike him less if he chose another path, if he took evasive action, but their disruption would only be meaningful while there was a life to be disrupted. Death would take his future life, but he wasn't going to give it his present. Evan Hatch, who hated being interrupted, would say to the Great Interruption: *What am I doing?*

6

Aiie, if only you'd phoned sooner, *payaso*. Daniel sent a postcard! We had a battered postcard from Bolivia! But it said he wouldn't be where he was for long.

How long?

Days. And that was a fortnight ago, said Yolanda, her voice crackly with *larga distancia*. She read out the old address and the name of the organization fighting water privatization Daniel was working with. Chano felt pride that he'd already heard of it. Where are you now? she asked.

Seattle, but tomorrow I'm leaving for New Mexico. Abiquiu.

Albuquerque?

No, *Abiquiu* . . . It's near Albuquerque.

How long for?

I don't know.

Give me the address right now.

My cousin Hector's meeting me at the bus station. I don't know it.
Let me know when you get there and let me know when you move.
Vale.

Chano wanted to ask Yolanda how she was but there was something
in that *payaso* (clown, fool) which forbade him.

7

In a *centro comunitario* in the Primero de Mayo neighbourhood,
Cochambamba, Daniel is one of many sweaty bodies on the dance
floor.

In the mix comes a high-hat sound like that noise made when a
magician opens a deck of cards wide as a chest expander and the
cards all flock together again. The high-hat's shuffle gets more and
more drawn out, the deck spreads ever wider in the magician's hands,
and the cards come flocking louder and louder. All Daniel has to do
is to be faithful to this sound. He doesn't know where his arms and
legs, head or neck, hips and knees are going next but he can't put a
foot wrong, every step is right and tight with a juicy marrow-tingling
tidiness. He ties his joints in knots, to unknot again like the satisfying
moment when a painted-in screw cracks its seal and turns.

He still has aches in his kidneys and lungs from the chemical
weapons, but hasn't coughed up any specks of blood for a week.
Fluent here, he feels he's evaporating the last of Seattle's gas to the
smoky, steamy air of the dance hall, whose low ceiling is slowly raining
sweat.

He's lost sight of Victor, a friend his own age. Victor, last seen by
the wardrobe-sized bass bins, has the bottle of water they're sharing in
the heat, but Daniel knows he'll only be thirsty when he stops. Arms
outstretched, palms aloft, a reed quivering in a rising hover-mist of
keyboards, a smile wreathes up through his face, having risen from
the small of his back, arms now waving like kelp.

To tonight's dance (a fundraiser for the Co-ordinadora against
Bechtel's water-privatization plans) has come hard-faced youth from
the *favelas*. A *vato* a few years older than Daniel is dancing in his
space. Is he trying to start a fight? Daniel wonders.

Crazy trumpets and trombones fly in from Tijuana. Daniel's arms swing in a contra-flow and he feels delicious cool hollows open in his spine, smooth as polished brass curves, like he's been cored. The trombones go galloping off on a stampeding bass drum and Daniel's along for the ride, bouncing higher and higher with the magician's high hat. When he looks again, the youth has melted away, and Daniel realizes that the *vato* had just been drunk and uncoordinated all along.

As he dances he feels an odd familiarity in shapes. His body draws ghost dances of the people he's seen dance. Oscar to the tune of the phone number song; Monica and Ramona in Clapton Priory; the headscarved woman on a dumpster singing *Ain't no power like the power of the people.*

This is my nature, he thinks, this dance is who I am.

And this was his dance: never knowing what will happen next; working through a huge job-lot of repetitive action; retreating to burst out somewhere unexpected; swerving and stalking his way out of enclosed spaces; now stepping gentle as a termite, now pounding; lifted by a force which feels like his own though he knows it never is. And as he dances faster on the brass and stamping bass-drum charge, he looks round and meets the girl's eyes. She scrunches up her face at him and bounces her fist in time to the music, as if to say *There you go, you're on it . . .*

The Co-ordinadora marches through Plaza de 25 Mayo toward soldiers sent out to defend Bechtel's water privatization. Daniel, stripped to his skinny waist, a T-shirt round his face as a mask, runs with a hundred others across the wide, deserted boulevard, hears the crack-crack of bullets and knows they can't touch him.

8

The café is still called El Café Fuente but only in the way that Rio Santa Katerina is still called Rio Santa Katerina. The fountain is dead. A defunct sculpture. A dusty climbing frame. And, just now, a high perch . . .

Alma-Delia's daughter Iriate is sitting on the fountain's top ledge, studying. She is wearing the same 77 T-shirt she wore the day Oscar cooked dinner in the back of his truck. An English text book is balanced on her raised knees. Gusts of wind ruffle corners of the page. She is frowning, either with concentration or with not being able to concentrate. She puts a hand behind her. Her back pocket is wet. *Pinche,* she curses. She drops down on to the next ledge and stands brushing clingy damp gravel from the cold seat of her jeans. She turns and looks at the fountain. Resting her hands on the top concrete leaf, she leans forward peering into the fountain's stem.

Ooze seeps out. She sees how the brown water gets corralled by the tiniest twigs; is overpowered by dust, grit, stones; has to go the long way round the chewed rims of a paper cup. She watches more dark bilge-water seep from the stem. Not from the spout but from the base of the top ledge, like a damp wall. Pushing her hands off the ledge, Iriate stands up straight, dusting her palms. She waits, as if any moment the fountain might spit the grit and dead leaves from its teeth and gush high into the dry air. She peers. Water seeps, but only what you'd get from treading on soaked tarpaulin. She climbs down from the fountain, hopping backward off the last ledge.

She runs in to tell her mother what she's seen but, after two paces, she slows, and just walks in.

9

He knew it was folly to walk to the docks. Someone would stop him. It would spoil his mood. But no one did and he walked past the dormant cranes and the last bank of bright red container crates, while far behind him Alaskan Way hummed a tune of container trucks.

It was a week since the town-hall meeting and Chano had just finished his last ever shift at the Broadway diner. In his anorak pocket was a yellow bus ticket the size of a business envelope. Abiquiu, standard single fare $136 dollars from the Greyhound terminus on Stewart Street. A two-night bus journey to New Mexico.

Pier 64 was silent. In twilight stillness he sat on the dock of the bay, dangling his feet over the drop. Chano gazed out at the still harbour.

He listened to the water plucking at the crenellated yellow steel of the harbour wall . . . and heard the knocking pipes in his Calderon *choza*. Once again he saw Marisa's skittish grin wreathing her young face when she knock-knock-knocked on the table legs in wordless comment on . . . what? Once again he came to the riddle of the knocking pipes . . .

Chano had made his home from bits and bobs. Like a trade rat, Marisa used to say. The observation was not quite as caustic as it sounds. Mexican wood rats or "trade rats" collect odds and ends for their nests. Best of all, the trade rat likes small, bright, shiny objects. Like a magpie, you might say, except with one difference: they always leave a swap for what they steal. If a trade rat carrying, say, a brass button in its jaws scurries past a silver San Cristobel, it drops the brass button and picks up the necklace. Thus the wood rat *appears* to pay hard brass for silver, appears to replace necklace with button, to swap, to trade.

They're called trade rats incorrectly, of course. What's called "trade" is an accidental byproduct of straightforward theft.

Chano's odd-looking home was his trade-rat monument to a rare chapter of local history; a social document of the time he'd felt most alive and fired by hope. (Over the years, however, the structure had reminded him of hope in name only, in the sense that a favourite song remains a favourite song long after we ever want to hear it again.) Specifically his trade-rat shack remembered the autonomous rescue groups set up after Hurricane Camilo went through Calderon and its surrounding villages in 1985.

The personification of hurricanes didn't seem at all odd to Chano. Years before, *campesinos* had been forced to build on the uplands when the lowlands were stolen; until, impatient of the timid people, the hills came to town on their behalf.

Next day, a red-brown sea went looking through the streets for a place to stay. A house gradually and thoughtfully gave way. Chano watched it resist being pushed over as dumbly as a cow, until it tipped, sploshing into the slowly flowing viscous waters, to become an underwater flat pack. Floating plants looked ready to bind themselves together into a new Mexico City. But when the waters drained away, the white wooden sides of the shacks on Calle Independencia were as filthy as cattle sheds. The more you scrubbed walls, he remembered, the filthier they got.

A city of mud. Black, red, brown, yellow, and white mud. Mangled foundations were churned by mud. The red siren of a patrol car stuck in the mud wailed hopelessly, its pompous siren no longer applied.

In the wake of Hurricane Camilo, the civil protection and emergency services never showed. The people from all the villages which the floods had swept off the map organized autonomous rescue groups. They were doing it for themselves.

Until then, the word "power" had been an abstract thing to Chano, as twice-removed as newspaper sealing up a steamed window in a café. But now he felt he could breathe it in the dehumidified air. The chemistry student believed power had been distilled. Here was a transfer he could sense: it seemed to hover over the mud-clogged, rubbled streets. Here was a community taking things into their own hands, right up to the sewage-sucking elbow. The government buildings and the banks had all been swept away by the flood, and with them, it seemed, the state, the army, the police and the PRI. They were on their own. They were free. And it seemed to Chano as though all the cinderblocks and corrugated iron had been put back in the reeking mix for a purpose. When he saw a man drying out a cellar with the naked flame of a six-foot red propane cylinder, he thought, yes, we are going to remould and fire a new order from this clay. Here and there little bunsen fires popped and plumed from cracked pipes. Consciousness quickened in the mud. He had never felt so alive.

. . . And there she was again. Chano was wading through mud when he saw her. She was standing on a corner of raised sidewalk, chatting and laughing with friends . . . until she stared back. For whenever they caught sight of each other, their faces took on a curious expression, more like listening than looking. The type of expression a late-night trucker might have seconds after hearing his fan-belt start to shred on a remote country road. They had still never greeted each other, but this, too, had begun to seem significant to Chano without him being able to say why. The new emotions she aroused in him were somehow connected to the changed world they now lived in, and as he walked past her on the raised sidewalk, his legs were still wading through mud.

One afternoon an old man laying a duckboard across a trench had cheerily called out to the young Chano: So much to do, so many told they cannot work!

And Chano had, he felt, known exactly what the old man meant. A sardonic joke about unemployment had been doing the rounds in the months before Camilo: "What do sperms and Mexicans have in common? There are millions of Mexicans, but only one will ever work." Now everyone was working together and all they had to do was all there ever was to do. What could they not now do together! It was as impossible to divide labour as it was to keep the mud from stopping where his T-shirt met his trousers. As many people were being helped out of a caved-in plot as were salvaging a stranger's icons, gas cylinders, or V-shaped guttering. It would have been invidious to pay one person and not another, and so the women began to cook up village meals. Stray cattle and chickens which had fled some *finca* were put in a pot before anyone came looking. Smallholders got together to find new land where they could corral their goats and cows. The police cells were used as stables. One minute land was being divvied up and the next? The next was that *people started building*. First they built a structure that would double as canteen and shelter, and then a school was going up. The next time Chano saw her, he was carrying a pile of white tiles from the bank for use in the new clinic.

The state had done nothing in response to Hurricane Camilo, but here was a seismic tremour it could not ignore: people were building. Now the emergency services came on Leviathan wheels with tire treads like the ridged backs of stegosaurii. Grabbers and pile-drivers shunted rubble or pulled foundation stumps out like bad teeth. Incontrovertible bulldozers levelled, flattened, and squared off the earth. This new diesel-Camilo also cleared away the makeshift shelters and canteen, and the clinic with its fresh, white tiles.

Troops tossed a few sandbags about for the cameras, but the student Chano quickly noticed how the troops only really came alive when spooling out the PASO PROHIBIDO tape; when telling people where to go and where not to go; when laying down the law in the arguments which seemed to flare at every intersection, like the little fires from buckled gas pipes, as people pointed out to the troops that they were hampering rescue efforts. But that was beside the point. They were not there for rescue. They were there for control.

Chano felt he now had a mission. He must stop people staring numbly at the civil protection services, bulldozers, and troops. They'd become spectators where previously they'd been controlling their own destinies. He must make them all as active as they were before. He felt that this one task was all; that somehow the whole struggle for the new community which they had been firing from this clay had now focused to a sharp point. The sole imperative was his hectoring, cajoling, persuading, and suggesting tasks that people could join him in; was that they all keep on doing what they'd been doing. He moved urgently through crowds of people who were watching what the clean, expert-looking paramedics were doing in the sealed-off street, until he realized *he* was just staring, too. A full body jolt would then course down his legs into his boots, and he'd set off to find an autonomous project.

But there were none. Not now. Once the professional equipment had arrived, the projects which had consumed everyone's efforts and brain power and discussions and arguments had all stopped. They only had the roof still to put on the improvized school, but to continue even with this by their own efforts seemed as hollow as going to the river for water when there's a stand-pipe at the end of the street. It was suddenly pointless. They were as demoralized as mountain climbers who find their route up the north face of the Eiger marked out by a new ski lift.

To climb would be a farce. Even in this instance: even if the mountaineers know that the authorities are only waiting for them to break up base camp and go home, before dismantling the ski lift and taking the motors, generators and arc lights some place else.

And then it was—at the point when it seemed to him that there was nothing left in this situation but individual salvage work—that Chano began to build his new home on the outskirts of Calderon, in what was then Ejido El Refugio El Reparo.

By a mesquite tree in a triangular plot of land, he'd found a single house-wall still wearing its straight shelves and prim cupboards. It even had a kind of wallpaper made from lacquered magazine pages painted over with azure and yellow. The external side of the wall was white plaster. Over the next few days, with Oscar's help, Chano gathered from here and there: a partition wall with door attached, a sink unit, guttering, power-point facings, window frames, shutters, a car seat, and miscellaneous floor tiles.

Halfway up a mud slide, one misty afternoon, Oscar and Chano had chipped away at what looked like a plaster raft and had found it to contain the intact fossil of a floor plan's worth of plumbing system. The plaster raft must have been the first floor of a municipal building, and its horizontal copper pipes still followed the fluent logic of the extinct structure. Using the steep incline, they slid and hauled the entire, excavated plumbing grid on to the maroon 68 Chevy flatbed Oscar drove in those days.

Longer and wider than Oscar's truck, the exhumed plumbing grid rattled, banged and clanked all the rutted way home. Copper bends and spouts jutted far out in front of the windshield. The plumbing grid trembled on the roof of the cab and nervously pan-piped, intermittent and tuneless, as if it knew of the dismemberment ahead.

Back at his new *choza*, pipes were sawn down and twisted off into brackets, joists, beams and clothes rails. Only a few sections of the maze were actually used for plumbing. In fact, when Chano tried to figure the "H" junction he would need below his sink for his kitchen taps, he found to his fury that none of the pipes he had left would fit. Humiliated, he realized that he would have to go back to the *vulcanizador* in Taxco Santos and buy more plumbing pipes!

Before Chano got to the *vulcanizador*, however, he passed a white Unión de Ejidos Uniones hall untouched by the flood. The door stood open. Above it shone a single, round light. Through the open doorway he saw lots of straw stetsons, white shirts, and headscarves. There were about forty men and women in the hall, talking in small groups of half a dozen, some sitting, some standing.

Chano passed under the round white light dotted with moon-walking moths and walked into a damp-smelling hall, whose wooden floor had been spread over with fusty straw.

And there she was again, and there were his legs wading in mud again.

One member from each group summarized the plans and ideas they had agreed upon. A forty-year-old man extemporized and was heckled by his table for omissions. Next came an older woman who read faithfully from a sheet of paper. Then another spokeswoman was called. And so her name was Marisa.

And Marisa was about to speak. At last he would hear her. What honey words would droppeth from that ripe mouth? What plangent music would embraceth the still-expectant air? What sweet poetry would calleth now unto his soul?

There was, she began, a general agreement for linking up with other autonomous rescue groups around the country to develop new organizational structures with which to coordinate collective direct action. There was a suggestion—here she corrected herself—*first of all* there was a suggestion that we make links with existing trade unions despite all the many reservations we have about them. But there were other suggestions instead, in favour of not doing this officially but—here Marisa glanced at her ink jottings on a paper towel—through those many individual rank-and-file members who themselves shared the experience of a community working together.

Chano cursed himself for not having been in on this meeting and for not having been part of the whole movement which had led to it. He hadn't known this organizational work was going on. He'd thought everything was just going back to how it was before. And so he'd missed out on the chance of getting to know Marisa.

This consciousness added a special bitterness to his self-reproach: Because I lacked faith in other people working together, I have been punished by the immutable laws of nature never to marry this woman. And that is only right. I have proved myself totally unworthy of the connection that existed between us. Because I lost faith that millions of Mexicans might work together I have made myself the sperm that will never work!

On which hazy reflection, the student screwed up his face and scanned the hall for the man who would be the luckiest of all the millions of Mexicans.

Seattle's Pier 64 had grown cold, the twilight had deepened, the sea was knocking and plucking against the crenellated steel harbour wall. He looked down at the brown water. Perhaps he knew now what she'd meant by knock-knock-knocking on the table legs, whenever he couldn't see something obvious, or when he was speechifying.

Perhaps I've worked it out Marisa, he said. No, not worked it out—I've learned it. I've learned the riddle of the pipes, the puzzle of the plumbing grid. I started sawing it up the moment I lost hope in collective action. I started doing things just for myself. But the plumbing grid, which had served many, didn't work for one. Knock-knock-knock. No one ever does anything on their own. I'd thought it was all over, all we'd been trying to do, all lost, and I was wrong, too hasty. When the trade rat picks up something new he leaves all he had behind. No point telling me, either, because it was something I had to learn . . . I've solved it, Marisa, I've solved the riddle of the knocking pipes.

And then he heard her voice say: *Shame you had to blow up more pipes to do it, eh,* corazon?

Chano threw back his head and laughter echoed over the still waters of the dock, and far out to sea.

Thanks and acknowledgements

My much-loved friend Wil Sanders (1936–2002) worked closely with me on the book and gave me, at last, the novel I thought I'd written all along but never had.

Special thanks go to my brilliant researcher Nicky Fijalkowska.

I've been fantastically lucky in the excellent editorial direction I've had from Richard Eoin Nash, Jane Hindle, Clare Alexander, and Kate Shaw.

Thanks too to Marisa Martinez, Oscar Salgado, Professor Susan George, Professor Doreen Massey, Mark Thomas, Katharine Ainger, Simon Lewis, El Flaco, Mehmet Dilloo, Greg Palast, Dom, Glenn Chapell, Brenda Kelly, Bobby Troman, Dylan Howitt, Leanne Klein, George Monbiot, Sarah Groff-Palermo, David Janik, Ammi Emergency, Hannah Griffiths, Nick North, Marcella de Ningunos-Caballos.

And to Reclaim The Streets, Plan International, Harmondsworth Support Group, The Refugee Council, *undercurrents*, London Tropical Diseases Hospital, Seattle Virginia Mason Hospital, Bosnia & Herzegovina Embassy in Washington, People's Global Action, *schnews*, and Corporate Watch.

I'm also directly indebted to the following publications from which I drew heavily: *Voces de la Frontera* (newspaper of the Coalition for Justice in the Maquiladoras), *Global Spin: The Corporate Assault on Environmentalism* by Sharon Beder (Green Books), *Toxic Sludge is Good For You: Lies, Damn Lies and the Public Relations Industry* by John C. Stauber and Sheldon Rampton (Common Courage Press), *Magical Urbanism: Latinos Reinvent the US City* by Mike Davis (Verso) and *Zapatista! Re-inventing Revolution in Mexico* by John Holloway and Eloina Pelaez (Pluto Press).

ROBERT NEWMAN was born in 1964. He is Greek-Cypriot, English, French, and American. He has worked as a farmhand, warehouse-man, house-painter, teacher, mail sorter, social worker, removal man, stand-up comedian, and broadcaster. *The Fountain at the Centre of the World* is Newman's third novel.